PRAISE FOR JOHN MARRS

'Provocative, terrifying and compulsive.'

—Cara Hunter, author of *Close to Home*

'Really clever concept and some great characters and twists. It's a real joy to read something totally original, smart and thought-provoking.'

—Peter James, author of the Roy Grace series

'One of the most exciting, original thriller writers out there. I never miss one of his books.'

—Simon Kernick

'Gorgeously written, and pulsing with heart.'

—Louise Beech, author of *The Mountain in My Shoe*

'This is a superb heart-pounding chiller of a thriller.'

—*The Sun*

'A brilliantly inventive thriller.'

—*Good Housekeeping*

'Gripping from the start and full of surprises, this kept us up long after lights out.'

—Isabelle Broom, *Heat*

'Full of twists, vividly drawn characters you'll love or love to loathe and pacy action.'

—*SFX*

'As topical as it is tense . . . No skill is required to recognise why John Marrs has become such a popular author, with his relatable characters, clever ideas, and smooth storytelling.'

—*Sunday Express*

'It's crammed with twists and turns that'll keep you guessing right until the very end. 5/5.'

—*OK!*

'If you're looking for a sleek, exhilarating ride, look no further.'

—*Financial Times*

'Marrs excels at thrilling readers by creating a real sense of tension and delivering a believable, harsh criticism of modern society through this dark and entertaining story.'

—*LA Times*

'Fun and compelling; I read the final pages while walking down the street, unwilling to wait until I got home.'

—*Wired*

'This will have you gripped.'

—*Woman's Own*

'Engaging concept, craftily executed.'

—Adrian J. Walker, author of
The End of the World Running Club

'Wonderful concept, ridiculously entertaining . . . an absolute pleasure, the malevolence and impishness of a young Roald Dahl.'

—T. A. Cotterell, author of *What Alice Knew*

'Fantastic . . . I can't remember the last time I was simultaneously this entertained and this disturbed.'

—Hollie Overton, *Sunday Times* bestselling author of *Baby Doll*

'[Marrs] writes tough, fast-paced, and twisty crime stories . . . If you like Simon Kernick, you'll love this.'

—*Peterborough Telegraph*

'Completely unputdownable . . . A must-read for crime fiction, psychological thriller, and thriller fans alike.'

—Books of All Kinds

'[*Her Last Move*] will suck you in . . . This is one of those books that will lead you to shirk responsibilities at home and work; postpone things like eating and sleeping . . . '

—The Irresponsible Reader

WHAT
LIES
BETWEEN
US

ALSO BY JOHN MARRS

WHAT LIES BETWEEN US

JOHN MARRS

THOMAS & MERCER

Text copyright © 2020 by John Marrs
All rights reserved.

Published by Thomas & Mercer, Seattle

www.apub.com

Amazon, the Amazon logo, and Thomas & Mercer are trademarks of Amazon.com, Inc., or its affiliates.

ISBN-13: 9781542017022
ISBN-10: 1542017025

Cover design by @blacksheep-uk.com

Printed in the United States of America

For Elliot

'A lie can travel halfway around the world while the truth is putting on its shoes.'

—*Charles Spurgeon*

PROLOGUE

I have stopped loving you. I have stopped caring about you. I have stopped worrying about you. I have simply . . . *stopped*.

This might come as news to you but despite everything, despite the cruelty, the selfishness and the pain you have caused, I still found a way to care. But not any more.

Now, I am putting you on notice. I no longer need you. I don't think fondly of our early days, so I am erasing these memories and all that followed. For much of our time together I wished for a better relationship than the one we have, but I've come to understand this is the hand I have been dealt. And now I am showing you all my cards. Our game is complete.

You are the person I share this house with, nothing more, nothing less. You mean no more to me than the shutters that hide what goes on in here, the floorboards I walk over or the doors we use to separate us.

I have spent too much of my life trying to figure out your intricacies, of suffering your deeds like knives cutting through scar tissue. I am through with sacrificing who I should have been to keep you happy as it has only locked us in this status quo. I have wasted too much time wanting you to want me. I ache when I recall the opportunities I've been too scared to accept because of you. Such frittered-away chances make me want to crawl on my hands and knees to the end of the garden, curl up into a ball on a mound of earth and wait until the nettles and the ivy choke and cover me from view.

It's only now that I recognise the wretched life you cloaked me in and how your misery needed my company to prevent you from feeling so isolated.

There is just one lesson I have learned from the life we share. And it is this: everything that is wrong with me is wrong with you too. We are one and the same. When I die, your flame will also extinguish.

The next time we are together, I want one of us to be lying stiff in a coffin wearing rags that no longer fit our dead, shrunken frame.

Only then can we separate. Only then can we be ourselves. Only then do I stand a chance of finding peace. Only then will I be free of you.

And should my soul soar, I promise that yours will sink like the heaviest of rocks, never to be seen again.

PART ONE

CHAPTER 1
MAGGIE

You can't see me from my place up here in the crow's nest. No one going about their business in the street can. I know that because I must have waved at my neighbours hundreds of times and they've never responded. To all intents and purposes, I'm invisible to the world. I don't exist, I have expired, I am a ghost.

I probably resemble one too, standing behind these shutters that mute the light entering my bedroom and turn me into a shadow. When the lamps aren't switched on outside, it's like dusk in here even during the sunniest of days. It's why each time I venture downstairs, I squint until my eyes adjust to the daylight. When the shutters were first installed, they made me claustrophobic; a barrier between the outside world and me. But I've grown accustomed to them. Given a little time, I become used to most things in the end. I'm that kind of woman; I've learned to be adaptable.

I refer to this room as the crow's nest because it reminds me of a ship's lookout point on the tallest of its masts. Sailors use them to see for miles across the horizon. My view extends as far as this housing estate.

Right now, I'm watching Barbara helping her mum Elsie into the passenger seat of a car. Barbara always makes time for her mum. Any parent would be proud of her. Elsie recently became reliant on a walking frame, one of those aluminium ones with castors attached to the front. I remember her complaining how the arthritis in her ankles and knee joints was escalating and that over-the-counter anti-inflammatories were no longer effective. I can't tell you the number of times I suggested she make an appointment to see Dr Fellowes. Once I even offered to pull a few strings in my job as the deputy practice manager to ensure she got an appointment on a day of her choosing. But she's a stubborn old coot. She thinks she's being a nuisance if she sees a doctor more than once a year for her flu jab.

I wonder if Elsie still thinks of me. I wonder if she ever questions why I just stopped going to her house for coffee every Thursday afternoon. Half-past three sharp, regular as clockwork; we stuck to that routine for years. I'd return home from work, grab my own jar of coffee from the shelf – she always served that bitter supermarket brand I hated – and we'd spend a couple of hours putting the world to rights or gossiping about the neighbours. I miss those chats. I've caught her looking towards the house on numerous occasions, so I like to think she hasn't forgotten about me.

Barbara's car moves off the drive, along the street and past number forty. The letting agency has taken its eye off the ball with that one. From up here, I can just about see into the rear of the property – and what a pigsty it is now. If the previous owner, Mr Steadman, knew what had become of his once-beautiful garden, he'd be turning in his grave. The lawn has grown into the borders he spent hours fussing over and they're filled with cans and takeaway boxes. Students have no respect for anything.

His grandson should have just sold the place. Or perhaps he couldn't find a buyer. Not everyone is content to live in a house where the previous occupant's dead body lay undiscovered for weeks. I was the only one who noticed the build-up of newspapers poking through Mr Steadman's letterbox and spotted that his curtains hadn't been opened. I would have raised the alarm myself but of course that's the last thing I can do.

Outside, a red car with a dent in the front bumper parks on the grass verge by the telegraph pole. It's Louise at number eighteen and when she exits, I can see the swell of her belly under her T-shirt. She's pregnant again and I'm delighted for her. She reached this stage once before, then one day, an ambulance arrived at her house and the next time I saw her, she had suddenly just stopped being pregnant. Her body returned to its normal shape as if nothing had happened. I can't imagine what it must be like to have to 'untell' people. I don't think you can ever be normal again after losing something you were so looking forward to loving.

I wonder if she is still working part-time at the cash and carry. I haven't seen her wearing her uniform for a while. I know that her husband is still a cabbie because his taxi's headlights frequently flash across my ceiling when he arrives home after a night shift. Sometimes if I can't sleep, I'll watch his shadow behind the wheel, engine switched off, his face barely illuminated by the dashboard. I often wonder, what prevents him from going inside straight away? Perhaps he's imagining a different life to the one beyond that front door. I can understand that; I often imagine my own alternative existence. But like that old song goes, you can't always get what you want.

There's nobody else to look at so I turn to face my room. There isn't much in here, but then I don't need a lot. A double bed, two side tables, two lamps, a wardrobe, a dressing table and an ottoman. The wall-mounted television has long since ceased to work and I haven't asked Nina for a new one because I don't want her to think I'm missing it. And without it, I'm no longer reminded of how much life I'm lacking.

I have my books to keep me company and sometimes I can convince myself they're enough. I don't get to pick what I read – I'm reliant on what she brings home for me. Every couple of days, I'll start and finish a brand-new one. I prefer detective or psychological thrillers, anything that promises and then delivers a twist. I like to get the old grey matter working and decipher who the bad guy is. I'm hard to please though. If I guess the culprit correctly, I'll be disappointed at how predictable the story is. If I get it wrong, I'll be annoyed at myself for not spotting it earlier.

I'd like to have written a book. I have many stories inside me and just as many secrets. But I doubt it will happen. A lot of things won't, like me leaving this house again. Try as I might, I just cannot manage it. And it's my own fault. I don't believe anyone who claims to have no regrets. They're lying to themselves. We all have them. If I was given the opportunity to go back and change something about my life, I'd be in that time machine quicker than you could say H. G. Wells.

Suddenly, I hear a door opening downstairs, then a voice. I must have missed her as she walked up the road.

'Good evening,' Nina shouts up the stairs from the first floor. 'Anyone there?'

'Yes, only me,' I reply and open the bedroom door. From where I stand under the architrave I spot two bulging carrier bags by her feet. 'Been shopping?'

'Very observant,' she replies.

'Have you had a good day at work?'

'The same as usual. I'm making chicken chasseur for dinner.'

I hate chicken chasseur. 'Sounds lovely,' I say. 'Is it my turn to eat with you tonight?'

'Yes, it's Tuesday.'

'Ah, I thought it was Wednesday. I'm getting ahead of myself.'

'I'll come and get you when it's ready. It shouldn't be long.'

'Okay,' I reply, and return to my room as she disappears from view.

I pause to count the liver spots on my hands. It's been so long since I've seen the sun that there are no new ones forming. That's a small plus among a long list of minuses. I take in my reflection in the dressing table's mirror and flatten down my unruly hair. It's been silver for so long now that I cannot visualise the colour it was before. Then I use a medium-red lipstick to paint on a smile, then add a little eyeliner. I dab blusher on to my cheeks but because my skin is so white, it resembles two red splodges daubed on a rag doll. So I wipe them off and leave my face bare.

I take a deep breath and prepare myself for the night ahead. Once upon a time we were the best of friends. But that was before *he* destroyed everything. Now the two of us are little more than the debris he left behind.

CHAPTER 2

NINA

I remove the glass lid from the dish on the bottom shelf of the oven and steam pours out. Inside, the chicken breasts appear white in colour and I prod them with a fork to check they're done. I know Maggie doesn't like chicken chasseur, but I do, and she's not the one who cooks in this house. Besides, her fake enthusiasm is amusing to me.

I empty the shopping bags before I take my coat off. She prefers neatly stacked cupboards and tidy drawers; I don't. I save my neatness and order for the workplace where I have no choice but to be organised. I don't have to do anything I don't want to in my own home. So I place the groceries wherever suits me best. Maggie isn't likely to rearrange them behind my back.

Sainsbury's was busy tonight, even more so than usual. Families were out in force; armies of beleaguered parents trying to do the weekly shop accompanied by sleeve-tugging children whining and demanding sweets, toys and comics. I watched some of these mothers, frazzled and rolling their eyes, thinking they didn't know how lucky they were.

One little boy with a mop of dark-brown hair caught my attention. He couldn't have been more than a year old and was sitting in a trolley, his chubby legs dangling through the hole in the rear, one shoe on and another lying on its side on a bag of satsumas. His smile was so broad it took up half his face. His mum left him for a moment as she went to another aisle. I imagined how easy it would be to grab him and carry him outside. When she returned with a bottle of ketchup, I had a good mind to tell her how careless she was.

There was a lot of food on special offer and close to its sell-by date tonight so I bought more than was on my list. However, as I couldn't walk home loaded with all those bags, I hailed a taxi instead, which negated the savings I'd made on my bill. I recognised the driver from his profile and the shape of his eyes reflected in the rear-view mirror. Nathan Robinson. I went to school with him – first at Abington Vale Middle and then, briefly, Weston Favell Upper. He hadn't changed much, except for his receding hairline and ugly tribal tattoos on his hands. He didn't recognise me and I didn't introduce myself. I was reluctant to spend the journey home reminiscing about people I've lost touch with or ruminating over where the twenty-four years have gone since we last saw one another. It was unlikely he'd remember me anyway. At fourteen, I turned my back on school and never returned.

As his cab pulled away, I took a moment to face my house and glance up towards the second-floor window. I know that much of Maggie's life is spent behind those shutters living vicariously through everyone else, and I wonder to what degree she misses interacting with people. Over dinner, she'll keep me up to speed with who she's seen and what they're up to, but does she ever long to be among them? Watching isn't living, is it?

I've tried to make her life a little more comfortable but she rarely asks for my help. She didn't mention when her television stopped working. It was only when I remembered I hadn't seen it switched on for a while that she admitted it was broken. I was about to offer to get it repaired when she informed me that the 'news is too depressing' and that she'd rather lose herself in a book instead. So I didn't bother. I know that if I were in her shoes, I'd have gone mad up there by now.

I leave the kitchen, make my way upstairs to the dining room on the first floor and set the table for two. I flatten out the lace tablecloth, the one Maggie's grandmother made her. She prefers to 'keep it for best'. I remind her that these days, there is no 'best' any more. We live in a time where everything and everyone is disposable. I return to the oven to serve up the food, and take the plates and a bottle of Pinot Grigio back upstairs.

I glance at my surroundings as I set the table. It used to be a bedroom and there's still a chest of drawers that I've yet to move. One day I'll make the time to redecorate. By most people's standards, this house is a little topsy-turvy. On the ground floor is a kitchen with a basement leading off it, a lounge, an empty room – formerly the dining room – and a toilet. The first floor contains two bedrooms, a family bathroom, a study and the new dining room surrounded by wall-to-wall bookshelves. Each book is housed inside a thick plastic cover. The second floor is the converted attic that Maggie calls home. It contains another bathroom that only she uses, a landing and her bedroom. And that's it. My home. Well, *our* home, I suppose. And love it or loathe it, neither of us is going anywhere.

I walk up another flight of stairs and find her standing by the window. There I remain, observing her and wondering what goes through her mind, alone up here. And for the briefest of moments, I am close to pitying her.

CHAPTER 3

MAGGIE

As I wait for Nina, I watch over the comings and goings of the cul-de-sac like a sentry guard but without the authority to report suspicious activity or to turn anyone away. I'm as much use as a toothless watchdog. I think back to when I first moved here some forty years ago now, and how most of the houses were identical in appearance. They were well maintained and had a uniform charm about them. Now they've got different-coloured garage doors, ugly plastic window frames and uPVC front doors. Most have replaced their lush green lawns with block paving to accommodate a second and in some cases a third car. They have transformed my once-colourful street into fifty shades of grey.

There's a pattern to the way I take in each property. Being at the far end of a cul-de-sac, I can see both sides of the road. I start with the houses on the left. They are pricier properties because they back on to school playing fields. Number twenty-nine is the last house I can see without squinting and the one that brings back the saddest memories. A little boy, Henry, almost died in a house fire there a few years ago. I remember him well: such a sweet, polite little lad.

Firefighters rescued him but he suffered terrible brain damage by all accounts. His mum never forgave herself and it tore the family apart. But I noticed her husband and their two girls, Effie and Alice, moved back in not so long ago, so I hope there's been a happy ever after for them.

Next, I'll continue with the other side. Elsie's house is next door to mine. She and I must be two of the street's longest-serving residents. We moved in three months apart and became firm friends early on. She knows more secrets about this house than Nina does. Of all the people out there going about their lives, I miss talking to her the most.

She never closes her curtains until she goes to bed, even when it's pitch-black. As an elderly woman living on her own, I'd assume she'd be more careful. I can just about spy a familiar green-and-white image on her large television screen and decide that it's the opening credits of *EastEnders*. Elsie likes her soaps, as did I. We used to chat about them over our Thursday afternoon coffees. I wonder, after so long out of the loop, how quickly I'd be able to pick up on the storylines I've missed. I think again about asking Nina to have my television repaired but do I really want her to think she is doing me a favour? Perhaps I'm cutting my nose off to spite my face.

A small white car with a dark sunroof briefly pulls up outside the house. It must have the wrong address because it quickly drives away again.

I'm suddenly aware I'm not alone and turn to see Nina, watching me. She tries to pretend that she's only just appeared but I sense she has been here for a few minutes. It's happened before, knowing that I'm being silently observed and likely judged, but I never ask. Neither of us ever says what we actually mean. Untruths and unwillingness to communicate effectively, that's how she and

I function. Or perhaps dysfunction might be a more accurate description.

'Are you ready to eat?' she asks, and I smile a yes. She takes my arm gently and helps me down the stairs, one at a time.

Nina sits at the far end of the dining-room table by the sash window while I am two chairs away and to her side. The window's top half has been opened a few inches and I feel a gentle breath of wind running through my hair. It sends goosebumps across my neck and shoulders.

The wine is an unexpected treat until she only pours herself a glass. She catches me looking at it for too long and knows that if she offered, I'd likely accept. But then she glances away so I don't mention it. I take a sip of lukewarm water from my plastic cup instead.

Nina has put ABBA's greatest hits album on the record player again. Some of the grooves have been literally worn away from the number of times she has played this LP with the same old stylus. Songs skip and crackles mask the words. I once suggested she bought it on compact disc without the clicks or interruptions and she looked at me in disgust, reminding me of who the album once belonged to and claiming it would be 'sacrilegious' to swap it. 'We can't start replacing things just because they're getting older, can we?' she asked pointedly.

I know the running order off by heart. The opening bars of 'SOS' begin and inside I chuckle. Gallows humour, I think they call it. Nina takes a serving spoon and awards me the larger of the two chicken breasts, along with an extra scoop of vegetables. She slathers them in more sauce than she gives herself. Later tonight, it will give me acid reflux. I thank her regardless and tell her again how lovely it smells.

'Do you want me to cut up your chicken?' she asks and I nod gratefully.

She chops it into bite-sized cubes with her knife, then returns to her seat.

'Did anything interesting happen at work today?' I ask.

'Not really.'

'Was it busy? I assume by the number of children playing in the street that they've broken up for the Easter holidays.'

'Nothing escapes you from up there in your little crow's nest, does it?'

'I'm just observant.'

My chicken is still pale pink inside but I don't complain. I dip it into the sauce to mask the raw taste.

'It was the under-sevens' club so it was busy this morning,' she expands. 'Some parents dump their kids on us like we're babysitters then disappear into town to do their shopping. The idea of the programme is to participate and read with their children. But some women aren't naturally maternal, are they?'

She holds her fork in her hand. A chunk of potato falls from it and lands on the tablecloth. She jabs at it twice with her cutlery, moving it around and spreading the sauce deeper into the ivory-coloured fabric. I hate it when she uses this tablecloth. It is made of lace and was the last thing my grandmother made before breast cancer took her life. However, I bite my tongue and try to ignore it.

'I see Louise's pregnant again,' I continue.

'Who's Louise?'

'You know, Louise Thorpe from number eighteen. Her husband's a taxi driver.'

'How do you know that?'

'Because he has one of those illuminated advertisements stuck to the roof of his car.'

Nina shakes her head. 'I meant how do you know she's pregnant?'

'Oh,' I chuckle, not genuinely, of course. 'I saw her with a baby bump. She's just starting to show as it wasn't there a couple of weeks ago.' Even as the words are coming out of my mouth, I regret bringing this subject up. I should have self-censored because babies are an out-of-bounds subject in this house and I know where conversations like this can lead.

'You don't remember when I started showing, do you?' she asks, her eyes narrowing.

'No, I don't suppose I do,' I reply, and turn my attention towards the plate. It is as if the temperature in the room has dropped several degrees.

'It probably wasn't until my sixth month that I really noticed it myself,' she recalls. 'I had no morning sickness, no tiredness, nothing. I suppose I was fortunate.'

I keep my head down. 'You were.'

'To a point,' she adds. 'I was fortunate *to a point*.'

Her tone ensures that the sentence hangs between us. I need to change the subject, but so soon into our dinner I'm already running out of observations.

She drops her knife and fork on her plate with a clatter, which makes me jump. She removes the second disc from the double album and chooses a song called 'Does Your Mother Know'. It's one of ABBA's pacier numbers and her face lights up as she hums along with the first verse. 'We used to dance to this, do you remember?' she asks. 'We'd each use a hairbrush as a microphone and sing along to it. I'd be the boy and you'd be the girl.'

She moves towards me. My instinct is to flinch until she stretches out her hand. I shake my head. 'I'm too old for that.'

'No excuses.'

Her fingers curl to beckon me and I reluctantly rise to my feet. We move to a clear space and she holds my hands as we start to dance. She takes the lead and before you know it, we are bopping around the room like a couple of idiots, albeit with my limited mobility. For a moment, I'm transported back to the late 1980s when, as we are now, we were jiving and singing along at the top of our voices. And for the first time in I can't remember how long, we are connecting. And it feels good . . . it feels *so bloody good*. Then I catch our reflection in the window.

Nina is no longer my little girl and I am no longer her mother.

And as the chorus begins to fade, so does the memory of what we once had. We find ourselves back in our chairs, eating a meal neither of us is enjoying, and me trying to make small talk.

I ask her what she has planned for tomorrow, then I throw a few of her colleagues' names into the conversation and by the time she has finished updating me on the lives of people I have never met, dinner is over. Already, I can feel the stomach acid beginning to creep slowly up my throat. I swallow it back down. I know it will keep me awake throughout the night and I'll spend much of it spitting foul-tasting saliva into the beaker next to my bed.

'Shall I clear the table?' I offer.

'Thanks,' she replies.

I begin stacking our plates and cutlery.

'I'm going to the bathroom, then I'll help you back upstairs.'

I look over my shoulder to check that she has gone and, in her absence, I take a swig of her wine from the bottle. It tastes as sweet as nectar, so I take a second gulp. Then I worry that she's done this on purpose, and it's a test that I've failed. So I replace what I have taken by filling up the bottle with the water from my cup. I fold the tablecloth and, using the last drops from the glass and a serviette, I dab at the stain the potato slice left.

'Don't worry about that,' she says dismissively when she reappears. 'I'll throw it in the washing machine on a high temperature.'

'But it's lace,' I reply too quickly. 'It'll disintegrate.'

'Then I'll throw it away and buy a new one.'

I want to retaliate, but I let it pass.

'Right, are you ready?' she asks. I look outside. It must be barely seven o'clock and it's still light.

Without warning, Nina grabs my wrist and digs her fingernails into it. I let out a yelp and feel them pushing deeper into me, pressing my tendons until the pain becomes too much and my hand unclenches from the balled fist it was in. The corkscrew I had partially hidden under my sleeve falls to the table with a clunk. Nina's hand remains where it is, her nails still drilling into my skin, and I bite hard on my tongue and try not to show her how much she's hurting me. Eventually, she lets go.

'I was about to put it with the dirty plates,' I say.

'I'll save you the trouble,' she says, but slips it into her back pocket. Her tone softens as if the last thirty seconds never happened. 'Come on then, let's get you back upstairs then, shall we?'

CHAPTER 4

NINA

I follow my mother up the staircase as she takes one step at a time. I notice the muscles tighten in her sinewy arms as she uses the bannisters to pull herself up. The last two years have really taken it out of her. And she's not as confident on her feet as she used to be. It's as if she is afraid that by going faster, she'll lose her balance and fall backwards. I'm here to catch her if she does.

Most of us at some point in our adult lives come to terms with the fact that we'll gradually watch our parents erode before our eyes and there will be nothing we can do to slow it down. I'm no exception. Despite everything that's happened between Maggie and me, it makes my heart heavy to know there will come a time when I'll no longer have her here with me. Sometimes I find myself standing at the bottom of her staircase with my eyes closed, listening to her feet pacing the bedroom floorboards and reading aloud from a book. I wonder if she makes her own noise to fill the empty space in her room.

I told her once that she's like a ghost haunting the house long before she's dead. She laughed and said she'll always be watching me, even from beyond the grave. I sensed a hint of malice in her delivery, but strangely, it offered me comfort. Sharing a house with a twisted spirit is better than being alone. Being alone scares me more than anything else in the world.

We reach her floor and she turns left along the short landing and pushes open the bathroom door. She tries to close it behind her, forgetting it will always be slightly ajar. I wait outside, sitting at the top of the stairs as the tap runs. It's a Tuesday night so she'll be preparing a bath. Set routines like this and our meals together are useful in that we know what to expect from one another. Except for when she veers from the script and does something stupid like trying to steal a corkscrew. Then it feels like one step forward and two steps back. Yet still I persevere.

I switched the immersion heater on when I got home but only long enough for the water to be mild at best. It costs a lot to run this house and my earnings and her state pension are limited. There was a cold snap in January and February, so her government winter fuel allowance ran out weeks ago. Once Easter is out of the way, we'll have summer to look forward to and we won't need to put the heating on as often.

'I brought you another book home,' I say from the landing, and hear a rattling from inside as she lowers herself into the water.

'Thank you,' she replies.

'I'll leave it in your bedroom.'

I head back downstairs to the ground floor and return with a book whose cover image is the chalk outline of a body. I question if her preferred reading material mirrors the darkness beneath her surface.

Placing the book on one of her two bedside tables, I gravitate towards the window. With the exception of a moving car, all is quiet outside. I spy the flickering of television screens in some of the neighbours' lounges and wonder what they're watching. At this time of night, it's probably the soaps. When I was a girl, we'd gather around the telly to watch *Coronation Street* and *EastEnders*. Well, Mum and I did. Dad would be catching up on the newspapers or sitting at his desk in his office upstairs designing buildings.

Outside, our neighbour Louise appears from her front door and collects something from the boot of her car. I spot her paunch in the streetlight – Mum's right, she is definitely pregnant. Without thinking, my hands reach for my own stomach and I find myself cradling it, as if there's a life growing inside me. I know there isn't; it's impossible. My insides are like a broken-down piece of old machinery with missing parts. However, it doesn't stop the longing.

I look up to the burned orange and purple sky and am happy the light nights have arrived. I saved up the money I receive as my Carer's Allowance and have treated myself to a new table and four chairs for the garden made of something called rattan. They should be arriving soon. I don't need all that seating; it's not as if casual visitors drop by. But one chair on its own would look pitiful.

For a moment, I picture Maggie and me eating dinner together in the garden one warm summer evening. It would be nice to do something that is different for us, but normal for other families. Then I dismiss the idea as quickly as it appeared. If I can't leave her alone with a corkscrew for a couple of minutes, then how can I be sure she won't be a danger to either of us if she's outdoors?

I glance at my watch; she's been in the bath for fifteen minutes and the water must be getting cooler. On my way to the bath-room door, I spot her reading glasses folded on her bedside table. Something glints and catches my eye so I step into her bedroom to look more closely. She has tried to hide a spring from her mat-tress under her glasses case, but the tip is poking out. *Good spot*, I think, pleased with myself but disappointed by yet another act of defiance I must now retaliate against. I use the bevelled end of the spring to unfasten the tiny screw that keeps one of the arms of her glasses attached to the frame. I slip both the screw and spring inside my trouser pocket and return her glasses, neatly folded, to where they were.

'Are you ready?' I ask from outside the bathroom door.

'I'm just putting my nightie on,' she replies, and I hear the clanking of metal again. Then she appears, clean and shiny. I follow her into her bedroom and she shuffles towards the window.

'Okay,' I say, 'lift your leg up', and she obliges, familiar with our well-practised routine. I remove a key from my pocket and undo the padlock attached to the clamp around her ankle. The chain falls to the floor with a heavy thump. I attach a second, much shorter clasp and chain to her ankle and lock it. This chain doesn't extend far from the spike. Once again, I have her confined to her bedroom.

'Right, I've bleached your bucket,' I tell her and look towards the blue plastic pail and toilet roll in the corner of the room. 'I'll see you in a couple of days.'

Later, I'll prepare tomorrow's breakfast and lunch and leave them outside her door before I go to work in the morning. Her dinner can wait until I return in the evening.

I lock the door behind me and stand at the top of the stairs with my eyes closed. I wish it didn't have to be like this, I really do. I think about a quote I read once in a letter written by one of my favourite authors, Charlotte Brontë. 'I can be on guard against my enemies, but God deliver me from my friends.' I wonder if that includes family members too.

PART TWO

CHAPTER 5

NINA

The number seven bus drops me off at the station in what used to be Northampton's fish market. Even though they've torn the old building down and replaced it with this brick and glass monstrosity, if I inhale hard enough I think I can still smell seafood, forever caught between the past and the present.

I make my way through an empty market square, remembering when I was a girl and this grey, rough-hewn cobbled space was the heart of the town. For three days a week, it was a hive of activity with traders selling affordable clothes, pet foods, music, fabrics, fruit and veg, and videotapes. Now, there aren't enough stalls to fill even half of it on the busiest of days.

I'm a quarter of an hour early when I swipe my way inside the library where I work. I head down the stone steps, following the grooves that thousands upon thousands of pairs of feet have made over the building's 150-year history. I use my security pass again to enter the basement and leave my bag and coat in the staffroom before I return upstairs to the main floor.

I bid a cheery good morning to my colleagues – I count twelve of us on shift today, all of us of different ages. As I watch them interact with one another, it strikes me that people have an anti-quated perception of librarians. They assume female employees are quiet, unassuming, bookish folk; that our wardrobes consist of a dull collection of cardigans and comfortable shoes; that we wear our hair tied back in tight buns and we spend our lives sitting behind desks shushing or fining people for late returns. Meanwhile, our male colleagues are equally dull, humourless virgins with beards, corduroy jackets and checked shirts, who still live at home with their mothers.

Nothing could be further from the truth. On the library floor, yes, we remain relatively softly spoken and professional and we do love our books. But that doesn't mean we live and breathe them. We have lives away from the written word.

One by one we discuss what we did over the weekend. Danielle shows us blue-and-yellow bruising across the skin above her rib-cage where she landed awkwardly zipwiring in Wicksteed Park. Then Steve arrives with five minutes to spare and proudly displays cling film wrapped around his forearm. He's been tattooed again, although it's hard to make out the design hiding beneath the wrap and Vaseline. Regardless, I tell him it looks nice. Joanna plays in a rock band while Pete is now in his fifties but training to be a yogi.

When Jenna asks about mine, I inform her my mum didn't have a great weekend so she took up most of my time. She nods sympathetically as if she understands, which of course she doesn't. I hate it when people pity the life they assume I lead. And it's not like it isn't pitiful . . . just not for the reasons they assume.

Many of us have worked in this building or in the library ser-vice for years. We joke that we'd have served less time behind bars for manslaughter. Some I am closer to than others but there's not one person here I can honestly say that I dislike. Maggie once asked me if I was lonely, not spending time with anyone my own age. For a long time, I was. But life has a habit of surprising you when you least expect it. And she doesn't know about everything or everyone I come into contact with. It's healthy to have secrets.

With one exception, I keep most people at arm's length for a reason. If you allow an emotional attachment to develop, eventually that person will disappoint you. They might not mean to, but if a better opportunity comes along, they will always leave you for it. I've learned the hard way that people – even loved ones – are transient souls.

As the library doors open and the first members of the public amble inside, the van containing a new stock of books arrives earlier than expected. Steve pushes a trolley containing boxes which need to be unpacked, serviced, jacketed, barcoded and catalogued. Then once they've been scanned, any books that have not been reserved are placed on another trolley. Today, I volunteer to stack the shelves with them.

There are thousands of books and hundreds of shelves and I know every inch of them. I've worked here for eighteen years, so I wouldn't be doing my job if I didn't. However, the library has changed beyond all recognition from when I first started. But I've moved with the times. I've been awarded a couple of promotions over the years but I didn't apply for them, they just sort of happened. I'm not an ambitious woman and I make no apologies for it. Some of us just aren't driven enough to climb the career ladder.

I assign almost all of my books to their correct shelves in their correct locations, spines neatly stacked up together and in alphabetical order by each author's surname. Sometimes I wonder why I bother trying to keep everything so orderly, as it won't be long before the public rummages around them like it's the last car-boot sale on earth.

Only one book remains on the trolley, so I make my way towards the War and British History section. It's often empty of customers, unless there's an anniversary of a famous battle approaching and interest is renewed. I remove a craft knife from my pocket, slip off the blade's protective sheath, slice the page out that contains the barcode and hide the book inside another. One of the benefits of my job is that I get to cherry-pick from the latest arrivals. I'll leave this one here and pick it up on my way out tonight. I'll slip it into my handbag to pass through the security barriers without setting the alarms off.

I could always just borrow the book, but I don't like giving them back once they're in my possession. I don't want anything that enters my house to leave it. I'm not one of those hoarders you see in TV documentaries who live like moles in their own homes, burrowing their way through skyscrapers of crap-filled boxes they can't bring themselves to part with. Maggie's a bit like that. The basement was like a rubbish dump until I cleared it out a couple of years ago. But meaningful things, like her books, I'm reluctant to dispose of even when she's finished them. So they remain forever on my shelves, their pages slowly yellowing, unlikely to be opened or touched again.

◆ ◆ ◆

My stomach roars and I note from the clock above the reception desk that it's lunchtime already. On my way to the staffroom, I notice an elderly person with a trolley by her side, one of those tartan-covered ones that every woman over the age of seventy pushes. Even from this distance, I can smell her. She leaves a bitter taste in my throat and for a moment I try not to breathe in around her. Her odour is the reason why no one is sharing her table.

Her hair is a shock of white and silver, matted in places, and reaches her shoulders. Her eyes are a milky blue, her skin a mocha brown and her clothes tatty and unwashed. I don't know her name and as far as I'm aware, she isn't a library member. But she is a regular here, more frequent in the winter months when she'll lurk at the back of the room absorbing warmth from the cast-iron radiators. She'll take her scarf, socks and shoes off and spread them out across the tops so that when it's closing time, her feet will remain warm for a little while when she's back in the unforgiving cold. She favours romantic fiction, especially those soppy Mills & Boon books. Sometimes she devours two in one sitting. It's a safe bet she's yet to find the same happy ever after as the characters she reads about.

I return from my locker with my packed lunch – a sausage roll, a red apple, ham and cheese sandwich and can of lemonade. I drop them into a plastic bag and place them on the table next to the old woman. When she understands what I've done, she looks up at me and for a second, I swear I can see Maggie in her grateful eyes. Without offering her an explanation or awaiting a thank you, I leave her alone.

'You shouldn't feed the pigeons,' says Steve as I pass him. He's seen what I've done. 'They're vermin.'

'I hate watching people suffer,' I reply, and make my way outside to buy my lunch instead.

I don't know what that woman has lost to end up trapped in the life she lives now, but I know how it feels to have your world thrown from its axis through no fault of your own.

CHAPTER 6

NINA

TWENTY-FIVE YEARS EARLIER

The weight of the textbooks in my schoolbag makes a heavy thump when I let it fall to the floor. I kick my ugly, clunky, black lace-ups into the cupboard under the stairs and rush upstairs to my bedroom and swap my uniform for my tracksuit bottoms and a T-shirt. While school uniforms are okay for kids, it's not fair that teenagers should be forced to wear them.

'Hello,' I shout as I head back downstairs, but there's no response. There must be somebody here because the front door was unlocked and Mum never works later than 2.30 p.m. at the surgery. She says she doesn't want me coming home to an empty house like she had to when I was her age. I keep reminding her that I'm nearly fourteen and that I can survive alone here for a few hours without burning the place down.

I pick up the remote control and switch on children's TV. The programmes are a bit babyish but I like background noise as I do my homework. Dad says he doesn't know how I can concentrate with all that noise; I remind him I'm a girl and it's been scientifically proven that we can multitask better than boys. I read it in *Just Seventeen* magazine so it must be true. Besides, I've only got an English lit essay about the Brontë sisters to finish tonight and they're my favourites. Although I do still have a soft spot for *Malory Towers* and Judy Blume. I'll do an hour before *Neighbours* comes on and if I'm lucky and Dad is late home from work, then I'll get to watch *Home and Away* too. He hates the Aussie soaps.

Mum has usually come to find me by now to ask me about my day. Half the time I mumble one-word answers and tell her to move out of the way of the telly. But her not being here means curiosity's getting the better of me, so I look for her instead. She's not in the kitchen, or upstairs on the first floor or in the attic they've just had converted. Everyone else has been getting conservatories, but we're the first house in the street to extend up *and* convert the cellar into a basement floor. Dad says when we come to sell in the next couple of years, the profit we'll make will have made the expense worthwhile. I keep trying to talk him into letting me swap bedrooms and move up there. He says no, but I'll wear him down eventually. I always do.

I gaze out from the window at the top of the stairs and into the garden, where I spot Mum. She's standing by the washing line, a towel in her hands and a full basket at her feet, but she's not moving. It's like I'm watching her on videotape and someone's pressed pause. I knock on the glass but she doesn't flinch. That's not like her.

By the time I reach the kitchen, she's made her way indoors. Her eyes are red and puffy, like mine when my hay fever kicks in and I want to claw them out.

'Didn't you hear me come in?' I ask, and I can tell that her smile is forced because I do the same when I get a birthday or Christmas present I don't like, so as not to offend. 'Is everything okay?' But I'm not sure I actually want to know.

'Just give me a minute to finish hanging up the rest of the washing,' she replies, and her voice is all sing-song-like. Like her smile, she's putting it on. She's acting weird; I don't like this.

I glance at the basket and all she's washed are bathroom towels, tea towels, dishrags, dusters and even those fluffy mats she puts under the toilet pedestal and by the side of the bath. I'm a bag of nerves as I wait until she comes back inside.

'Come here,' she says, and beckons me to join her at the kitchen table. She sits by my side, removes a tissue from under her sleeve and dabs at her eyes with it. I don't know what she's about to say.

'There's something I need to tell you,' she begins. 'It's about your dad.'

My stomach does backflips and I clamp my hand over my mouth so quickly that it hurts my lips. Now I know what she's going to say and I want to throw up. The same thing happened to Sarah Collins at school last Christmas. She was called out of geography class and then Mrs Peck told her that her dad had been in an accident on his motorbike and her mum was on her way to come and collect her. She's the first person I know who has lost a parent.

My dad is my world and I don't want to be in a world without him. 'Is he dead?' I ask.

Mum shakes her head and suddenly, there's hope. 'No,' she says. 'He's not, darling. But . . . but I'm afraid your dad and I won't be living together any more.' She puts her hand on my arm. Her skin is cold. 'This morning, when you were at school, your dad told me he couldn't be with us any longer and that he had to leave.'

'He's gone?' Tears prick my eyes and my voice trembles. 'Why?'

'We haven't been getting on very well lately.'

'But why does he need to leave?'

'Because he thinks it will be for the best.'

'Where's he gone to?'

'He's found somewhere else to live up in Huddersfield.'

'Where?'

'About two and a half hours from here.'

'When can I see him?'

'You're not going to be able to for a while. But he has left us an address that he said you can write to.'

'I don't want to write to him! I want to see him now.' Mum's grip tightens on my arm. It doesn't hurt and I think she's trying to reassure me but it's only making me more afraid. 'You're getting a divorce, aren't you? Mark Fearn's mum and dad did that and he went to live with his mum and now he only sees his dad at week-ends and it's not fair.'

'I know darling, I know.' Mum can't control her tears either and she cries with me. Her hand moves towards mine but I snatch it away before she can make contact.

'It's not fair,' I shout. 'Why couldn't he have waited until I came home and told me?'

'I know how close you two are. I think he might have found it too difficult.'

'I want to go and live with him.' I want to hurt her like she's hurting me. It works, because her eyes flicker as if she wasn't expecting to hear that.

'I'm sure you'll be able to stay with him during school holidays, once he's settled.'

She has already set the kitchen table for tea and it's only for two places. The anger inside me boils over and I sweep the cutlery and crockery off it with my arm and it clatters and smashes across the floor tiles. Now Mum looks scared, almost terrified, and I clamber to my feet. 'I hate you!' I yell, but I don't mean it. 'You shouldn't have let him go. This is *your* fault.'

I run from the room and I hear Mum following me, but I'm too quick and I'm up the stairs and inside my bedroom before I slam the door shut. Then I lie on my bed, my face buried in the pillow, sobbing my heart out.

She leaves me alone for an hour or so and when she finally comes upstairs, she knocks before she enters. I turn away, ignoring her and the smell of chicken pie and gravy she carries with her. I watch her reflection in the mirror as she places a tray of food and a drink on my desk and turns to leave without saying anything.

'Why?' I ask again. 'You never argue, you're always doing stuff together, you seem really happy.'

'When you get older you'll understand that sometimes appearances can be deceptive,' she replies. 'You can never really know a person, no matter how much you love them.'

I feel like there's something she's not telling me because it still doesn't make any sense. 'Why didn't you try harder? For my sake.'

'You still have me and we still have our home and everything else is going to carry on the same as it's always been.'

'But it's not, is it? Without Dad it's never going to be the same again.'

Mum opens her mouth but I'm done with listening to her. I close my eyes until she leaves. Then I grab my notebook from my desk and write Dad a letter, demanding that he comes home or at least calls me. He will listen to me, I know it. I'm his 'only girl'. He's called me it for as long as I can remember. He won't leave his 'only girl' here without him.

Later, Mum puts his address down on an envelope, sticks a first-class stamp on the front and promises me that she'll post my letter in the morning on her way to work. If Dad hasn't called by tomorrow, then I'm going to write to him again telling him it's not too late to change his mind and that he can come home. I bet Mum would take him back in a heartbeat.

When it's time for bed, Mum comes in and lies next to me with her arms wrapped around me and we quietly cry together. The last thing I remember before I fall asleep is her kissing the top of my head and telling me how sorry she is. 'Please don't hate me for being the one who stayed,' she whispers.

'I won't,' I reply, and I mean it. No matter what I said to her earlier, I could never hate her. She's my mum.

CHAPTER 7

MAGGIE

I don't know what time I awaken, as Nina removed my watch and the clock from my bedroom months ago. The clock was a gold carriage timepiece that once belonged to my mother. I ended up with it after she died, and my sister Jennifer took the china figurines. I kept it on the chest of drawers in here. Then one evening when I'd returned from my bath, it had disappeared without explanation.

I'm not yet ready to leave my bed. Last night was a restless one. There was nothing restful about reading, as I had to hold my book with one hand and use the other to keep my glasses with the broken arm perched on my nose. The spring I'd picked out of the mattress had vanished from my bedside table and I told myself off for not having hidden it better. I assumed Nina was punishing me by making reading – my one pleasure – more difficult.

Even my sleeping tablets weren't fit for their purpose. They used to knock me out within minutes of my head hitting the pillow, but I've built up a tolerance to them over the years and now, most nights my sleep is fitful. I'll also wake up at least twice a night to urinate in the bucket in the corner of the room and only if I'm lucky will I manage to get off to sleep again quickly.

As I move myself up into a sitting position, the chain attached to my ankle rattles against the floorboards. The cuff strikes my other shin and I curse. That'll add to the colourful tapestry of other bruises I've given myself with this damn restraint. You might think I'd be used to it by now and for much of the time I am. But sometimes I forget.

Rubbing my shin, I slowly swing both legs over the side of the bed and my toes feel the cool wood of the floorboards. I shuffle towards the window and begin my first watch of the day. I'd rather be up here in the crow's nest and with a bird's-eye view than living down in the basement like a worm underground.

The day I woke up in here, Nina informed me that the glass was shatterproof and soundproof, not that I'd be able to reach it anyway through the dense shutter slats. Neither the chair leg nor lamp I smashed against them even scuffed their surface.

I rise to get ready for the day. I clean my face with a damp sheet from a half-full packet of wet wipes, then use three more to clean my body. The orange scent from last night's bath lingers on my skin and while I don't welcome it – I hate citrus smells – I suppose it's better than not smelling of anything. I change out of my nightie and choose a pink and red floral dress from the wardrobe. I don't wear knickers any more because I can't get them over the chain or ankle cuff. Likewise tights or trousers. Everything I slip on must be something I can pull over my head or wrap around my waist.

The wardrobe is still full of my clothes, but they're of more use to the moths than to me. I'm sure Nina has left them as a reminder of what I once had; along with heels, scarfs, gloves and coats, they're no longer fit for purpose. There are just seven ensembles I rely on, one for each day of the week. Every Friday, I leave a neat pile of my dirty washing outside my door and the following day, it's been cleaned and pressed and returned to me. It's like room service at a hotel I can't check out of.

On the wall and an inch or so below the ceiling is a photograph of my husband Alistair that has been glued to the wallpaper. He's smiling at the camera. When I first ended up in here, it was as if his eyes were following me around the room. I couldn't escape him. I hated it and I hated him. But the length of my chain makes it too far out of my reach to tear it down. I threw a glass of orange juice at it once, but all that did was give the photo a sepia effect, like it had been taken a hundred years ago. In fairness, that's how long ago our marriage feels.

I cover my bucket with a towel to contain the odour of last night's expulsions. Nina only empties it once every two days but I've got used to the smell. Soon after this all began, I lost my temper and tried to throw the contents over her. But because I hadn't got used to the restriction of the chain, I tripped over it, lost my balance and covered the floor with my own waste instead. Nina laughed until the tears fell from her eyes and refused to bring me anything to clean it up with until the next day.

She also used to leave me a can of air freshener until I tried to spray it into her eyes and blind her. She dodged the stream just in time and I never saw another can again. Instead, she leaves me car air fresheners to hang around the room, making it smell like a showroom. And they're citrusy, of course.

Nina alternates between two chains of differing length to keep me prisoner. I don't know what they're made of, but they're a solid, toughened metal that I've tried and failed to break or prize apart countless times. They're comprised of links attached to a cuff that is secured to my ankle with a padlock that only she has the key to. They're almost medieval in appearance.

My daytime chain is affixed to a metal spike in the centre of the room that's secured to what I assume to be a joist under the floorboards. It stretches exactly the same distance in both directions, to the window and to the door on the opposite wall. I suppose that's why she doesn't lock my bedroom door. She knows I'm not going anywhere.

The second chain is only used when I join her for dinner, every second evening. It reaches down the staircase, along a first-floor landing and into the dining room. It also allows me into the bathroom on my floor for my twice-weekly baths. However, it won't go as far as the next staircase or the ground floor.

I open my door to find a book and two transparent Tupperware boxes on the carpet. 'Hotel room service has been while I slept,' I say to myself. Inside the smaller of the boxes is breakfast. Two slices of cold, buttered, toasted white bread, a tin of fruit cocktail and an apricot yoghurt. The larger box contains a green banana, a ham and cheese sandwich, a satsuma and a packet of cheddar-flavoured crackers. There is no cutlery. I take it inside and sit on the bed, nibbling at the toast first, before I pick the fruit out of the tin with my fingers and drink the yoghurt. Later, I'll make the lunch last throughout the afternoon until dinner arrives.

The longer I spend at this window, the more I realise I'm becoming like Jeff, the wheelchair-bound character James Stewart plays in the film *Rear Window*. Like him, I have little choice but to spend my days spying on my neighbours. Jeff thinks he has witnessed the murder of one of his neighbours. But the only thing dying in this street is me. And nobody knows that but my daughter.

Where did it all go wrong for us? I think. I'm aware of the answer; I just don't want to be reminded of it.

I turn to pick up today's book. It's *Room*, by Emma Donoghue. I read the dust-jacket synopsis and find it's about a mother and son who live in a single locked room together. *Very droll of you, Nina.* Every now and again she amuses herself with book choices like this. In the past she has left me biographies on Anne Frank, Terry Waite,

J. Paul Getty III and Nelson Mandela – she favours anyone who has been held against their will or locked in a confined space. I can tell which books talk about ways to escape because they're the ones with pages ripped out.

As I make my way to the bed to begin reading, something on the floor underneath it catches my attention. I hesitate, unsure at first whether my tired eyes are imagining it. No, it's definitely there. I move closer and recognise what it is – a wooden memory box that Alistair made Nina some thirty years ago. He even stencilled her name on the lid with gold lettering. I haven't seen it in decades.

I crouch to pick it up and its contents shift as I place it on the bed. How long has it been under here? I've searched every square inch of this room looking for a means to escape, so I can't have missed it. Nina must have put it under my bed one night when I was in the bath. Where did she get it? Then I remember – it was in the basement.

My stomach sinks. Already, I don't like what this box represents: things that I'd rather forget and maybe my daughter doesn't know. The hinges quietly creak as I lift open the lid. The first thing I spot among the contents is a reminder of the first time Nina broke my heart.

CHAPTER 8

MAGGIE

TWENTY-FIVE YEARS EARLIER

I'm perched on the edge of the sofa, unaware the television channel has finished broadcasting for the night, until I catch a glimpse of coloured on-screen text pages offering last-minute holiday deals. I turn it off.

It's an ugly habit but when I'm anxious, I bite at the skin around my fingernails. Tonight, I've gone too deep and the metallic taste of blood is on my lips. The room is now dim, so I can see out of the window and along the darkened road. Directing my eyes towards the streetlights, I spot someone. I spring to my feet and press my face up against the glass, then sigh. It's not Nina.

The clock on the mantelpiece reads past 2 a.m., and my teenage daughter still isn't home. She is somewhere out there in the dark and I don't have the first clue where. The police won't do anything until she has been missing for at least twenty-four hours and it's only been six since I saw her go upstairs to bed. At some point, she must have crept back out and left the house. The policewoman I spoke to was sympathetic but deep down, I know she was judging me. I don't blame her because I'm judging me too.

It's already been an awful day filled with lies. I've had calls from Alistair's credit-card company and his employers pursuing me for money owed and the repayment of wages he was given before he disappeared. I keep trying to tell them that I haven't seen him in months and that he is no longer my responsibility. But when I contacted the Citizens Advice Bureau this afternoon, they advised that, legally, these parasites have every right to chase their money. I hate the mess he has left me and Nina in.

A few minutes pass before a car pulls up outside the house. I hurry to open the front door as a man I don't recognise exits the passenger side. He pulls Nina out from one of the rear seats. When she can't stand up unassisted, he leaves her slumped in a heap on the path like a bin bag.

'What have you done to her?' I yell, and dash towards her.

He shrugs. 'Take a chill pill. She's just drunk.'

'But she's only just turned fourteen!'

'Don't let her out then,' shouts the driver from an open window as his friend rejoins him. The car pulls away, repetitive music blaring from the speakers.

Nina reeks of booze and cigarette smoke. I can smell vomit on her too. I reach down to grab her before the neighbours see.

'Fuck off,' she mumbles and tries to push me away.

'I need to get you inside, Nina. You cannot stay out here all night.'

'You can't tell me what to do,' she slurs, but she's not in any fit state to protest. Eventually she surrenders and allows me to help her to her feet. I slip my arm around her waist and we walk slowly and unsteadily towards the house.

She virtually falls on to a kitchen chair and rests her head on the table with a thump. My relief that she is home and safe tempers my fury. But I'm at a loss as to know what to say to a girl I don't recognise. I wish that I could dismiss tonight's behaviour as a one-off occurrence but it's not. It's not even close. Her unmanageable attitude is becoming frequent and I'm powerless to stop it. I've tried yelling, reasoning, crying and begging but my protests are falling on deaf ears.

I control the impulse to shout at her. It's pointless because she's unlikely to remember it in the morning. Instead, I take a glass from the cupboard and fill it with cold water, then place it in front of her. She pushes it away.

'It'll help with the hangover tomorrow,' I advise.

'I don't get them,' she replies.

'Darling, you can't continue like this. It's not fair on either of us.'

Her eyes are closed but she hears me. 'I can do what I want. You can't stop me.'

'You aren't old enough or responsible enough to be going out and behaving in this way. You're going to get yourself in trouble.'

'I was in town with my mates. We were having a laugh.'

'Where? In pubs?' Her lack of response gives me my answer. 'It's against the law, Nina. And look at the state of you; who knows what might happen when you're this drunk? Who were those men who brought you home?' She shrugs. 'Do you even know their names?'

'They said if I gave them a blow job they'd drive me home.' She bursts into a fit of laughter as I take a step back, hoping to God she's joking. I wait for her to admit she's being crude to hurt me. But she doesn't. She catches my slack jaw and wide eyes. 'Don't look so freaked out,' she says dismissively.

'Who are these animals? What are their names?'

Nina shrugs. 'What does it matter?'

'Because you're a child!'

'I'm fourteen. That's what girls my age do.' Her version of fourteen and mine are worlds apart. 'And I take precautions.'

'What do you mean?'

'I make them wear a rubber . . . sometimes.' She opens her eyes, stares at me and lets the statement hang before she laughs again. 'Oh my God, you think I'm still a virgin, don't you?'

I don't say anything. Nevertheless, the fact that she is so blatant about her sexuality hits me with the sharpness of a slap. I can't believe I haven't been able to see what was happening right under my nose. I don't need a psychologist to tell me why Nina is behaving like this. Her transformation from my beautiful, fiercely intelligent, empathetic daughter to this obnoxious, drunken teenager is happening because of her father; because of things I know and that I can never bring up with her. Now I am paying the price for doing what I must. What he has done to her breaks my heart, but for the sake of both of our sanities, she must remain in the dark. I must protect her at all costs.

Her bad behaviour began quickly, with the raising of her school-skirt hemlines; then she pierced her ears without asking my permission. Soon, reports from her teachers arrived about her failure to complete homework, playing truant and bullying a younger girl. I'm not sure whom I was trying to convince when I assured them it was a passing phase.

The first night she came home after her 9 p.m. curfew, I grounded her. Her response was to tell me to 'get fucked'. When she did the same the following week, I imposed the same punishment again and this time she laughed in my face. I wasn't aware she'd started sneaking out of the house until a police car brought her home a fortnight earlier. She was with a group of friends drinking cider near the parade of shops in the next estate. Then came the multiple love bites that appeared on her neck and shamelessly made their way down to her chest. But I told myself she wouldn't have gone any further; she was just too young.

And now she's offering oral sex for car rides home. Fury erupts inside me when I think of how these men have taken advantage of my child; I want to find them and make them pay for what they have done. She has suffered enough without now being easy prey for perverts. I continue glaring at her, trying to decide upon my next approach. I want to yell but it will do neither of us any good. 'Let's get you upstairs,' I suggest, and she tries to swat me away like a fly. I approach her again and this time she attempts to slap me. She misses.

Eventually, she rises to her feet of her own accord. I remove an old blue bucket from under the sink and follow her as she stumbles up the stairs, using the bannisters to pull herself up. Almost as soon as her head hits the pillow, she is asleep. I roll her on to her side in case she vomits while unconscious. I leave her in her clothes and place a glass of water on her bedside table. The bucket is on the floor if she takes ill.

As I leave, something catches my eye inside the rubbish bin by her desk. I do a double take.

It's a pregnancy test.

I turn to ensure she is still asleep before I bend over to pick it up. I scan the discarded box's instructions and my worst fears are realised when I spot two blue stripes in a plastic window. I clasp my hand over my mouth and my knees threaten to buckle beneath me. My chest aches like my heart has broken. I steady myself with the doorframe, put the test back where I found it, leave her door ajar and try to reclaim my breath.

◆ ◆ ◆

I spend the next few days with a mind as numb as my body. I put a brave face on it at home and at work, but it's eating me up inside.

This is the worst possible outcome. Even if the circumstances were less horrific, Nina would be nowhere near ready for motherhood – and the circumstances are in every way a horror. Trying to reason with her will be pointless as she is too stubborn to listen to anything I have to say. I wonder how far along she is, or if she even knows when she is due. I cannot take the risk, so there is only one solution. I must deal with this for her.

I wouldn't have thought it possible, but my hatred for my husband has sounded new depths. I'm glad he is never coming back because Nina deserves better. I just need to make her understand this.

CHAPTER 9

NINA

The swimming pool is almost empty. I am in one lane and a teenager being coached by a vocal parent is in another. The boy is like a dolphin, flying up and down the pool practising the butterfly stroke. His dad follows him from the side, a stopwatch glued to his hand. Between lengths, he keeps trying to motivate his son with reminders like 'think Team GB' and 'the next Olympics'. He is a pushy parent and his son is no doubt sick of it, when he should be grateful. At least he still has a father in his life. Even after all these years, I still feel the absence of mine. My memories of him didn't disappear just because he did.

I slip my waterproof earplugs back in, kick off from the side of the pool and launch into the breaststroke. I like to swim at the Mounts pool two or three times a week before I go to work. It's only a ten-minute walk from here to the library and I have set myself a goal to complete fifty lengths non-stop before the summer arrives. I'm not yet half the way towards reaching my target, but I'm getting closer.

This morning I manage nineteen and a half lengths before I cheat and walk the last half. My heart races and my lungs burn but it's a satisfying pain, although I don't think I'll be troubling Team GB anytime soon.

I push my goggles to the top of my head, leave the pool, shower and once I've retrieved my clothes from the locker, I find an empty cubicle. I peel off my black one-piece swimming costume and stand there, naked, staring at myself in the mirror. Someone has daubed the words 'ugly bitch' on to the reflective surface with a red marker pen. It comforts me to know they have lower self-esteem than I do.

The self-help books I've read advise you to take time each week to stare hard at your moles and wrinkles, cellulite, spots, lumps, bumps and stray hairs. Apparently, owning your imperfections is a valuable exercise in gradually accepting them as perfections. What a load of old crap. They're all just ugly.

I grab my love handles then cup my breasts and hitch them back up to where they're supposed to be. I'm not even forty and they're like a spaniel's ears. I dread to think what I'm going to look like in another decade if I don't start firming up now.

Three months ago, when I plucked up the courage to stand on my first pair of scales for years, I peaked at just over fourteen stone. And at five feet four inches tall, I struggle to carry it off. I didn't consciously pile on the pounds with greed. At twenty, when my body went through an exceptionally early menopause, the hormone replacement therapy that followed made my weight balloon. It's only recently that I've decided to do something about it. And through healthy eating and exercise, I'm thrilled to have lost almost a stone.

I move my face closer to the cubicle mirror and use my thumb and forefinger to peel down my bottom lip and read what's tattooed inside. Only I can see it; nobody else has ever noticed it, aside from perhaps my dentist and her assistant and they didn't pass comment. It wasn't professionally inked; the lines have bled over time and parts of it have faded.

I wish I could remember the name of the man who scarred me, but each time I try and put a face behind the needle, I draw a blank. The middle of my teens are like a jigsaw puzzle with too many missing pieces to form a full picture. Sometimes it feels like I'm living a half-life, never knowing if what I've done today I've done before.

My weight loss has been coupled with a desire to update my appearance. It surprised Maggie almost as much as it surprised me when I turned up at her bedroom door asking if she could teach me how to apply make-up. I could have watched a YouTube tutorial or visited Boots and asked one of the overly made-up mannequins behind the counter to offer me a demonstration. But this felt like something she and I should have done back when I was a teenager.

'I can show you how to do your nails as well if you like,' she suggested, and I agreed. I returned to the room with a file and let her shape them and paint them baby pink. For a moment, it was as if we were an ordinary mother and daughter again. There were no lies or pussyfooting around one another, we were just two women enjoying a conversation about make-up.

It was only when I was leaving that I understood Maggie had palmed the nail file. She tried to pretend that she hadn't, but it was easy to locate inside her pillowcase. I tutted at her, waved my finger in an exaggerated manner and took it back before she could do any damage with it. Then I stole her pillows as punishment.

Before I know it I'm changed and standing outside the Mounts building. I look at my watch. I'm too early for work so I take the long route in, passing the fire station, Campbell Square Police Station and the Roadmender venue. The latter is another place in this town that I know is tied to my youth but which I only vaguely recall. I think I spent a lot of time there watching music acts perform but I couldn't give you any of their names. Well, with the exception of the one that changed my life. I often wonder if my best days might be the ones I can't remember.

Soon after I arrive at the library, I assist a middle-aged, silver-haired man to compile his CV on one of the computers. While my client types with one finger and squints at the screen, a young woman with a pushchair and a child strapped inside it passes us. I leave him for a moment and gravitate towards them. I use the word 'woman' but the closer I get, the more I realise she can't be much more than fifteen. *Babies having babies*. It might be her age or her fluctuating hormones that are causing a strip of acne to emerge and spread across her forehead. Her attempts to mask it have failed and her make-up resembles caster sugar sprinkled across the uneven surface of a cake.

The child is a little girl. She's dressed in a green *PAW Patrol* sweatshirt and jeans, and she is clutching a bag of sweets. There's a ring of white chocolate spread around her lips. She has a huge smile and just two teeth, one at the top and one at the bottom. When her big brown eyes lock on to mine, she bursts into a fit of giggles and I cannot help but pull a silly face and laugh with her. She seems clean, well nourished and happy, so her mum can't be doing a bad job even at her age. It doesn't stop me from resenting her for having this healthy, cheerful child and against all the odds, keeping it alive. It's more than I ever managed.

I'm not ready to bring an end to this playfulness so I casually follow mother and daughter towards the magazine shelves. Mum leafs through the celebrity mags, stopping only to glance at the photos of people I've never heard of.

I like being around children but less so babies. I remember last summer when our area manager Suzanne paid us a visit during her maternity leave. She turned up with her infant son in a sling wrapped around her body. Had there been prior warning, I'd have booked the day off. I spied her just as she passed through the sliding doors, and I quickly slipped away and locked myself in the disabled toilets until mother and son left and it was safe to emerge.

If I'd stayed, I'd have been expected to behave like the others and coo over the baby and patiently await my turn to hold him and tell Suzanne how beautiful her son was. I couldn't put myself through that. If I held him in my arms I might never be able to let go.

Without so much as a warning sniffle, this child in the pushchair lets out a huge sneeze and a large string of green snot shoots out of her nose and hangs from her nostril like a stalactite. It's disgusting but funny at the same time and she's oblivious to it. Her mother is too lost in an article about the Kardashians to notice, so I take a paper tissue from my pocket and wipe her daughter's nose clean.

'What are you doing?' The girl has turned around and she sounds angry.

'She had a snotty nose,' I reply. 'I was just giving it a quick wipe.'

'Back off,' she says loudly. It gets the attention of other users. 'I don't want you touching her without my permission.'

'I'm sorry,' I reply, taken aback by her aggression. My face reddens and I fight a sudden urge to cry. She waits for a moment until I leave, humiliated.

I take a handful of deep breaths until I am back in control of my emotions. Instead of shame, I'm now annoyed by that poor excuse for a mother. How dare she speak to me like that? What is it with women who, once they have a child, automatically think they're superior to the rest of us? If she'd kept her eye on her daughter's well-being then I wouldn't have needed to step in. Well, she's going to regret that.

My opportunity arrives much sooner than I anticipated when a few minutes later, the child is alone again. I pick two random books from a shelf and, checking that nobody is watching, I slip them into the shopping pouch under the pushchair by her daughter's feet.

When the girl is ready to leave, I'll make sure to watch as the barcoded books set off the electronic alarm. I doubt the police will be called, but she will feel as humiliated as she made me.

CHAPTER 10
MAGGIE

The bedroom is uncomfortably stuffy. The windows are triple glazed and the locks are glued shut, so the only way to allow new air to circulate is to open the door between my room and the landing. But even that makes little difference tonight.

I lift an electric fan that's been sitting unused on top of the wardrobe for months and place it lower down on the dressing table. Months ago, I prized the safety guard from the front so I already know the blades are plastic and of little use to me as a weapon. Neither are the exposed floorboards. It's impossible to prize up the nails, so I can't use them or the wood to my advantage. I plug it in and point it in the direction of the bed and I watch as specks of dust dance inside the current of air it creates. It dawns on me that perhaps I'm using my preoccupation with the room's ventilation as an excuse for feeling restless, and it's Nina's memory box that is really the cause.

Dinner with her earlier this evening passed without concern. But neither of us mentioned the box and I wonder which one of us will break first. I did ache to ask her why she had left it for me because her actions always have a reason. I try and read between the lines but I can't imagine the box's purpose. I keep trying to pluck up the courage to take another look, if only to dip in and out of it, but I haven't managed it yet.

I fan my face. I can't ask her to lower the heating temperature, because about an hour ago I saw her leave the house. Every other week, albeit on different days, she goes somewhere but never mentions it. I think that she enjoys having this little secret to herself, so I don't ask what it is. I'm usually asleep by the time she returns.

Even if she was downstairs, she wouldn't hear me if I yelled because the door and partition wall separating the second floor from the first have been professionally insulated and soundproofed. And for good measure, she's even stuck cardboard egg boxes to the walls. I have yet to hear a peep from downstairs, and I assume it's the same for her with me. If I'm away from the window, the first I'll know of her arrival home is when the first-floor door unlocks and she appears.

I take off my top so I'm sitting in just my bra and wraparound skirt and think of how well I've adapted to my imprisonment. I wonder if I've surpassed Nina's expectations. Spending so much time alone has given me the opportunity to learn a lot about myself. I want for little, which is fortunate, as it's exactly what I'm given. I don't have many luxuries, but I appreciate those in my possession more than I did when I was living a normal life.

Sometimes I wonder if Nina hasn't stripped me of absolutely everything so that when she decides I need punishing, she still has objects to remove. It's what happened with my perfumes, hairspray, transistor radio, shoes, pillows, some make-up and jewellery. One by one they all went to 'teach me a lesson'. But I no longer allow her to witness how her cruelty upsets me. Maybe I've been taking the wrong approach. Perhaps she needs to believe she has broken me before this all ends. Exactly how it will end, though, remains unclear.

I think back to the box again and what else, aside from a twenty-five-year-old pregnancy test, might lie inside it. As soon as I saw that, I closed the lid and slid the box back under the bed. I both do and don't want to know what else is in there. I have to take my mind off it.

I notice for the first time that the fan is making something rustle on one of the bedside tables. I turn my head and I spot that Nina has left me a refill air freshener and a packet of wine gums. She must have put them there when I was in the bath earlier. I haven't tasted sweets since my ordeal began and seeing them here excites me like a child. In my hurry to tear open the packet it splits and the contents spread across the duvet like an edible rainbow.

I am about to pop a red one into my mouth when I hesitate. I've fallen for this before, a random act of kindness that turns out to be anything but. I'm reminded of when she left me a beaker containing a strawberry and banana smoothie. It was as equally unexpected as the wine gums. By early evening, the chronic diarrhoea began and I realised she had laced the drink with a laxative. I still don't know what I'd done to prompt it.

Regardless, I throw caution to the wind, sucking gently at first on the soft sweet in case she's hidden a drawing pin or small piece of glass inside it. Then I can't help but smile at how much pleasure such a simple treat is giving me. Perhaps Nina is taking a new approach in trying to break me, by showing me what I am missing, one small treat at a time. It won't work. I have come to terms with this being my lot. And it's pointless trying to second-guess her. Sometimes there is just no rhyme or reason to what motivates my daughter.

I recall how for my first two months in here, I was convinced that Nina was watching my every move through a camera attached to the coving. It was a small black box containing a glass lens and a tiny red light that flashed every couple of minutes. The thought of her being able to view and relish my misery whenever she liked wound me up like a coiled spring. But as much as I tried to remove the camera, my chain wouldn't stretch far enough to allow me to reach it. I tried hurling a mug at it once, but it missed by inches. Nina's punishment was to make me use the plastic lids of my hairspray and deodorant cans as drinking utensils instead. Then one day, the camera fell from the wall, just like that. It landed on the floor, its case breaking open. I picked up the pieces and saw that it wasn't real. It was just a shell with room for a battery to operate the red light. More of her games.

Back then I questioned how long I was to remain in here and whether her threat to keep me locked up for the next twenty-one years was genuine. I'm sixty-eight now, so the chances of me living until I am eighty-nine are slim, especially with a minimal diet, lack of exercise, no access to fresh air or natural sunlight. I have very little chance of making it to a decade, let alone another thirteen years on top of that.

Of course I've considered suicide – who wouldn't if they were me? But I am the only person in Nina's life. No matter what hardships she puts me through, I can't leave her alone. It doesn't mean I'm not going to fight my way out of here if the opportunity presents itself. Then we can be together on my own terms after I find her the help she needs. She will always be my little girl, no matter how cruelly she treats me.

And there's a part of me that knows I need to be punished for what I have taken away from her.

CHAPTER 11

MAGGIE

TWENTY-FIVE YEARS EARLIER

It's Monday morning and Nina has been crippled by stomach cramps since the early hours. I've already informed the school she won't be coming in today and I phoned in sick myself at the surgery.

I've been padding around the house unable to settle in one place for more than a few minutes at a time. I hear her in tears behind the bathroom door and I'm in two minds over what to do. Eventually, the primal urge to comfort my poorly child becomes too much and I can take no more. I knock, half-expecting to be sworn at and told to go away. 'What's wrong, darling?' I ask.

'It hurts, Mum,' she moans and immediately I want to be the one aching, not her.

I turn the door handle but it doesn't open. 'Unlock the door,' I coax.

I hear her shuffle towards it before it opens. When I see her, I want to hold her and never let go. The heavy eyeliner she has taken to wearing is streaking down her face like ink stains. She is clutching her stomach and her knickers are still around her ankles. I can't remember when I last saw her so vulnerable. I wrap my arms around her, bring her in to my shoulder and rub her back.

'My baby girl,' I say as my eyes well.

'It's never hurt like this before,' she says, pitifully. 'Why am I bleeding so much?'

I take a deep breath. 'I think you're having a miscarriage,' I reply as softly as I can.

She stares at me, shocked that I am aware of her pregnancy. And in that instant, I know I wasn't supposed to find out. Leaving the positive test in the bin wasn't a cry for help as I'd told myself it was; it was a careless mistake.

I reassure her that I'm not here to lecture her but to help her through it. I take her by the arm and lead her back to the toilet but make the mistake of glancing into the bowl. It chills me. Some things you can never unsee. I quickly flush and hope that she didn't see it either before I sit her back upon the seat.

Her face contorts as her cramps flare up again. I place my hand gently on her forehead as I would when taking her temperature as a child. She is burning up – it's normal, one of the side effects. I dampen a cold flannel and dab her face with it, then hold it there. I'm taken back to when she was a five-year-old and caught measles during an outbreak at primary school. A year later it was chicken pox and I remember how Alistair and I took it in turns to take care of her, smother her in camomile lotion and make sure she didn't scratch her pustules and scar. She may be a teenager, but to me she's every bit as defenceless now as she was then.

The silence between us swells, only broken by her sobs and groans as we remain where we are – her in discomfort and me stroking her hair and kissing the back of her head – until nature has taken its course. I know that if I call one of the doctors at the surgery, they will offer to make a home visit. But I don't want their help. I have let her down before; now I must prove to myself that I can be the mother she needs. We will get through this on our own. Lately, Nina may not have thought she needed me, but she does now and that's all that matters. I cannot and will not let her down more than I have already. *This is a fresh start for us*, I tell myself. It has to be.

An hour passes before we move into her bedroom. And as I lay her down, her body folds in on itself like a fragile sheet of origami. I pull the duvet over her and up to her chin, then remove two pain-killers from a packet, offering them to her with a glass of Lucozade. 'Thank you,' she mutters. It feels like so long since she last showed me gratitude for anything, so I cling to it. For the first time since her father disappeared from her life, I feel a bond between us. I love her more than anything I have ever loved or will ever love again. And nothing she does will ever change that.

But there's something I have to tell her, while the memory of what is happening to her body is fresh and in case she is tempted to be careless again.

'I need to explain something that's not going to be easy to hear,' I begin. 'And I'm sorry because I should have told you a long time ago. But I've never known when to bring it up.'

'What?' she asks. 'Is it about Dad?'

'Yes, and no,' I reply.

Her eyes widen, the whites still red. She is desperate for even a fragment of information as to his whereabouts. His silence has dev-astated her and I blame him for setting her on this self-destructive path just as much as I blame myself.

'Do you know why I haven't heard anything from him apart from the birthday card?'

I shake my head. 'No, I'm sorry, I don't,' I lie. 'This is about something that Dad carried inside of him and which he's passed on to you.' I pause to choose my words carefully. 'Your dad was the carrier of something called estroprosencephaly. And it means that if he has a daughter and she falls pregnant, her baby would be very, very poorly if it managed to survive the full nine months.' Nina looks at me, perplexed. I place my hand in hers and hold her fingers tight. 'A baby with estroprosencephaly is likely to be born with a lot of problems, Nina. And I mean *a lot* of problems.'

'Like?'

'Like severe facial disfigurement and with its brain not properly developed. Most babies pass away before they're born and that's probably what's happened today. So while it doesn't feel like it, this is the best possible outcome. Your body knew something was wrong and rejected it. The worst-case scenario is that you would've gone the full nine months and been forced to have a baby that died as soon as it was born.'

'How . . . how do you know this?' she asks.

'When you were a little girl, your dad had these horrendous stomach pains and he ended up in hospital for a time. Eventually and after all sorts of blood tests, the specialists told us he was the carrier of a chromosome deficiency that was causing it and that he may well have passed it on to you. And then they told us what happened to babies born with it.'

'But why was I born okay?'

'It's complicated,' I reply. 'It has to do with how many of the faulty chromosomes you're carrying, and when you were tested as a girl, we learned you are carrying a high number.'

'So I'll never be able to have a normal baby?'

I pause, then answer her quietly. 'No, I'm afraid not.'

I feel the rustle of her duvet as she draws her knees closer to her chest. 'I want to go to sleep now,' she says.

'Shall I stay?'

'No, thank you.' I kiss her on the forehead and reluctantly leave her be.

I make my way back downstairs until I am in the kitchen. I need to take my mind off this hellish day, even if it's just for a few moments. There are dirty dishes lying in the sink from yesterday. *I'll wash them*, I think. But before I do that, I take a box of tablets from my handbag. 'Clozterpan' reads the label, and inside there are three empty spaces in a strip. I slip it into my pocket and make my way to the basement door. I pull the light switch and a bulb illuminates the storage area.

As I head towards the suitcases hidden away under the stairs, I am grateful for my job as a doctor's receptionist. It allowed me to slip into Dr Fellowes' office when he was on call and tear off a blank script to write my own prescription. After using the surgery stamp on it, I forged his signature that I am so familiar with and later had it dispensed by a chemist in town. Last night, I crushed the tablets with the back of a spoon and added them to the gravy I poured over Nina's Sunday roast. She didn't notice any difference in taste.

As I watched her eat, I questioned whether forcing my daughter's body to miscarry without her knowledge was the right thing to do. My mind goes back to 1981 when I was two years into my midwifery training and fell unexpectedly pregnant with Nina. My plan to return to complete the course never materialised. But I know for sure from my studies that Nina has been pregnant for much longer than she thinks. I swallow a good measure of bile rising from the pit of my stomach.

You did the right thing, I repeat. In taking this away from her, I have given Nina so much more.

CHAPTER 12

NINA

Madonna's greatest hits album *Celebration* plays through my headphones on the bus home from work. When I was six years old I'd take the lace doilies hanging over the back of the sofa and put them on my head, tie shoelaces around my wrists and pretend to be the Queen of Pop. Apparently, Dad didn't like hearing his little girl miming about being 'Like a Virgin' so Mum and I would tease him by singing 'Papa Don't Preach' in response. The memory tugs at my heart and I feel myself taken over by a longing to return for even a moment to those innocent times.

Still, after almost a quarter of a century without him in my life, there's so much I miss about Dad. A lot has faded as the years march on and it saddens me that I draw a blank when I try to recall his voice. Mum disposed of all the photographs of him and I, apart from the one I have kept tucked away inside my purse.

I remember when it was taken. He drove us into town so that he could get a new passport picture in a photobooth. I waited outside while the flash went off behind the curtain. In the fourth and final photo, I squealed when his hands suddenly grabbed me and pulled me inside. That's the one I have kept all these years: the two of us laughing our heads off. Mum doesn't know this private moment between us was captured on film. And I treasure it because without it, I might not remember his face either.

My phone vibrates and an email icon appears on the screen. My inbox says it's a Google News alert and my body stiffens. I set it up for when stories appear about one person only. I'm scared to open it. I remove my earphones and start tapping my feet against the metal floor of the bus. Then as I clutch the phone to my chest, I suddenly feel clammy and queasy and I crave fresh air.

I push my way through the commuters holding on to rails and exit through the rear doors three stops earlier than my scheduled one. I need time to read why he has made the headlines and to digest it before I return home for dinner with Maggie. Standing by the side of the road with my eyes half-closed, I read the email.

'Troubled singer dead,' says the headline. Underneath, it reads: 'Convicted killer Jon Hunter dies after an 18-month battle with leukaemia.'

I am vaguely aware of traffic and pedestrians passing me, but I am simultaneously frozen in the present and welded to the past. I couldn't move even if I wanted to.

Jon's photograph is familiar. It's the one the newspapers used at the time of his trial but which I only saw for the first time years later. It's unflattering and doesn't do his good looks justice. He's scowling in it and to someone who didn't know him like I knew him, he'd appear empty and soulless. I don't remember much, but I know he was more than that.

Without warning, a series of images appear in my head, like pictures hanging from string in a photographer's studio, slowly developing. I struggle to put them in order. *I'm somewhere at home*, I think, sitting down while Maggie is standing behind me. She moves closer and she's talking, only her voice is quiet and I can't make out what she's saying. As quickly as they arrive, the images fade.

Without realising it, my fingers have moved towards my lips and the tip of one is tracing the tattoo hidden inside my mouth.

CHAPTER 13

NINA

TWENTY-FOUR YEARS EARLIER

He is moving across the stage just a few metres in front of me and he is so beautiful, I literally cannot breathe. I gasp as he turns his head sharply and the sweat from his shoulder-length dark hair flicks across my face. I can taste him on my lips. You can kill me now because nothing is ever going to feel as good as this moment does.

When he cups the microphone with both hands, I notice his fingernails have been painted black. I'll do the same with mine tomorrow. And when he moves his mouth closer to the mike, I imagine he's holding my face and is about to kiss me. He isn't as tall as his bandmates and he's kind of skinny, yet he dominates the whole stage.

The heat coming from the frenzied crowd in the Roadmender's main hall creates condensation that falls from the ceiling like warm raindrops. At the halfway point of the song, he slips the mike back into the stand and lets the lead guitarist take centre stage for a solo. But even then, all eyes are still on him when he lifts his T-shirt over his head and throws it into the crowd. Now he's standing here, shirtless. None of the boys I've been with are anything compared to him, and I blank them from my mind. He is the only one who exists and I want to be with him like I have never wanted anything else in my life.

I love you, Jon Hunter.

Saffron is jumping up and down next to me; her screams are so hysterical, she's going to make me deaf at this rate. She doesn't realise that she's digging her fingernails into my arm so hard that it hurts. But I don't complain. She, like every other girl in this audience, is fantasising that each word coming from Jon Hunter's beautiful lips is being sung just for her. But she's wrong. They're all wrong. Because he is going to be mine, not theirs. It's me who he's looking at right now with those piercing grey eyes, not anyone else. It's me he sings the words 'crazy little woman-child' to. He knows me better than anyone and we haven't even met. If my best friend or any one of these crazy bitches thinks they stand a chance with him, they're idiots.

Saffron and me have been following Jon's band The Hunters for months now, ever since she first spotted their picture in the *Chronicle & Echo* newspaper. Its music reviewer gave their EP five stars out of five and said they were the most exciting thing to come out of the town since Bauhaus back in the eighties. I don't remember them. The Hunters are supposed to be the next big thing in Britpop, and I reckon they could be even more popular than Oasis or Blur. And it's all down to Jon. Right now, he is everything. And he is going to fall in love with me like I have fallen for him.

Saffron arrived here much earlier to start queuing so that we could get the best spot at the front. Since Dad walked out on Mum and me, Mum's upped the strength of her sleeping tablets. I reckon they could knock out an elephant. I wait for her to fall asleep before I spring to life. It doesn't take much to sneak out of the back door unheard.

Mum never stops thinking about Dad. She doesn't admit it and she never brings him up in conversation but sometimes, I watch her when she goes quiet and gazes out into the garden and I'm sure he's on her mind. Husbands and dads don't walk out on their families for no reason, which makes me think she treated him so badly that he had no choice but to leave us both. It's because of her that he can't bring himself to see me or to reply to any of my letters. It's been seven months since he vanished and all I've had from him is a birthday card saying 'Love, Dad' inside. No letter, no phone call, no nothing. I hate her for whatever it is she's done. It's not fair.

I've been letting her think that things between us are back to the way they used to be before the miscarriage. And now that she trusts me more, I can get away with doing what I want to do and she doesn't have a clue.

As the band finishes its encore and Jon leaves the stage, I'm scared to take my eyes off him because once I do, he'll go back to being a fantasy again. And it's a good job I keep staring because when he reaches the wings, he turns around, his eyes connect with mine and he gives me a smile. I smile back. Then he flicks his head as if to say, 'Follow me.'

'Nina, what are you doing?' shouts Saffron as minutes later, I leap over the barrier and on to the stage. Behind me, the rest of the audience is beginning to make its way home, but my night is only just beginning. I can feel it. My heart wants to beat its way out of my chest and I hear Saffron yelling something else behind me, but I don't reply or turn around to acknowledge her.

Behind the stage, the breeze-block walls of the corridor have been painted white but there's graffiti scrawled across them, including song lyrics, names, signatures and doodles. I keep going, dodging the crew and sound technicians until I spot Jon towel-drying his chest and hair as he walks into a room. My legs are wobbling as I follow him inside. He turns to take me in from top to bottom, then sits on a packing case, removes two cigarettes from a packet of Marlboro Reds, lights both and hands one to me.

'What's your name?' he asks, and blows a smoke ring into the air above his head. It's like a grey halo and he's my saint.

'Nina,' I reply weakly. I clear my throat. 'Nina,' I repeat, this time with confidence.

'Nice to meet you Nina-Nina. I'm Jon.'

'I know,' I say, and take a long drag of my cigarette. I'm no stranger to smoking but tonight I've been singing for so long and so loudly that it burns the back of my throat. I fight not to let it show.

'It's got a kick to it, right?' he says. I nod, worried that if I say anything, I'll cough and make an idiot of myself. 'It's got a little extra something packed into it.' He laughs and raises his eyebrows like I should know what he means. I don't, but I laugh along regardless. 'What did you think of the show?'

'Amazing,' I reply. 'It's not my first time though.'

'I bet it's not.'

He winks and I realise my innuendo. I will myself not to blush. 'I meant I've seen you play a few times.'

'So you're a fan then?' I smile my yes. 'You're hot,' he adds and this time I have no control over my reddening cheeks.

'Thank you,' I reply. 'So are you.'

'I mean you've sweated through your T-shirt,' he continues, and suddenly I'm aware of what a mess I must look. 'Take it off,' he says, and without really thinking I peel it from my wet skin. Now I'm standing here in just my bra and jeans. I normally need a few alcopops inside me to make me this confident. But Jon Hunter is bringing something out of me. He throws me his damp towel and I use it to dry my hair. I wait until he turns around and can't see me before I breathe the towel in. Then he takes a spare T-shirt from a rucksack and hands it to me. Only I don't put it on. Instead, I stand there, looking longingly at him as he looks back at me. Then he makes the approach I've been longing for.

CHAPTER 14

MAGGIE

According to my old carriage clock, now in its new home on the dining-room sideboard, I've been sitting alone at the table for ten minutes. Nina rarely leaves me this long because she doesn't trust me. I don't blame her; I've given her good reason not to. So what is the cause of this change of heart?

I use one hand to pull at the metal cuff locked around my ankle while I rub antiseptic cream into an area that's been chafing. Last year, the cuff was so abrasive that my ankle developed an abscess. Despite me suggesting I might need to see a doctor, Nina was reluctant to help. It was only when I warned her that if it became infected or septic, things could become particularly unpleasant for both of us, that she finally agreed and bought me the cream. Now, she rotates the cuff between ankles every week or so.

The minutes tick by and I begin pacing the room. The last time I spent so much time in here of my own volition was when I was a free woman. I'm tempted to shout downstairs to check that all is well, but I decide to savour the time alone in a place that isn't my bedroom for as long as I can. The top of the window is slightly ajar and I hear birdsong coming from outside. It sounds like a blackbird from here and, curious to see if I'm right, I approach the window and look into the rear garden, but I can't see where the noise is coming from.

Then it hits me – *she has left me alone in a room with an open window!* I know the glass is shatterproof because I once hurled a dinner plate at it when we argued. But it's always been shut and fastened with a lock unless she is in here. Until now.

My immediate reaction is to stand on a chair and start screaming for help at the top of my voice through the gap. But I'm only likely to get a few words out before Nina barrels up the stairs and drags me away. Or is this a test? I've learned to be wary of opportunities, be they a packet of wine gums or an open window. I weigh up the pros and cons and decide this isn't a risk worth taking when the chances of anyone hearing me are so remote. My efforts need to be smarter. I hope I don't live to regret this.

I remain where I am, looking outside. Dark clouds are dominating the silvery sky and I predict we are in for a storm later tonight. It isn't until the invisible blackbird restarts its song that I acknowledge just how long it's been since I've heard a noise not created by either Nina or me. A dog's bark, squealing children playing in the street, a radio DJ's voice, a car engine turning over or even the rustling of a plastic bag caught in a tree . . . they're all things I took for granted.

I remember being constantly surrounded by clatter at the surgery. Patients with hacking coughs, screaming toddlers, the telephone ringing or filing cabinets opening and slamming shut as we gathered records; it was rarely a peaceful environment. But I loved that job, which is why I remained there for thirty-two years. You don't stay in one place that long without making friends with colleagues, and some patients too.

I hope I am still missed. Soon after placing me under house arrest, Nina took delight in recalling how she'd informed everyone

I knew that I'd developed 'vascular dementia' following a series of 'sudden mini-strokes'. She said the damage caused to my brain was irreversible and that I was going to be cared for by my sister Jennifer, a retired nurse, in Devon. I wonder if anyone still contacts Nina to ask after me. If they do, she hasn't told me, and I haven't given her the satisfaction of saying 'no' by asking.

Finally, the quiet of the dining room is broken by Nina's footsteps climbing the stairs. I remain by the window and don't turn to greet her when she unlocks the door and finds me standing there. I spy her reflection; with one glance she sweeps the room and she's dismayed by her carelessness at leaving me alone with an open window. Now she's on the backfoot, assessing whether I've taken advantage of her neglect.

'I haven't done anything,' I say, and face her. She's carrying two plates on a tray, trying to determine if I'm being honest or if she needs to take remedial action. Eventually, she appears to believe me.

As I return to my seat, she slides one of the plates to me with plastic cutlery. She learned not to trust me with the metal ones when I stabbed her in the arm with a fork shortly after this all began. To this day, I maintain that I didn't mean to do it; that the Moxydogrel she used to keep me docile also made me hallucinate. I thought that she was a wild dog trying to rip my throat out. I still don't think she believes me.

It's lasagne for dinner and it comes with two slices of garlic bread apiece. I admit, it genuinely smells appetising. But she knows of my gluten intolerance and I assume the meal is not free from it. However, I'm so hungry that I tuck in regardless and I'll deal with the after-effects privately in the bucket in my room.

'Thank you,' I say. 'We haven't had this in a while.'

She nods but says nothing. With no ABBA and little conversation, Nina is clearly preoccupied.

'How was the library today?'

She shrugs. 'Same as usual.'

'Did you talk to anyone interesting?'

'No.'

'How does Steve's tattoo look now that it's had a chance to heal? Is it better than his last one? You weren't keen on that, were you?'

'I haven't asked to see it.'

Clearly, she has little interest in conversing with me. But as she will be my only source of conversation for the next two days, I pursue it regardless. Reticent company is better than no company at all.

'You missed all the drama this afternoon,' I continue, and recount how bailiffs evicted the students and their belongings from Mr Steadman's old house. 'What did they expect?' I add. 'They treated that place dreadfully. Their parents should be ashamed of them.'

Nina breaks from eating, rises and opens a drawer containing her old compact discs. She slips one into the tray of the hi-fi and presses play. It's a lot louder than ABBA, with clanking guitars and heavy drums. The singer wails rather than trying to hold a tune. I don't like it one bit and it makes me crave the Swedes.

'Who's this?' I ask politely.

She side-eyes me as she retakes her seat. 'The Hunters,' she replies, as if I should know.

A breath leaves my lungs and I don't try to replace it.

'Do you remember them?'

'Vaguely,' I lie.

I wonder how much she remembers. I hope it's the bare minimum.

'Saffron and I used to see them play live all the time.'

'That's a name I've not heard you mention in a while,' I respond, hoping to steer the conversation into safer waters. 'How is Saffron? Are you two still in touch?'

'No. We haven't been for a long time.'

'That's a shame, she was your best friend.'

'You hated her.'

I don't know where this conversation is heading but it's not sitting comfortably with me. 'I didn't think she was a good influence on you at the time,' I say. 'She was leading you astray.'

'It was more like the other way around.' The corners of her mouth rise ever so slightly, as if a specific memory has stirred.

I smile too, as if I know what she's referring to, but I don't have the first clue. There is so much about that period of her life that I am not privy to, nor do I want to be. I know all that I need to know and even after so much time has passed, it still feels like too, too much.

'You hated me too back then, didn't you?' Nina continues. 'Go on, admit it.'

'Of course not. I could never hate you. You're my daughter.'

'Surely you must hate me by now for keeping you locked upstairs?'

'No, I don't.'

'I don't believe you.'

She is looking to pick a fight that I don't want to have. 'You're my flesh and blood. I don't always have to like you, but I have never stopped loving you.'

Nina tears her garlic bread in half and stares at me, her head slightly cocked, like my words have resonated and are creating a warm spot inside her. For a split second I think I can see my daughter again, not my captor. How I miss her. 'Well, I hate you,' she replies and I realise I'm wrong.

We don't speak again until all four songs on the CD have played in their entirety.

'You haven't asked me why I've dug this out,' she says.

'I thought perhaps you fancied a change from ABBA.'

'Do you remember the band's singer?'

'Not really,' I lie again. I can picture his body, as clear as day, nearly naked, his legs splayed, slumped upon the sofa in his basement flat. I can't see his face though.

'Jon Hunter. He was in the news today.'

Hearing his name makes my stomach churn. I mask it by taking another mouthful of lasagne. Moments ago, it tasted delicious. Now it takes effort to swallow it.

'Oh really,' I reply, but don't ask why.

'Yes, he died.'

I stop chewing and look at her. That's knocked me for six. I hope she's telling the truth, I really do, but you never can tell with Nina. 'What happened?' I ask.

'Cancer. Leukaemia, to be exact. It came up as a news alert on my phone. He died in prison, still protesting his innocence.'

'Well, the evidence was stacked against him.'

'I thought you didn't remember him?' she says.

'I recall the story. Vaguely.'

'I only remember bits and pieces about that time.'

'The brain is such a complex thing. It has the ability to store so much, and also to tuck away certain things that don't need repeated examination.'

'They're called repressed memories,' she says. I keep my face a blank. 'They are memories that have been subconsciously blocked because they are so stressful or traumatic. But by hiding us from them, they keep us shackled to the past.'

'Oh,' I say, nodding.

'I've been thinking of going for therapy to see if I can unlock mine.' She glares at me, again, waiting for a reaction. I swallow hard and she catches me do it. It's a giveaway and she has what she wanted. Nina has rattled me.

'Whatever you think best,' I say. But I don't want her to remember anything from back then. It will do neither of us any good if she does.

CHAPTER 15
NINA

It's getting late and the wind and rain have started rattling the windows. I close the curtains and pull down the blinds to keep myself hidden. Even as an adult, storms make me uncomfortable. And tonight, I'm already unsettled as I continue to process the news about Jon's death.

I'm doing everything to delay the inevitable clicking on my phone's news alert and reading more than just the headline. It's as if learning the whole story will make the truth all the more real. At present, they are just words on the Internet and we all know how much the Internet lies. So for a moment, I try and convince myself this is fake news. It doesn't work.

I stare at my reflection in the bathroom mirror as I direct the electric toothbrush along my bottom row of teeth, before pausing it and pulling out my lip. I examine my tattoo for the second time this week. *Lolita*, it reads. I recall visiting the library and borrowing Jon's favourite book by Vladimir Nabokov, to understand why Jon chose the nickname for me. I was flattered when I understood how much the protagonist was imprisoned by his love for that girl.

Nobody can ever convince me that Jon wasn't driven by the same passion for me.

There are a handful of memories I've been able to piece together from back then, such as the night I got the tattoo. It was at a house party and Jon was keen that I got something permanent to show how much I loved him. He was insistent it was the word Lolita because it would mean something to both of us. I eagerly agreed.

It was in a bathroom not dissimilar to the one I'm in now, when I sat on the lid of a closed toilet, listening to the gentle tap of excess Indian ink against the jar as one of his friends prepared to pierce my skin. It didn't hurt – the pills Jon gave me made my body tingle and it was like I was lying on my back and floating in a warm ocean with the sun shining down on me. Minutes later when he was finished, several hands connected with mine as his friends high-fived me, telling me I was a 'cool bird' for having it done. Then I rinsed the blood and sour-tasting ink from my mouth with a bottle of vodka, and it stung like hell. I spat it into the sink and examined my branding in the mirror as I'm doing now. Jon's face radiated with pride. I'd proved my commitment to him as he'd asked me to.

I asked him to get one inside his lip saying Heathcliff, my favourite-ever Emily Brontë character, but he shook his head, laughed and never offered a reason why he refused. And that's where the memory ends. Like so many others, it's just another snapshot of a time past and never bettered.

I finish cleaning my teeth, sit on the rim of the bath with the phone in my hand and take a deep breath. I can't put it off any longer, so I click the email link to the news story.

'Convicted killer Jon Hunter dies after an 18-month battle with leukaemia,' the story begins. 'Hunter, 46, was convicted and jailed for life 23 years ago for the murder of his girlfriend. She was found . . .'

'No!' I hiss. Seeing her name infuriates me so I stop reading because I know the lies the article is about to repeat. I glimpse two photographs of Jon used to illustrate the story. One is of the man I loved, performing onstage where he belonged. The second was taken by a fellow inmate and sold to the papers. Jon's hair is still long but now it's white, along with his beard. Even in such a grainy image I can tell the light has long been extinguished from his eyes. I guess being locked up in one room for so many years can do that to you. I'm already beginning to see it happen with Maggie and she's only been upstairs for a fraction of Jon's time.

I scroll further down without reading any more until I reach a photograph of *that girl*. She's sitting on a beach, wearing a blue bikini, and a pair of mirrored sunglasses is balanced on the tip of her nose. She is smiling like she doesn't have a care in the world, because I suppose she didn't. The resemblance between us back then is uncanny.

I hold the phone to my chest and rack my brain, trying my hardest to remember her, but I still don't think our paths crossed. She didn't hang around with the band, I didn't meet her at any gigs or parties and I know for a fact that she wasn't Jon's girlfriend like the papers said because *I* was. Ask anyone who hung around us at that time and they'll tell you that we were besotted with one another. So it frustrates the hell out of me when they keep referring to them as a couple.

An unwelcome thought creeps into my head. *Or perhaps I just don't want to remember her? Perhaps they did have a relationship that I didn't know about and she's one of the missing pieces of my history?* I shake my head until the suggestion dissolves. 'No,' I say aloud. It simply isn't possible. My memory might be vague but I'm not stupid.

Jon wasn't my first partner and I certainly wasn't his, but he was the first man I ever loved. He was also the last. Imagine that, living a life without love for all these intervening years. I don't need anyone to tell me how pathetic that sounds.

He'd known soon after the first night we slept together that I was fourteen, even when I'd tried to convince him I was eighteen. He was twenty-two and I hadn't wanted to scare him off by admitting the truth. When Saffron opened her big jealous mouth and gave it away – to try and split us up, I assume – I could have slapped her. However, her truth had the opposite effect and Jon admitted it excited him knowing that what we were doing was forbidden. 'I like my bananas green,' he'd said with a grin.

He made me promise not to tell anyone at school about us – no easy feat when you're a teenage girl who wants everyone else to be envious of your relationship with the singer of the hottest band in town. But Jon warned me that if it ever came out, he would deny it for the sake of his career, then he'd dump me. Boasting wasn't worth the risk.

Sometimes when Jon and I met in town after school, he'd sulk if I'd changed out of my uniform in the bus station toilets first. He preferred me to keep it on. I don't think we would've got away with our relationship in this day and age. They'd accuse him of grooming me and would throw around words like paedophile or child molester. But he wasn't any such thing. Unless you were in our relationship, you couldn't possibly understand what we meant to one another. He loved me, he looked after me, and he wanted what was best for me. He was my boyfriend, my best friend and my father all rolled into one. And I've never since allowed anyone to make me feel as special as Jon did.

It was false accusations that ruined Jon's life when I was facing my own battles. There are so many blanks and Maggie is to blame for all of them. If she hadn't done what she did to me, I could have defended him. I could have told the world he wasn't capable of doing the awful things he was jailed for. It's because of her that he has died in prison and half his life was wasted. As a result, so was mine. I might not be behind bars, but I might as well be.

His loss burns like I'd only been with him this morning. I notice that I'm no longer clutching the phone to my chest. Instead, my hands are pressed against my stomach. And I'm rubbing it gently and remembering my second pregnancy. I'm remembering the child I had with Jon.

CHAPTER 16
MAGGIE

Hearing Hunter's name come from my daughter's mouth has left me flustered and unable to sleep. Now as I lie in the darkness of my room, my fingers anxiously kneading bunched-up ripples of duvet, I keep replaying the sound of him laughing at me the first time we came into contact.

Tonight, the news of his death has come so out of the blue that I didn't have time to rehearse a suitable reaction. I'm not a vindictive woman but I hope his end was a long, drawn-out, agonising affair. I'm relieved that after all this time, the three of us no longer share the same space on earth. We are free of him and he's incapable of hurting Nina again. It's over. Perhaps now, there's a chance she can try to push past whatever memories she keeps of him and reclaim normality amid the chaos she's created. Well, as much normality as there can be when you keep your mother chained up like a Russian circus bear.

Her eyes drilled through me as she conveyed Hunter's fate, trying to identify falseness in the ignorance I was feigning as to the depth of my memory of him. Of course I remembered Jon Hunter as clear as day. A lifetime could pass and I'd never forget a parasite like him. Yet for some reason, I am struggling to picture his face with clarity, which doesn't make sense because I have spent two decades following his story. For three weeks, I sat in the Crown Court public gallery, in the furthest seat away from him in the dock, listening to the evidence against him, hoping he wouldn't recognise me under my wig and differently made-up face. Each time his eyes scanned the courtroom, they didn't hover over me any longer than anyone else.

Despite the severity of his charges, he retained the same arrogance he had displayed during our confrontation well over a year earlier. Later, when a jury found him guilty of murder, it was all I could do to stop myself from sprinting across the room and hugging each member, one by one. Instead, I wept silent jubilant tears. My daughter was finally safe from that predator.

Then, as Hunter was led from the court and into a van to transfer him to a prison in Durham, I watched as his family and fans protested his innocence while the relatives of his victim cried for their lost sister and daughter. I felt their pain. He had tried to take my daughter away from me too, but I had snatched her back from under his nose. I had won, but I have paid for it with twenty-three years of guilt.

So why can I remember everything about him but his face? I'm overcome by an urge to see him one more time. I turn on the bedside lamps, take a deep breath and remove Nina's memory box from under my bed. I purposefully skipped past this the last time I looked inside it, but now I don't. Here is Hunter, pictured with his band on a flyer for a performance. I check the date – it was one of their last. Now his grey eyes, thin red lips and pale skin marry with my memories of him to form a complete picture of the times our paths crossed.

Over the following years, I read about each appeal and was relieved by each rejection. Although I admit to being surprised by his refusal to admit his guilt and earn an earlier parole. It meant that he languished behind bars longer than he had to. Perhaps beneath the snake's surface lay a backbone after all. The irony that he ended his days incarcerated is not lost on me. We have both been punished for the same crime – for loving Nina.

Hunter's conviction came at a time when she was only just beginning her journey back to me. I had kept her out of harm's way and under my protective eye for the best part of two years before she discovered the truth. I remember the conversation as clear as day.

'Why didn't you tell me what happened to Jon Hunter?' she had asked tentatively over supper. Her delivery was cautious, as if she were unsure whether to bring his name up.

'Because he's a part of your past now,' I said. 'I didn't want to upset you.'

Nina struggled to look me in the eye. 'I read about what they said he did and I don't think he did it. He wasn't a violent man.'

'Sometimes we don't know the people we think we are closest to.'

'But . . . I knew Jon.'

'And I thought I knew your father.'

'Jon couldn't have killed anyone.'

I pushed my cutlery to one side. 'That's not what the police or the jury decided. And from what I gather, he could wrap girls around his little finger. I don't blame them because at your age I would've been over the moon to get attention from a pop star like him. But he had a girlfriend who he lived with so he was leading on anyone else who thought they were in a relationship with him.'

Nina opened her mouth as if there was more she wanted to say, then changed her mind. I knew this version of my daughter couldn't be certain of anything any more. The last few months had left her scarred and unable to trust her own judgement. And that meant I had done my job properly.

I close the lid on the memory box and put it back under the bed; it's enough for one night. I turn off the lights and stare blankly at the wall ahead of me. The streetlights cast moving shadows of trees in the wind; the storm is raging both outside and inside this house. I wish I knew what Nina is thinking. What can she remember about him? Which of her memories are as clear as day and which are a jumble of patchwork squares that she can't sew together? I hope her talk of seeing a therapist to unlock 'repressed memories' was an empty threat. Because if she is serious, expert help might enable her to put two and two together. And I can't have her realise the lengths to which I have gone to protect her.

I close my eyes tighter and Hunter's face, once again, vanishes. But even though he's dead, he's going to come alive again in my dreams tonight, I know it. Because he and his girlfriend do that a lot.

CHAPTER 17

MAGGIE

TWENTY-FOUR YEARS EARLIER

Mother's intuition warns me that Nina is hiding something. And while I can't put my finger on what it is, I don't think I'm going to like it.

It's terrible timing because I've had to shift my focus away from my daughter and towards our financial situation. We're a one-income family and our fixed-rate mortgage has been replaced by a variable one, hiking the monthly charge up. Hell will freeze over before I ever consider selling this house, so alongside working as a receptionist at the surgery, I've swallowed my pride and am now also working after-hours as its cleaner. But needs must and my colleagues who know my marital situation have been very supportive. And I'm going to apply for the deputy practice manager's job when Lizzy retires next year.

As a result of my expanded hours, Nina and I have been passing like ships in the night. She's been returning home from school each day to an empty house, and by the time I arrive, she has already eaten her tea and is upstairs behind closed doors doing her homework. I dislike living this way, but I have little choice.

Making my way towards the post office, I realise it's been about a year since Nina miscarried and I still find myself treading on eggshells around her. Young people grow up much quicker than they did in my day, so I'm trying to move with the times and be a more modern parent. I've placed fewer restrictions on where she goes and I've given her generous curfews for when she goes out with her friends. I've asked her to limit her alcohol intake and made her promise that if she's going to be intimate with a boy, then it's not while she's drunk and to make sure he wears protection. I don't think she's ready for this adult world but short of locking her in the attic, what else can I do? I only hope that if I offer her a long enough lead, she'll always have the means to find her way home.

Maybe I'm placing too much emphasis on trying to be her friend and not enough effort into being her mum. But I want her to like me and to stop seeing me as the enemy who drove her dad away or told her she'd never have a family of her own. Of all my regrets, telling her that when she was at her most vulnerable is up there with the biggest of them.

I hope we are over the worst of Alistair's aftermath, but I'm a realist. Perhaps I'm being hyper-vigilant but I'm constantly on the lookout for signs that she's up to something I wouldn't approve of or is lying to me.

Last night, she passed me in the corridor as she left the bathroom, clad in an oversized white dressing gown. She hadn't worn it for months, but suddenly, it's fallen back into favour. When she spotted me, she pulled her sleeves down and wrapped it up tight and for a second, it crossed my mind that she might be hiding her arms for signs of needle marks. Then I told myself she couldn't be that stupid to be a drug abuser. It would explain her mood swings.

But still, I can't shake the feeling that something is happening under my own roof that I don't know about.

Nina weighs so heavily on my mind that I don't hear or see the car when I step out into the road until it blasts its horn at me. I step back and catch the driver giving me the finger. Motherhood will be the death of me.

'Are you all right, Maggie love?' a voice from behind me asks. I turn to see Saffron's mum, Erica.

'Oh hello.' I smile.

'That was a close call.'

'I was away with the fairies.' I note that she's dressed in her Tesco's uniform. 'Are you finishing or about to start?'

'Just finished,' Erica replies and rolls her eyes. 'I was there for seven a.m. so now I'm done for the day. How are you?'

I want to answer, 'I'm broke, I can barely afford the mortgage, my daughter hates me and the life I loved has turned to crap.' But I don't. 'Oh, you know,' I reply vaguely.

'How's Nina?'

'She's staying over at yours tonight, isn't she?'

'Mine?' She appears puzzled.

'Yes, it's Tuesday, isn't it? She usually stays over at yours tonight?'

Twice a week, on a Tuesday and a Friday, I've given Nina permission to sleep at Saffron's house. While I'm not keen on her friend – she is far too opinionated for my liking – I decide it's best if I pick my battles. This isn't one of them. At least if Nina is under Erica's roof then I know she is safe.

'Is that what she's been telling you?' says Erica. 'I'm sorry, love, but she's not slept over at ours in weeks. She and Saffy had a right old ding-dong over some lad and I haven't seen hide nor hair of her since.'

I hesitate, unable to recover fast enough to pretend I'm aware of this already and had simply forgotten. I feel my face flush. Neither of us knows what to say next. So I give Erica an awkward half-smile and leave the conversation at that.

◆ ◆ ◆

Nina times finishing her dinner with the closing credits of *Neighbours*, then she hurries upstairs to grab an overnight bag and her schoolbag. She mumbles 'See you tomorrow' before closing the front door behind her.

I hover in the lounge, peering at her from behind the curtains and allowing her a head start before I grab my coat and handbag and follow her. Ignoring my advice not to wear headphones when she's outside is working in my favour, because she has no clue her mother is on her trail. She cuts through the Racecourse Park before skirting around the perimeter of the town centre, then reaching Greyfriars bus station. I follow her inside the cavernous red-brick building and hang back by a vending machine as she enters the public toilets. She leaves ten minutes later with a full face of make-up and a different set of clothes. Nina is favouring the baggy look at the moment, which does little for her figure. Her jeans are ripped at the knee and I can see her bra straps on her shoulders. She stores both bags in a locker and continues her journey without hesitation. These movements are too choreographed for her not to have done them many times before. How stupid of me to have trusted her.

Nina makes her way into the town centre and enters the Prince William pub. It's been here for as long as I can remember but I have never been inside. There are at least a dozen motorbikes parked parallel to one another on the street outside. Nina smiles and chats to the doorman as if they are familiar with one another. He doesn't ask her for proof of age and points her towards the back of the rock music venue.

I am tempted to follow her inside but the risk is too high of her spotting me, and I don't want to cause a scene in public. From my position across the street, I watch as she walks through the pub and into the beer garden at the rear, then out of view.

I can't leave her like this. I take a few steps back and survey the area. To the right of the pub is a fast-food cafe on two floors. A sign on the door informs me it's open until midnight. I order a cup of tea and a lukewarm sausage roll, then make my way upstairs and sit at a table by the window that overlooks the pub garden where I can see Nina. It feels intrusive watching people from up here, but I can't take my eyes off my daughter and her friends. She's draped herself across a long-haired man who, even from this distance, I can tell is significantly older than her. Around their table are more men and women, none of whom are in her age bracket. I wonder if they know she is only fifteen.

She keeps her hand entwined in his but when she thinks no one is looking, she slips it under the table and strokes his groin. Part of me feels ashamed of her; the rest blames myself and her dad for driving her to such brazen behaviour.

The only silver lining to this dark cloud of an evening is that Nina is the only one drinking from one of those distinctive circular Orangina bottles. The rest drink from pint and wine glasses. And while they smoke cigarettes, Nina refrains.

I remain focused on her for a good couple of hours until she and her male friend are the first to rise and prepare to leave. I hurry back down the stairs and into the street when I spot them walking towards me, arm in arm. I freeze as they stop, my heart skipping a beat when I think Nina has seen me. She hasn't. Instead, she pushes him into a doorway and kisses him. I hide behind a van, panicked and weighing up my options. I want to drag her back home with me, but my rational side warns me against it. Our relationship is so fragile that pulling at any of the remaining threads that bind us might tear us apart for good. I could try reasoning with her, but I know from experience that she won't listen to me. Or I can do what I'm doing now – nothing. Until I have time to weigh up the pros and cons of my next move, I choose the latter. So I remain where I am until they pass me and disappear into the night.

I feel awful and utterly useless. But before I leave, I return to the pub and find the same doorman is still on duty. 'Hello,' I begin. 'The couple who just left, do you know who they are?'

He looks at me quizzically.

'Oh, I'm not an oddball,' I point out, 'but I think I used to be his teacher. He looks familiar.'

'You've probably seen him in the papers,' he replies. 'Jon Hunter. Sings with The Hunters. Pretty good by all accounts.'

'Ah, my mistake, thank you,' I say before making my way home, alone.

CHAPTER 18

NINA

I open the side gate to the back garden to allow the two Argos delivery men entry.

One of them is mixed race with the most beautiful glowing light-brown skin I've ever seen. His biceps are fit to burst from his tight blue T-shirt. The other is short and squat and reminds me of a Super Mario brother. They place the boxes containing the furniture I ordered next to the patio under the kitchen window. I'm not sure if I'm imagining it when the hunkier of the two appears to wink at me as he hands me the delivery note. It's only when they leave that I see he's written his phone number on it. I'm flattered but wonder how often he does this. I won't be calling him.

I've dated sporadically over the years, but I've yet to find anyone who has excited me in the way Jon did. Besides, most men only want two things from a woman – no-strings-attached sex or to start a family. And when they discover I can't fulfil one of their criteria, they rapidly lose interest.

I was nineteen years old and a few months away from taking my A-level exams when I learned that not only was I cursed by faulty chromosomes, but my entire reproductive system was giving up the ghost. With little warning, my periods became sporadic until eventually, they all but vanished. At the same time, I was finding it harder and harder to sleep. My skin felt as if it was burning up at the strangest of times and when my anxiety levels shot through the roof, I actually feared I was having another breakdown. I vowed I would rather die than go through that again.

After a series of tests at Northampton General Hospital, a specialist advised me that I was going through a highly premature menopause. 'This is the earliest I've ever seen it happen,' she explained. 'It's called premature ovarian failure. It's such a rare condition. I'm very, very sorry.'

I was going to ask her if it had anything to do with my estroprosencephaly, but whether it did or it didn't would not make any difference. It was happening, it was shitty and there was absolutely sod all I could do about it. So I didn't bring it up.

I didn't mourn for my lost periods and dried-up eggs. Relationships were the last thing on my mind anyway. It wasn't until the end of my twenties that I felt ready to find someone. The advent of dating apps made meeting the opposite sex much easier for someone like me who was ripe and not ready to wither and rot on the vine.

There were only two men I ever went further with than swiping right on Tinder. But despite putting my all into those affairs, they turned out to be huge disappointments. Then, soon after swearing off all relationships and even new friendships, someone came along who changed everything. For the last two years, he has been the only person who matters. Even just thinking about him brings me out in a broad smile. He is the reason why I want to lose weight and get fit. I don't need anybody's approval but his. And he is the biggest secret I keep from the world, an even larger one than Maggie.

I slice through the plastic strips binding the patio furniture boxes, then cut the cardboard into sizes that will fit the recycling bin. The set needs no assembling so after arranging it on the decking, I test the seats out one by one, taking in different views of the garden. Then I pour myself a glass of sparkling white wine and enjoy the late spring Saturday afternoon by myself.

Next door, I hear Elsie tunelessly singing along to her kitchen radio. It sounds like a Michael Bublé song or some other middle-of-the-road crooner who makes women of a certain age weak at the arthritic knees. I snicker when I hear her back door unlock, as I know what's coming next. Through the gaps in the wooden fence panels, I catch glimpses of her as she struggles to negotiate the doorstep with her frame to reach the garden. She wears one of those red plastic pendants around her neck which, once pressed, alerts a switchboard that you need help. Mum used to be one of her crisis calls, but when she 'moved to Devon' I asked Elsie to take our number off the list. I'm not going to any trouble for a woman I don't particularly like.

I sit very still and hope that she doesn't look over the fence, but of course she does. 'Oh hello,' she begins, spying me with my feet up on the table. 'I haven't seen you in a while.' She regards me, as ever, with suspicion. She has never completely believed my story about Mum's illness.

'How are you, Elsie?' I ask politely.

'Not bad, despite my ailments. But Barbara comes over every morning and evening to help. I'm lucky to have such a good daughter. Some mothers aren't so fortunate.'

It's not hard to read her disdain for me.

'Been splashing out, have we?' she continues, and points to the furniture.

I ignore her. 'Send Barbara my love,' I say and turn my head, indicating the conversation is over. But Elsie doesn't take the hint. Or if she does, she chooses not to acknowledge it.

'How's your mum?' she continues.

'Not great at the moment.'

'Do you visit her very much? Most weekends you seem to be here.'

Nothing escapes you, does it? Apart from your best friend locked away in the attic. 'Once a month I take the train down there,' I say. 'But it's quite expensive.'

'You can't put a price on family.'

'You can when a train ticket costs close to a week's wages. Besides, Mum doesn't remember who I am now.'

'Perhaps she might if you saw her more often or hadn't sent her so far away.'

'As I've explained many times before, Elsie, it was Mum's decision to be with her sister. She wanted to return to Devon where she grew up. And there are some lovely views of the coast from where she's living now. It's very private, not like here.'

Elsie pulls slices of bread from a plastic bag and scatters them across the lawn for the birds. 'I still don't understand how quickly it came on,' she says, shaking her head. 'She was always sharp as a pin.'

'That's the brain for you. Everything can change in a heartbeat.'

'So you say.'

For a moment, our cold stares mirror one another's. She has always regarded me with mistrust, even when I was a teenager, and I've never known why. Eventually she offers me an insincere wave goodbye as she makes the slow walk back to her kitchen door. I promise myself that when winter comes, I'll throw water at that doorstep until it freezes. Then we'll see how much use she gets out of the emergency alarm when she's lying on her back with a broken hip and hypothermia.

Alone again, I survey the garden. Like all the others on this estate, the proportions are much more generous than you'll find in a modern equivalent, because space wasn't at such a premium in the 1930s. By covering the borders with a weed-proof membrane and woodchip, I've kept it low maintenance so that in the summer months, I only have to mow the lawn and trim the edges fortnightly.

A path of concrete paving slabs runs from the back door further up the garden and disappears behind a row of crab-apple trees. Out of view is Dad's shed. The roof now leaks and the door must be yanked hard before it will open. Inside are his cobweb-covered tools and the cardboard-like remains of a hornets' nest from last spring. The seven-foot fence at the very back has a row of conifers growing around it that are so tall, no one living behind or next door to us can peer into that part of our garden, and vice versa.

I take my glass of wine with me as I walk to that secluded area, and then sit on the grass by the only flower bed in the garden. I often find myself spending time there, recalling all that I've lost and what's to come, as the hours pass. I love the privacy this corner offers and I understand why Maggie chose it. It's the one blind spot – and perfect for a grave.

CHAPTER 19

MAGGIE

Do I know you? I think as I stare from the window at the man standing outside our house. I'm aware that spending so much time in here alone means I've started to become a little confused about past events out there. And while I'm usually good with faces, I'm struggling to remember why his is resonating with me. I rack my brains but I just can't place him.

From this distance, he doesn't look very old. His clothes appear modern and he's standing with his hands on his hips, surveying my home like an estate agent might. For a split second I wonder if Nina has put the house up for sale. But of course she hasn't. Imagine the agent's surprise when he looks around to measure up and discovers it comes with its own ghost in the loft. I pinch the back of my hands just to remind myself I'm not actually a ghoul. It stings, so that's a good sign.

He looks as if he wants to come closer, but stops himself from walking up the path to the front door. It gets me to thinking, what would happen if a burglar was to break in? Would they reach the first floor, see the locked door and assume there must something valuable in the attic? Would temptation prove too much and is that how I'd be found? Would I be able to talk them into setting me free?

It's all speculation because this man turns his back, climbs inside the little white car he arrived in, does a three-point turn and drives away. I spot the black sunroof and remember it being here a few days ago. Something's going on, I can sense it. And I admit the thought of being burgled does rather excite me.

As I turn to pick up a Tupperware container with sliced apple inside, Nina's memory box catches my eye again. But it doesn't repel me. Today I feel strong, today I feel ready for it. So I place it on the bed, lift the lid and start removing its contents one by one. Among school reports and drawings, there's a photograph of Alistair and I taken as we left the registry office; I wonder where she found it, as I thought I'd thrown all these photos out. It brings back an unexpected happy memory of the day itself and how there were only a handful of guests, but that was enough for us. It was such a joyous time, but I don't allow myself to dwell on it or any of my other years with him. They have all been tainted by everything that followed.

Also inside is a birthday card he made for his 'only girl' – his nickname for her makes me shudder. There's a bottle of coloured sands that Nina filled on a holiday to see her Aunty Jennifer in Devon, school portrait photographs of her throughout the years, and an English exercise book and essays. There's a small wooden figure wearing a blue suit that I remember was one of the toys she used to replicate me, herself and her dad in her doll's house. All three toys used to be inseparable. There's a dried red carnation from when she was a bridesmaid at Jennifer's wedding, and a Sweet Valley High pencil case with photos of the cast on the side.

It dawns on me that everything here is related to events that happened before she turned thirteen. It might as well have been sealed tight at that point. Could this be its purpose, to remind me of what was taken away from her the last night she saw her father, the night I let her down? Is it possible that, after all this time, she is starting to remember what happened? Are the events of that night – and what she lost – represented by this box? Maybe she's piecing things together and is asking me for help to push her over the finishing line?

Or perhaps I am giving her too much credit. Yes. More likely – no, almost certainly – this memory box is just another way for her to pile guilt upon my shoulders.

'Well, it's not going to work, Nina,' I say defiantly. 'Nothing you can do can make me feel any worse than I do already.'

I replace everything in the box, with the exception of my wedding photograph and the flyer of The Hunters' performance with *his* picture on it. I don't want his or Alistair's pictures in this room, reminding me of what they took from me. I rip them in half, then into tiny shreds until they're like a small pile of confetti lying on the floor.

CHAPTER 20

MAGGIE

TWENTY-FOUR YEARS EARLIER

I don't know the first thing about modern music or what kids listen to these days. But I do know that the man Nina is spending time with is in a local band. I rack my brains as to where I can find out more about them before I come up with a starting point. I make a few shortcuts while cleaning the surgery and finish early, then hop on a bus into town. From there, it's a short walk down the hill to Spinadisc, a record shop that Nina talks about.

There are a dozen or so teens here, still in their school uniforms and flicking through racks of CDs or trying on T-shirts with band names I don't recognise emblazoned across the front. Rock music blasts from wall speakers and rattles my bones. I wonder how the staff can focus on their jobs when they're surrounded by this noise day in, day out.

I question when I became so out of the loop with popular trends. At forty-four, I am prehistoric compared to everyone else in this shop. I know by sight the difference between Oasis and

Blur when I see them performing on *Top of the Pops* and of course I remember the hangers-on from the 1980s like Madonna, George Michael and Prince. But the rest of these new faces stacked up in racks are alien to me.

I flick through the CD singles until I find one by The Hunters, and recognise Nina's friend in the centre of the cover picture. I look at my surroundings and the walls are plastered with brightly coloured posters. Some are advertising the release of new records, others are posters you can buy. There's a section dedicated to the local music scene. I scour the walls and find a much larger image of Hunter's band. Below it is a list of tour dates they are playing across the county this month. One immediately captures my attention – it's for a gig tonight, only a ten-minute walk away from where I am now. I look at my watch. It's 5 p.m. I wonder if Jon Hunter is already there with his band setting up equipment. It's an unexpected opportunity. I hesitate as I think this through. As far as I can see, I have no choice but to confront him. I need him to leave Nina alone.

My hunch is right. When I arrive, the front doors to the Roadmender are locked shut, but around the corner and to the side, there is a fire door propped open by red extinguishers. Two greasy youths are carrying amplifiers and guitar cases from a transit van into the building. I hover on the pavement, partly because I want to see Hunter in neutral territory, and partly because I'm still unsure of what to say. Five, ten, then fifteen minutes pass before he finally appears from inside and makes his way to the corner of a small car park, turning his back to the street as he lights a cigarette with a match. I take a deep breath before I approach him.

'Jon Hunter,' I begin, the words almost sticking in my throat.

He turns to look at me. The whites surrounding his grey irises are pinkish and framed by dark rings. His skin is so pale, it's as if he hasn't seen sunlight in years. His cheeks are sunken and he's as thin as a rake, but despite these flaws, he is startlingly pretty for a man. He takes another drag from his cigarette and from its smell, it's clear that it doesn't contain only tobacco.

Saying nothing, he raises his eyebrows as if to ask, 'And who are you?'

'May I have a minute of your time, please?'

'What about?'

'My daughter.'

'And she is?'

'Your girlfriend.'

His expression tells me he is unsure who I am talking about, which indicates that either he and Nina aren't serious, or he is not the monogamous type. His occupation suggests the latter. 'Nina Simmonds,' I clarify.

Momentarily, his bravado is replaced with defensiveness. 'I don't know what's she's told you, but—'

'Please don't insult me by denying your relationship,' I reply, enjoying the feel of the upper hand. 'I know that you two are dating. I've seen you both with my own eyes, canoodling in a pub.'

'*Canoodling*,' he repeats, and laughs at either the word or at me, I can't be sure. 'You've got nothing to worry about, we're not serious.'

'I should hope not, she is a fifteen-year-old schoolgirl,' I say. 'But does she know that?'

'Know what? That she's fifteen? I'd hope so. Anyway, she told me she was eighteen so it's hardly my fault.'

With my added confidence comes added frustration. 'Don't talk to me like I'm a fool. Does she know that she's probably one in a long line of other gullible girls?'

'Look, I'm really not comfortable with this conversation,' he says. 'What do you want?'

'I want you to promise not to see her again.'

Hunter lets out another laugh and smoke gushes from his mouth. 'You want me to *promise*? How about I go one better and give you a pinkie swear? Or a Brownie's promise?'

'Perhaps you would prefer it if I went to the police and reported you?' I snap.

The smile falls quickly from his face. 'I don't think you'll do that.'

'No? Campbell Square station is a five-minute walk from here. I'll go right now.'

I turn, then feel his hand on my shoulder. He swings me around. I'm about to protest but he speaks first, his face far too close to mine for my liking. I smell the tobacco on his breath.

'I don't think you will. Do you honestly believe Nina will appreciate you interfering?'

'Eventually she'll understand.'

'Don't kid yourself. All you're going to accomplish is that you'll see even less of her. She'll hate you for breaking us up and she'll keep running away from you to come back to me.'

'She's my daughter, not a toy for you to play with.'

'She's both. She tells me how much she hates being with you and how you drove her dad away. If I click my fingers, she'll be living with me and you'll be left with nobody.'

'The police won't allow that to happen.'

'If they investigate me, then they're also going to tell Social Services about the risk you've put her under by allowing her to sleep at my place.'

'But I didn't know she was with you! She said she was with a friend.'

'It doesn't matter. You see, your daughter is a pleaser, she likes to keep people happy. Not you, of course. But she's terrified that I'm going to disappear like her daddy did. And that means she'll do anything I say to keep hold of me. And if that means lying about you, then she'll do just that. Fuck with me and I'll fuck you right back.'

He releases his grip of my shoulder, takes a long drag from his cigarette and flicks it up into the air. It lands behind a clump of dandelions. 'I assume we've reached an understanding?' he says, and I'm powerless to do anything but nod.

'By the way,' he adds as he walks away, 'it's a shame you don't have any more daughters. A year or two younger would've been just right.'

Then he winks at me and saunters back inside.

CHAPTER 21
MAGGIE

I'm alone when I spot it. It's in the corner of the dining room, wedged between the carpet and the skirting board. Nina doesn't use hairpins, so it must be an old one of mine that's lain there for years. Perhaps she accidentally loosened it with the vacuum cleaner, which is why I can see it now.

Its positioning is too subtle to be another of her tests. Not like when she left her mobile phone on the dining-room table partially covered by her handbag while she was downstairs in the kitchen. I frantically dialled 999 only to discover she'd removed that little card inside that operates it.

I arrive at the conclusion that I've stumbled upon this by chance. Nina is preparing dinner so she doesn't hear my chain rattling as I move to grab and keep it, like a magpie taking a shiny object back to its nest. I hold it up to the light; it's metal and could be just what I need to remove this padlock from my ankle.

I am a bag of nerves at this find, and I slip it inside the left cup of my bra. Nina removed the underwire from all my bras when she found one missing as she did my washing, evidence of a previous failed attempt to undo this padlock. However, that metal was not as strong as the one used to make this pin.

Taking a few deep breaths to calm myself, I glance around the room; it's my equivalent of a prison's exercise yard. If Nina gets her way, I'll be trapped in this house for the rest of my life. But my spirit is too strong to give up hope: hope of an escape, hope someone might find me and hope she has a change of heart and accepts that what she is doing to me is so, so wrong. Without hope, I have nothing. And I am not there yet. *I have not given up.*

I've been housebound for two years now; at least that's what Nina tells me. The days, weeks and months blur, so I can't be sure. To mark my first anniversary, she ordered me a two-tier sponge cake and paid the baker to ice it with decorative prison bars and a lit candle. The second year, when I cut into it with a plastic knife, I found a nail file inside. Well, an emery board, because I can't use that to my advantage. I wonder what she has planned if I make it to a third year. Perhaps this small hairclip is all I need to ensure I won't be here that long.

When I look back at my other attempts to escape, they were reckless and born out of desperation. The first time wasn't long after all this began. In a fit of frustration, I hurled a stool at the shutters. But it was no match for their strength. Two legs snapped off and fell to the floor. As much as it pained me to do it, when Nina opened the bedroom door later that night to change my chain and allow me out for dinner, I used one of the stool's legs as a weapon. But as I swung it, she caught sight of my shadow and ducked so it hit the top of her arm and not her head. She wrestled the stool out of my hands and used it to beat my ribs black and blue. The rage in her eyes petrified me because I have witnessed first-hand what it can lead to. And that is much, much worse. However, instead of putting me off, it made me all the more determined to get away from her.

A spur-of-the-moment decision to throw my dinner plate and smash the dining-room window saw her retaliating by hitting me over the head with a wine bottle and knocking me out cold. I awoke to find myself with my chain not only attached to my ankle but wrapped around my body too, binding me like an Egyptian mummy. For two days I remained like that, lying in my own filth, until finally she decided to free me.

I've used everything at my disposal to get out of here, even smashing batteries with the cistern lid in the hope that the acid they contain might dissolve one of the chain's links. Needless to say, it only blistered my skin. The one thing I haven't tried is burning my way out of here and that's only because I haven't had access to anything flammable.

I've flooded the bathroom and blocked the toilet to force her to call someone out to repair them. When the plumber arrived, he had no idea he was working feet away from his client's bound, chained and drugged mother.

On and on our dance has continued, me on the lookout for new opportunities for escape, and her thwarting me and dishing out a punishment to fit the crime. Perhaps the hairpin will shift the balance of power.

Finally, Nina appears with two plates of another mediocre hotpot. Dinner passes with polite, meaningless conversation about nothing. To my relief, there's no mention again of Hunter or his death.

Despite the stilted awkwardness of it all, a part of me looks forward to these moments as they are my only means of human interaction. At sixty-eight, the thing I'm afraid of most is losing my faculties, and sometimes I feel I'm already missing some of the details of the past. Loneliness has been proven to exacerbate the advancement of dementia and Alzheimer's, so keeping my brain active with conversation and books can only be a positive thing. I'd hate to end up a prisoner not only of Nina's cruelty but of my own mind, too.

However, tonight is an exception as I can't wait for our encounter to end. I decline dessert, claiming I have a headache and asking her if I can return to my room. In a rare moment of compassion, she disappears and returns with two headache tablets. They're still in their blisterpack so I know they aren't laxatives. She helps me upstairs, swaps the chain on my ankle for the smaller one, and wishes me a good night. I have two days to free myself with this hairpin.

I immediately set to work, unfolding it from its V shape and into a straight line, but bending one end ever so slightly into a hook. I wear my glasses with the missing arm and shine the LED bedside lamp into it so I can see what I am doing. Not that I actually have the first clue as to how to pick a lock, other than what I've seen in films. I start by simply wiggling it about and the result is, predictably, nothing. I'd be suspicious if it worked that quickly.

I try moving the pin in alternate directions; clockwise, anti-clockwise, up and down, back to front, trying to catch something inside that might make the lock spring open. I'm not sure how long I'm at it for, but it's dark outside when I look up. I'm just about to call it a night when something inside the cylinder makes a clicking sound. I take a sharp intake of breath. *This is it!*

My eyes widen and I pull at it but the lock holds firm. I wiggle the pin around a little more and it feels loose inside. Why hasn't it opened? I remove the hairpin and examine it closely. The hooked end has snapped off and is still inside the padlock.

'Oh no,' I mutter, and clasp my fingers together in front of my face as if in prayer. I hold the lock upside down and shake it, hoping that the broken piece will fall out. It doesn't budge. I bang it against the bed and then the wooden floor and it still doesn't appear. *Don't panic*, I tell myself. *I still have two days to get it out, and then I can try again with the other end of the hairpin.*

I hope to God it works, because I'm not sure how much strength I have left to fight my daughter again.

CHAPTER 22

NINA

I sense something is wrong the moment I open Maggie's bedroom door to invite her downstairs for dinner. Her gaze is like that of a frightened rabbit's, caught in my headlights. Immediately, I am on high alert. She has done something she shouldn't have. I don't have time for this, as I have plans for tonight. But now we must play our cat and mouse game again until I find out what she's up to.

'Hello,' I begin in a deliberately friendly tone. I survey the room for signs that something is out of place. Aside from the corkscrew incident, it's been some time since she last tried to escape from me. I had wondered if it meant that I'd finally broken her. But that in itself would've been a double-edged sword. Because while it means I've won, I need her to crave the world she sees from her window. Once she stops wanting everything she can't have, she's no longer being punished. I can do without being stabbed by a fork or having a plate of dinner hurled at my head, but at least those defiant actions show she has fight left in her. And while there's fight, I know that she's hurting. I need her to hurt for her to understand what she's done. 'Is everything all right?' I continue.

'Yes, thank you,' she replies, a little too quickly for my liking.

I choose to wrong-foot her with kindness. 'Do you still have that headache? I can get you some more aspirin if you like?'

'No, I'm fine.'

'Perhaps you need some fresh air. Maybe we can think about going into the back garden for a few minutes?'

'I'm okay for the time being. I just need to lie down on my own for a bit.'

Now I know for certain that something is askew because she has begged me in the past to allow her outside, even if it's only for five minutes. 'Okay then,' I respond, and cautiously, I make my way towards her, scanning the room again. I even look up to the ceiling to reassure myself that a cartoon anvil hasn't been rigged up to fall upon my head.

She rises to her feet, turning around so her back faces me, and I slip my key into the padlock and prepare to swap the shorter chain for the longer one. Her leg has a slight tremble to it, but I'm not sure if it's because she is scared or has been seated for too long. However, the key won't fit. My brow furrows as I try again, but still it won't go in the whole way. I look up at Maggie and finally it makes sense. It's not the first time she's tried to pick the lock; she's attempted it twice before with a bra wire and by snapping a pair of tweezers in half. *There's life in the old dog yet*, I think, and mask my respect.

'What did you use?' I ask.

'A hairpin,' she replies without hesitation.

'Where did you find it?'

'On the dining-room floor, between the skirting board and the carpet.'

'And the rest of it?'

She lifts the bottom sheet of her bed and hands it to me.

'Okay,' I say calmly. 'You're going to have to give me a few minutes to find Dad's toolbox.'

I leave her alone to stew as I search the basement for it. Then I carry a set of bolt cutters back upstairs, assuming she's aware there will be repercussions for this. I remain outside her door for a few more moments, taking joy in building the tension.

It takes three attempts before I cut through the padlock bar and it falls to the floorboards with a clunk. That's when it happens. That's when I take my eye off the ball.

Without warning, Maggie raises her foot and kicks me sideways in the face so that the chainless metal cuff secured to her ankle hits me square on the cheekbone. I yell in pain; the force of the impact and the shock of it knocks me to the floor. By the time I grasp what she's done, Maggie is making a run for it.

She is surprisingly agile for a woman of her age and before I can get to my feet, she is across the room and heading down the staircase. I remain at the top, watching her at the bottom turning the doorknob that separates the second floor from the first. I've locked it. She grabs at it again, more frantically this time, but I remain where I am, watching her and nursing my aching cheek. Christ, it hurts. I can taste blood and I run my tongue against my teeth. I think she's cracked one.

Suddenly, Maggie begins yelling for help and screaming with an energy I've not heard or seen in her before. She pulls at the empty egg boxes glued to the door and walls and tosses them behind her. Her throat sounds hoarse and she's crying as she screams.

Maggie hasn't thought this through properly. She has panicked and I reckon kicking me was a spontaneous action that has backfired. And now she knows that she is about to pay dearly for it. I prolong what's about to come by descending the stairs slowly, one at a time.

She turns her body so that her back is now pressed against the door, her left arm and hand are covering her face and the right one is flailing and trying to make contact with me. It doesn't take much for me to grab a hold of it, twist it behind her back and frogmarch her up the stairs. I'm surprised by how thin her skin feels to my touch.

I push her into the bathroom and then, gripping her by the neck, I shove her into the bath. Somehow in the tussle she falls in back first and throws her hands out to stop herself from landing awkwardly. But it's too late and we both hear the crunch of bone against the metal of the taps. She has hit her head, and she's hit it hard. For a moment, we are united in our wait for what will happen next. Nothing, as it turns out. She moves her hand to the back of her head and then brings it towards her face to examine it. There is no blood. It sounded worse than it is.

Her arms start flailing and her hands grip the rim of the bath-tub to pull herself up. All I can think about is how much my cheek and my, I assume, cracked tooth are hurting because of her. But for the second time tonight, I'm not fast enough to pre-empt her and she hurls a bottle of orange bubble bath at my head, striking my face in almost the exact same position as the metal cuff hit me. This time, a horrendous pain shoots up the side of my face as part of the same tooth breaks and rattles inside my mouth. I spit it out into my hand.

Now I'm moving without thinking. Anger and adrenaline are propelling me forward as I grab Maggie and thrust her backwards, her head hitting the tap for a second time. 'You think that's going to stop me?' I hear myself scream.

I spit while I yell, my words firing like bullets from my lips, and I start slapping her around the head and face. I no longer have any control over my own temper as I unravel and spin. I want to hurt her in ways I have never done before. Maggie shields her face again with her arms as I grab a bottle of bleach from the side of the toilet and unscrew the safety cap.

'You're making me do this!' I roar. 'You made me think that I was unlovable, that I deserved everything that came to me, but you're wrong!'

'Please, Nina, no,' she begs and she looks pitiful trying to claw her way out of the bath, her cuff clanging against the plastic bottom as she struggles.

'Why must you keep doing this?' I continue, directing the nozzle of the bleach bottle at the top of her head, ready to squirt it. One more slight movement and it will cover her face and neck. 'Why do you keep trying to leave me?'

'I'm sorry,' she whimpers. 'I'm sorry, it won't happen again, I promise I'll stay. I'll be good.'

Suddenly I can only see the colours of the world in two shades – red and black – and I fear I am about to pass out. I become fixated by Maggie, because now she is covered in blood. There is so much of it, it's as if she's soaking in it. It must be coming from where she hit her head. But how has it spread so quickly? I panic as I look around the room, and there's more blood oozing across the surface of the floor and streaks of it have splashed against the walls. The towels and bath mat are also soaked in red. I look back at Maggie in disbelief and for the first time, I notice there's a knife in her hand. I back away quickly until I collide with the wall – how the hell did she get hold of that? As I try to force what I am seeing to make sense, I feel my body starting to convulse as if I am having a seizure.

I blink so hard that my eyes want to roll back in their sockets and when I open them again, the blood has disappeared. There's no trace of it anywhere or the knife she was holding. There's only Maggie, begging me not to douse her with bleach. I drop the bottle and it falls to the floor, leaking liquid on the mat.

We glare at one another, our breathing short and rapid, our hearts beating so loudly we can almost hear one another's. I realise I am also crying and I don't know why. For a moment, I see Maggie as my mum again, the woman who told me she loved me every day of my life until I locked her inside her bedroom. And briefly, I realise I've missed hearing that.

I move towards her but this time, she doesn't recoil. She recognises I've returned from the spell I was under and nervously offers me her hand. I help to lift her leg over the side of the bath and back to her feet.

She slips her hand through my arm as we walk slowly towards the bedroom. 'Dinner will be in half an hour,' I say quietly, and I lean down to attach the longer chain to her ankle cuff. 'I'll get you some more painkillers.'

CHAPTER 23
MAGGIE

I'm shivering, not because I am cold, but because I am in shock. I am sweating and dizzy and unsure if it's because I've hurt my head or because I've borne the brunt of the fury of a Nina who terrifies me.

I also don't know whether I want to cry, to vomit or to scream . . . or perhaps do all three. But I can't in front of her. Instead I ball my fists and dig my fingernails into the palms of my hands until I think I'm about to draw blood. *I must stay strong. I must ride this out.*

I don't protest as she attaches the extended chain to my ankle with a new padlock, nor do I turn to watch as she leaves the room. I don't want to look her in the eye because I don't know who might be looking back at me. Already I'm dreading the moment when she calls me down for dinner. How can I sit opposite her and make conversation after what has just happened?

I rub at the back of my head again where it twice hit the taps. A bump the size of an egg is rising to the surface. I'm suddenly overcome by immense fatigue and I want to lie back on the bed and close my eyes, but I know there's a danger of concussion. So I force myself to remain awake.

I've seen my daughter consumed by her dark side twice before and I prayed I'd never bear witness to it again. The first occasion was as much of a surprise to me as it was to Alistair. It was so swift neither of us could've seen it coming. And, truth be told, I can't blame Nina for it. That's why I wasn't going to allow what she did to destroy the rest of her life.

When the rage reared its head for a second time, I wasn't there and I'll regret that for the rest of my life. But I mopped up the aftermath. It's a mother's duty to protect their child from themselves.

Tonight, Nina's darkness has made its presence felt once again. And I was the one who drove her to it. And again, I cannot blame her; I can only blame myself. I wasn't thinking when I kicked her in the face. I panicked – it was a case of fight or flight, and I chose both. And it was the worst thing I could've done.

I close my door and lie back on the bed, but I can't stand it for long because my head hurts so much. Instead, I curl up on my side and into a tight, impenetrable ball. I try to gather myself, taking deep, calming breaths and wrapping my arms around my body to stop it from shaking. Neither works. *Just get through dinner,* I tell myself. *Just get through dinner with her and everything will go back to the way it was.*

I only wish I could believe that to be true.

CHAPTER 24

NINA

I leave Maggie in her bedroom and make my way down the stairs, trying to convince myself that tonight's events are par for the course and that we have lived through this situation many times before.

But even I know that my reaction was extreme.

For a minute there, I lost it. I actually lost all control of myself and I don't know how it happened. It was more than just anger or blind rage. It was something much, much darker. And I'm frightened. She dredged up something from deep inside of me that I never want to experience again.

I lock the landing door behind me and make my way down the second set of stairs, using the bannisters to support myself. My hands, my arms, my back . . . my whole body feels weak. *What happened up there?*

I enter the kitchen, trying to piece it all together. I know I had every right to be furious at Maggie. Whether lashing out at me was premeditated or not, she crossed the line. More than two years after she woke up to find herself in there, it appears I'm no closer to making her understand that the time she took away from me *must* be repaid. There are no two ways about it. She owes me another nineteen years.

I've always managed to maintain a tight rein over my emotions, even when Maggie has pushed me to the brink. Not once have I ever lost it like I did tonight. I'm covered in goosebumps as I replay the moment I held that bottle of bleach above her head, fighting the voice inside me telling me to squeeze hard and burn her. It was as if someone else had crept inside me and was pulling my strings.

I lean over the kitchen sink, turn the tap on and throw some cold water over my face, then pat it dry with a tea towel. I rinse my mouth out with water and wince at the sharp pain of the damaged tooth. I'm supposed to be making dinner; instead, I'm now replaying what I thought I saw in the bathroom. The blood in the bath, the red-stained towels on the floor . . . it's all so vivid.

I cannot stop picturing Maggie's terrified face and fight the urge to check on her well-being. Through all of our battles and skirmishes, this is the first time I've felt something akin to guilt. It's also the first time in years I've thought of her as my mum and not as Maggie. Something in my head has shifted and I don't know how to push it back into place.

I am supposed to be seeing the one who centres me tonight, but as much as it pains me to cancel, I reach for my phone and text him my apologies. Once a fortnight we meet for dinner, drinks or days out; although he has postponed a couple of times recently, which has concerned me. I have never pulled out of our get-togethers, but I am in no fit state to see anyone. I can't explain the bruise and lump that's already rising on my cheek. He's too perceptive to believe I simply fell over. Besides, my broken tooth must have exposed nerve endings because it's absolutely killing me. I take some cotton wool from the first-floor bathroom to use as padding and I bite down upon it to stem the bleeding.

I smell burning from downstairs and remember I've left the chilli too long in the pan. By the time I reach the kitchen, it's hard around the edges. The water in the rice has boiled away and some of it is black. I can't be bothered to start anything new now.

I take another look at my reflection in the glass and struggle to recognise myself. How did I become *this* woman?

CHAPTER 25

MAGGIE

When I hear Nina's footsteps coming back up the stairs to get me for dinner, I recoil. I hurry into the corner of the bedroom, picking up the bedside lamp before positioning myself. If she is returning for round two, I am not going out without a fight, no matter how much this chain restricts my movements.

When she reaches my closed door, I hear the clatter on the tray as she places it upon the floor. I wait until I hear her head back downstairs before I let out a breath. I'm glad she changed her mind about making us eat together; I'd rather have no company at all than be at the mercy of her fury again.

I wait a few moments until I hear the downstairs door lock before I open mine and see what she has left me. There are three home-made turkey sandwiches, a bowl of crisps, two apples, a packet of Mr Kipling cakes and a single-serving plastic bottle of red wine. It's the first time she's given me alcohol. Is this her way of apologising? Does she know she went too far and perhaps even frightened herself?

Nevertheless, I remain on my guard and barely get a wink of sleep. I'm too afraid to take a sleeping tablet and become a sitting duck if Nina is ready to go into battle again. It's happened in the past – we have argued, she has stormed out, and then much later that evening, she has appeared over my bed, hurling abuse at me after continuing the dispute in her head.

At some point in the night, I must have drifted off because I awake in the morning with a start, disorientated and sure that she is in the room with me. I open my eyes, relieved to see she's not. Then I wait with my ear pressed against the bedroom door, just in case she is lurking outside it. But I don't hear anything to indicate that she is. I am alone. I urinate into my bucket and then make my way to the window just in time to spy Nina walking away from the house. I spot the milkman and I try and work out what day it is; he's knocking on doors to collect his money, so it must be Saturday.

Nina never works weekends so I wonder where she's going. It doesn't really matter because when she's not under this roof, I am safe. I can't help but wonder, though. Is she off to meet someone? Has she made a friend? Has she found a boyfriend? Or perhaps it's not a man she's seeing but a woman. Maybe she's gay and doesn't want to tell me because she thinks I'm too old-fashioned to accept it. But I wouldn't care if she were, I really wouldn't. I used to own several Dusty Springfield albums, so I've always been quite open-minded.

I'd like her to know how it feels to be loved in a romantic sense, at least once in her lifetime. Despite everything, she deserves that. We all do. I thought that having a baby meant that I would always be loved by someone until the day I died. I was wrong. Being a mother is no guarantee of anything.

CHAPTER 26

MAGGIE

TWENTY-THREE YEARS EARLIER

'Good morning.' I smile, and note that her pregnant belly is now poking out from beneath her white T-shirt.

'Hi there,' she says, then emits a long sigh.

'Are you feeling it today?'

'Oh yes,' she replies and nods her head. 'I've been up with heartburn most of the night and a stomach ache I can't shift.'

'I used to get exactly the same thing when I was carrying Nina,' I reply, hoping to reassure her that it's perfectly normal to feel awful in the last few weeks.

It hasn't been the easiest time for her and she's been a frequent visitor to the surgery throughout the duration of her pregnancy. She is only eighteen years old and far too young to be a mother if you ask me. She's a pretty girl with elfin features and she reminds me a lot of Nina. She wears a silver nose piercing that my eyes are drawn to each time I look at her face. Her chestnut-brown, shoulder-length hair is scraped back into a ponytail and held in place with a scrunchie. No matter how crummy the baby is making her feel, I've yet to see her without make-up on.

'Are you here to see Janet the midwife?' I ask.

'Yes, but I haven't got an appointment. Could you squeeze me in?'

I look at the register and spot a cancellation. The surgery is only just starting to transfer all its patients' paper files alphabetically on to a computer system and I don't think we have reached hers yet. 'Can you remind me of your surname, Sally Ann?'

'It's Mitchell.'

I nod. 'Janet's free in half an hour. You'll be upstairs in room eight.'

She smiles gratefully.

A few minutes later I drop her files off at Janet's office. Sally Ann is in the waiting room, reading one of Nina's old *NME*s that I've brought in from home.

'They were my daughter's,' I say. 'I've never heard of most of the people in them.'

'My boyfriend's in a band and their new single is reviewed in here.'

Of all the times we've chatted, I've never asked her about the father of her baby. She doesn't wear a wedding ring and he hasn't accompanied her to any appointments so I assumed he was no longer in the picture. 'Are they popular?'

'They're working their way up,' she says, and it's hard not to recognise the pride in her smile.

'Can I have a look?'

She passes me the magazine. 'That's them, The Hunters,' she points out.

My heart starts to race. 'Which one is your boyfriend?' I ask, hoping that it's the long-haired man pictured in the centre who only recently warned me there was nothing I could do to stop his affair with my underage daughter.

'That's him. That's Jon.'

I pause for a moment until I know my voice won't sound thin. 'I bet the girls love him,' I say.

'Tell me about it. He gets a lot of attention.'

'I don't know how I'd cope with that if I were you. Is he away from home a lot?'

'He is going on tour a couple of months after we have the baby. But I trust him. He knows which side his bread is buttered.'

'I'm sure he does. How long have you been together?'

'Since I was fourteen, but don't tell anyone that.' She giggles. 'My parents don't like him and think I'm making a massive mistake settling down so young. But when you know something's right, you just know, don't you?'

I nod my head, but I don't mean it. Hunter is doing to my daughter exactly what he has done to this poor girl. I wonder how many others he has, dotted about the town. I have the urge to tell her she's being made a fool of and that her pervert boyfriend is a cheat. But I can't bring myself to be the one to break her heart in her condition. So I leave with a smile and make my way back to reception.

The end of my working day can't come quickly enough and when the clock reaches 5 p.m., I grab my coat and I'm out of the door. En route home, I rehearse what I'm going to say to Nina. I'll slip Sally Ann into the conversation over dinner. I'll casually ask Nina if she's heard of The Hunters, then tell her I met the singer's pregnant girlfriend in the surgery. Her imagination will do the rest.

Since discovering their relationship, I have said nothing to her about it. She has continued to lie to me about staying at Saffron's house, and I have continued to play along with it. Hunter has me over a barrel. I can't risk losing her.

I slip my key into the front door lock, but it's already open. I take a deep breath and tell myself that if I remain poker-faced, this should all go like clockwork. 'Hello?' I shout, then work my way around the ground floor of the house until I reach the foot of the stairs. It's then that I hear it – a moaning coming from behind Nina's closed bedroom door.

I stop in my tracks, listening closely and hoping to God that she doesn't have Hunter under my roof and in her bed. She knows that I return from work at around this time – is she really so deep under his spell that she would take such a risk? I climb the stairs and falter outside her room. There's another moan followed by a shortness of breath. I cover my mouth with my hand, furious at the position she's putting me in. But I cannot just walk away and pretend this isn't happening. I cannot let Hunter get away with it. I bang on the door with the palm of my hand.

'Nina,' I say loudly and firmly. 'Get dressed, I'm coming in.'

It's the way in which she whimpers the word 'Mum' that alerts me to the fact that I may have got this all wrong. I grab the handle and open the door, and find Nina alone. But I struggle to make sense of what I'm seeing.

She is wearing a T-shirt and tracksuit bottoms and I gawp at her exposed, swollen stomach. It's then that I realise that not only is my daughter pregnant, but she is in labour too.

CHAPTER 27

NINA

TWENTY-THREE YEARS EARLIER

I hear Mum's faint 'Hello' from downstairs and I know that I can't keep my pregnancy a secret from her any longer. I've done everything I can to hide it but I'm in too much pain, and I need her. As she opens the door, it takes her a moment to realise what she's seeing.

'I'm sorry, I'm so sorry,' I begin before I start howling again.

'You're . . .' she says, but she can't finish her sentence.

'I think it's coming. It's early and I don't know what to do.'

There are only two other people in the world who know I'm pregnant: the woman at the family planning clinic who confirmed it and who wouldn't let me leave until I'd stopped hyperventilating, and Jon. And he only learned of it a few weeks ago.

I was lying on my back on a mattress at his friend's house where we crashed after a party. My head was facing Jon when I awoke in the early hours. He was naked, sitting upright and smoking a cigarette. Sometimes I think he never sleeps or that he's like a vampire who only comes alive at night. I watched his eyes making their way around my body. I thought I'd covered myself with a sheet, but I'd left a section of my stomach exposed. When I realised, I yanked it so it covered me completely, but it was too late. Jon was focusing on what I'd spent weeks hiding, the morning light capturing it perfectly. The game was up – he knew that I was pregnant.

I heard the crackling of the cigarette as he stubbed it out against the wall, red-hot ash falling to the floor. Then I felt his warm hand against my tummy. He made eye contact with me but I couldn't hold his gaze.

This is it, I thought. *This is where our story ends*. Until recently, I'd been lucky, as I'd barely shown. Then, as I gradually expanded, I took to wearing thicker, baggier clothes everywhere. I always kept my clothes on during sex, especially my school uniform, something Jon found a massive turn-on.

I wasn't ready to have this conversation with him because I knew it would drive him away, just like whatever Mum did to upset Dad that made him leave. That's what men do, isn't it? When something big happens that they can't handle, they use it as an excuse to leave you and you never see them again. Like Dad. Over and over he'd tell me that I was his 'only girl', but I wasn't enough to make him stay. Maybe that's why I started sleeping around almost immediately after he left – I wanted someone to love me as much as he did. I just went about it the wrong way.

And I didn't know how I was going to deal with Jon going next because he is everything to me. I can't lose anyone else. So I closed my eyes and rolled on to my side.

'You're . . . pregnant?' Jon asked. 'Is it mine?'

I turned my head sharply to shoot him a look. He knew it was the wrong thing to say.

'I can't believe it,' he said, shaking his head. 'It's brilliant. I'm going to be a dad.'

I hesitated, convinced I'd misheard. 'What?'

'I'm going to be a dad,' he repeated. 'It's amazing.'

'Really?' I gasped. 'Do you mean that?'

'Why wouldn't I?' He cupped my cheeks as he passionately kissed me. I didn't want it to end. But when it did, he lit up a spliff and after a few drags, I moved my hand to take it from him and have a puff. He pushed it away. 'You can't be smoking this stuff with a baby inside you,' he warned. 'No smoking or drinking and no more pills, it's all got to stop. They can damage it.'

Damage it, I said to myself. *Damage it.*

The reality check was crippling. I wanted so much to be happy that for a moment I'd forgotten about my condition; that this unborn baby was already damaged beyond repair. Even if I carried it to full term, it wouldn't live. I'd already researched my condition in a library medical journal and seen a photo of a baby with estro-prosencephaly. I wanted to be sick. I learned it won't have a usable brain and its face will not really be a face but a bit of mouth here and nose somewhere else and an eye in the middle of its head like a Cyclops. And it'll die within minutes of being born. So it doesn't matter if I did all the Es and whizz and coke and smoked all the spliffs in the world, I can't hurt my baby any more than my body has already.

But I couldn't tell Jon any of this because I didn't want to lose him. I started crying again.

'It's okay.' He soothed and spooned me, his hand still cradling my stomach. 'My Lolita is having a little Lolita of her own,' he said softly.

◆ ◆ ◆

Weeks passed and my body expanded. It was as if Jon's awareness gave it permission to blow up like a bouncy castle. And instead of dwelling on the inevitable, I allowed myself to imagine a happy-ever-after for the three of us.

I started telling myself that Mum and the tests I had when I was a kid were wrong and that I wasn't carrying a bunch of faulty chromosomes. I talked myself into believing that last year's miscarriage wasn't down to my broken insides, it was just bad luck. And when this baby came out, it would be healthy. The fantasy was a far better place to visit than the truth, and I kept returning to it.

'What's going to happen after I have it?' I asked Jon one afternoon. We had met in a truckers' cafe just outside the town centre. He was wearing his reflective sunglasses inside and his hair was scraped back with wet-look gel. He looked every inch the rock star. A spot of blood had seeped through the long sleeve of his white T-shirt and left a stain.

'What do you mean?' he asked. His voice was slurred as he stirred sugar into his coffee. I was too exhausted to see him play last night and I assumed he had a hangover.

'I mean where are the three of us going to live? Can we come and stay with you?'

He yawned and slumped into his seat. 'My flat is no place for a kid, you know that.'

'I don't because I've never been there.'

'And you wouldn't want to because it's a shithole and it's where the band rehearses. It's no place for our child, that's why I doss at mates' houses. Why can't you stay with your mum?'

'Because she is going to go ballistic when she finds out I'm pregnant.'

'Then put your name down for a council flat. They're obliged to look after teenage mums.'

'We could get one together,' I offered hopefully.

'You know I can't do that.'

'Why?'

'Because of your age. You're fifteen and I got you pregnant at fourteen. Once that gets out, I could be arrested and it'll be the end of you and me and the band. And we are so close to getting signed by a major label.' He put his thumb and index finger close together as if to emphasise his proximity to success. 'You wouldn't want to ruin that for me, would you? I'm doing all of this for us. You just have to wait it out and then we can get somewhere together. I promise.'

I gave myself a moment to imagine the house and the life we could share and how content we might be, before reality hit home – it didn't matter what I told myself, the doctors weren't wrong. I wasn't destined to have the life I badly wanted.

I started crying and I expected Jon to ask me why I was suddenly so upset, but he didn't say anything. Then as the sun caught his eyes behind his sunglasses, I saw they were closed. He had fallen asleep.

I'm glad it's Mum who's with me now, but I still want Jon. Once she gets over the shock, she will know what to do. She always does. And she will be able to tell him that what's happened to our baby isn't my fault. She will make him understand and he won't leave me.

CHAPTER 28

MAGGIE

TWENTY-THREE YEARS EARLIER

I gasp. 'You're . . .' But I can't finish the sentence.

'I think it's coming,' Nina cries. 'It's really early and I don't know what to do.'

Pain contorts her face and body and she clutches her stomach. Suddenly the truth hits me as to why I've been writing so many notes to excuse her from gym at school over the last few weeks. She blamed period pains when in reality it was quite the opposite. She didn't want anyone to see her in PE kit and notice her belly. How many other things has she lied to me about?

'Get Jon, I need Jon,' she begs me.

'I don't know who Jon is.' I shouldn't feign ignorance while she's at her most vulnerable, yet I find myself doing so. I might be in shock but I know I don't want that bastard anywhere near her or this house. 'Just concentrate on your breathing.'

She is sobbing now and short shallow breaths punctuate her sentences. 'His name is Jon Hunter and he's my boyfriend,' she pants. 'His address is in my coat pocket. I need him, I can't do this without him.'

I recoil at her reference to their relationship. 'Do you have a telephone number for him?'

'No.'

'Then I don't think we have time for me to find him. And I don't want to leave you alone.'

She isn't as convinced as I am. 'Should we call an ambulance?' she says, and her body folds in on itself as the latest wave of contractions plough through her.

'We can do this, you and me, together,' I assure her. It isn't the answer she's expecting. On the surface I appear calm, but underneath I'm frantic because I don't know what to do. My fifteen-year-old daughter is pregnant for the second time but I can't nip it in the bud with illegally obtained medications as I did before. This baby is on its way.

I need to get a hold of myself, take control and do what's best for Nina. And it isn't calling for an ambulance. I don't want to bring undue attention to our lives. If Social Services become involved, their questions might be too much for her to cope with. Undue stress might lead to catastrophic repercussions and they could take her away from me. I have too much to hide.

So there is only one thing I can do. I will deliver my grandchild myself. I assisted in bringing babies into the world during my midwife training and although it was under supervision, I doubt much has changed procedurally over the last sixteen years. Only if there are any complications and Nina's health is at risk will I call for help.

She looks at me and she's so scared right now. I need to get over my shock and reassure her. 'I promise you that we can get through this. Have I ever lied to you?' She shakes her head and I thank God she doesn't know the truth. I move towards the door and hear her panicked voice.

'Where are you going? Please don't leave me,' she pleads, and the fact that she needs me so desperately makes me feel overcome with emotion.

'I'll be back really soon, I need to get a few things together,' I say.

I stand at the top of the stairs with my hand over my mouth, trying not to let her hear me as I break down. What kind of mother am I to let this happen for a second time? And not to have noticed her condition until it's gone this far? This is all Alistair's fault. Given the chance I'd kill him with my own bare hands for the mess he has made of our lives.

I return to her room as quickly as I can, making several journeys carrying clean towels and sheets, bowls of water containing diluted antiseptic and sterilised scissors. Then I prepare myself and the room for what is to arrive.

As the hours pass, I stroke Nina's hair like I did when she was a little girl and she was poorly. I reassure her that everything is going to be okay even though I know that from the moment this baby appears, her life is going to be far from that.

'I'm frightened of what'll happen,' she says.

'It's going to be all right. I'm here.'

'No, I mean when the baby's born. I've been reading about the condition, about the estroprosencephaly. I've seen pictures of what she'll look like.'

'She?'

'I think it's a girl. It's what Jon wants.'

'Let's not worry about what she looks like now,' I say, but it's only natural that Nina is terrified.

'I don't think I can watch her . . . die.'

I don't know what the right thing to say to her is. 'Okay,' is all I can manage. 'I'll be with her.'

'Promise me.'

'I promise.'

In between her contractions, Nina offers me a glimpse of a life I have been shut out of for so long. She explains how she met Hunter and how she wasn't aware she was pregnant until it was too late to do anything about it. She reveals how she kept the pregnancy secret from me, that her boyfriend can't wait to become a father, but how it will break his heart when he discovers the baby's deformities. She expresses her guilt for the way she has behaved. I forgive her everything.

Evening moves into night-time and then to early morning until finally, I know the baby is imminent. And soon after it begins to crown, it's only a matter of minutes before I am holding my grandchild in my arms. Now that Nina's hard work is complete, I take charge.

'Is it a girl?' she asks as I cut the baby's umbilical cord with scissors smeared in antiseptic Savlon and clamp it with the plastic clip I use to seal freezer bags. After so much pain, Nina is now almost motionless, too scared to sit up and see the face of her child.

'Yes it is,' I reply.

'And is she . . .'

'I need to leave the room, darling,' I reply, wrapping the child in a warm blanket I'd kept on the radiator and heading for the door. 'I'm so sorry.'

'She's not making any noise,' Nina says quietly. 'Can I see her?'

'It's best that you don't,' I reply, and close the door behind me.

I hurry down the stairs. I don't want to wound Nina any more than she's been hurt already. But not allowing her to see her baby has to be for the best. This is the most difficult decision I have ever made and now I must stick to it, for Nina's sake.

I leave my grandchild alone in the basement, then return to help Nina deliver the placenta and place it in a washing-up bowl to throw out. I check her tear and considering her age, she has been fortunate. It's small and she hasn't ripped any muscles, so it should heal by itself. Nina isn't crying, in fact she is not expressing any emotion at all. I give her two tablets and a glass of water and wait for her to swallow them.

'Dylan,' she says suddenly. 'Dylan.'

'What's that?'

'My baby. That's what I'm calling her.'

'It's an unusual name for a girl.'

'It's after the singer Bob Dylan. He's Jon's favourite.'

'Then that'll be her name.'

She tries to move her legs to get out of bed. 'I need to tell Jon what's happened,' she says, but I encourage her to stay where she is. 'But he'll be worried about me.'

I doubt that. I want to keep them apart for as long as I can. 'There will be plenty of time to explain everything to him,' I say, and she is too weak to argue.

'I'll be back soon,' I whisper, then return to the basement to do what needs to be done.

CHAPTER 29

MAGGIE

TWENTY-THREE YEARS EARLIER, TWO DAYS LATER

It's an unfamiliar area of town to me, even though it's only ten minutes' driving distance from where we live.

An A-to-Z map stored in the glove compartment guides me to the address written on the scrap of paper I found in Nina's coat pocket. Also inside are a pair of Alistair's leather driving gloves, which I slip on. I park close, but not too close, to the street and then wait. It's early afternoon, so I have missed much of the lunchtime traffic and the teatime rush hour has yet to begin. I know time is of the essence, but if I hurry and make a mistake then I risk being seen. I allow a few minutes to go by and when nobody passes me on foot or by bike, I gather myself and exit the car. I leave it unlocked so I can hurry back inside when I am finished.

The row of four-storey houses faces the Racecourse, an historic parkland a stone's throw from Northampton town centre. The homes here date back to Victorian times but many of them have been split into flats. The address on the paper reads 14a Winston Parade, so I assume the occupants live in a converted building. My palms grow clammy as the house numbers decrease until finally, I'm here. A set of stone steps leads up to the ground floor. Another set leads down to the basement flat, where I need to be.

Outside the entrance to 14a, I take one last look around me to assure myself I haven't been spotted, then I press the intercom buzzer. It makes no noise and I wait just in case I can't hear it but the occupants can. There is no answer.

I peer through the window but venetian blinds block the inside from the world outside. I turn to knock this time, and as soon as my hand makes contact with the front door, it gently falls open. I've seen this happen in enough films to know that no good comes from a door that opens with such little effort. But leaving is not an option. I love Nina too much to do that, so I press on.

'Hello,' I half-whisper, half-speak. I desperately want someone to reply, but they don't. My fingers are trembling so I ball my fists to make them stop. Now, my whole hands shake. I slip them inside my coat pockets. 'Hello?' I repeat and again, there is nothing.

The interior is neat and tidy. The walls of the corridor leading to what I assume is the lounge ahead have been papered with wood-chip and painted a fresh magnolia. To the right, the galley-style kitchen is clean and jars of spaghetti and pasta are lined up next to a breadbin. There's a tea towel with a printed dog pattern hanging from an oven door and a handful of dishes on a draining board.

I continue to walk with caution, passing a bedroom. Inside is a double bed that's been made and covered with a brightly coloured duvet. I pause to take a closer look. I don't know quite what I expected but it wasn't something as well kept as this. I notice make-up and perfumes scattered about the surface of a chest of drawers. They are the inexpensive Yardley and Avon brands. Perched on a radiator cover there's a framed photograph of Jon Hunter, a pair of dark sunglasses on the crown of his head. He's kissing the cheek of his pregnant girlfriend Sally Ann Mitchell, who is smiling for the camera.

I poke my head around the door of the second bedroom. All it contains is a large cardboard box with a photograph of a baby's cot on the side and four framed drawings of Disney characters that have yet to be nailed to the wall. *She is nesting*, I think, and for a moment, I'm heartbroken for all that Nina is missing out on.

It's only when I reach the lounge that I realise I'm holding my breath. I let it go, then sharply inhale when I spot him. Hunter is sprawled across the sofa wearing only his underwear; his legs are spread wide, his head is drooping forward and his breathing is shallow. He is either unconscious or fast asleep; I can't be sure. The curtains are partially closed, making it difficult for me to see him properly, so I move closer.

The sound is turned off but the television remains on, the picture flickering and casting infrequent bursts of light across the room. I spot an overturned blackened spoon lying on the glass coffee table; next to it is a cigarette lighter. Wrapped around his sinewy arm is a piece of rubber tubing and a needle is still lodged inside a vein. The sight of such depravity jars against his home's domesticity. Hunter's chest rises and falls and I decide he must have passed out while high. How in God's name did my daughter fall for this mess of a man?

I'm startled by a noise behind me. My head turns and I spot another door. It's slightly ajar and appears to be a bathroom. I'm no fighter but I'm prepared to protect myself if needs be. However, the noise isn't coming any closer. The sound is like that of a deflating car tyre, only more sporadic. I make my way towards it, using my foot to push the door open, then quickly I take a step backward in case someone bursts out of it.

The hinges creak before the door suddenly stops. Something is blocking it from opening completely. I inch towards it and that's when I see Sally Ann Mitchell. She is staring right at me, her big blue eyes as wide open as they can be. She is clearly as shocked to see me as I am to see her and for a moment neither of us moves, each waiting for the other to react first.

I have little choice. Fingering the vegetable knife in my pocket, I move swiftly towards her.

CHAPTER 30

NINA

TWENTY-THREE YEARS EARLIER, ONE WEEK LATER

I can't think in straight lines any more. My brain zigzags instead, leaving me muddled. It's like a shaken wasps' nest with angry, uncontrollable thoughts flying in all different directions. Everything is such a blur right now – it's like the world is still moving as normal but I'm in slow motion, unable to speed up and rejoin it.

When I'm awake, Mum is never far away and she chats to me but I can't process everything she says. My mind is as weak as my body and I don't have the energy to ask her to repeat herself, so I just nod and fall back into my own little confused world. Sometimes I wake up and I think I hear noises and hushed voices, but I'm never sure.

I don't know how long I've slept for today or how I even got into the bathroom, but I'm assuming Mum helped me. I find myself sitting inside a warm bubble bath that smells of mint. My back is facing her. She is shampooing my hair, and flashes of memories appear of Dad doing this when I was a little girl. I briefly tune in to what she's saying and she's naming people she saw when she went to get a prescription for me at the chemist.

She asked if I remembered Dr King coming to visit. I honestly don't. When she saw it was stressing me out not being able to recall it, she said not to worry and filled in the blanks for me. She hadn't told Dr King I'd lost a baby; instead she said I was struggling to come to terms with Dad leaving us. The doctor diagnosed me with 'major depression' and told Mum it's as if my brain is struggling to cope with loss, so it's protecting itself by shutting down for a while. It's like when an electrical device overheats; sometimes it has to be switched off and left to rest before it's turned on again.

If I don't take the tablets he prescribed for my depression and anxiety, I want to curl up into a ball and die. But when I do take the tablets, they create a fog that's so dense, I can't separate what's real from what I'm imagining. When I explained this to Mum, she admitted Dr King tried to talk her into sending me to stay in a special hospital that might help to sort me out quicker. I know the one she means, it's St Crispin's on the other side of town. Everyone knows that's where they put the nutters. We learned about it at school – when it opened decades ago, it was a mental asylum for insane kids. And while it's not used for that any longer, if I'm sent there, I'll never shake the stigma. I begged Mum to look after me and she promised to, as long as I help myself and keep taking the pills.

Mum turns the shower attachment on, waits until the water is nice and warm and rinses the shampoo from my hair. When she opens the bathroom cabinet and reaches for the conditioner, I spy the breast pump on the shelf. She says I need to use it a few times a day because my stupid, insensitive body is producing milk for a baby it killed. It'll dry up soon enough, she promises.

The grief appears in waves and I can't control when or why I start crying. Like now. I'm suddenly overcome with emotion and start to weep again. Mum doesn't say anything, but she places her hand on my shoulder as if to reassure me. I put my hand on hers. I used to think that I was so grown-up, but I'm not. And I'm certainly not strong enough to carry this pain alone. I don't know where I'd be if I didn't have her to share it. Actually, I do. I'd be throwing myself from the roof of the Grosvenor Centre car park.

Guilt continues to eat me up: guilt at what my stupid body did to my daughter, and guilt for letting Mum take her away without me even holding her first. When she wrapped Dylan's tiny body up in towels, all I saw of her were five pink toes poking out. I wanted to reach out and touch them. Only now do I acknowledge that I never said hello or goodbye to her. She just sort of left my body and that was it.

Part of me wishes I'd felt her warm skin against mine, even if just for a second. I owed it to her to look at her properly, even though Mum thought it best I didn't. I guess she was right because this way, she can be whatever I want her to be. In my imagination, she is a beautiful, perfect little girl who wasn't strong enough for this world.

Like Mum said, perhaps it's best she died before she was born as I'd hate to think of her suffering, even for a second. I hope she slipped away while she was sleeping inside me and that all she felt during her short life was the love between me and Jon.

'Where is she?' I ask.

'Don't you remember?' Mum says. I think hard, but shake my head. 'I chose a really nice spot in the garden because if we tell anyone about her, they'll take her away from us. This way, she stays here and we can visit her whenever we like.'

'I want to see her now.'

'Why don't you wait until you're feeling better?'

I have no concept of time. 'How long has it been?'

'A week.'

I'm suddenly struck by Jon's absence. 'Have you heard from Jon?'

'No, I'm sorry, I haven't,' she replies.

'But you promised you were going to see him and tell him what happened.' My words slur as I fight to release them.

'I promise you I saw him, but he wasn't interested in coming to visit. I'm so sorry, my darling.'

I start to cry again.

◆ ◆ ◆

A few days later, Mum helps me out of bed and leads me into the garden. The warmth of the sun reaches my face as she walks with me, her arm wrapped around my waist for support. She leads me along the path until we reach the far end, past the crab-apple trees and close to the shed. In front of me is a flower bed. It's full of brightly coloured plants and a small rose bush has been planted in the centre. It has one yellow bloom.

'Why don't we sit down?' she suggests, and I do. I allow the palms of my hands and fingertips to run across the soft blades of grass. For a moment, I feel alive again. However, it's fleeting.

'And she's here?' I ask, gazing at the plants.

Mum nods. 'I chose somewhere secluded where you could come and sit and talk to her where nobody else can see.'

I consider how hard it must have been for Mum to deliver her granddaughter, then hold her lifeless body in her arms. She never talks about what my faulty chromosomes did to Dylan's appearance, but I have no doubt that it can't have been easy for her to see. 'What did you bury her in?' I ask.

'I put her in an old Babygro of yours that I'd kept and I wrapped her in that patchwork quilt that Elsie made for you when you were a baby to keep her warm. And then I washed a box I found in the shed and carefully tucked her up inside it.'

Dylan. My Dylan. I let the earth she is buried under run through my fingers and scatter.

As the medication begins to wear off, I understand that it's always going to be like this. Everyone I have loved or will ever love is going to leave me. Dad. Jon. My daughter. I'm never going to carry a healthy child or settle down and start a family because no man will ever want someone as broken as me. Jon didn't, so why should anyone else be different? The only constant I'll ever have is Mum and even she won't be around forever. At least while she's here, she will always put me first. She will never let me down.

Without warning, it all becomes too much for me. I look at Mum and instinctively, she knows what to do. She helps me to my feet, escorts me inside and upstairs to my bedroom and offers me another couple of tablets.

I think I'm beginning to prefer the blur because it hurts less.

CHAPTER 31

NINA

The kitchen is rich with the sweet aroma of a chocolate cake I'm baking. I've blended the flour, eggs, sugar, cocoa powder, baking powder and salt together with a wooden spoon and good old-fashioned elbow grease, just like Dad used to do. Now the two halves are cooling down on a wire rack on the worktop.

I can't resist scooping what's left in the bowl with my finger to taste before I begin the washing up. I haven't eaten much in the last few days since the dentist removed the root and shards of the tooth Maggie broke. The swelling has gone down but there's still bruising.

I've been thinking about Dad a lot this week, and being in the kitchen makes a childhood memory of him surge to the surface. I'm standing by his side with a red tea towel in my hand and he's passing me wet dishes to dry. I can't be more than ten years old and we are singing along to ABBA's greatest hits album playing on the hi-fi in the lounge next door. Every weekend, Dad made us either a cake or a loaf of bread from scratch, and I'd help.

Now, when I'm baking, which admittedly isn't that often these days, I imagine that I'm standing where I am right now, in front of the sink, and my child is next to me, every bit the willing helper as I was. I can see Dylan in the reflection of the window and I find myself explaining aloud which ingredients need to go into the bowl first and why, and that we have to be patient while the cake bakes and not keep opening the oven door to check on it. When I blink, she vanishes.

I remember very little after Mum carried Dylan away from me. I know that I shut down and for almost a year, I disassociated myself from everyone. Shortly before my sixteenth birthday, Mum helped wean me off the antidepressants and I made my slow return to the world. But it soon became apparent that I was no longer fitted for the life I once had. I couldn't slip into the same routine, same cliques or the same school. I had suffered too much loss to be that girl again. So I had to become someone else.

Maggie began working three jobs to pay for a private tutor to get me up to speed. And after a year of effort, I scraped through my exams with seven GCSEs. It was enough to get me to Northampton College to study for A-levels in English literature and English language.

For the sake of my sanity, I'd pushed Jon out of my mind. I no longer listened to music – his or anyone else's. I didn't go into town, I didn't keep my old friends or read magazines or newspapers. I stopped doing anything that reminded me of the life that had ended so painfully. It didn't stop me from worrying that I might just bump into Jon one day in the street. However, I was sure he was some big globetrotting rock star by now and had left this small town way behind him.

It was a new friend I made at college who shattered that illusion.

'Did you see the local news last night?' Stacie Denton began over lunch in the canteen. She was a plump girl who dressed in dark Goth clothing and as a result, strayed a little too far from the norm to have many friends. But our shared love of Charlotte Brontë gave us common ground. 'You remember that local guy who used to sing in the band The Hunters?'

A buried image of Jon performing onstage at the Roadmender burst to life in my head. 'Just about,' I said.

'Do you recall when he was jailed for killing his pregnant girl-friend? Well, he launched this massive court appeal to get a retrial but it was turned down yesterday. I used to quite fancy him.'

It was too much information for me to process at once. Feigning illness to get out of classes, I said goodbye to Stacie and hurried towards the *Chronicle & Echo*. There, I sat in the reception area flicking through old issues of filed copies, catching up on what I had missed. So much of the story didn't make sense. I was his pregnant girlfriend, not this Sally Ann girl, and I was very much alive. Jon was never the slightest bit aggressive with me. And when he was using, he was too out of it to move, let alone hurt anyone. I could only assume Mum had known about it, but didn't tell me because she didn't want to hurt me.

My mobile phone rings and brings me back to the present. I don't know how long I've been lost in thought, but the washing-up water is now lukewarm and my hands are white and wrinkled. The phone's screen reveals that Aunty Jennifer, Mum's sister, is calling. I let it go to voicemail. She rings every fortnight for an update on Mum's 'condition', as Jennifer's own disability – multiple sclerosis – means she can't travel to visit Maggie in the care home that I've invented. I leave a notepad of things I tell her each time we speak just so that I don't contradict myself. But Christ, keeping up with your own lies is difficult. I give Maggie grudging respect for managing it successfully for so many years.

I dry my hands, send a text message and place a couple of fingers on top of the cake to check that it's the right temperature before spreading chocolate mousse across the base. I take the piping bag and fill it with buttercream, then start to decorate it with the name Dylan. Finally, I add twenty-three candles that I bought from the supermarket yesterday, one for each year since I gave birth.

'Happy birthday,' I say, and I allow them to burn for a minute or so before blowing them out myself. And I make a wish that could never come true.

CHAPTER 32
MAGGIE

The sight of him is enough to make my pulse race.

Who he is and what he's up to, I don't know. But for the third time, he has turned up here in his white car and is simply staring at my house. Only today, he's slowly making his way up the path. I crane my neck to get a better view but the bloody shutters are making it difficult. I drag the ottoman over and stand on it so I am right at the top of the window, looking down. I can just about see him; I think he's looking in through the lounge window while I'm looking out from up here. If he's a burglar, then he's not a very good one because he's far from subtle. Perhaps he's a plain-clothed police officer or even a private detective? Maybe someone I know doesn't believe Nina's claims that I'm now living with my sister on the coast? Perhaps they are missing me?

Suddenly someone else comes into view – I think it's Elsie. She's a one-woman Neighbourhood Watch scheme and very little happens without her knowing about it. She uses her walking frame to approach him, although I have no idea what they're saying. Now she's pointing to the telephone in her hand and he's beating a hasty retreat back to his car. I know she's only trying to be helpful, but if he was planning to break into this house, she might just have scuppered my chances of being discovered.

As his car pulls away and Elsie returns to her house, I scan the street again and a room in the home opposite hers catches my eye. I don't know the family at all; they moved in some months after I ended up in here. Two adults and two children, a boy and a girl, likely under the age of ten. I've never really liked the look of the husband. He's a chubby man with tattoos up and down his arms and even from this distance, I recognise an arrogance in the way he swings his shoulders as he walks. I can't see his wife's face clearly but I picture her to have harsh angular features and to look as equally unpleasant as her spouse. And I've never seen the kids playing out in the street like Nina did when she was their age. I suspect they're not very good parents.

I watch both of them in an upstairs bedroom with the daughter. The light is on but the bulb has no shade. They're decorating the room and the window has watered-down emulsion on it that stops you from seeing inside while the curtains are down. Only from this height and angle, I can see through the upper section of the sash window, which they haven't bothered to cover.

The wife has my attention; her finger is pointing aggressively towards the girl and she is leaning towards her as if she is shouting. But when her husband turns to leave, something happens. I can't see what's gone on behind him until he passes, but his daughter is falling into the wall and I watch helplessly as she collapses to the floor, out of my sight. I think her mother has just smacked her hard. In fact I'm sure of it. 'No!' I shout.

I ball my fists and will the girl to clamber to her feet. Her mother's mouth opens wide again as if she is still yelling at the poor mite, then she too leaves and pulls the door behind her. Eventually, and to my relief, her daughter rises back into view; she's rubbing her eyes and then the side of her head that hit the wall. She moves towards the door and I assume she is turning the doorknob, but it won't budge. She tries a few times before accepting that she's been locked inside. My heart bleeds for her as she disappears again.

She wants to look out of her window and wipes some of the temporary paint that's obstructing her view. I think how terribly alone she must feel, incarcerated and with nobody knowing how much she is hurting. I want her to know *I* am here and that *I* care.

An idea comes to me.

I grab the bedside lamp and drag the cable towards me, then start flashing the lamp on and off, over and over again in rapid succession, in the faint hope that it will catch her attention. I have tried this many times before but nobody has ever noticed, not even Elsie and especially not in daylight. I think it must be the positioning of the slats that won't allow light to be seen below from certain angles. 'Come on, come on,' I repeat anxiously before I hear a noise that takes the wind from my sails. It's a ping. The bulb has blown.

'No, no, no, no!' I yell. Without thinking, I put my hand on the bulb to turn it in case it has only come loose. It burns my fingertips and I curse. I move swiftly to grab the other bedside lamp, but it won't stretch as far as the window. I unplug it but the cable is caught behind the cabinet. I pull the furniture away with a tug but lose my balance and my foot becomes entwined with my chain, causing me to fall face first on to the bed.

I climb to my feet and plug the lamp into the second socket and start again. A good fifteen minutes pass before finally, the child turns to look in my direction, squashing her face up against the glass. Even if she can't see my face behind the shutters, she knows someone is up here. Then she places the palm of her hand to the window as if to say hello.

I am overcome with emotion. Aside from Nina, this is the first interaction I have had with anyone for two long years. Finally somebody outside of this house knows that I exist! I struggle to stem my tears. I don't want it to end.

The girl's hand moves from left to right, like she is waving at me. She disappears out of sight for a moment and her room goes a little darker. I squint until she switches her light on and off and then returns to the window and I do the same with the lamp. Now I am practically bawling.

But our interaction is cut short by her mother appearing at the door; she catches her daughter playing with the lights. She grabs her by the arm, the light goes off and the girl vanishes again. I vow to myself that I am going to help that child. And in doing so, perhaps she can help me. But I won't be able to do it on my own.

CHAPTER 33

NINA

'I need to show you something,' Maggie says with urgency. She scuttles towards the window, her chain rattling like Marley's ghost's. 'Come here.'

Despite the facial bruising and my lost tooth, I decided tonight that we need to move forward and eat together. It's the first time we have come face to face since she tried to escape ten days ago. This is not the welcome I expect, and I regard her with my usual suspicion.

My eyes dart around the room. The ottoman has been moved to under the window and its padded cushioning has an impression that suggests she's been sitting there a lot. Nothing else appears out of the ordinary. It doesn't mean that it isn't. I can only trust Maggie as far as I can throw her. However, after the events of the other night, I take a chance that she won't make the same mistake twice.

'What is it?' I reply and remove the key for her leg cuff from my pocket. She's not listening. She's standing by the shutters, pointing towards the house opposite Elsie's.

'You see that window?' she asks, and I think she's referring to the one with white paint covering much of it. 'I can see directly into it.'

'And that's your big news? Who shall I call first, the *Daily Mail* or CNN?'

'I haven't finished,' she snaps, then recognises that she shouldn't have. She waits to see if I react, but I let it slide.

'Okay, go on then.'

'Have you ever met the family who live there?'

'I've said hello a couple of times when I've walked past, I think. I haven't paid them much attention.'

'Because I saw the mother smacking her little girl last night.'

'What do you mean by "smacking"?'

'I mean exactly what you think I mean.'

'What, like a smacked bum or a clip round the ear?'

'I mean I'm sure she slapped her child around the face so hard that she hit the wall and fell to the floor.'

My hackles rise. I cannot abide cruelty to children, animals or the elderly, although I appreciate the irony of the latter. I move to the window for a clearer view.

'And you're positive you're not mistaken?'

'Yes, I'm sure that's exactly what happened.'

'You keep saying "I'm sure", but did you actually see the slap?'

She hesitates for a split second, too long for my liking. 'Despite what you may have told the world about my fictional mental state, I'm still compos mentis,' she replies in a way that suggests I've offended her. 'That little girl was locked in her room all night until this morning. She is being abused and neglected.'

Maggie meets my stare as we both recognise the similarities between her own circumstances and those of the girl. The difference between them is that no child can ever have done something that warrants such aggression. 'Have you seen her tonight?' I ask.

'She was locked inside again for about an hour earlier. Then her dad came and let her out. We have to do something, Nina.'

If Maggie is being honest, then no, we can't let a child suffer. But what if she's confused or wrong? Or what if this is another one of her escape plans? Is she capitalising on my big heart to lull me into a false sense of security?

'I'll be back in a few minutes,' I say, and leave her. I pause at her bedroom door and turn around, again looking for a sign that I'm right to be cautious. But she isn't paying me any attention. She remains where she is, glued to the window. I want to think that she's telling the truth.

I return with a tray containing both of our dinners. We sit side by side on the ottoman, eating sausage and mash from plates on our laps and watching the girl's window over the road. Neither of us mentions our fight.

It's the first time I've eaten with her in her bedroom. She picks up a metal knife to cut into a sausage and at the same moment, we both realise that I've forgotten to give her a plastic one. I'm angry with myself – only moments ago I was telling myself to be vigilant and here I am, handing her a weapon. She turns the knife around and passes it to me, handle first.

'It's okay,' I find myself saying, so she continues to use it.

'This is nice,' she comments. 'What's in these sausages?'

'They were on offer in Sainsbury's,' I say. 'They've got chilli flakes in them.'

'Chilli? Fancy that. You used to love sausage and mash when you were a girl.'

'These days they call meals like this "comfort food".'

'My comfort food is beef, Yorkshire puddings and roast potatoes.'

'I can never get my Yorkshires to rise like yours did.'

'It's all in the heat. If the oven temperature is too high, they won't go up enough. You know Alistair couldn't cook to save his life.'

The mention of Dad surprises me. She brings him up so casually, it's as if we discuss him on a regular basis. And she never refers to him as 'your dad'. She's stripped him of his parental title. In return, I have done the same to her.

'Yes, he could,' I counter. 'He was always in the kitchen at the weekends. I used to help him.'

'He was. But they say you're either a baker or a cook, and he was definitely a baker. What about the time when I was ill with shingles and he made dinner and put the fish fingers in the microwave for fifteen minutes? When they came out they were like doorstops.'

That brings a smile to my face. 'I wasn't that much better,' I say. 'Do you recall my home economics class when I had to make vegetable soup? You packed the spice jar in among my ingredients, and I thought I had to pour the whole thing in.'

Maggie laughs. 'We were barely able to keep a straight face when you brought that home. One spoonful and our mouths were on fire.'

I'm suddenly overcome by the need to ask the question I have asked many times before but which she's steadfastly refused to answer. She has never told me the truth about Dad. My mouth opens, only this time, I have second thoughts. I'm so used to being consumed by resentment towards her that this ceasefire has come out of the blue. And I find myself appreciating the moment we've found ourselves in.

'She's done it again!' Maggie yells, bringing me back to the present. My eyes dart back to the window. 'Did you see it? She just slapped her daughter again!'

I was too busy looking at Maggie to see it, but looking across the road I recognise another argument taking place between mother and child. I watch carefully, waiting for another physical outburst, but instead there's only shouting. Did Maggie really see what she thinks she's seen? Can I take her word for it?

'We have to help her,' says Maggie adamantly. 'We need to call the police.'

I'm swayed by her passion but I shake my head.

'Why not?'

'Because they'll want to know where I witnessed the attacks and I can't see into that bedroom from the ground or the first floor.'

Maggie glares at me, and I feel like a child who has disappointed a parent with naughty behaviour. But I can't afford to fly above the radar and put myself at risk of outside scrutiny.

'What if you were to contact Social Services?' she says. 'Anonymously.'

'I don't know. They must get malicious tip-offs every day. How long does it take to investigate an allegation? Both parents are going to deny cruelty and if there are no obvious injuries and the girl doesn't back up my claims, they'll get away with it and make things worse for her.'

'Well, we can't just do nothing.'

I feel her frustration. 'I'm not saying that. I'm saying I need to think this through.'

'I'm not going to be able to rest knowing what she's going through on my doorstep. She and her brother will be better off in care than living in that house. They should give those kids to someone who wants to look after them properly . . .'

She trails to a stop mid-sentence, aware of her error. Now she won't look at me.

'Go on,' I say. 'I assume you were going to add, "Look after them properly like a foster parent would." That's another opportunity you took away from me, wasn't it?'

CHAPTER 34

NINA

TWO AND A HALF YEARS EARLIER

I'm so nervous my hands are trembling. I slip them inside my jacket pockets so that no one else can see.

I am having second thoughts. What if they take one look at me and reject me on sight alone? What if they tell me I'm too old or too unqualified or don't even give me a reason before turning me down? Now I don't think I want to go inside, but the sensor has already picked up on me and the sliding doors open. Heads turn to look at the latest arrival and I'm greeted with warm smiles. It temporarily disarms my apprehension.

Northamptonshire County Council's building recently opened and has that new smell attached to it. It's in stark contrast to the mustiness of my library. I'd forgotten that workplaces can smell of thick carpets and wooden furniture and not just old pages and people. Lining the corridors are movable noticeboards, each with details of tonight's event. Most have posters pinned to them containing images of children – models, I assume – of all ages, and there are pamphlets and information packs on trellis tables.

'Hello there, I'm Briony,' a chirpy woman begins as she approaches me. She thrusts out her hand and her smile swallows the lower portion of her face. She's probably about the same age as me, but she has fewer creases around the eyes.

'Nina,' I say. 'Nina Simmonds.'

'Nice to meet you, Nina. I assume you're here for the adoption and fostering open evening?'

I nod.

'Great, and have you registered with us online yet?'

'No, I haven't. I only decided that I was coming as I left work.'

'Not a problem.' She hands me a clipboard and a biro to write down my details. 'Bit nervous?'

I nod again.

'Well you don't need to be, we're all very friendly here. We just need your basic contact details, it's nothing intrusive.'

As I begin writing, I'm tempted to give them my work address as I don't want anything mailed to the house before I get the chance to tell Mum what I'm doing. And I also want to be sure in my own mind that this is the right thing for me. I spot a compromise and tick the box that says I'd rather be contacted by email than by post.

I'd seen the poster for the open evening pinned to the notice-boards in the library for weeks. Every now and again it caught my eye, and I'd imagine how it might feel to be the parent of the desperate little girl pictured on it. The more I looked at her, the more I thought of Dylan. And the more I realised that just because my faulty body had ruined my chances of becoming a biological mother, it didn't mean I couldn't raise someone else's child. I've lost a lot, but not my maternal instinct.

Sometimes my desire to be a mum becomes all-consuming and I crave the need for a child's love above all else. I want to shape them, guide them into adulthood, help them to not make the same mistakes that I did. Even when they're grown and have flown the nest, I want to believe they are out there thinking fondly of me and grateful that I chose them. Parents and boyfriends can walk away, but a child stays in your heart forever. Take Dylan. She *is* my heart.

I complete the form as Briony reassures me I'm not alone and that there are plenty of other prospective single parents like me here tonight. She leads me to a drinks station and invites me to help myself as she explains what fostering and adoption entails. My eyes wander to some of the others in the room. All ages and ethnicities are represented here; most are couples but there are a handful of us singletons. I wonder what their circumstances are. Perhaps they have bodies like mine that kill babies.

'I'll leave you with this,' Briony says, and hands me an information pack. 'It'll give you an idea of what to expect from the interview process and the stages ahead should you wish to move forward. Now, if it's okay with you, I'll pop your name down on the list to have a chat with two of our adopters. Don't worry, it's an informal conversation and they'll answer any of your questions. It's about a ten-minute wait, is that all right?'

'Yes, that's great,' I say. I pour myself a cup of tea and she leaves me alone to flick through the info. When she eventually returns, she has a young couple in tow. She introduces me to Jayne and Dom and I follow them to a seated area. They adopted twin sisters three years ago, Briony explains, and encourages them to recall their experiences.

'I'm not going to sugar-coat it and say it's been easy,' admits Jayne. 'When we decided we wanted to give them a home, they were aged four and had a lot of behavioural difficulties.'

'Like what?'

'They'd been left to run wild by their biological parents. There was neglect, a lack of rules and boundaries, no schooling, they ate

160

junk food, they didn't go outside and play and they couldn't read or write. We've spent the last three years helping them to catch up with other kids their age.'

'And how's it going?'

'We are getting there,' says Dom with pride in his eyes. 'They're about a year behind where they should be development-wise, and while it's been a tough slog, it's also been incredibly rewarding.'

'You must need a lot of patience,' I say, quietly questioning whether I could ever be as good as them.

'Yes, patience is important, but above all, they needed love,' Dom continues. 'That's all these kids need, to know they are safe and secure with you and that you aren't going to abandon them.'

I can do that, I think, because I know how it feels. We chat for longer, and then I meet another adoptive couple and finally a social worker. And before I know it, it's past 10 p.m. and the night is drawing to a close.

'How are you feeling then?' asks Briony with a smile as I slip my jacket back on. 'Have we put you off or are you still interested?'

'I'm definitely still interested,' I say, and I mean it. Dylan aside, I don't think I have ever wanted anything more.

'Is it just adoption, or would you consider fostering?'

I shake my head. I could never throw all my love at a child only to have it taken away from me a week, a month or even years later. I've experienced too much loss to voluntarily offer myself up for more. 'Adoption appeals to me the most,' I reply firmly. 'So what do I need to do now?'

'Well, I have your contact details, so we'll email you later this week and we can start the process. There will be more forms to fill in, criminal record checks, references, interviews, psychological evaluations, home visits, courses to attend . . . It's a long journey and there are no guarantees. It can take months to go through all the processes and then it might be years before we match you with a child that is right for you.'

'I don't mind,' I reply. 'I have all the time in the world.'

As I leave and make my way to the bus stop, I'm buoyed by an enthusiasm I can't ever remember feeling before. I might just have found my calling. I have a feeling I'm going to be a mother after all.

CHAPTER 35

NINA

TWO AND A HALF YEARS EARLIER

A social worker by the name of Claire Mawdsley sits opposite me in my lounge. A frayed tan-coloured handbag crammed with folders lies by her feet and paperwork is open upon her lap.

At her request, I have already taken her on a tour of the house and garden. When she made a note of the shaky bannister, I felt compelled to point out that I'd booked a handyman to repair it. I haven't, but I'm going straight on Google to search for one the moment she leaves. She also noted the lack of guard in front of the open fire and the sharp corners of the wooden coffee table. I assured her they will be easy to childproof.

Nothing escaped her trained eye. 'That's not poison ivy, is it?' she asked, pointing to green leaves climbing up the shed at the bottom of the garden.

'Oh no,' I say, but in truth, it could be. I'll dig it out this afternoon, just to be sure. When I noticed her shadow looming over the flower bed, for a moment I wanted to apologise to Dylan and tell her that I wasn't trying to replace her. But I couldn't, because that's exactly what a part of me wants to do.

As Claire searches for the next form to fill in, I think of the horror stories I've read online from some prospective parents whose social workers have judged their houses unfit for a child. Some have been forced to move before being granted permission to adopt. While I don't plan to live here forever, I hope our home passes, as I can't afford to go it alone just yet.

I watch quietly as she starts writing, and I place her in her early forties. Deep horizontal lines are etched into her forehead and her hair is wiry and greying, leading me to assume she's seen a thing or two in her job that's prematurely aged her.

'If you continue with this process, there will likely be five visits from us in all,' she says. 'The rest of today will be made up of me asking questions about who you are, what your reasons behind wanting to adopt are, your strengths and weaknesses, etcetera.'

We discuss my relationship with my parents and I explain I've had no contact with my dad since he left us. She asks me how I feel about it and I tell her that I'm no longer concerned about why he did it or where he went, because he has missed out on more than I have. It's a lie, of course. Aside from that wilderness year after Dylan's birth and death, I don't think a day has passed when I haven't wondered how different my life might've been were he still a part of it. I miss him every bit as much now as I did then.

I really want Claire to like me, but I know that lying about Dad isn't going to be the only untruth I'll offer in this process.

'Can you tell me a little about your past relationships?' she asks.

'What would you like to know?'

In truth, there is very little to say. I got pregnant at fourteen by a man I loved who was almost a decade older than me; my botched body killed our baby months later and I never saw her dad again because he went to prison for murder. If I mention any of that, we won't be able to move in this room for red flags.

'Have you been in many long-term relationships?'

'I've had three.'

'How long did they last and why did they end?'

I think on my feet, as I was not expecting to be asked details. 'My first, Jon, was when I was a teenager and we were together until my early twenties,' I begin. 'We met at school, then after we finished our A-levels, we lived together for a while in a flat in town . . .'

I find my voice trailing off as I picture a basement flat in a townhouse opposite a large green open space. I see Jon and me inside it, going about our daily lives, me reading a book as music floats through the air when he plucks at his guitar strings. The image feels so authentic that I wonder if it's actually a long-forgotten memory. *It can't be*, I decide, and I return to Claire's question. I clear my throat. 'Sorry,' I say. 'I have a lot of happy recollections from that time. Anyway, Jon was a musician so he was away from home a lot, and we gradually drifted apart.'

'And the others?'

Instead of telling the truth, I create imaginary lives for two of my fantasy exes. 'My second long-term boyfriend was Sam. We met through friends and we were together for a couple of years.' I try tugging at her heartstrings. 'He really wanted a family and as I explained earlier, my medical condition means that it's something I couldn't give him. So in the end, we split up. And most recently there was Michael. Again, the family situation came between us and taking our relationship any further. It's hard to find a man who doesn't want children if he doesn't already have them from a previous relationship.'

'This isn't a nice question to ask,' Claire continues, 'but I wouldn't be doing my job if I didn't bring it up. Is there a part of you that hopes that by having a child, albeit one you've adopted, you might be a more attractive prospect to a potential partner? A sort of ready-made family? Or that it's because you want to do better than your own father and mother did?'

An image of Dad flashes into my mind; it's the second time I've thought about him today. Earlier, while searching for a jumper in the bottom of my wardrobe, I found a padded envelope of old birthday cards that Dad has sent me over the years. Each message is the same: it simply reads 'love, Dad'. His use of the word 'love' and the fact that he never forgot the date meant that no matter how far he has moved on, he still thinks about me. Even if it's only annually, it's something. Many times I've thought about trying to find him, perhaps hiring a private detective or applying to be on one of those television shows that reunite long-lost relatives. But as the years go on, the more I accept that too much time has passed.

I give thought to Claire's question before answering. 'That is absolutely not the case. I want to give a child a home because it's something that I can do. Even if I had a biological baby, I'd have still gone down this road eventually.'

Claire appears satisfied with my conviction. She asks more questions, but at no point do I mention Dylan as then she'd check the records and no records of her exist. My little girl was never officially registered or named. To all intents and purposes, she was only a part of Mum's and my world. But only I know how the loss of her shaped the rest of my life.

Mum has no idea about my adoption plans or that a social worker is sitting in her lounge while she is at work. I know I'll have to tell her soon, but I've enjoyed keeping this to myself. Initially me and my son or daughter will live here, but at the earliest opportunity we'll move out to a place of our own. I don't want to spend the rest of my life living under this roof. A change would do all three of us good.

'Okay,' Claire says in a manner that indicates this first assessment has come to an end. She takes a final sip of her tea, which must be cold by now, then picks up her bag with my completed paperwork. Her expression remains friendly, so I think I have passed this stage. I rise to my feet with her. 'I'll need you to email the names and addresses of six people, three of whom aren't family members, who can give a testimony as to why they believe you are a fit person to adopt.'

'Leave it with me,' I say. I have prepared for this and have already lined up three people from work who said they'd be happy to assist.

'We'll also need to speak to a couple of your ex-partners,' Claire adds casually.

This is news to me. 'Why?' I ask.

'It's normal practice.'

'But I don't even know where they live now.'

'It's okay, you can give me a few more details later and leave it to us to find them.' She tells me I will hear from her soon. 'As you and your mum share this house, we will also need to speak to her, of course. But don't worry,' she adds, 'you're doing great.'

Her reassurance should appease me. However, when I close the door behind her, I do start to worry. I start to worry *a lot*. The truth behind my relationship with Sam was that I knew he was married when I pursued him. But I'd fallen in love with the images of the three children he plastered over social media more than I did with him. I reasoned that if I could have him, I'd have a ready-made family too. Then when I told his wife about us, she forgave him and he dumped me. And Michael ended it when he caught me following him on a work's pub crawl. He wasn't answering his phone or replying to my texts and I assumed the worst: that he was with another woman. It was the straw that broke the camel's back, apparently, and he branded me 'too possessive'. It was only when he contacted the police a few months later that I stopped turning up at his work and flat unannounced.

So I'm going to have to find a way around Claire's request. And I also need to think how I am going to get Mum on board. Every parent wants to eventually become a grandparent. And I bet that once I convince her how certain I am that this is what I want to do, she will support me all the way.

CHAPTER 36

MAGGIE

TWO AND A HALF YEARS EARLIER

I read the letter once, then look at it again line by line, just to make sure my eyes aren't deceiving me. The council's logo at the top of the page suggests that it's genuine. There's a telephone number for two named members of staff. I lift the phone's receiver, withhold my number and call them one at a time. The first answers in person and I hang up; the other is a recorded message. Both women are real. This is not a prank.

I slump on to the sofa, allowing this information to sink in, and try to process it. The last thing I expected when I arrived home from work was to read a letter from Social Services informing me that Nina wants to adopt a child. It has come completely out of the blue.

Surely this can't be a spur-of-the-moment decision? She must have given it a great deal of thought before applying. So why hasn't she spoken to me about it? Perhaps she didn't want to say anything because she thought I'd try and talk her out of it. The letter says they require a reference from me and to discuss her suitability as a parent because the child would be living in a house we share. I will also undergo a criminal record check and they will poke around into my background, too. I close my eyes and shake my head. I don't like this one bit.

It's a long three hours before Nina arrives home from work, and another two before we sit down to eat and I bring up the letter. 'I'm not going to lie, it came as quite a surprise,' I add.

'I've been mulling it over for a number of weeks,' Nina replies.

'And you didn't think to mention it?'

'I would have, eventually.'

'The letter says that a social worker has already been here to assess you and our home. So when were you going to tell me?'

'I was going to wait until I found out if I'd made it through to the next stage.'

'Nina,' I say, more forcefully than I mean to. 'You make this sound like a bloody *X Factor* audition. This is a huge decision you've made and I had a right to hear it from you. Don't you think that adoption is going to affect me too?'

'I assumed you'd want a grandchild?'

'Of course I do, but that's not the point! This is a big decision for you to have made on behalf of both of us.'

'Well, if it happens, it's not like I'd be living here for much longer anyway.'

She is full of surprises. 'What do you mean?'

'I mean that I don't want to spend the rest of my life with you, Mum. I'm thirty-six and time is running away from me. If I don't do something about it then I'll end up . . . sorry to say this, but like you.'

'Me?' I say. 'What's wrong with me?'

'You're lonely.'

'I'm not lonely!'

170

'Only because you have me here. How many relationships have you had since Dad left?'

References to Alistair are like hearing nails being dragged down a blackboard, even after so long. 'You know the answer to that.'

'Exactly. None. Sometimes I think because you and I have each other, we're holding one another back from getting on with the lives we should be living.'

'And you think adoption will help you move on?'

'Yes, I do.'

I have lost my appetite. I nod slowly to mask an ascending fear. This idea of hers is wrong on so many different levels, yet I can't tell her why. I hear the lump in her throat when she explains how she hides from colleagues who bring their children to work because she is so envious of them. She tells me how she has never got over Dylan's death and the gaping hole she left in Nina's heart. She admits to creating an imaginary world in which her daughter still exists; sometimes she pictures walking her to school, reading to her and tucking her up in bed at night.

Her disclosures knock me for six and I want to hold her and never let her go. Neither of us mentions Dylan any more so I had no idea how much her child plays on her mind all these years later. I assumed the secret to Nina's survival has been her ability to compartmentalise and consign her baby to the past. But it turns out I've been too blind to recognise the strength of her maternal instinct. I was naive to assume a dead child means you're no longer a parent.

There are things I want to tell her, things that I keep from her. I too have imagined an entire life for my grandchild, wondering if they would have taken after Nina or if they had the faults of their father. We both lost so much that day.

Watching Nina choke back the tears, I want to cry along with her. But instead, I swallow my pain. The more she reveals of herself, the more of a compelling case she makes and I gradually understand that adopting is something she is desperate to do.

And that also makes me more determined. Determined that I will not allow this to happen. When she talks about further interviews and psychological evaluations, I know for sure that I can't let anyone inside her head. Because if I do, they might release something that I have spent the last twenty years trying to contain.

CHAPTER 37

MAGGIE

TWO AND A HALF YEARS EARLIER

The front door slams and I hear the picture frame rattle against the wall in the hallway.

'Why?' Nina growls as she storms into the kitchen. I brace myself; *she knows*.

'Is everything all right?' I ask, when we both know that it's not.

Her cheeks are flushed with anger. She hurls her bag on to the floor and some of its contents spill out. 'Tell me why you did it.'

'Why I did what?'

'Why you told Social Services that I wouldn't make a good parent.'

'That's not what I said.' I remove my hands from the washing-up bowl and wipe off the soap suds with a tea towel.

'My case worker Claire says that in your reference, you talked in detail about things I'd kept from her. She says she has no choice but to turn down my application.'

'She told you that *I* said things about you?'

'Well no, not you, but who else could it have been? Who else knows that much about me?'

'And what were you keeping from her? Aren't you supposed to be honest throughout the process?'

'Not about everything!' Nina says, raising her voice. 'Someone told her about the miscarriage, that my ex-boyfriend was a murderer and about my breakdown and they didn't think I was ready to take on the responsibility of a child. How dare you!'

'Darling, I didn't say you weren't ready, I said that you had very little experience with children, so much so that you avoid your friends' babies.'

'Why would you use something I've told you in confidence against me? Adoption was supposed to be my chance to catch up with a world that's moved on without me. But you've destroyed it all.'

'They'd have found out about Hunter eventually.'

'How? We were together a lifetime ago! There was absolutely no need to tell her about the miscarriage either, because only you and I knew about it.'

'I didn't tell them about Dylan,' I offer.

The name alone is enough to bring her to the brink of tears. She has no idea this is hurting me as much as it's hurting her. I feel so bloody awful for what I've done. I want to tell her that I have always had her best interests at heart even when it doesn't appear so, but I can't. The weight of the secrets I carry are almost too much to bear.

'This was my one chance at happiness, Mum. You are supposed to want what's best for me. So why have you taken it away?'

'I didn't want to, Nina, but I had to answer their questions honestly. I don't think you're prepared for what being a parent entails. What experience do you have?'

'I can learn.'

'And what about problem children? Kids who've come from terrible backgrounds, who have had some horrible, horrible things done to them? How would you cope with that?'

'Social Services organises training courses and workshops to help you prepare for whatever issues come your way.'

'Training courses are no substitute for the real thing. Raising a child is stressful . . .'

'I can cope with stress.'

'Can you though?' I fold my arms and hope that she will realise I'm being honest with her because she isn't being honest with herself. 'How would you cope if you're given a child who behaves like you did when you were a teenager? I was a single parent too when you went off the rails. I went through hell with you; two years of absolute hell. God knows there were times when I wanted to give in, but I didn't because I had the strength to see it through. Would you? Because I have seen what happens when you suffer extreme anxiety, when the stress of what the world throws at you becomes too much. You regress. You close the doors. You shut down. You cannot do that when you are a mother.'

Nina shakes her head as if she cannot believe I have brought this up. 'Are you really using that time in my life against me? I was fifteen years old, Mum. *Fifteen!* I was a girl – I'm thirty-six now. I'm a grown woman. I can deal with anything that comes my way.'

'You can't know how you'll react to such pressures when you've not had any for most of your life. You don't have a mortgage to worry about, a family to feed, a job that takes up all your time or a relationship to maintain. You don't have the first clue about pressure.'

'And that's just how you like it, isn't it? That's what this is all about, me remaining dependent on you. If I don't move on, then it means you don't have to either. And with me still living here, you'll never be on your own.'

Her bitterness takes me by surprise. But there will be time for me to replay this and criticise myself later. For now, I cannot afford to let this escalate.

'I'm sorry if you think I was trying to hurt you, darling, but I didn't say anything to the social worker that's inaccurate. I've been honest with her for the sake of you and any child that might be placed here.'

'Don't kid yourself. You did it because you want to keep me this way . . . this teenage woman with nothing and no one to her name. This pathetic shell who has no life because she's an extension of you. You did it because you are as lonely as I am. You are too bitter and too cruel to let me better myself. I will never forgive you for this.' She storms out of the room.

Alone, I cry, quietly, because she will never understand how much I have sacrificed for her. I can never explain why I've done what I've done.

I did the right thing, I say to myself. *I did the right thing. My daughter cannot be trusted.*

CHAPTER 38

NINA

Maggie and I are perched on the ottoman in her room eating from a plate containing triangular slices of Marmite on toast.

'I've not had this in years,' she says, savouring each mouthful. Her eyes are fixed on the house opposite Elsie's. 'Do you remember your Aunty Edith?'

'No. Whose side is she on?'

'Mine. She's my cousin. Anyway, her son Alan used to eat Marmite by the gallon. She took a few jars with her to California when he was working in that city with all the computers. Sylvanian Families or something.'

'Silicon Valley.' I chuckle.

'Yes, that's the one. But when customs officers singled her out to search her suitcase, all three jars had broken in transit, covering every single piece of clothing. She had a devil of a job trying to explain to them what it was and that she hadn't been caught short and used her suitcase as a commode.'

We laugh together, but don't look at one another. We have been sitting in the same position for three mornings in a row now. My handbag is already over my shoulder, my coat and trainers are on and the envelope is in my pocket. Then suddenly, we spot figures moving downstairs in the front room of the neighbours who are abusing their daughter.

'They're about ready to leave,' says Maggie. 'Are you ready?'

'Yes,' I reply, and pat my pocket to reassure myself the envelope is still there. 'I'll see you tonight.'

'Good luck,' Maggie says, and touches my arm. I don't recoil. I grab another slice of toast to eat on the go and hurry down the stairs, locking the landing door behind me. Then I leave the house and at the same time, my neighbour appears with both children. They are well presented in their red school V-neck jumpers, charcoal-coloured trousers and black shoes, and there is no visible bruising to either of their faces. I wonder what damage lies beneath.

This is the first time I've seen them walk to school – their father normally gives them a lift. The mum is too consumed by her mobile phone to hold their hands or notice me behind them. The kids are too close to the road for my liking, their heads down, not conversing with one another.

This common cause means Maggie and I have spent more time together over the last few days than we have in the last two years, debating how to help that little girl. It doesn't mean I've had a change of heart and am ready to give her life back to her. But I can't deny I have enjoyed her company. Finally, we agreed upon a plan that I'd approach the child directly with a letter we composed together.

'To the girl at Number 2,' it began. *'Please don't be scared, but I want to help you. I know what has been happening to you at home. I have watched your mummy hurting you and I want you to know that she shouldn't be doing it. Good mummies and daddies don't treat their*

children like you are being treated. And no matter what they might be telling you, it's not your fault. I want you to promise me that you are going to ask a grown-up for help. And I want you to do it as quickly as you can. At the bottom of this letter is a telephone number. Dial it and you can speak to a kind man or woman at a place called Childline who will help you. You don't have to give anyone your name if you don't want to, but you can tell them what has been happening to you. If you can't use a phone, then please tell someone you trust, like a teacher or a friend's mummy or daddy. They will help you and your brother. I know this isn't going to be easy for you because you love your parents, but you have to believe me when I tell you that the moment you start being brave, everything will get better. Yours, a friend.'

There hasn't been an opportunity to execute our plan and get the girl alone until now, when the family makes a detour and stops at a newsagent. Their mother makes her children wait outside and I half-expect her to tie them to a lamp post like she might a dog. They wait, reading postcard advertisements taped to the window. Through a gap, I spot their mum queuing at the counter. I'm going to walk into the girl, knock the bag off her shoulder and as I help to pick up its contents, I'll slip the letter inside.

I take one last look around to make sure nobody is watching me, and then I make my approach.

CHAPTER 39
MAGGIE

I lingered at the window for most of yesterday, only leaving it to urinate in the bucket or to stretch my legs. Even when night fell, I kept at my post, hoping and praying that the girl might have found and read the note Nina slipped into her schoolbag and sought help.

I waited for a police car to pull up outside the house to take her awful parents away, or at least an official visit from a Social Services team. But there was nothing. The only person to knock on their door was a parcel delivery man. As the night drew in, I knew it was too late for anything to happen, yet still I remained where I was sitting with the lamp in my hands, ready to flash the bulb to show her I was still there. But I only saw her briefly as she entered her bedroom, then her mother turned off the light. Assuming that she was safely tucked up in bed, I left my viewing platform and got changed myself.

Just as I was wondering why I'd yet to be updated by Nina, I spotted it, lying half inside my bedroom and half in the landing. A white envelope with no name on it upon the floor. I knew what it was before I opened it. Inside was the letter Nina and I had written for the girl. She hadn't given it to her. It explains why nothing has happened all day; no one has come to the girl's aid because she doesn't know that she has options. Despite what Nina had witnessed, she'd chosen not to believe me and not to help. And she didn't have the guts to admit it to my face, either.

While helping the girl escape an unsafe environment was my priority, a part of me hoped it might lead to my freedom, too. I imagined her telling whomever she confided in about seeing someone in the attic of the house across the road flashing a light. It's ridiculous, now I think about it. Regardless, I let out a long, defeated sigh.

Tonight, when Nina came to my room to bring me downstairs for dinner, it was like nothing had happened. I considered confronting her, asking why she doubted the abuse, but what would have been the point? Once Nina makes up her mind about something, she never changes it. So instead, we ate, she told me of her day voluntarily and we reminisced about when she was a child and recalled old memories because we are unable to make new ones.

Two other occurrences have also left me without answers. Earlier, while I was enjoying a warmer-than-usual bath, Nina installed a new television in my room. She hadn't mentioned she was planning to do it or offered an explanation as to why. I just entered the bedroom and there it was. Then, when I faced the opposite direction with my ankle raised, waiting for her to swap my long chain for the shorter one, she didn't. She just left the room with a 'See you on Friday.'

I was suspicious of the gesture, as I am with every random act of kindness. Both this and the new television can be taken away as quickly as they have been given. But while the chain remains, I can leave the confines of this room and use the bathroom whenever I want to. I have access to a toilet again instead of using the bucket in the corner of my bedroom.

I awake later in the night with the urge to spend a penny. And instead of using the bucket, I sit down on a cold toilet seat and cry my heart out as I urinate. It is such a small act, but enough to make me feel like a human being again.

CHAPTER 40

NINA

I wonder if, on a much smaller scale, this is how it feels to be a dictator, the head of a regime in which you always get your own way. Nobody challenges the decisions you make and those that do are swiftly taken down. It's how living with Maggie makes me feel; that I am the leader of this autocracy and the weight of responsibility for both our lives is firmly upon my shoulders. For most of my life, she was the one in charge. But dictators are almost always eventually toppled. So despite improvements in our relationship, I'll never rest on my laurels when I'm around her. I can't allow the balance of power to shift full circle.

With her back in her room, I take the opportunity to enjoy the mild weather and new garden furniture outside, hoping Elsie hasn't spotted me. I can't be bothered with her forked tongue and poorly disguised accusations tonight. I've brought my glass of wine with me and take a couple of mouthfuls before closing my eyes and enjoying the silence.

I think about the little girl across the road and hope I made the right choice in not slipping the letter into her bag. I was only a couple of footsteps away from knocking the bag off her shoulder when her mum suddenly appeared from the corner shop with two chocolate bars and brightly coloured comics in her hands. Her excitable kids hugged her to say thanks and the three of them continued to school holding hands. Because I'd only witnessed the aftermath of the alleged violence, I couldn't be 100 per cent sure that the smacks weren't the result of Maggie's overactive imagination. Perhaps being cooped up in the attic is beginning to play funny tricks on her mind. Because I'd stake money that the woman I saw with those two children yesterday was not someone who'd inflict violence. It's hard for me to put into words, but I could just tell theirs was a relationship based on love and quite unlike mine and Maggie's.

An alarm sounds on my phone, reminding me to do something. I reach into my pocket and remove a blisterpack of tablets. I pop one from its foil wrapping and swallow it with a swig of wine. I know that I'm not supposed to drink with my meds, but I'm sure it can't do that much harm. I hate taking tablets so I swallow it quickly. It was supposed to be a quick-fix solution, but two years later I'm scared at what might happen to me if I stop.

CHAPTER 41

NINA

TWO YEARS EARLIER

The new GP sitting opposite me scrolls through my medical notes on a computer. He's at least a decade younger than me and there's something white and pea-sized stuck to his hair just above his ear, as if he missed a spot when he was styling it this morning. I stop myself from leaning over and ruffling it until it dissolves.

It's the first time I have seen him or any doctor since changing surgeries from the one where Mum works. I assume she knows I'm no longer registered there; not that either of us have mentioned it. It's none of her business. In the aftermath of her sabotaging my adoption plans, I don't want her knowing anything about my life or poking through my records.

A rift has opened up between us, even larger than the one when Dad left. Every spare penny I earn I am saving to get the hell out of that house and far away from her. My failure to adopt has hurt me in ways I didn't think possible. For months, I have lived under a black cloud that I can't escape. Dr Kelly is my last resort.

Despite his youthful appearance, I'll give him his due – he has the sympathetic bedside manner of a GP with many more years' experience. He listens when I tell him of my endless despondency.

'And you've been feeling like this for how long?' he asks.

'A few months.'

'Has it ever manifested itself into suicidal feelings?'

'No.'

'Not at all?'

'No. I don't want to kill myself.'

'Have you had any desire to self-harm?'

'No.'

'Do you go out and socialise much?'

I want to lie and say yes, as it sounds better than admitting I spend most nights watching television with a parent I resent. 'No,' I answer truthfully.

We talk about some of the potential causes of what has left me feeling so flat. I touch on how I'm thirty-six years old and living a vastly unfulfilled life, but I stop short of telling him about Dylan's death or the failed adoption application.

He returns to his screen. 'I see you went through the menopause very early,' he says. 'Did you deal with the emotions attached to that diagnosis properly at the time?'

And as I give it thought, I realise I didn't. I accepted it for what it was, put my head down and got on with living without Jon or Dylan. 'Probably not, no,' I concede.

'Why would you like me to prescribe you antidepressants?'

'Because I'm running out of options,' I admit. 'I've tried so hard, but I can't bring myself out of this on my own.'

After the year I lost on high-strength antidepressants after Dylan's death, I prefer to shy away from most medicines – even cold or flu remedies. So these are a last resort. My feelings of inadequacy have left me considering whether Maggie was right when she said I couldn't handle stress. Perhaps I don't have the coping mechanisms ordinary people have to deal with the day-to-day acceptance of failure and disappointments. Maybe that's why I never tried to find Dad; it was the fear of taking a risk and being rejected by him a second time.

'Have you thought about group counselling as a strategy? The NHS waiting list is lengthy but it's shorter than for one-to-one and I'm happy to set the wheels in motion.'

'I'm quite a private person, so I'd rather deal with it myself.'

I can tell that he's still unsure, but eventually he wavers.

'I don't want a high dose,' I point out as he begins typing up his notes. 'I was prescribed them as a teenager and the side effects knocked me out for the best part of a year.'

'When was that?'

'In the mid-1990s. I don't want to go through that again.'

Dr Kelly shakes his head. 'They shouldn't have those side effects,' he says. 'It's normally drugs like lithium and valproate which do that. And they are only prescribed for conditions like bipolar. Are you absolutely sure they were antidepressants?'

'Yes. I was taking them for about ten months.'

'There's nothing in your records to confirm this.'

I frown. 'It was Dr King who prescribed them.'

'Nope, there's no mention of it at all. From what it says here, you didn't see a doctor for around three years over that period.'

I sit back in my chair, puzzled. Why has it been omitted from my records?

'I must have got my timings wrong,' I say eventually, before Dr Kelly prints out my prescription and hands it to me.

'I would still like you to consider counselling, though,' he adds as I rise to my feet. 'Sometimes it's good to open up what you've got locked up in there.' He taps his head. I thank him and leave, promising to give it consideration.

◆ ◆ ◆

Later that night, my medical notes play on my mind. My eyes gravitate towards Mum on the sofa chuckling at a daft TV sketch show, her legs tucked under her bum. I wonder if I should bring the subject up.

For years I've believed Dr King made a home visit and, seeing my distress, prescribed me strong medication. But I can't recall ever witnessing him here in the house or talking to me. Nor do I remember any follow-up house calls. I just accepted Mum's word for it. As for his warning that if I didn't take the tablets, the alternative was to commit me to a mental hospital – that also came from her. In fact, all of this came from her. Has she spent the last twenty-one years lying to me? *No*, I say to myself, *there is no reason for her to do that. She must have just misunderstood what tablets he was giving me.* I want to believe that, yet the niggle remains.

A Facebook alert gets my attention; a friend request from somebody I don't recognise. I click the decline button because misery doesn't always love company. It's not fair of me to expect anyone else to share the space under my dark cloud.

CHAPTER 42

NINA

TWO YEARS EARLIER

I'm sitting in one of the library meeting rooms flicking through my phone when a second Facebook friend request pops up. This time I don't ignore it. I push my packed lunch to one side and take a closer look.

It's the same profile picture as yesterday, and belongs to a Bobby Hopkinson. I check to see if we have any friends in common but we don't. Why is he so persistent? I assume he's mixing me up with someone else. However, curiosity gets the better of me so I click the 'Confirm' icon; I can always block him later if necessary.

I'm not a regular user of social media. I have taken charge of the library's Twitter feed and Facebook page but I do the bare minimum. In fact, I only took them on because nobody else could be bothered. As for my own Facebook account, I forget that I have it half the time. I set it up years ago on a whim and don't look at it from one month to the next. Occasionally I'll stalk some of the girls I went to school with in the hope that their lives have stalled like

mine, but more often than not, their profiles are littered with photos of husbands, children, nice homes and sunny holidays. Then
I block them in case they are tempted to make contact with me.

I take a peek at Bobby's profile. He lives in the neighbour-
ing county of Leicestershire, about forty-five minutes away from
here. I check to see if it might be a fake profile but if it is, whoever
is behind it has gone to a lot of effort because there are dozens
and dozens more photos of him in albums dating as far back as
2011. It doesn't mean that he hasn't stolen someone else's online
life, though. The truth is, it could be anyone behind that keyboard.
You read about people being catfished all the time. Perhaps he's
really a prisoner with access to a mobile phone, a serial killer or a
professional scammer on the other side of the world. My paranoia
is working twenty to the dozen today.

'Hi,' he says on Messenger.

Imaginative opener, I think.

I pause. Do I really want to engage in conversation with a
stranger? I have nothing better to do for the next fifteen minutes
until a client arrives, so I reply with a 'Hello.'

'How are you?' he asks.

'Good thanks, yourself?'

'Great. I'm Bobby, by the way.'

'I know. I've looked at your profile.'

'Ah, okay.'

I'm not really sure what he expects me to write next or why
I'm humouring him.

'Are you busy?' he continues.

'I'm on my lunch break.'

'What do you do?'

'I work in a library. You?'

'I'm a reporter.'

'Who for?'

'A newspaper in Leicester. I'm the news editor.'

'Is this a work-related message then?'

'No, not at all.' He adds a smiley face emoji and I glance at his photograph again. Perhaps he has no hidden agenda and is genuinely just being friendly. 'I should probably leave you in peace,' he says. 'I've got a deadline approaching.'

'Okay,' I reply.

'Chat again soon?'

'Sure.'

'Great.' He signs off with an 'x' which I don't read anything into. However, back upstairs in the business suite, I log on and find he has profiles on Twitter and LinkedIn. I also find his photo byline in the *Leicester Mercury* online newspaper.

Later that night and back at home, I hear Mum downstairs loading the dishwasher while I'm watching television in my room. My phone pings with another Facebook message from Bobby.

'Hey!' he writes.

'Hello there,' I respond. I'm not sure why, but I am pleased to hear from him. Surely the antidepressants can't be working after just a day? They are barely in my system.

'What are you up to?' he asks, and for a while we chat about television programmes. We both favour gritty dramas; we have the same taste in thriller films, actors and actresses. The conversation is effortless and flows and it's as if I'm talking to an old friend. I flick through his photographs again, but this time to see if he has a significant other. I know I'm older than him and it's mainly girls around his age who appear in his albums. His relationship status confirms he's single and there haven't been any pictures of just him with the opposite sex in more than a year.

Despite our similar tastes, he and I have our differences. While I'm no wallflower, I'm not the kind of woman who catches a man's eye, either. He is young and attractive while I blend into the background. He wears fashionable clothes that reflect his age, and I favour what still fits and that I've had in my wardrobe since Britney and Justin were still together.

Our Messenger conversation is interrupted by Mum's voice coming up the stairs. 'I'm making a hot chocolate before bed; do you want one?'

'No, thank you,' I reply. I shake my head. She is a reality check. I'm kidding myself if I think this Bobby is interested in someone who still lives with their mum. What do I have to offer? When our conversation inevitably runs its course and he figures out what a dullard I am, he'll stop responding to my messages and I'll feel like crap. So what's the point of this?

Taking charge, I turn off my phone for the night.

◆　◆　◆

By the time the clock radio alarm wakes me in the morning and I switch my phone back on, there are already two messages waiting for me. One is a continuation of Bobby's and my movie chat from last night. The second is a cheery 'Morning!' and a smiling sun emoji. 'Did you have an early night?' he asks.

'Yes,' I lie. 'Sorry, I was shattered.'

Against my better judgement, I indulge him and allow the conversation to continue in between me showering, dressing for work and making a packed lunch. Mum eyes me in the kitchen hunched over my phone. I don't offer to explain who I'm talking to and she doesn't ask. After the adoption disaster, she is no longer welcome to know anything about my private life.

'I'm enjoying talking to you,' he writes when I'm on the bus. I feel the same but I don't admit it. Instead, I turn on him.

'I'll be honest with you,' I reply. 'I'm wondering who you really are. I'm not a prolific social media user, we don't have any joint friends and our paths have never crossed. So how did you find me?'

'I was looking up some old friends in Northants and you were a "people you may know" suggestion.'

It's plausible, I suppose, but I get the feeling he is holding something back. 'So do you message a lot of random women out of the blue then?'

'No, no, not at all,' he protests. 'You just looked friendly.'

Looked friendly, I repeat to myself. Friendly, like an old reliable dog you want to approach and pet. 'And you got that from my photograph?' I ask. 'You saw it and thought, "Oh, this older woman *looks friendly*, why don't I say hello?"'

'Well . . . yes. I'm sorry, I've offended you, haven't I? That wasn't my intention.'

'I'm at work now so I'd best go.'

I log out of Facebook so that I can't be casually tempted to check whether he is messaging me again. But it doesn't stop me from thinking about him.

CHAPTER 43

NINA

TWO YEARS EARLIER

Ignoring Bobby didn't last for long. In fact, I managed just a day. Maybe it's the antidepressants working their magic after all, but talking to someone new adds a little brightness to the clouds above me. In such a very short space of time, I've come to look forward to hearing from him.

And for the best part of a week, the messages have bounced back and forth between us like a table tennis ball. Barely a waking hour has passed since we haven't chatted or made each other laugh. I like him, he's fun. Sometimes I resent our jobs for getting in the way of our conversations. But I am still none the wiser as to what he wants from me.

I'm no stranger to talking to men through dating apps and websites, but the conversations dry up quickly and I block them if they send me a photo of their penis. Bobby seems different. He appears genuinely interested in what I have to say. There's quite an age gap between us but we share a lot of similar likes and opinions.

We are also both quite independent souls, even if his Facebook photos indicate he's a lot more gregarious than I am. However, there are questions I want to ask him, but don't.

Where is this going? With two billion active Facebook users online each month – I've researched this – why did he decide to strike up a conversation with me? Each time I've broached the subject, his answer is vague. And that makes me suspicious.

Last night I found myself thinking about what it might be like to meet him in person. I played the whole scenario out in my head, from the French restaurant on the Wellingborough Road where I'd suggest we meet, to the bar where we'd enjoy a nightcap, before he'd drive me home and we'd smooch in the car like teenagers. I quickly realised how silly I sounded and shook my head until the fantasy evaporated. And that's the reason I've made a decision to put an end to this. While my head is fragile and I need chemicals to balance me out, I must protect myself. Mid-conversation, I have simply stopped talking to him.

Bobby must have sent a dozen messages yesterday before he realised I was no longer responding and stopped. But I awoke to find another two this morning asking if I was okay and claiming he was worried about me. I can't recall the last time a man said that, even Jon. I want to ignore this new message, hoping that he takes the hint and gives up. But whoever he is, whatever his game, I decide to end this like an adult. I shouldn't ghost him; I'm not a cruel person.

My fingers hover above the phone's keyboard before I eventually type, 'Hello.'

'You're there!' he replies, and I can feel his enthusiasm. 'This was going to be my last message. When you didn't reply to the others, I was worried that I was getting on your nerves.'

'Sorry,' I say. 'I've been busy.' I correct myself. 'No, that's not true. I haven't been busy. I've been avoiding you.'

'Why? Whatever I've done, I'm really sorry.' He adds a frowning face emoji.

'You're not telling me the whole truth, are you?'

He is usually quick to respond – his replies take seconds. This time, it's minutes. A nervous feeling emerges from the pit of my stomach and slowly crawls up the back of my throat. I both want – and don't want – the truth. The longer he takes, the more afraid I become.

My phone pings again. 'No, I haven't,' he replies. 'I'm sorry.'

I sigh. Even though I knew it in my heart, I'm still disappointed. He's probably sitting in an east European Internet cafe hoping I'm one of those desperate, gullible lonely women he can get money from in the promise of a future that'll never arrive. I used to think these women were stupid to fall for it, but after a week of speaking to Bobby, I understand why. When you think you're making a connection, even with a complete stranger, your imagination can lead you astray.

'So who are you then?' I ask.

'I am who I say I am,' he replies, which adds to the confusion.

'Why did you start messaging me?'

'Will you meet me so we can talk about this in person?'

'Meet you?' I frown as I type quickly. 'No! Why on earth would I want to meet you when you've just admitted you've lied to me?'

'I haven't lied to you, honestly, Nina. But I'd rather explain face to face than by message.'

I shake my head and offer him an ultimatum. 'You either tell me now what you're playing at or I block you and we never speak again. It's your choice.'

'Please don't do that.'

'Why shouldn't I?'

'Because you're my sister.'

CHAPTER 44
MAGGIE

From the day I gave birth to my daughter, I have strived to have a better relationship with her than my mother had with me.

Mum wasn't a nice woman; she admitted as much long after I'd ceased allowing her to have power over me. She was on her death-bed when the words came, unprovoked and in a rare unguarded moment. It wasn't so much a confession, more of a statement of fact. A fact that my sister Jennifer and I already knew all too well.

We were sitting in armchairs on either side of Mum's hospice bed. A catheter tube poked out from beneath Mum's sheets, leading to a quarter-full plastic bag of brown urine. She was so dehydrated that an IV had also been inserted into her arm. A plastic mouth mask lay close to her hand, within easy reach for when unaided breathing became too difficult. Her bed faced a floor-to-ceiling window, and she stared out across the garden and towards a copse on the grounds' perimeter.

'I didn't have the capacity for love,' she said without apology. 'I never cared for either of you as I should have.'

I was neither surprised nor disappointed to hear it. I don't recall her ever cooing over us, kissing us, picking us up when we fell over or proclaiming her love. She kept us fed and watered, our house was always clean, and she ensured we both got the best education we could. Perhaps that was her way of expressing love, or maybe it was born out of duty. Either way, that's where her responsibilities ended.

'Having a family was the done thing back then,' she continued. 'You were expected to marry a man you might not even love, start a family and not discuss how you really felt. You just got on with it without complaint. Before you were born, I thought perhaps that when I held you in my arms for the first time, something inside me might click, like a light switch turning on a bulb. But it didn't. And then I hoped it might happen with Jennifer, but again, I remained in darkness.'

'When I look back on our childhood, I feel like I should resent you, but I don't,' said Jennifer. 'I just kind of feel sorry for you for everything you've missed out on with us. It wasn't all bad, was it?'

'No, it wasn't,' Mum replied. 'I couldn't have asked for better children. Despite everything, you're both here with me now. But I wouldn't have blamed you if you'd left me here to die alone. I blamed both of you for me not living the life I thought I deserved. That was for me to shoulder, not you.'

'Did you ever love Dad?' I asked.

'Perhaps, in my own way. Although I don't think I ever really got to know him. He was too busy at the bookies or chasing other women for any of us to be involved in his life. You didn't get the parents you deserved.'

For the first time, Mum reached out her hands to grasp both of ours. Her skin was ice-cold and I felt her surface-level veins protruding like liquorice laces. 'Learn from my mistakes, girls. You're lucky to have Vincent, Jennifer – be happy together. And Maggie, I truly believe you will always have Alistair to support you. He won't let you down. He'll give you everything you didn't get from your dad and from me.'

Only a few short years later I learned that among Mum's many failures, she was a truly awful judge of character.

There were just four months between Mum's diagnosis and her death. If detected earlier and when she had first found the lump in her breast, she might have survived, with treatment. Instead, she said nothing and hoped it would disappear as quickly as it had arrived. To many people of her generation, a cancer diagnosis was akin to being unclean. So when she finally sought help, it was too late.

Now, like Mum, I have a lump in my breast, too.

Since discovering it this morning by chance, my emotions have been all over the place because I've witnessed what it can do. As well as Mum, this disease killed my grandmother and my aunt. So the odds aren't in my favour. Mum was a prisoner of her own denial, whereas I am a prisoner of my daughter.

I'm caught between a rock and a hard place. Things between Nina and me are on an even keel right now. I don't know how long it's going to last, but I'm not ready for it to end. If I tell her what I've found, it's going to complicate matters. But if it is the worst-case scenario, it might also be a blessing in disguise and just what I need to get out of here.

CHAPTER 45

NINA

Maggie is getting on my nerves tonight. It's not what she's done; it's what she is not doing – and that's talking. When she's this quiet, it puts me on edge. The last time it resulted in a blow to my face from her ankle cuff and a series of events I can't quite piece together. I hoped we had turned a corner since then. Maybe I'm wrong.

As she stares blankly at the dining room wall, I give her the once-over. ABBA's greatest hits album is spinning around the turntable, but even I am starting to get a little fed up of hearing the same tracklist every time we eat. I first started playing it to taunt her, because I knew how much it reminded her of Dad. And she hates to be reminded of him. Now I think it's just irritating us both.

I need to find out what's on her mind in case it's a threat to me. However, I'm momentarily sidetracked when I notice how quickly she seems to have aged lately. Her hair and eyebrows are now completely white and the cream-coloured jumper she wears hangs from her bony shoulders like a bedsheet, giving her a cartoon-ghost-like appearance. For a moment, I imagine I am Bruce Willis in *The Sixth Sense* having dinner with his wife. Perhaps only I can see

Maggie; maybe I've gone completely mad and she only lives in my imagination. It's not as if I have anyone to ask to verify her existence.

I'm tucking into my food while she pushes her beef stroganoff and mushrooms around the plate like she's placing chips on a roulette table. She scrapes her fork against the surface and it takes us both a little by surprise, because it's still peculiar to hear her using metal and not plastic. Neither of us comments on this luxury now being the norm.

I'm overcome by the necessity to fill the void. 'Is the food okay?' I ask pointedly.

'Yes, it's lovely,' she says and gives me a smile I recognise. It's the one she relies on when she's trying to reassure me that everything is okay when it's not. She used it on the day Dad left; it's part apologetic and part trying to minimise something seismic.

'I bought fresh meat instead of the frozen stuff and I made the sauce from scratch,' I continue. 'I found the recipe in one of Jamie Oliver's books.'

'It's delicious,' she says, and that bloody smile returns.

It's the last straw. I put my cutlery down on the plate and dab at the corners of my mouth with a paper napkin. 'Are you going to tell me what's wrong? Because clearly something is bothering you.'

'It's nothing,' she replies, but she can't, or won't, make eye contact with me.

'Mum,' I continue, then quickly correct myself. 'Maggie. Let's not play these games. I'm not an idiot.'

She takes a deep breath and pushes her half-full plate to one side. 'I've found a lump in my breast,' she says.

That, I was not expecting. I take my time searching her face for an indication that she is lying to me.

'A lump,' I repeat.

'Yes. In my left breast.'

'How large is it?'

'It's about the size of a pea.'

'When did you find it?'

'A few days ago.'

'Why haven't you said anything before?'

'I didn't want to worry you.'

A persistent doubt remains. There's only one way to know for certain. 'Show me,' I say.

She appears disappointed that I'm not taking her word for it, but I don't back down. Dictators never do. So she removes her top and remains bare-chested and seated and as vulnerable as I have ever seen her.

'Where?' I ask, moving closer to her and reaching out my hand. She guides me towards it and I can immediately feel it between my thumb and forefinger. It's definitely a lump.

'Shit,' I say without thinking.

'Can I get dressed, please?'

I nod my head and she does.

I return to my seat, neither of us passing further comment. I am aware that my thoughts are of the selfish kind because this discovery puts me in a very difficult position. The plan was to keep Maggie upstairs for either twenty-one years of her life or until she died, whichever came first. At her age, it was likely to be the latter, but now it looks as if it might happen much sooner than I anticipated. I'm not sure how to feel.

My conscience pipes up out of the blue: am I the cause of this? Has the stress of what I'm putting her under built up and up and culminated in her potentially developing cancer? I shake my head. *No*, I think, and I remind myself that it's a curse that's blighted her side of the family for three generations. It's why Maggie taught me from an early age to check myself regularly, and why I never miss an appointment for a mammogram as I'm at a higher risk than most women. Then I realise I'm assuming the worst. It could be anything from a boil to a cyst. A lump doesn't necessarily mean cancer.

When it comes down to it, I suppose the cause of this lump doesn't matter. The fact is that it exists, and if it's the worst-case scenario, then I'm not sure what to do. I think of Bobby and I want to call him and tell him what's happened, but I can't. Doing so would mean opening up a can of worms I'd never be able to put the lid back on because even if I told him the full story, I don't think he'd ever be able to understand why I've done what I've done. Besides, I can't make him complicit in my behaviour. Maggie has put him through enough already.

CHAPTER 46

NINA

TWO YEARS EARLIER

Flute and violin folk music floats from the ceiling speakers. I'm alone and rereading Bobby's Facebook messages for what might be the thousandth time. It's as if by looking at what he wrote again and again, I might be able to interpret his words in a different way.

Because you're my sister, he wrote. With the best will in the world, there's no way to misconstrue a statement like that.

I place my phone face down on the table and try to move my mind away from what might come by taking in my surroundings instead. The layout and the garden are familiar, but the generic decor is at odds with my hazy memory. Jon and I came here back in the day, but when it was a rock music venue and not the badly put together Irish-themed pub it is now. Nothing in here has come within fifty miles of the Emerald Isle, not even the Guinness it promotes so heavily.

I pick up my phone again and glance at the time. I'm still fifteen minutes early and already I'm a bag of nerves. I take a sip of my lemonade and regret not choosing something to take the edge off how I'm feeling. But I need to keep my wits about me.

Because you're my sister.

Those four words have sent my head spinning for the last twenty-four hours. I look at my phone again and remind myself of the response I sent him, telling him in no uncertain terms that I was an only child.

'I don't think you are,' Bobby replied.

'Listen, I don't know what kind of game you're playing, but I don't find it funny,' I responded.

'I have proof, can I show you . . . please, can we talk about this in person? I can come to you,' he begged. 'And then if you don't believe me, you never have to speak to me again.' He seemed so genuine in his belief that eventually, I agreed.

'Meet me tomorrow after work,' I replied, and sent him the address of a town-centre pub.

And that's where I am now. I've been over and over it to the point of exhaustion, trying to make some kind of sense of it. While I can't remember much after Dylan's death, Mum couldn't possibly have been pregnant, so he can only be Dad's son. Perhaps Bobby's mum was the real reason why Dad disappeared – he chose her over us. I've always assumed Mum was holding something back from me when she said he left because they hadn't been getting on. Now I think she was too ashamed to admit she had been replaced.

I've spent my entire adult life blaming her for me having no father. And I don't know how I'm going to begin to make it up to her if what Bobby is saying is true.

'Nina?' A voice startles me. Like me, Bobby is early. I stare at him as if he is the first human I have ever come into contact with. I'm relieved to see he looks the same as his Facebook photos. His smile is as nervous as mine as he holds his hand out. Our same-shaped eyes and lips and shared chin dimples are more evident in the flesh than they are in his online photographs. Everything that I want to say and that I've spent all day rehearsing vanishes from my head, because instinct tells me that I've just met my half-brother.

'Can I get you a drink?' he asks, and I politely decline. He leaves a black leather satchel at the table and my eyes burrow through him as he waits at the bar. Suddenly, I'm ashamed of myself for the inappropriate thoughts I had about him before he made his announcement.

He returns to the table with a glass and bottle of lemonade and takes a seat opposite me.

'Did you find the pub okay?' I ask, unsure of why this is my first question when there's so much else to discuss.

'Yeah, I just followed my sat nav.'

'Where did you park?'

'In the Grosvenor Centre car park.'

'I hope you made a note of the floor you're on. Otherwise it's a nightmare trying to find your car afterwards.'

He shows me his phone. He's taken a photograph of the wall showing the painted lettering 4B. I'd have done the same.

I honestly don't know what to say next, but I don't need to worry because he speaks instead. 'It's like going on a blind date, isn't it?' Then his face reddens. 'Not that I've ever been on a blind date with my sister,' he adds.

Nobody has ever called me that before. A part of me likes the way it sounds.

'Why do you think we're related?' I ask.

'Mum and Dad have always been honest with me from as far back as I can remember,' he says. 'So I've always known that I was adopted.'

'Adopted?' I repeat.

'Yes. You sound surprised.'

206

So both of our mums were abandoned by the same man. If our blood wasn't enough to bond us, then this shared rejection by our father is. I'm overtaken by an urge to throw my arms around Bobby, but I hold back. I want to ask him why he has sought me out ahead of his biological parents. Unless he has already found them and they've denied him? But I'm sure we'll get to that.

He goes on to tell me more about his life. His family moved to Leicester when he was an infant; he has two older brothers and a sister who weren't adopted; he was an average student but excelled in English. He explains how he always wanted to be a journalist, how he's saving up enough money to travel the world.

He asks me about my life and I offer him selected highlights, which are honestly few and far between. He seems as interested in my every word as I am in his. He has already accomplished so much more than I have. I wonder if it's normal to be proud of a person you have only just met.

Flashbacks of Dad slide in and out of my head as he chats. For the first time, I now have a snippet of a life Dad had away from mine. I wonder how many more of us are out there; how many more half-brothers or half-sisters has he created and abandoned? We could walk past one another in the street and not have the faintest clue of the blood we share. I want to know what Bobby has learned about him.

'I've thought about Dad a lot over the years,' I begin. 'In spite of myself, I still miss him. Have you ever tried to find him? Do you know if he's still alive?'

He looks at me, puzzled. 'Dad?' he asks.

'Yes,' I reply. 'He must have had you around the same time as he left my mum and me.'

'I have no idea who my father is,' he replies, and now it's my turn to be puzzled.

'Then how are we related?'

'We share the same mum.'

I push back in my seat. 'Mum?' I repeat. 'I think there's been some mistake. You and I share the same dad, not mum.'

'Not according to my birth certificate.'

'That's impossible.'

'Please, take a look.' He reaches inside his satchel and withdraws a brown padded envelope stuffed with papers. He rummages around until he finds the one he is looking for. It's a birth certificate, issued in Northampton. It says 'unknown' under his father's name, but his mother is listed as Margaret Simmonds. It's also my mum's date of birth, but her occupation has been left empty. 'It can't be her,' I say.

Bobby nods his head. 'I looked her up on the electoral register and found her here in Northampton, and discovered she also had a daughter still living with her. I did a bit of research through Facebook and found you, as I didn't know if I should approach Margaret or not. I'm sorry, this must be coming as a shock.'

'Bobby,' I say firmly. 'I'd have remembered if my mum had been pregnant and had another baby. That's not something you can hide.'

Then I think back to how I had hidden it from my mum up until the day I went into early labour. Could she really have disguised something like this from me? After all, it must have been around the time my world collapsed in on itself. Then I think again about what the doctor said last week about the antidepressants I thought I was taking at the time. Surely she couldn't have been drugging me to hide that *she* was pregnant? No, that's ridiculous.

But when I look again at the birth certificate, a cavern opens up inside me. Bobby's date of birth matches the one I'll never forget. Then I realise I haven't looked at the name he was given on the certificate. When I read it, my stomach drops like I've been hurled from the top of a skyscraper – Dylan Simmonds.

'Dylan?' I gasp.

'Yes,' he replies. 'Bobby is a nickname I've had since I was a kid because of my Christian name. You know, as in Bob Dylan.'

We have both got this so very, very wrong. Bobby isn't my half-brother. Bobby is Dylan. And Dylan is my son, not the lost daughter I have pined for all these years.

CHAPTER 47

NINA

TWO YEARS EARLIER

My brain doesn't know what to do with itself. It has never been more confused, angry or elated, all at once. Unless this is an elaborate and cruel scam and Bobby's birth certificate is a forgery, the daughter I have mourned for twenty-two years never existed. *She* was in fact born a *he*, and *he* is still very much alive. The baby my mum told me was stillborn was no such thing. How do I begin to make sense of this?

I arrive home and close the front door as quietly as I can. I need to get my thoughts in some kind of order before I confront Mum. But I've been heard.

'Is that you, Nina?' she says from inside the kitchen.

'Yes,' I reply, my jaw tensed.

'You're late.'

'One of the deliveries was delayed,' I lie.

I hear the clinking of dishes and the running of water. 'There's some hotpot left if you're hungry, it's still in the slow cooker,' she says. 'Oh, and there's an apple crumble in the fridge too. The sell-by date was yesterday but it should still be good.'

Her tone is light and almost melodic, as if nothing out of the ordinary has happened. Like everything is perfectly normal. And in her world, it is. But mine has been turned upside down and had its insides ripped out. Things have been done to me that I have no idea about, and it makes me so frustrated and isolated that I want to hurt myself just to relieve the pain.

Her voice alone makes me want to scream and slap her across the face. I need to hold back. I need cold, hard facts before I decide what to do next. I need to go back to the start.

She comes into view, wiping her soapy hands on her apron. I'm looking at her with fresh eyes. 'Whatever's the matter?' she asks.

'Why?'

'You're as white as a ghost. Are you coming down with something?'

'I have the start of a migraine coming on.'

'Oh, sweetheart,' she says. 'You've not had one of those for years. What's brought that on?'

'Probably the strip lights in the library basement. I've been down there a lot today.'

'Have you taken anything for it? I've got some aspirin somewhere . . .' She turns her back to me and moves towards the cupboard where she keeps all her medicines. Inside is a shelf crammed with packets and bottles. She is her own pharmacy.

I need to keep a lid on the anger I'm feeling towards her right now. It wouldn't take much for me to grab the first movable object I see, like the kettle, and hit her across the back of the head with it.

'Yes, I have taken tablets,' I reply. 'I might lie down for a bit.' I don't wait for her to reply as I hurry up the stairs, scared as to what I might do if I am alone with her any longer.

Once behind my closed bedroom door, I finally unclench my fists. *Poor Bobby*, I think. *How confused he must be right now.* Earlier tonight, and after realising that I might be sitting next to my son and not my half-brother, I panicked, made my excuses and left without explanation. It was too much to take in all at once. I promised him it wasn't anything he'd said or done and that I'd be in touch soon, but I had to go. I didn't even give him a chance to reply before I hurried out of the pub. I will explain everything to him as soon as I figure it out myself.

When I came out of the fog after Dylan's death, almost everything from my previous life had vanished from the house. 'We need to start you again,' Mum had informed me. 'So I've taken away things that might upset you.' By 'things' she meant photographs, clothes and music. She had casually tossed away my whole life. But I was still too fragile to argue with her. She was doing what was best for me, or so I thought.

However, there was something she missed; something I found by accident many years later. It was a flyer for a Hunters gig that I promised Jon I'd go to. Among the blurriness I remember that clearly, because it was the afternoon I went into labour. And despite the fear and the pain, I kept thinking how disappointed Jon would be not to see me there. The flyer was kept pressed between the pages of *Wuthering Heights*, my favourite novel as a teenager. Now I open the pages and find it still there, a sheet with a fold along the centre and a photograph of the band on it. I pause to take in Jon's image. The likeness between father and son is subtle, but it's definitely there.

I thought Mum was putting my feelings first by hurrying my child away before I even had the chance to hold her. But now I know why. She didn't want me to hear my baby's first breaths or cries. She was already planning to give her grandchild away. There are so many questions I need answers to, all rattling around in my head at once. I know she's unlikely to give them to me, so I need to find them elsewhere.

◆ ◆ ◆

It being a public record, ordering a copy of Bobby's birth certificate was a simple online process and it arrived within two days. It proved the copy he had shown me was genuine. His name was Dylan Simmonds, he'd been born the day I gave birth and Maggie was listed as his mother. Twenty-two years ago she wouldn't have been able to predict the scope of the Internet or how social media could shrink the world.

'There's an envelope for you on the dining-room table,' Mum says.

'Thanks,' I reply and pick it up for closer inspection. It's white, about half an inch thick and, as I requested, hasn't got a surgery stamp on it. It's only taken five days to order a printout of my medical records. She hovers, as if expecting me to tell her what's inside. I don't.

I've said nothing of what I've learned so far. But every moment in her company is spent going through the motions, and it's pushing me closer and closer to breaking point. I'm on the edge and it won't take much for me to step over it. And from then on, there will be no coming back for either of us. I am sure of it.

I close my bedroom door and tear open the envelope. My heart pounds through my chest as I read each page, my entire life documented from my birth to my recent request for antidepressants. Everything is listed, from measles to mumps and pneumonia. Everything except the reason why I have requested these files in the first place.

Dr Kelly was right – it says here that between the ages of fourteen and sixteen, I did not see a doctor. The home visits Mum told

213

me Dr King had made? There is no record of them. His prescription for antidepressants? No mention. My breakdown? Not a word. It's as if I have just fictionalised an entire chapter of my life. I even double-check the page numbers to make sure some haven't been left on the surgery printer. Was Dr King doing Mum a favour and treating me off the books? If so, for what purpose? I can't confront him and ask him the question because he died years ago. Only Mum knows the truth.

Another of the many things I don't understand is why Dylan was born healthy, when I'm a carrier of estroprosencephaly. I search back a few pages to read up about my diagnosis but I can't see it charted anywhere. I return to the very start as I'm sure that Mum said I was tested for it when I was seven. But there is definitely no mention of it. Surely the specialists or my parents would have informed my GP? Something this important must have been documented.

I pick up my phone and for the first time, I google estroprosencephaly. Having the condition isn't something I've given much thought to for years. The last time I researched it was in a library medical journal when I was pregnant with Dylan and wanted to know more about what to expect. Only when I saw the photographs of disfigured babies, I couldn't read on. Now I wish I'd continued. Because if I had, I'd have known much sooner that Mum was a liar. It says here that estroprosencephaly is not passed on from father to daughter, nor is it genetic. There is no rhyme or reason as to why it occurs. It is a condition that cannot be tested for. In fact it's so rare that only five babies are struck by it per year in the world. The chances of me having it are less than one in a billion.

I think of the place in the garden where Mum told me she buried Dylan, and all the comfort that visiting this spot has given me over the years. Only each tear I shed there for my child was a wasted one. I wasn't crying over a grave, I was crying over a flower bed. All that time, Dylan was alive and living forty miles away from me with somebody else's family.

Perhaps I should take time to digest this, I think. But I can't. Too much of my life has been wasted already for me to delay this any longer. My bedside alarm clock tells me it's only 7.40 p.m.; I have a couple of hours to wait before I can act. Mum is usually in bed by 9.30 p.m. and the high-strength sleeping tablets she's dependent on take a half an hour before she is out for the count. Then I will get to work.

Suddenly, it hits me. I have what I always wanted. A child. *I am a mother.* I smile for the first time in days, then force myself to rein it in. There will be plenty of time to enjoy this later.

CHAPTER 48

NINA

TWO YEARS EARLIER

When I hear Mum's heavy breathing from the other side of her bedroom door, my search for the truth about who I really am and what happened to me begins. You can't just give a baby away without there being a lengthy paper trail. I need cold, hard, legal, irrefutable proof of what she has done. If she's been sensible, she'll have destroyed everything. But knowing what a hoarder she can be, I'm hanging on to the hope that she might have forgotten something.

Using my phone as a torch, I make my way into her room, tiptoeing across the carpet. I feel my way around inside her chest of drawers and wardrobe, though I know it's unlikely to be that easy. As expected, I find nothing incriminating in there or in the two empty bedrooms, dining-room sideboard or writing bureau in the lounge. When I finish in the kitchen empty-handed, all hope rests on the basement.

I turn on the light switch and make my way down the concrete steps. I can't recall the last time I had a reason to come down here.

It's a sizeable space and runs the entire length of the ground floor of the house. One of the first things Dad did when we moved here was to get a damp course fitted, electrics installed and the walls plastered. It was going to be 'his space', only he never got around to installing the snooker table he always wanted. Now it's just a dumping ground for our family history and is crammed with clutter. I don't know where to begin.

It's been swallowed up by decades of objects and old tables and chairs that Mum hasn't thrown away. There are abandoned sets of broken garden furniture, two of my old bikes, shelves of half-empty paint cans and a broken tumble drier. Yet there is something strangely comforting about being among so much that reminds me of my childhood. Down here I feel impervious to what upstairs has to throw at me.

I set to work, sifting through dozens of cardboard boxes. They are all unlabelled, so only when I peel off the brown tape and open the flaps do I discover what's inside. Some are files containing paperwork, but they're only old bank statements and bills. Others contain Mum's out-of-fashion clothes, my and her school reports, and old rolls of partially used wallpaper.

A box of my school exercise books sidetracks me, and I remove one at random and flick through it. I stop at an English assignment where my eight-year-old self is asked to write an essay on where I hope I will be at the age of thirty. I smile at my naive ambitions. Back then, all I wanted was to marry George Michael, live together in a house by the seaside and look after sick ponies.

My search risks becoming a trip down memory lane as I stumble across boxes of my old toys too. Barbie and Ken dolls, Sylvanian Families, Beanie Babies and board games all bring back long-lost memories. There's a three-storey white doll's house that I used to spend hours playing with. I remove from its kitchen one of the three wooden figures that make up the perfect family; he's dressed in a small blue suit, carries a briefcase in his hand and I've drawn a red smile on his face in felt-tip pen. I realise I've been painting on my own smile for most of my adult life.

I wonder why Mum has never thrown any of this away. Perhaps it's her way of holding on to a past she longs to return to, when she was happily married and mother to a little girl who hadn't lost her innocence.

It brings a lump to my throat when I stumble across a memory box my dad made for me. Inside are posters and song lyrics from *Smash Hits*, postcards, birthday cards and other odds and ends. I choose meaningful objects from the other boxes in front of me and add them to the box. I long to remain here in a thirteen-year-old's world and never leave, but I have a mission.

I'm unaware of the time until I glance at my watch – it's past 1.30 a.m. and I've already been down here for hours. Yet I'm no closer to uncovering the depth of Mum's lies. Another hour, and yet more boxes pass until there is nothing left to search. I sit on an old wooden stool with my head in my hands, defeated and frustrated by failure. The only place I haven't looked is outside in the garden shed. But I'm sure I'd have spotted paperwork in there over the years.

I rise to my feet and let out the longest of yawns. I'm shattered, but I don't think I'll be able to sleep tonight with so many questions left unanswered. As I return to the staircase, I catch sight of a dustsheet draped over objects in a shaded gap under the stairs. Curious, I pull it aside; underneath are six upright suitcases and Dad's golf bag. The latter gives me goosebumps. I read the cardboard labels tied with string to the luggage handles. I can just about make out Dad's writing in the faded ink: his and Mum's names and address. They also contain flight luggage tags from Spain, France and Germany, all places I've never been to but which they must have visited before I was born. Sometimes I forget they had a life before me. All have small padlocks attached, and it doesn't take much force to snap them open with the heel of my shoe. I lay the first suitcase on the floor, unbuckle the sides and lift the lid.

Inside are scores of empty white-and-red medication boxes. They all appear to be for the same tablets. Each one has a typed name and address label on it; the same four strangers' names and addresses are repeated over and over again. It takes time, but I examine each of them; the earliest dates back to July 1995 and the most recent is for May 1996. The last few packets are still sealed. The labels reveal they've been provided by seven different chemists located in different parts of town.

I pull my phone from my pocket and google the drug's name, Moxydogrel. It's a medication that has been withdrawn from use. I read a Wikipedia entry:

> *Moxydogrel was a sedative licenced in 1993 and available by prescription only until 1996. Developed primarily for long-term usage by adults with behavioural issues and/or crippling anxiety, its purpose was to keep patients sedated and in a more manageable, pacified and less aggressive state. If used on an ongoing basis, it could lead to long periods of dormancy, memory loss and compliance.*

I let out a breath I'm unaware I am holding and look at the box from all angles. 'She was using it on me,' I say out loud in disbelief. Mum must have been stealing prescription pads from work, making them out in different people's names and rotating her way between chemists to have them filled. It explains why antidepressants weren't in my medical records – I hadn't been prescribed them. This Moxydogrel is the reason why so much of the period after Dylan's birth is hazy. She was drugging me.

I return to my phone and carry on reading the web page, when the words 'side effects' catch my attention.

Moxydogrel was withdrawn from the worldwide market in November 1996 when it was discovered that long-term usage can bring about early menopause, and infertility in both sexes. It is unknown how many victims of the drug there have been, although a number of out-of-court cases have been settled.

'Infertility. Early menopause.'

I repeat those words over and over again, just to be sure that the lateness of the hour and the stress of the last few days aren't combining to mess with my thinking. I don't want to believe it, so I park it to process later.

I'm about to close the suitcase when I notice one box is different to the others. It's called Clozterpan. Again, I rely on websites to explain that it's a medication used to induce the termination of a foetus. *'It will help the user to miscarry at home.'* Mum must have given it to me the first time I fell pregnant. Nature didn't make me lose the baby; she did.

I have no frame of reference to know what to do next, so I sit on the floor, dumbstruck. Not only did Mum kill my first baby, but she gave my second away, then made me infertile. I have no control over the tears streaming down my face.

Now the dark cloud above me swallows me whole. I don't want to be down here any more. I don't like the truth because it hurts too much. I'm ready to crawl on my hands and knees up two flights of stairs, lock myself in my bedroom and never come out again.

Yet I find strength from somewhere to continue. I break open the padlock to another suitcase, and inside are adult clothes and brown envelopes containing paperwork. This is what I have been searching for – files and documentation relating to Dylan. There's also another copy of his birth certificate.

I read the summary page of a social worker's reports on Dylan and Mum.

> *Following several meetings at her home, Margaret has made it clear that her son was unplanned and unwanted. She has steadfastly refused the opportunity to be reunited with him and explained that she is married but that the child was born as the result of an extramarital affair. Her husband worked away and she did not want him to know about the baby. Despite our best efforts, she has remained determined not to see the child and would not reconsider keeping him.*

By the date of the reports, these meetings and discussions were all taking place just metres away from me while I was drugged and unconscious upstairs.

There are two suitcases left and I don't want to open them. It comes as a relief to discover they're filled with more old clothes. Musty-smelling shirts, jeans, T-shirts, underwear, socks, coats and shoes are crammed inside, balled up as if they've been put there in a hurry. I rummage through them and find more than a dozen white envelopes in my handwriting. They are stamped and addressed to my dad but there are no postmarks. Every letter I wrote and that Mum told me she posted to him never made it further than the basement.

I'm about to close the fifth and final case when it dawns on me that they only contain men's clothing. And then a coat catches my eye. It's a denim jean jacket that Dad often wore. I remember the patch on the elbow where he caught it on a barbed-wire fence and Mum repaired it with a needle and thread. Now I can picture him wearing some of the other items, like his Adidas trainers and work ties. Finally, in a coat pocket, I find his passport and his wallet. Inside it is £65 in notes that are no longer legal tender, his expired credit cards and driver's licence. It doesn't make sense. Why would he have left all of this behind when he disappeared? Even his golf clubs? You don't leave one life for the next without taking something with you.

Then it hits me.

Unless Dad never left us.

CHAPTER 49

NINA

TWO YEARS EARLIER

Cold shivers race across the surface of my skin and I place my hands flat on the floor to stop myself from toppling over. I take deep breaths but my vision is beginning to blur and the colours around me are changing into shades of black and red. I tighten my fists and concentrate hard so as not to black out.

Eventually, I rise to my feet and, still shaking, I use the handrail to pull myself up the stairs until I reach the kitchen. The digital clock on the oven reads 3.39 a.m. and it will be light outside before I know it. I continue using my phone's torch as I unlock the back door and step outside. It's silent out here and there's only the barest sliver of a moon to help illuminate the path that will lead me to the flower bed at the end of the garden.

Snail shells crunch underfoot until I reach my sanctuary; the place I've come to for more than two decades to mourn Dylan's loss. Since discovering that my child didn't die, I've assumed this flower bed was empty. Now, I'm praying that it is.

I grab a spade from the shed, lay the phone on the ground and set to work, digging. Adrenaline charges through me as I shovel spade after spade of flowers and dirt on to the lawn. Each time the tool hits something that isn't loose earth, I take a closer look and am relieved when it's not bone. Sweat pours down my face and unused muscles in my arms burn as I dig further and further down, wider and wider, until eventually, I'm knee-deep inside the hole.

And then it happens. My spade makes a dull thud and goes no further; I know that it's not soil beneath me any more. I shine the torch into the hole. I've reached a brown fibre which, when I rub it between my fingers, I realise is the stuffing from a duvet. Much of it is rotting away and leaving brown feathers, like the wings of a fallen angel.

I put a muddied hand over my mouth, leaving a film of grit on my lips. I need to see for myself what lies inside the material and I'm desperate for it not to be what I think it is; not something else my mother has taken away from me. I crouch and brace myself, then tear the tape that binds the remains of the duvet together and open it. The torch reveals flashes of a faded pale colour and something familiar. I pick it up and brush the dirt away; it's Dad's house keys. They're attached to a key ring with my school photograph inside it that I gave him for Father's Day. I hold them in my hands for a moment, then slip them into my pocket.

I know what I'm going to find next, yet I cannot prepare myself. I push away soil and stones with my hands until I can make out what I am seeing. It's the ribcage of an adult. I am standing over my missing father's body.

CHAPTER 50

NINA

I peer into her room and find Maggie lying on her side on the bed, gazing in the direction of the television, but I don't think she's actually watching it. She is somewhere else instead.

I can guess what's occupying her thoughts because it's been the only thing on my mind too. For now, I've stopped thinking of her only as the enemy, and instead as my vulnerable, elderly mother. This clouded judgement doesn't sit comfortably with me.

I startle her when I say hello, then she frowns. 'I wasn't expecting you,' she says. 'We only had dinner last night.'

'I know,' I reply. 'But look.' I lift up a supermarket bag I'm carrying and she stares at it, unsure how I'm expecting her to react. 'Move over,' I say, and she hitches herself up the bed. I pour the contents across the duvet; there are at least a dozen packets and boxes. She slips on her recently repaired reading glasses and picks them up one by one, reading each label.

'I've been looking online for alternative treatments and therapies for breast cancer,' I explain. 'I had no idea there were so many different options.' I start reading aloud. 'Camomile, omega-3 fatty acids, probiotics, St John's wort, ginger . . . lots of websites suggest similar things, so there must be something in it.'

'We haven't had a diagnosis yet,' she says.

I ignore her. 'A study by a university in Colorado suggests echinacea, garlic, turmeric and flaxseed can help, so I'm going to start cooking with these ingredients more. And I've bought you a flask which I'll fill with hot water so that you can drink green tea. It's full of antioxidants.'

Maggie lacks my enthusiasm; I see scepticism in her eyes. 'Nina,' she says hesitantly, but I cut her off. I know what she's going to say; working in that surgery for half her life has brainwashed her into believing that man-made medicines are the answer to everything. They're not. She has no knowledge of the huge leaps forward that've been made in naturopathy. I must convince her to keep an open mind.

'You're going to say that you don't believe in this kind of thing. But you have nothing to lose by giving them a try, have you?'

'No. But—'

'I photocopied some recipes from a book I found at work called *Cooking for Cancer*. It has tons of suggestions. And in my lunch break I did an online shop and ordered us lots of fresh organic stuff from Waitrose that'll be delivered tomorrow night. Also vitamin D is supposed to be good, so perhaps at the weekend, and if it's sunny, we could go outside into the back garden for a bit?' Her eyes widen ever so slightly at the offer and I reel myself back in. It was a spontaneous suggestion. I've been getting carried away. I haven't thought this through properly, especially with Elsie next door. I guess there's a chance I can get Maggie to the end of the garden where it's private without her being spotted. 'I've been reading up on the statistics of breast lumps,' I add. 'Eighty per cent are non-malignant. So chances are yours is just a cyst or fatty tissue.'

'Nina,' she repeats, but this time more assertively, like she does when I'm not listening. It works and I stop talking. 'You know our family history,' she says. 'You know this type of cancer can be genetic. They call it "inherited altered genes". I'm around the same age as when my mum and grandmother died of exactly the same thing, so I know the odds of this lump being malignant are much higher than most women's. And I know how high the survival rates are when it's caught early. If it's cancer, it isn't something that's going to vanish with a few healthy meals and some vitamins. But before we do anything else, we need a professional diagnosis.'

'Homeopathic medicine has been used for thousands of years,' I counter. 'Native Americans have always used fungis, herbs, lichen etcetera to treat themselves.'

She reaches out to touch my arm, but I pull away from her before she connects. I don't understand why she's not keeping an open mind and it's annoying me.

Maggie must see she's upsetting me because she takes another look at what I've bought her. 'Thank you,' she says. 'I'm grateful, I really am.' A small part of me wants to pull her into my chest so that we can cry together. I dismiss it. There's too much water under the bridge for that to happen. Instead, I stand firm, rise to my feet and move all the boxes back into my bag.

'I'll call you when dinner is ready,' I say. And from the corner of my eye, she nods.

I leave her door open behind me and make my way downstairs, reminding myself once again that she is locked up there for a reason. I can't let this health scare ride roughshod over everything she's done to me. However, I am not ready for another person in my life to leave me.

CHAPTER 51
MAGGIE

I don't think I ever really appreciated how much I missed having a bath until the luxury was taken away from me. Until recently, I was only allowed to fill it with lukewarm water and bathe twice a week. But with Nina allowing me to keep my longer chain attached, not only do I get to use the toilet instead of a bucket, I also have the use of my beloved bath again whenever I like.

I've started taking baths during the day after Nina leaves for work, filling them up with as much hot water as is left following her shower downstairs. As a precautionary measure, I normally wait until I've seen her disappearing up the road before I start to run one. Not that she has forbidden me; in fact, she hasn't said a word about it. I just don't want it to be used against me in the future.

As I kneel naked by the bathtub waiting for it to fill, I turn to look at the day's worth of food and alternative medicines she has left in Tupperware boxes outside my bedroom door. I can't say I'm not disappointed. A handful of almonds and some green teabags aren't going to rid me of my lump. But a doctor might.

I sink into the bath, my leg raised and resting on the side so that I don't wet my chain. Nina has replaced the orange-scented bath foam with one that smells of lavender. It's much more pleasant. I lie back, placing a folded towel for a pillow behind my head, and locate the lump in my breast again. Perhaps I'm hoping for a miracle and that it might have miraculously vanished overnight. It hasn't, of course.

I honestly don't know how I am supposed to react to Nina's remedies. I believe there's certainly a place for complementary medicine, but it is alongside, not instead of, modern medicine. I am someone who has spent more than three decades working at a doctors' surgery and witnessing how medicines can prolong lives and fight cancer. Nina is clutching at straws. And I don't know what I can do to make her understand that.

I can still taste the garlic in last night's chicken Kiev in the back of my throat. It was so overpowering and I wonder if, going forward, that's how every meal is going to be – crammed or coated with some 'miracle' cure. Throughout dinner, each time she brought up something she had read online that might help, I wanted to grab my plate, hurl it at the wall and scream at her to shut up. But I don't, partly because I don't want to hurt her feelings and partly because I need to keep her onside.

I struggle to relax so I climb out of the bath and dry myself, slip a dress over my head then return to my room. Too wound up to sit, I pace up and down instead.

I've counted them and there are three potential directions I see my future heading in. The first is that I am going to leave this house in a wooden box. The second is that I'll persuade her into allowing me a proper professional diagnosis and, if necessary, treatment. Presently, the former seems more probable because Nina has inherited many of her dad's traits, one being his stubbornness. The third is that I am going to help myself. To date, each of my escape plans has been thwarted. So I need to be smarter.

As I scan the walls, floors and ceiling with a fresh perspective, I'm distracted by the photograph of Alistair that Nina glued to the wall just under my bedroom ceiling. With my extended chain, it's no longer out of my reach. I balance on the ottoman and tear at it. It comes off in two strips. I take it to the toilet and flush him away.

I know every square inch of my bedroom, but not so much the bathroom. I look around. I don't even know what I'm searching for or how it might help me get out of here. But Nina has taken precautionary measures. The mirrored door of the bathroom cabinet has been unscrewed and removed, as has the heavy lid of the porcelain toilet tank.

Suddenly I start to cry. I don't want to die at sixty-eight. If my time is up, I want it to be out there, not stuck in here. I don't want to spend my remaining days mimicking my mother's final moments in a hospice deathbed, mourning a life I never had the chance to finish properly.

And what will I have to apologise for when my day of reckoning comes? Will I be sorry for what I did, or for what I didn't do, in the name of a mother's love? Will I be forgiven for how I let my daughter down, for my sheer bloody ignorance? How can I ask for forgiveness when I truly believe that what I did was the right thing to do?

CHAPTER 52

MAGGIE

TWO YEARS EARLIER

Something is putting an immense amount of weight on my head, pushing it deep into the pillow as far as it will go and preventing me from moving it. I try to lift my arms to push myself up, but they are as weak as a baby's. I slowly reach for my scalp to push away whatever is holding me down, but all I feel is my hair. It's matted and greasy to the touch. Then I realise the pressure isn't coming from the outside, but the inside.

I begin to panic. This is what a stroke must feel like; blood has stopped pumping to my brain and my cells are slowly dying. I need to get help. I attempt to move my neck but it's as stiff as plywood. A shooting pain runs up the left-hand side of it and then spreads across the back of my head, making the pain even more excruciating. I want to open my eyes but it's easier said than done. Eventually both sets of eyelashes unstick and everything is bright again, but my eyes struggle to focus. I am completely disorientated. Wherever I am, it's grey and gloomy, and unidentifiable objects surround me. Gradually, I push my way up whatever it is I'm lying on; they're soft to the touch, like cushions, maybe? I don't get very far because every inch releases more sharp bursts across my head. I don't have the strength to continue.

A voice comes from nowhere, alarming me. 'Let me help you.' It sounds as if it's coming from a tape recorder played at half-speed. 'Give me your arms, Maggie,' it continues, and I suddenly realise who it is. Nina is here, but she sounds different.

'Thank God,' I mumble, my throat dry and crackly. I slide my hand around until I eventually find hers. 'I need an ambulance.'

Nina's hand leaves mine and I feel the warmth radiating from her body as she leans across me, places her hands under my arms and lifts me until I am in a slightly raised position. The pain in my head switches sides, forcing a sharp intake of breath. I'm beginning to wish she'd left me where I was.

Her fingers gently part my lips and something small and with a smooth texture is placed between them. The next thing I feel is something wet and cool pressed against my mouth, then liquid running down my chin.

'Take a sip of water and swallow,' Nina says.

It feels like such a monumental effort to ask her again to call 999, so I do as she says without question. If she is here with me then I am safe. So I close my eyes again and drift back into sleep and dream of her when she was my baby girl. All I ever wanted was my beautiful baby girl . . .

◆ ◆ ◆

I'm barely conscious again, but my head still throbs like a jackhammer is pounding the living daylights from it. I reach out my hand until I feel Nina's and it calms me in an instant. This time when

I open my eyes and take a deep breath, the space around me no longer smells stale. There's a familiarity about it, but also a newness.

'Take it slowly,' Nina advises and helps to lift me up into a sitting position. She tilts my head back and the stiffness in my neck makes me cry out. 'Open your eyes a little bit more,' she says, and I feel a cool wet cloth dabbing at them. Then two cold drops sting each of them. 'It's okay, they'll help,' Nina adds.

In a croaky voice I tell her that I have a splitting headache, so she offers me a tablet. My mouth is parched and I guzzle water from the bottle like I've discovered an oasis in the desert.

Eventually my senses begin sharpening and I'm comforted to see I'm at home and in my own bedroom. It's darker than usual.

'What happened to me?' I ask.

Nina's fingers entwine within mine. Hers are warm while mine are cold. 'Moxydogrel,' she whispers.

'Moxy . . . what?'

'Moxydogrel,' she repeats. There's a pause as my muddled mind lurches from one half-baked memory to another and tries to recall why I recognise the word. Suddenly it hits me and I know that she can see it in my expression because her fingers dig deep into mine like claws.

My hearts pounds like my head and it wants to burst through my ribcage.

What does she know?

I don't want to be in here any longer; I have to get out. I try and push myself up the bed but Nina keeps her fingers firmly locked around mine to the point where if I move any further, they will snap like twigs.

What does she know?

With my one free hand I rub at my eyes and examine her face. She is deceptively calm. But I know there is something lurking beneath the surface because I have seen it before. A familiar detachment. We remain like two scorpions, each circling one another, poisonous tails aloft and waiting for the other to strike first. But I am too weak to fight her, and she knows that. Because she has made me this feeble.

What does she know?

I look towards the window and I am confused by the absence of the net curtains and why they've been replaced with white shutters. The carpet has also disappeared, leaving exposed floorboards. Everything else in the bedroom appears to be the same.

Finally, Nina lets go of my hand and takes a step back. I swing my shaking legs over the side of the bed and sit upright. For the first time, I am aware of something heavy attached to my ankle and weighing it down. I lift my leg up and I see something like a cuff and a chain.

'What . . . what have you done to me?' I ask, my eyes now stinging with fear.

'I should be asking you the same thing,' she replies.

'Nina, you're scaring me. Why are you doing this?'

She shrugs then, and the smile she gives me is as cold as the Arctic. 'You can pick a reason. There are plenty to choose from.'

What does she know?

CHAPTER 53

NINA

TWO YEARS EARLIER

I watch in fascination as my mother's panicked eyes flit around the bedroom trying to place what has changed since she was last in here, ten days ago. I have left her with the same furniture and bed but I've taken away her creature comforts. There's no longer any jewellery inside the mother-of-pearl box on her dressing table, little make-up in her bag, no knickers in her drawers nor shoes in her cupboard. But she will find all of that out for herself later. It has taken so much effort and organisation over the last few weeks to get to this point and her reaction is making every moment of it worthwhile.

New triple-glazed and shatterproof windows have been installed in the landing, bathroom and bedroom, and a carpenter has fitted shutters in here that allow Maggie to see out but no one from outside to see in. The builder I employed didn't question what it was for when he inserted a steel joist in the centre of her bedroom floor and welded a metal ring to it. I use it to attach Mum's made-to-measure chains that I ordered from a German fetish website. And I told the woman who installed the soundproofed ceiling, partition wall and door on the first-floor landing that it was to block out the noise of my son, an amateur drummer.

It was only the night before work on the house began that I drugged Maggie's food for the first time with Moxydogrel, the same medication she plied me with all those years ago. Given that the use-by date stamped on the packaging warned that the drug had expired some thirteen years earlier, I had previously tested one myself and when it wiped me out for the entire evening, I knew I could use them on her. I kept her locked in the basement until the workmen completed their jobs. I clothed her in adult nappies in case she wet or soiled herself as she remained unconscious, and I set the alarm on my phone to every eight hours so that when she stirred, I could make her drink, spoon-feed her easy-to-digest baby food, then pump her with more medication.

I called in at her surgery to inform them that she was sick with a flu-like bug. And when two of her colleagues turned up at the house with Tupperware containers of home-made soup and a bunch of flowers, I told them that Maggie had just been taken to hospital following a suspected stroke. Further tests revealed that it was likely to have caused vascular dementia. Maggie's colleagues never saw or heard from her again.

I later told the surgery – and Elsie next door – that I'd taken her to Jennifer's house in Devon to recuperate. Then I contacted Jennifer and repeated the diagnosis but changed the locations and tearfully explained I had no choice but to put Maggie into a care home.

With work complete on the house, it was time to move Mum upstairs and to the room where she will be spending the rest of her life. After a devil of a job dragging her unconscious body up three flights of stairs, all that was left to do was wait for her to wake up.

I had options. I could have said nothing and got the hell away from her; contacted the police or even killed her. God knows, I seriously considered the latter. I ran through the options of how I might do it, and decided I'd bury her body next to the father I loved and the man she murdered. But no matter how much I hate her, I am not like her. I am not a killer.

So instead, I decided to remove her from everything and everyone she loves. I am separating her from her job, her colleagues, her friends, her freedom, her home and motherhood. I want all her needs to be almost within touching distance, but just that little bit too far out of reach.

Each time my conscience questions what I'm doing – and it has, frequently – I recall finding Dad's fractured skull. Whatever she did to him was swift and brutal, and what I'm going to do to her will be long and drawn out. But she will pay for taking my dad and my son away from me.

CHAPTER 54

MAGGIE

TWO YEARS EARLIER

This must be what a panic attack feels like because I'm hyperventilating and my skin is on fire. I want to be sick but I can't inhale deeply enough to retch.

Even with this debilitating headache clouding my judgement, it's fast becoming obvious that Nina has discovered at least one of the secrets I've kept hidden from her for most of her life. Her deliberate mention of Moxydogrel means that she has pieced some of her past together and realised I used this medication to keep her sedated. But does she know why? I cannot defend myself until I learn how much she is aware of. And I don't want to be the first one to blurt out the whole sorry story in case I'm offering her new information that she can use against me. Showing her my hand could have a catastrophic effect on her fragility. I don't want to be responsible for destroying the thing I love the most in the world.

I must get out of this room and clear my head. She doesn't try to stop me when I stand. Instead, she watches with amusement. I try to regain control over my breathing and use my hands to steady myself against the surface of the bedside table, then against the wall as I move forward. I turn to look her dead in the eye, using her face as my focal point while I wait for the room to stop spinning.

Carefully, I make my way to the door and turn the handle. It's unlocked. But as I attempt to cross the threshold, the chain around my leg tightens. I pull at it and it pinches my skin. I bend over to pull at the padlock's curved bar but it won't budge.

Nina continues to glare at me as I return, defeated, to the bed. If she's telling the truth and has used Moxydogrel on me, there must have been leftovers among the empty boxes in the basement suitcases. I curse myself for not having thrown them out years ago. I'd planned to take them to the rubbish tip along with Alistair's clothes and any other incriminating items. Only I never got around to it and over time, I forgot. How stupid of me to leave my secrets and lies in one place and under this roof, yards away from the person they affected the most. I left a trophy cabinet of my failings as a mother for her to find.

'I did it for you,' I say first.

'Which part?' she replies.

'Every part.'

'Spell it out for me. The part where you made me miscarry? The part where you told me my daughter was born dead, only she was a he and you gave him away? How about the part where the medication you force-fed me made me infertile? Or the part where you killed my dad and sent me a birthday card every year pretending to be him? Precisely which part of any of that did you do for me?'

She knows almost everything. 'I had to protect you,' I say.

'From what?'

I want to say *from yourself* but I can't. Instead I find someone else to blame. 'From Hunter.'

'You did all of this just to keep us apart? Well, that's a lie because I hadn't met Jon before you killed Dad. I know why you did this. Because you couldn't stand having to share me with anyone else – not Dad, not Jon and not my son. You hated it when anyone else threatened to come between us. Even when I wanted to adopt.'

'No, Nina, you have it all wrong.' I can no longer hold back my tears.

'Then tell me why, Maggie,' she snaps. 'Tell me why you did these things.'

But I cannot. I can't give her my reasoning. It is too tightly bound with chains and padlocks like those on my ankle and which I will never open. Nina cannot learn the truth. The lies must continue. 'Hunter was wrong for you. He was going to hurt you.'

'He wanted to be a father.'

'He didn't deserve to be one. He was a paedophile who groomed you. He had a girlfriend that he didn't tell you about and who he went on to kill. You could have so easily been Sally Ann Mitchell. You must be able to see that?'

'You didn't know him like I did.' Nina adds a dismissive wave of her hand. 'Jon loved me.'

'You wouldn't have stood a chance with him and a baby. By taking you out of that situation, I gave you a second chance at life.'

She gives an unamused laugh. 'A life? Is that what you call this? You're the reason I have nothing to show for my life.'

'Is that what this is all about?' I say, grabbing at and rattling my chain. 'You're doing all this to punish me for trying to give you a better life? For giving my grandson better opportunities?'

'That wasn't your decision to make! He was *my* baby and you gave him up.'

'You were in no fit state to be a mother.'

Nina rises to her feet and jabs her finger in my chest. 'You didn't give me the opportunity to try! It was not up to you to decide that for me.'

I know what she is capable of and I am a sitting duck. I need to calm her but I don't know how to control the narrative. I am out of my depth. 'I'm your mother,' I say. 'I did what I thought was best for you.'

'What, like telling me I had dodgy chromosomes that would kill any baby I became pregnant with?'

'I wanted to frighten you into being careful.'

'Why not make me go on the Pill?'

'I couldn't make you do anything back then. You couldn't even take precautions after I told you about your condition.'

'The condition that I never actually had because you made it up? Where did you even come up with such a thing?'

'It was a case study I read about during my midwife training. It stuck with me.'

'Were you ever going to tell me the truth?'

'Yes, when you were an adult.'

'I'm thirty-bloody-six! How much longer did I have to wait?'

I can't answer that.

'Why did you tell me I had a daughter, not a son?' she continues.

'Because I wanted to give you something that you really wanted.'

'Careful, Maggie, it almost sounds like you cared.'

'I did care! I do care. I've always cared. Perhaps too much.'

'If you didn't trust me to be a parent then why didn't you help me to raise him?'

'You wouldn't have allowed that.'

'How do you know? Because again, you never asked.'

'Because you were too obsessed with Hunter and he wasn't good for either of you. And because you didn't listen to a word I said. You did as you pleased, coming and going at all times of the day and night. Pregnant twice by the time you were fourteen? How can you honestly tell me that you or that drug abuser were in any fit state to be parents?' She knows I am right because she changes the subject instead of countering.

'How long was Dylan here for?'

'I don't remember.'

'Of course you do.'

'It was a long time ago.'

'You wouldn't forget something like that.'

'Two, maybe three days.'

'How did you look after me and him? How did I not hear him crying?'

'I was careful.'

'You mean you knocked me out with drugs.'

To her evident frustration, I don't answer this, or any of the other questions about those few days or even how I found Dylan his new family. So she changes direction.

'Did you know the Moxydogrel was going to put me in early menopause? That by nineteen, I wouldn't be able to have any more children of my own?'

'Of course not. Nobody knew the side effects before it was too late and it was withdrawn from the market.'

'But if you hadn't made me take them, I could have had a family.'

'I know, and for that I'm sorry, Nina, I am so, so sorry. You have to believe me.'

'I don't have to believe anything. Are you sorry for giving Dylan away?'

I hesitate and choose my words carefully. 'It was the right thing to do at the time.'

'You even denied me my name on his birth certificate. Why did you use your own?'

'In case one day he tried to find his mother, so he would find me instead. I thought it would be too stressful for you to deal with.'

'You mean for *you* to deal with. And you'd have lied to him like you lied to me. And what about Dad? Why did you kill him?'

I look away. I'm not sorry he is dead, not one bit. But telling her this would not be wise. 'I'm sorry that things ended up the way they did.'

'Why did you do it?'

I shake my head but I don't reply.

'Why?' she spits, but I can't explain. My lips remain sealed and I turn my head to look away from her.

My lack of response is all it takes for Nina to lose control. Without warning she lunges towards me and there's nothing I can do to stop her.

CHAPTER 55

NINA

TWO YEARS EARLIER

The culmination of everything I have learned about Maggie in the last five weeks is released in one swift action which I can't contain.

I grab her by the neck, push her back on to the mattress and straddle her. Her arms remain weak so she is easy to pin down. My fingers wrap themselves ever tighter around her throat.

I don't know who I've become but I am no longer myself. It's as if the real Nina is standing in the corner of the room watching someone resembling me strangling my mother. My hands are tightening and her windpipe is contracting and not allowing any new air to enter her lungs. Her mouth opens and she attempts to speak but her words are hard to make out. One of her legs flails behind me, kicking in all directions, but it falls short of making contact. The other shakes and rattles the chain attached to her ankle. 'I hate you I hate you I hate you,' I repeat in a voice that doesn't sound like my own.

At first I don't think I have ever felt a rage like this before, until a flash of déjà vu strikes. It's a blur of fast-moving, dimly lit, black-and-red-tainted images that suggests this isn't the first time I've been overcome by a need to lash out and hurt. However, I can't pinpoint when or why. As quickly as it appears, it vanishes and I'm back in the present. And I'm aware that if I don't release my grip on Maggie's throat soon, it's unlikely I ever will. I'll end up killing the woman who gave me life but who went on to take so much of it away from me.

Bit by bit, my fingers slacken until my hands are still around her neck, but I'm no longer putting undue pressure on it. I climb off her but continue to loom over her. She gasps for the air I've starved her of while I am drawing my first breaths as a new woman. I take advantage of her frailty, remove a key from my pocket, unlock the padlock, and swiftly replace the chain on her ankle with a much longer one stored under the bed.

Now I'm upright again and, grabbing her arm, I pull her from the bed and to her feet. I have never seen Maggie as weak and petrified as this and I'm surprised at how much satisfaction it brings me. I maintain enough self-awareness to recognise this isn't how normal people behave, but Maggie is no normal mother and she has given me no choice; she has turned me into this monster. I am an extension of her.

I haul her across the bedroom and on to the landing. This second chain allows me to pull her down the staircase until we reach the dining room. I push past the sideboard and table until we reach the window that offers a view of the back garden. I clamp my hand upon the back of her neck and direct her line of vision towards the flower bed Dad is buried beneath, hidden behind the trees.

'You let me spend my entire adult life believing Dad abandoned me,' I yell. 'You stood over my shoulder watching me write him letters, begging him to come back to us. You wiped away my tears and promised that I'd hear from him. And all the time you knew that he was out there because you killed him.'

'I had no choice,' Maggie sobs.

'Of course you did! I was the one who had no choice because you made those decisions for me. And later, what were you thinking when you watched me sitting by what I thought was my child's grave? Did you ever feel remorse?'

'Yes, of course I did. I have spent every day of my life since feeling guilty about everything that's happened to you.'

I can't tell if she's crying because she's telling the truth or because I have finally unravelled her lies and she's getting her comeuppance.

'I am sorry,' she says. 'You must believe me, Nina, it's much more complicated than you understand.'

'Then tell me. Why did you kill my dad? Did he cheat on you? Did he hit you? Did he gamble your money away? I need to know, I need to understand. Surely you must see that?'

Maggie opens her mouth as if she is ready to reply, then hesitates. 'It's not what you think,' she says quietly and shakes her head, defeated and resigned to her fate.

And now we are crying together. 'I have seen him, Maggie,' I say, trying to appeal to her better nature. 'I have held my dad's bones in my hands and wiped the dirt from his skull. I have lost him twice now. I have lost everyone I have ever loved and the common denominator in all of this is you.'

'But I'm still here,' she says. And for a moment, I believe Maggie thinks she is all I need; that her presence as a constant in my life makes up for all she's done. 'Despite everything, I've never left you, I have never deserted you, I've always been here for you even when you didn't want me to be.'

'And you have never been enough,' I reply, deliberately trying to hurt her. 'I have had five weeks to try and get my head around a lifetime of your lies. For more than twenty years I have been kept

246

away from my dad and my son and now I'm going to take that same time from you. This is going to be your prison in the same way you have imprisoned me. You won't see your friends, go outside or speak to anyone other than me, ever again. For all intents and purposes, you are frozen in time like you have frozen me.'

'Please,' Maggie weeps, 'Nina, darling, please don't do this. You know that it's wrong.'

I take her by the arm again and frogmarch her back upstairs. Once in her bedroom, I make her turn around and lift her foot while I replace her long chain for the shorter one that won't stretch beyond the doorway. And then I leave her alone to adjust to her new life. Her cries gradually fade away and by the time I have closed the soundproofed door behind me, the house is silent again.

CHAPTER 56

NINA

That lump. That bloody lump in Maggie's breast. It's all I can think about.

All morning I've been making silly mistakes while trying to input new titles on to the library's computer system because I'm worried about what she's found and its potential to ruin everything. At her age, ill health is always going to be a risk, but I didn't expect it to happen so soon. My shifting attitude towards her is also a concern. I was supposed to despise Maggie until the day she died. Instead, I find myself worrying about her.

Despite everything, she and I have built a type of co-dependent relationship, not so much a friendship but an alliance. So now, when I think about her dying before her time, it pulls at me. Maggie has been my only constant in thirty-eight years and I don't know if I am ready for her to leave me yet.

It's my lunch break and I'm hunched over a desk in an empty research room. A yellow notepad lies open in front of me. I draw a line down the centre of a page with a red biro and on one side, I write 'Ways to help' and on the other, 'Risks involved'.

I begin with 'Make Maggie an appointment with her GP'. Straight away, I know this wouldn't work because her employers and ex-workmates think she has dementia and is living on the coast 300 miles away. If she were to reappear without warning, they wouldn't need to spend much time with her to know that she's a long way from losing her marbles.

Next, I write, 'Take her to a walk-in centre'. On the other side of the column I add why this is pointless. They wouldn't give her a mammogram or perform a biopsy. They would refer her to a specialist breast clinic.

And the only way for either of those options to work would be if once out of the house, Maggie says nothing about where she has been for the last two years. Can I trust her stay quiet? No, of course I can't. If it were me, once outside I'd be running up the path and down the road faster than Usain Bolt.

I stare at the page and I lose track of time, trying to come up with another suggestion. Eventually, I write down the only choice left open to me.

'Do nothing'.

CHAPTER 57
MAGGIE

I haven't eaten with Nina in days. Instead, she has returned to leaving my three meals alongside vitamins and powders outside the bedroom door when she knows I'll be asleep. I know why. It's so she doesn't have to face me and tell me what she plans to do about my lump. She is torn, and while she is feeling this way, I have a chance of getting through to her. But not from behind a closed bedroom door.

The clock on breakfast television tells me it's just past 8.30 a.m., but I have yet to see her leave the house and set off for work. She is rarely this late, even if she is working a different shift. She is also never sick. My mind briefly wanders . . . what if she *is* sick, though? What will happen to me if something happens to Nina? I've read stories about single mums who have died suddenly, and their infant children have starved to death because they didn't know how to raise the alarm. Their situation hardly differs from mine. I too am totally dependent on someone else to keep me alive. If Nina had become incapacitated, how would I know? And even if

I did, I couldn't help either of us while the landing door is locked. It's another thing to add to my list of worries.

I am hovering by the window waiting for her to leave when a moving car draws my attention. I think I recognise it – it looks like the same white one with the sunroof that's been here three times before. The last time, Elsie said something that warned him off and he scuttled away with his tail between his legs. Then my house was empty, but today I believe Nina is still here. I stand on my tiptoes as he makes his way up the path, before Nina emerges to meet him halfway. Then they give each other a tight hug. This is a turn-up for the books.

I try to get a better view of my daughter and I'm noticing something different about her. She usually prefers to blend into the background with plain blouses, sweatshirts and jeans. But today she is wearing a colourful dress and heels. They walk to the car and she slips her handbag from her shoulder into the car's footwell before climbing inside. As she closes the door, I catch her turning her head to look upwards to where she assumes I will be watching. She's right; I am. But it doesn't stop me edging backwards like a peeping Tom who has just been caught. Her companion's car pulls away and they disappear up the road.

Who on earth is he? When she first put me under lock and key she couldn't wait to tell me in minute detail about everything that went on in her life as a reminder that the world was turning without me. But this man has been conspicuously absent from her conversation.

Returning to the dressing table, I spot a small plastic tub of flaxseed that I forgot to sprinkle upon my soaked oats breakfast pot. It's on the tray alongside a book called *Fighting Cancer through Good Food and Positive Living*. I roll my eyes at the title. Positive living! I skim the back of the jacket. Apparently, the author reveals how you can fight the disease simply by changing your lifestyle and diet. I don't get past the contents page, where I see no mention of ultrasounds, biopsies, X-rays, MRI scans, chemotherapy, radiotherapy, hormone therapy or any of the other weapons I need in my arsenal to fight this thing inside me, if cancer is what it is. And chapter headings such as 'Outdoor exercise' and 'Support from friends' are as much use to me as a scuba-diving kit.

I feel my chest tighten as I think of how I'm growing ever more resentful of Nina. She is burying her head in the sand if she thinks this is the way forward. And I'll be damned if I'm burying myself next to her. I know that every day counts. The longer I wait for a diagnosis, the more advanced it could be.

I can't leave the damn lump alone. Half a dozen times a day I am touching it, working my way around it, moulding it with my fingers, wondering if it has gone up or down in size or remained consistent. Sometimes when it's dead silent in here I think I can feel it growing, stretching my skin and expanding beneath the surface. Perhaps it's like a dandelion head, casting its cancerous little seeds about my body to rest and sprout in all my nooks and crannies. Whatever this thing is, I want it out of me. And I want out of here.

I wander into the bathroom to refill my water bottles. On the way out, I notice there's still half an inch of water left in the bath. I push down on the press-in plug but it doesn't budge. I try again and this time the whole thing pops out from its socket. Curious, I examine the plug's mechanism to see how it operates. My eyes light up when I take a look at what fits the two pieces together – a two-inch screw with a sharp pointed end. It's loose so I can take it apart. Both this and Nina's companion might be my ticket out of here.

CHAPTER 58

NINA

TWO YEARS EARLIER

I sense Dylan has arrived before I see him. I look to the glass panel in the pub door and recognise the shape of his shadow behind it. It opens and he spots me sitting at a table, alone, and waiting for him. My heart flutters as just for a second, all I see is Jon Hunter in his son's face.

He goes by the name Bobby now, I remind myself. He approaches me with a nervous smile that replicates my own, followed by a 'Hello.' I have a lemonade waiting for him, alongside my own glass of the same. He removes his coat and takes a seat opposite me.

Six weeks and two days have passed since the one and only time we have met. I really wanted to see him sooner but I had so many revelations to process that it wasn't fair on him to meet when my head was in such a state. I needed to come to terms with all I'd learned, then punish Maggie before I could allow him into my life. I wanted him to meet the best possible version of myself, and now

I'm ready. After we first met I messaged him just once, promising I'd be in touch, but that he needed to give me time. And bless him, he did just that.

His eyes are directed towards the tabletop rather than towards me. I don't blame him. He's mustered up the courage to risk rejection twice now.

'I wasn't sure if I'd hear from you again,' he begins.

'I'm sorry,' I reply, 'I really am. And I'm also sorry that I left you in the pub that night without explaining why.'

'I understand it must have been difficult for you.'

'I panicked, but you didn't deserve to be treated like that. Please remember, before then, I had no reason to believe you existed.'

'It's okay,' he says, but I can see in his face how much my reaction hurt him, because I wear the same expression when I've been let down. I vow never to wound him again.

I have had a lot of time to consider the different ways I can explain my story to Bobby, but each one comes with risks. I'm desperate not to lose anyone else from my life, but I have to be honest with him. However, only up to a point. There are some truths I must be economical with. I take both of his hands in mine and clear my throat. 'There's a lot I need to tell you and very little of it will be easy for you to hear. So before I start, I'd like to offer you something that was taken away from me – a choice. You and I can either carry on as we are, getting to know one another, or I can explain everything and you can make up your own mind if you want to continue this.'

Bobby replies without giving it any consideration. 'I'd like to know everything, please.'

'Are you sure?' I ask again, and he nods. 'Okay.' I take the biggest breath my lungs will allow. 'Well, to begin with, I am not who you think I am.'

His hands tense as if I am about to renounce him again, and I think he wants to slide them from under mine. I hold them firmly in place.

'We are related, Bobby, but not in the way your birth certificate suggests. I am not your half-sister. I'm your biological mother.'

I release my grip and he withdraws his hands. His posture tenses as if being drawn by invisible strings. 'I don't understand,' he says. 'It says . . .'

'I know what your birth certificate says,' I continue softly. 'But it's a lie. My mum didn't have a baby on that date; I did.'

'You?' he asks, and I nod. 'But you were . . .'

'. . . I was fourteen when I fell pregnant and fifteen when I gave birth to you. But I was told that you were stillborn.'

He shakes his head. 'Who told you that?'

'My mum – your grandmother. Let me explain.' I return to the start and recall all I know, but I leave out his grandfather's and grandmother's fates. I finish by describing the special place in the garden where I'd go to mourn his passing. It's no wonder that by the end of it, he looks as if he's gone twelve rounds in a boxing ring.

'Do you need a few moments?' I ask, and he says yes. Then he makes his way outside while I remain seated, my heart beating twenty to the dozen, doubting myself and questioning whether I've done the right thing. I take a little comfort when I notice he has left both his phone on the table and his coat on the back of the chair. After an interminably long period of time, he returns.

'Why did your mum do that to us?' he asks as he sits. Now, his eyes are locked on to mine like magnets.

I adapt the truth and tell him I've been in touch with my Aunty Jennifer who confirmed the truth. 'She said that Mum didn't think I could cope with a baby,' I say. 'Back then I was what you'd call a wild child; I accept that. But I was acting up; I was angry and

255

upset at Dad leaving us, so I took it out on her. You have to believe that I really wanted you. I know that I was so, so young, but given the chance, I think I might've been a good mother. I couldn't have given you the opportunities your adoptive parents have, but I'd have loved you and that would have counted for something.'

'Did you have any more children? Do I have brothers and sisters?'

I shake my head and explain how the Moxydogrel brought on an early menopause. The hatred I feel towards Maggie is every bit as raw as it was six weeks ago when I unlocked those suitcases. I worry it's going to reveal itself in my face. I don't want Bobby to think that I'm bitter, although it's exactly what I am. 'My mother was a conflicted woman,' I continue, 'and I don't think I'll ever be able to forgive her for what she did.'

'Does she know I found you?'

'She died a few years ago,' I say quickly. 'Breast cancer.' As much as I hate myself for lying to him, he cannot know what I've done to her. I deserve someone in my life who sees only good in me.

'What about my dad?' Bobby continues. 'Are you still in touch? Does he know about me?'

Even now, my default setting is to smile fondly when I think of Jon. 'I wish I had better news. Your dad was reliant on a lot of substances back then. At the time, everyone in the music scene was doing it so he wasn't alone. It's only with hindsight that I can see it was a problem for him. I don't know all the details but Jon became involved in an altercation with a girl he knew and she died. He was adamant that he wasn't to blame but he was found guilty of murder and has been in prison ever since.'

Bobby lets out a long breath like a whooshing sound.

'For what it's worth,' I add, 'the Jon I loved and the Jon the newspapers wrote about weren't the same person. He was sweet and sensitive and I never saw any violence in him.'

'Shit,' he says. 'Do you visit him?'

'No, I've never been.' My face flushes with guilt as if I've turned my back on him. 'For my own recovery, I had to let him go.'

I don't tell him that I wrote to his solicitor soon after I discovered he was jailed to ask Jon for a visitor's permit. I don't mention that I was turned down because his client 'didn't recall who I was'.

'Does he know about me?'

I shrug. 'I hadn't seen him for two years when I discovered what he'd been accused of. Over the years I've followed his case and his numerous appeals and I've wondered why he never got in touch. He knew I was pregnant but he didn't know I thought I'd lost you. I like to think he was trying to spare us from the life he is trapped in.'

We sit in silence; this is an incredible amount of bleak information to take on board in one sitting. Until tonight, he thought he'd tracked down his long-lost sister. Instead, it turns out I'm his mother and I'm carrying more baggage than a jumbo jet.

'Would you like me to leave?' I ask. 'I've given you a lot to think about. I'll understand if you need time to yourself to process it.'

'No,' he says. It trips off his tongue too quickly for him not to mean it. 'You could have just glossed over everything but I'm glad you didn't. I'd rather know than not know. I appreciate your honesty.'

There are many things I am able to give my son. Unconditional love and support are just two. But complete honesty will never be one of them.

CHAPTER 59

NINA

EIGHTEEN MONTHS EARLIER

It's hard to stop myself from smiling when I feel so much joy. Most parents have hundreds, perhaps thousands of moments when their child has brought them the happiness I'm feeling right now. But it's all still new to me so every minute I spend with Dylan is a precious one.

The only thing threatening my happiness is Maggie. I didn't expect it to be an easy transition for her, but months into our new arrangement she's not being as compliant as I'd hoped. When she becomes particularly troublesome, I've taken to using the remaining Moxydogrel tablets, crushing them into a fine powder and stirring them into her food to sedate her. Like last night. Through my clothes, I rub at the Band-Aid which covers the wound where she stabbed me in the arm with a fork. Later, she claimed she was confused and hallucinating and it must've been the fault of the tablets. We both know that's untrue; she just wanted to leave me. I've taken all metal cutlery away from her.

The transition for me hasn't been that much easier. Holding Maggie captive is harder than I thought and I'm not getting as much satisfaction from it as I'd hoped. In fact I'm starting to resent the energy she's sucking out of me. When I'm around her I'm constantly on my guard or second-guessing what she'll do next. My life outside that house should be about Dylan and spending time with him. Instead, I find myself trying to keep one step ahead of her and wondering what she's up to while the cat's away.

Today it's my turn to visit Dylan in Leicester. We have been meeting fortnightly for the last seven months and take it in turns as to who goes to see who. If I had my own way, I'd be with him every day. But I'm mindful that he has a family of his own that I'm not a part of. I'd like it – in fact, truth be told, I'd *love* it – if he shouted from the rooftops that he'd found his real mum. However, navigating the periphery of his world is better than not being a part of it at all. Our relationship must be on his terms and I've learned to be patient. Most of the time.

He is waiting for me at the coach station when my bus pulls into the bay and he greets me with a broad smile and a hug. The family dog, Oscar, bounces up and down in the back of the car and greets me with the same enthusiasm as his owner. Dylan drives us to a village a few minutes away and we attach Oscar to the lead and set off arm in arm for a country walk around the plush grounds of a stately home. To the people who pass us, we must look like lovers.

I know how inappropriate that sounds but it's how I feel. When we are apart and I think of Dylan, my heart swells with such happiness. I want to be with him all the time. I want to hear what he has to say, study his mannerisms, make him laugh, make him feel as if he is loved with every fibre of my being. I want all the things a couple in a relationship want from one another. Except we are not a couple. And sometimes, when I feel the lines starting to blur, I have to remind myself that we are mother and son.

According to the Internet, I'm reacting typically to our situation. I hate the term genetic sexual attraction and that there are websites and message boards devoted to it. It's because we didn't have that gradual mother-and-child bonding experience when he was a newborn. My love for him, my longing not to be apart and the elation I feel when we're together is happening all at once and in a much more condensed timeframe. I'm hoping in time it will pass.

I catch our reflection in a window of the manor house. With his slim frame, dark hair, his angular face and his piercing grey eyes, it looks as if I am on his father's arm. My grip becomes that little bit firmer. Now I have my son, I am never letting go of him.

A month after our second meeting we took a DNA test for our own peace of mind. And of course it came back as a positive match. And each time we're together, I'm constantly searching for new things that we have in common. Today, I notice our earlobes are exactly the same shape and that his two bottom middle teeth overlap ever so slightly, as do mine. These simple things bring me a warmth.

We walk through woodland until we reach the river Soar. A gaggle of Canada geese waddle past us on the muddy bank, reluctant to return to the water until a canoeist paddles by. The mother keeps turning her head to check that her chicks are still behind her. It sounds silly but I realise I have something in common with her. I too have someone to look after.

'Are you dating at the moment?' I ask. 'You've not mentioned anyone special.'

He's hesitant at first before he replies with a 'No.'

'Your dad had so much female attention at your age,' I continue. 'He had to practically beat the girls off with a stick. Well, perhaps I was the one holding the stick. And you look a lot like him.'

'I've seen photos of him online.'

'You've looked?' I ask, and I don't know why I'm surprised. Of course he'd want to know more.

'Yes,' he says. 'Do you think he and I would get on?'

'I'm not sure. You're very different people. Jon could be quite cocky and arrogant but I don't know how much prison has changed him. He was also very caring and very protective of me.'

'Do you miss him?'

I nod my head and we fall into a comfortable silence, which eventually he breaks. 'By the way, it's not really girls I'm interested in, if you catch my drift.'

I don't, until he gives me one of his dad's knowing smiles. 'You're gay?' I ask, a little more taken aback than I should be.

'Uh-huh,' he replies. We walk in the direction of a cafe. 'I started seeing someone a few weeks ago but I don't think it's going anywhere.'

'Why not?'

'It's not the right time. With work and getting to know you, I don't have the time to invest in a relationship.' My heart warms when I hear this. I am a priority for him. 'Does it bother you, you know, me liking guys?'

'Of course not,' I say, and I mean it. I'm glad I won't have to share him with any more women.

'Mum and Dad aren't bothered either. They're pretty chilled.'

I have mixed emotions when he speaks of his adoptive parents. I want to hear about his childhood and the stolen years. But I don't like to think of another mother picking him up when he fell over, reading him bedtime stories or cheering him on from the sidelines at school sports day. It should've been me doing those things, not a stranger. It's irrational and unfair but I resent a woman I have never met.

We take a seat inside the cafe and I return from the counter with a pot of tea and two cups. We take it the same, a splash of milk with two sugars. He removes an envelope from his jacket pocket and passes me an assortment of photographs.

'They're me as a baby,' he says.

He is lying on a rug wearing just a nappy, grinning. His chubby arms are stretched wide and his legs are bent and mid-air. Even at an early age, he has a mop of dark hair like Jon's. Other pictures reveal the first time he sat up unaided and the moment when he took his first steps. In that one, his adoptive mother is standing behind him, her hands holding his, helping him remain upright. Her face isn't in the picture, which allows me to pretend that I'm there, not her.

'You can keep them if you like,' Dylan offers, and I thank him. He spots the tears forming before I feel them. 'I'm sorry, I didn't mean to upset you,' he says.

I remove a packet of tissues from my handbag, dab at my eyes, shake my head and change the subject. 'It's a nice cafe,' I say. 'Have you been here before?'

'No, we live on the other side of town. One of my colleagues writes the pub and restaurant reviews and said it was a decent place.'

I sense there's another reason why we are here. 'And you're not ready for us to be seen together, are you?'

His face flushes.

'It's all right, I understand,' I add, and I do. But it stings a little. Like me, he's sensitive and he recognises it in others.

'I haven't told my mum and dad about you yet,' he says.

'How do you think they'll react?'

'I don't know. We're a close family but I don't want to hurt them.'

'Then what made you want to find me?'

'Curiosity . . . a way to put all the pieces together to see the full picture. To learn where I came from, who I might look like, what we might have in common . . . it's not as if I feel that I don't belong in my family, I just have a natural curiosity. Maybe it's the journalist in me.'

'And by finding me, have you satisfied that curiosity?'

'I have,' he replies.

Fear rears its ugly head. Is this his way of saying he has everything he needs from me? We've met and he's learned what a messed-up world he was conceived in. Was I just an itch he needed to scratch? 'Okay,' I reply, and my eyes begin to well again.

He places his hand on my forearm. 'And I'd still like to keep getting to know you,' he says. 'I'm not looking for another mum, I have one of those, but I'm always open to new friends.'

I can no longer hold my tears back. 'So am I,' I sniff, and dab at my eyes with a second tissue. But I'm not crying because he wants to continue in the way that we are: it's because I see him as my son, but he will never see me as his mother. And it strikes me that, for as long as I live, no one is ever going to call me 'Mum'.

CHAPTER 60
MAGGIE

It's mid-afternoon by the time Nina reappears with the man who arrived at the house this morning. I strain my eyes to see what's happening between them, but I think they're only talking. This is followed by a peck on the cheek before she exits and returns to the house, alone. I wonder if Nina has told him about me. Has she told him she lives here alone? Have I been buried, written out of her history, or does she say we are estranged?

There has been one significant development today. Earlier, when she left my food, it was just breakfast and lunch, which indicates we are to dine together tonight. It offers me hope that she has made a decision on having my lump examined by a professional. And I'm prepared for the worst.

When the landing door eventually opens, we greet each other politely before I make my way downstairs. However, I can instantly tell there's a distance between us. I hide my disappointment even though it comes as no surprise. So if she isn't going to help me, I am going to help myself. I steel myself because I know this is going to get ugly.

'You look nice,' I say as she passes me a bowl of pasta. 'Is that dress new?'

'It's a couple of weeks old,' she replies.

'You don't normally wear such bright colours.'

'I fancied a change.'

'Is it for a special occasion?'

'No, not really.'

'How was work?'

This time she hesitates, as if she is trying to decide whether I indeed watched from the crow's nest as she left and returned with that man. I don't give anything away.

'The usual,' she replies.

'Nothing out of the ordinary then?'

'No. A typical day in the library.'

We both know she is lying.

'Did you read the book I left you?' she asks, changing the subject.

'Not yet.'

'Why? Struggling to find time in your busy schedule?'

I side-eye her as if to say I don't appreciate her sarcasm, but she isn't fussed by what I think. She's annoyed with me. 'A lot of it wasn't applicable to my circumstances, like going outdoors, getting exercise, seeing friends and generally remaining positive.'

'Maggie, you've got to meet me in the middle.'

My hackles rise and my reply comes through gritted teeth. 'I appreciate that you are trying to help, but it's not books or healthy food I need, it's a proper diagnosis.'

'If you're not going to help yourself, then why should I?'

My frustration and resentment towards her rises with the speed of a rocket. If she won't let me out of here then I am going to need to fight my way out. I have what I need on me. I slip my hand into my cardigan pocket and feel a sharp prick from the plug and screw I've been carrying. I place the half of the plug with the screw protruding from it between my thumb and index finger and grip it so the end protrudes and almost penetrates the fabric. My heart is already racing.

'Sometimes I don't think you appreciate everything I do for you,' Nina continues, oblivious. 'You know that my hands are tied when it comes to what we can and can't do, so when I go out of my way to find alternative ways and you ignore them, it feels like you're throwing it back in my face. It's like banging my head against a brick wall.'

An ever-increasing part of me wants to bang *her* head against a brick wall, over and over again until she either sees sense or falls unconscious. Then I can grab the keys to my ankle cuff and escape her once and for all. But I need to get this clear before I make a decision that will change everything for the both of us.

'So what you're saying is that you are not going to help me?'

'The books, the vitamins, the alternative medicines, the food – if that's not helping you then what is?'

'Getting me an expert diagnosis!' I snap.

'You have to remember that you have put yourself in this predicament, not me. Killing Dad, taking my son away from me . . . the guilt you feel from everything you've done to us all is likely to have eaten you up inside. And from the studies I've read, that kind of stress could be a contributing factor towards the development of cancer.'

'And you don't think locking me up here for two years might have had anything to do with it?'

She laughs. 'Are you really trying to blame me?'

Bite your tongue, I tell myself. *Wait for your chance*. I grip the plug and screw so tightly, my pulse hammers inside my throat.

'You haven't answered, which indicates you know I'm right,' Nina adds. 'It's time you stopped fighting against me and started working with me. I'll help you, but we are doing it on my terms. And I'm sorry, but that won't involve you leaving this house.'

She places her knife and fork on her empty bowl and sees that I have stopped eating. 'I assume you've finished,' she says, and points to my barely touched salad.

'I've lost my appetite.'

Nina rises to her feet, picks up my bowl and I spot the fob where she keeps the key that unlocks my chain poking from her dress pocket. The fob used to belong to her dad and I hate that she exhumed it when she exhumed him.

It's now or never. I knock my fork to the floor and she bends over to pick it up. This is my opportunity. Within the blink of an eye I could withdraw my weapon, catching her completely unawares and stab her hard in the back of the neck. It might take a few jabs until I can completely overpower her and set myself free, but I can do it. I want to, oh Christ I *want* to, in fact I want to do it so badly that it's like a fire burning me from the inside out. In the next five minutes I could be out of that front door and a free woman again.

Compared to my past efforts to escape, I know this one has the potential to be the most debilitating or even lethal. Realistically I could kill my own daughter if I hit her in the right spot. But as much as I want to raise the plug above her head, I just cannot bring myself to do it. I brought her into the world, I cannot take her out of it. I can hate her, resent her and despise her, but I cannot end her life to save my own. Because above all else, Nina is still my baby girl whom I have loved every minute she has been in this world.

As she turns her back to me and leaves the room with the dishes, I want to weep in frustration or use the weapon against myself as punishment for my inability to act. Cancer might as well ravage me because life would not be worth living if I had her blood on my hands. And for her sake, I cannot allow her to know of the blood she has on her hands, either.

I cannot kill as she has killed.

CHAPTER 61

MAGGIE

TWENTY-FIVE YEARS EARLIER

I awake with a start, unsure of what's prompted my eyes to open so quickly.

Over the last year or so, I've had a lot of trouble getting to sleep. It's as if the touch of the pillow against my head sends a message to my brain urging it to burst into life, no matter how tired I feel. So I've started using sleeping tablets as a temporary fix to help me get a good night's rest; otherwise my tossing and turning will keep Alistair awake. And typically, I'm out like a light and rarely wake up until morning. But tonight is an exception. Something isn't quite right, I can feel it.

The alarm clock on his side of the bed reads 12.45 a.m., so I've only been out for the count for a couple of hours. 'Alistair?' I whisper, and feel around for him in the darkness. He isn't curled up next to me, but that's not unusual. When his work as a civil engineer isn't taking him to different parts of the country, he's often squirrelled away in his office downstairs until the early hours.

Lately he hasn't had much time to spend with Nina or me. He hasn't even been able to visit his mistress, the golf club, as often. His golf bag has been leaning against the landing wall between Nina's room and his office for the best part of a fortnight, waiting to be either used or moved. And it's become an unspoken battle of wills between us as to who is going to fold first and shift it to the basement. Neither of us have yet backed down.

Climbing out of bed, I slip on my dressing gown and promise myself I'm going to drag him to bed whether he likes it or not. Sometimes, for his own sake, he needs me to point out if he's been burning the candle at both ends.

I make my way to the first floor and reach the bedroom he has converted into a home office. I don't see a light shining from beneath the door and wonder if he fell asleep in there. It wouldn't be the first time. I push it open and switch the light on. Inside is a desk, two filing cabinets, reams of paperwork and walls covered with sketches of buildings, bridges and tunnels. But there's no Alistair.

I return to the corridor and am about to head downstairs to see if he's dropped off in front of the television when I notice Nina's door is slightly ajar. An orangey glow spills from the cracks, which suggests she's fallen asleep reading those *Sweet Valley High* and Judy Blume books that she's obsessed with.

I let out a long yawn as I make my way towards her room to switch the lamp off. Suddenly, Nina's door opens quickly and I jump. The light illuminates Alistair's face and he is as shocked to see me as I am to see him, if not more so.

'You scared me to death,' I exclaim. He doesn't respond, and I can't determine what the look on his face means. 'Are you okay?'

'Yes, yes,' he says, and curls one half of his mouth into an awkward smile. It fails to reassure me.

'Why are you up so late? Is Nina all right?'

He nods too quickly. 'She's fine.'

'Why were you in her room then?'

'I . . . I thought I heard a noise.'

'And?'

'And what?'

'And did you?'

'No, I was wrong,' he replies.

My father was a natural-born liar but my husband is not and I see straight through him.

'What are you not telling me, Alistair? Please tell me she doesn't have a boy in there?'

He shakes his head but offers nothing else. Then I recognise his expression. It's guilt, like when he tells me he's taken the bin out but has actually forgotten, or says he's been working late on site when I can smell booze on his breath. Only tonight, Alistair's guilt is compounded by fear. He is the calm rational one in our relationship. Nothing worries him. He doesn't fret about money or his career, he doesn't get angry and he doesn't dwell upon sadness. But I have never seen him like this before. He is terrified and he is doing a terrible job of trying to hide it. My eyes burrow so deeply into his that I wonder if I might find his soul.

'What's going on?' I ask in a firmer tone. 'What were you doing in Nina's room?'

But before he can answer, a shadow appears behind him. A form in motion, first taking a step away down the hall, then sweeping back towards us with something swinging high above Alistair's head. He registers my reaction, but before he can turn around to see what it is, there's a dull thwack and he falls, face down, to the floor at my feet. I've taken a lurching involuntary step back to allow him to drop. It's only then that I see Nina raising the thing above her dad. Alistair stretches an arm out in front of him as if hoping to crawl to safety, but he isn't given the opportunity. His daughter rains two more blows upon him, one across his back and another to the head, until he stops moving.

Then without saying a word, Nina drops the object to the floor and retreats to her bedroom as quietly as she appeared.

CHAPTER 62

MAGGIE

TWENTY-FIVE YEARS EARLIER

I want to scream but when I open my mouth, nothing comes out. Not even air. I move my hand to turn on the light switch but I'm shaking so violently that it takes several attempts.

When the light shines upon Alistair's body sprawled across the floor, it's worse than I imagined. The right-hand side of his skull is concave and has a small piece missing. The hole is filling with blood and trickling over the side and into his hair. I look around and blood is everywhere. I pinch myself; I must be dreaming. *This isn't happening. Oh, but it is.* His eyes are saucer-wide and inert. He is most definitely dead. There are streaks across the wallpaper, spots on the Artex ceiling, and it's seeping into the carpet and creating a red circle around his head. Next to him is a golf club with a metal head that Nina used to hit him with.

Finally my voice returns. 'Nina!' I yell. 'What have you done?'

I don't know what to do. I should run downstairs and call 999 but something stops me. It's my daughter. The steel of the club briefly reflected street light into her eyes with the second blow, revealing a deadened rage of the like I have never witnessed before in Nina or anyone else. What dreadful thing must have happened to instigate it? I steady myself against the wall as I move towards her room, my legs threatening to fold beneath me.

Now my baby is sitting on the edge of her bed, catatonic. Her eyes are wide open but almost lifeless and her cheeks, forehead and pyjama top are splattered with blood. I choke back my grief and just about manage to say her name aloud. She is non-responsive. 'Nina,' I repeat, but still she remains mute.

My daughter is not evil; she is not cruel. I have never encountered a bad bone in her body. So why would she want to hurt her father? A wicked thought springs to mind. It's the worst explanation. No, it can't be that; I don't even know how I could think such a thing. I want to believe that I'm tired and confused and my imagination is running away with itself. Alistair and Nina are so close, but he would never do anything he shouldn't. I know my husband inside out and I wouldn't have married him if I'd had even an inkling he was . . . he was a . . . I can't even think the word. I'm wrong, I have it very, very, wrong. I try and cast it aside but it lingers . . . it's growing . . . I have given it life and now it's expanding.

'My baby, my poor, poor baby,' I sob. 'What has he done to you?'

She offers no response.

I give in to gravity and fall to my knees, wrapping my arms around her, feeling her rigid limbs against me and her almost imperceptible breaths on my neck. I never want to let her go, but I know that I need to put this right. I need to think. What do I do first? I have to wipe the blood and her father's evil from her skin.

I help her to her feet but it's as if she is running on autopilot. To reach the bathroom, we are forced to step over Alistair's body.

I don't want her to see him again, but she has retreated so far into herself that there's little chance she is registering anything.

I guide her into the bath, strip off her bloody pyjamas and wash her with warm water from the shower hose and use an orangey shower gel to take the metallic smell of blood away. She allows me to clean her without comment or conflict. I avert my eyes from her body and pray that Alistair hasn't damaged her permanently. I sit on the edge of the bath as I dry her, help her into fresh bedclothes and guide her back into her bedroom. I lay her down under the duvet and remain by her side until eventually her eyes flicker and she falls asleep.

It's only when I close her door behind me that I ask myself whether I should have already called for help. I know it's what I'm supposed to do, but I'm terrified as to the further psychological damage it could do to my already fragile child. I cannot watch as a police car takes her away for questioning or an ambulance carts her off to a psychiatric unit. Besides, in my haste to make her clean again, I have washed away the evidence. But perhaps that was my intention?

I have made such a mess of this already. I lean against the door and slide to the floor, my hands covering my mouth so neither the living nor the dead can hear my sobs. I have never felt guilt like this before. Nina might be thirteen but she is still my little girl. I should have known; there must have been warning signs that I didn't want to acknowledge. I have let her down as badly as her father has. What if I have lost her forever? Or what happens when she wakes up and remembers what she or Alistair has done? I don't know how I'm going to deal with either. All I know for certain is that I cannot allow this one night to shape the rest of her life. I have to make this better.

I run around the house grabbing every towel and tea towel we have. With Alistair's heart no longer pumping blood around his

274

wretched body, he has stopped bleeding out, but there is still a hell of a mess in the hallway. I have to face him but I can barely bring myself to take him in. I see flecks of something white in his hair and I don't know if it's bone fragment or brain. I fight the urge to vomit.

I return to the landing and place the towels across the floor. As they soak up the blood, I drag a duvet from the spare room and spread it next to him. I roll Alistair on to it, tuck it snugly around him, then go on rolling. Just doing this much helps; with him hidden away, I could be rolling up a carpet. When he's done up tight, I set about wrestling packing tape around and under his body like a spider might with a captive insect. Only when I'm sure the duvet is sealed do I attempt to drag him downstairs. He is at least three stone heavier than me and it takes all my strength, interspersed with many breaks, to shift him. My muscles strain and burn as we move, the last thing we'll ever do together. As his head hits each bump of the staircase, the reality of what is happening right now threatens to derail me.

This is my dead husband. When I went to bed, this was the man I was going to spend the rest of my life with. Now I must get rid of him as if he never existed.

I want to break down again but I can't give in; I must see this through. I'll have all the time in the world to think of myself and process this later.

It's only when I reach the kitchen do I realise I have no idea what to do with a dead body. It's highly unlikely that I'd be able to carry him far enough into a field or woodland to dump – even if I could get him inside the car. I don't have the stomach or the apparatus to cut him up and dispose of him piece by piece. Now I understand why so many people try to cover up domestic murders by burying the victim in the garden. Alistair is no victim but at least here, I can prevent him from ever being discovered.

I take the torch from the kitchen drawer and slip it into my dressing gown pocket, then open the back door. I scan the neighbours' houses for signs of activity before I drag Alistair over the step and up the path. It's too dark to do anything with him now other than to store him in the shed.

Back in the kitchen, the clock on the oven warns me it's past 5 a.m., and I'm mentally and physically exhausted. But this hellish night isn't over yet. I throw all the bloody towels into the washing machine and turn it on to a ninety-degree heat. Then with a bucketful of cleaning products and hot water, I get to work scrubbing the carpet and the walls with all the household products I can find. Every few minutes, I open Nina's bedroom door to check on her, but she is still fast asleep.

◆ ◆ ◆

By 8 a.m., I'm on my fourth coffee and sitting at the kitchen table, staring from the window towards the shed at the end of the garden. I've decided where in the garden I'm going to bury Alistair. But first, I need to deal with Nina. I don't know how to help her, though. I am so far out of my depth that I'm drowning. Perhaps I could ask one of the doctors from the surgery for advice? But how do I avoid explaining the cause of her breakdown and what she did to her dad?

'Why didn't you wake me up?' The voice comes from behind me. I scream and drop my empty mug on the tabletop, breaking the handle.

I turn to see Nina, dressed in her school uniform, approaching me.

'Clumsy,' she says, and I watch her in disbelief, my jaw slack as my narrowed eyes follow her. She takes two slices of bread from a loaf and slips them into the toaster. 'Why does everything in the house smell like bleach?'

'I . . . I spilled something,' I say. 'I was cleaning up.'

She takes a carton of fresh orange juice from the fridge and pours herself a glass. I'm on tenterhooks, watching, waiting for something, anything unusual, to happen. She glances out of the window and for a second, I think she senses where I've left Alistair. But if she does, she gives nothing away. Instead, she tells me about her forthcoming day at school and a science project that's proving challenging. I nod and shake my head in what I think are the appropriate places. The truth is, I'm not listening to her. I can't marry the girl who killed her father with the one before me now.

She slathers her toast in raspberry jam and informs me she's going to eat it upstairs while she gets her books ready for school.

'You're going to school?' I ask in disbelief.

'Yeah, where else would I be going?' Her eyebrows draw together. 'Why are you acting strangely?'

I shrug. 'I wasn't aware that I was.'

'And they say teenagers are supposed to be the weird ones.'

As she heads back upstairs, I collapse at the table. Did last night actually happen or did I imagine it? Am I having a breakdown?

I wait until she shouts 'Bye, Mum!' and hear the front door close before I lock it, slip the chain through the latch and hurry into the back garden. Alistair is still in the shed, confirming that no, this is not all in my imagination.

It takes a good hour and a half before I've dug a hole to a depth of about five feet and the length of his body. I'm exhausted and sweat is dripping down my back and chest. But I can't rest until I've dragged his body from the shed into the hole in the most secluded part of the garden. It's hidden by conifers and even Elsie can't see beyond them. Then without any last words or a goodbye, I toss his keys in with him. I use the spade to smother him in a blanket of soil until the ground is level. The excess I spread across the borders. And suddenly, this part of the nightmare is coming to an end. Nina no longer has a father and I no longer have a husband. I wish it could be over as quickly as that.

I'm filthy and am desperate to wash away the stink of death clinging to my skin, but there's something else I need to do first. I grab the suitcases from the basement and stuff Alistair's clothes into them. I want every shoe, shirt, tie, pair of trousers and jumper out of my sight. Then along with his golf clubs – including the one Nina used to kill him – I hide it all under the basement staircase until I can decide what to do with them. Finally, I park his car about half a mile away before returning home.

I drag my feet into the bathroom where I sit under the shower and remain there until the hot water turns cold. My world has caved in on itself and I'm buried under the rubble. All I know is that I must continue to breathe under its weight because Nina needs me. I must protect her from the truth at all costs.

CHAPTER 63

MAGGIE

TWENTY-FIVE YEARS EARLIER

I know how much of a mess I look. I've not eaten a proper meal in five weeks, I can only sleep when I've trebled my dose of tablets and when I look into the mirror I barely recognise the drawn, exhausted shell staring back at me.

The girls at work have started to notice. To their credit, they've rallied around me since I told them Alistair had walked out on me and Nina. Lizzy, the practice manager, suggested I took a week off to gather myself. I thanked her but declined; I'd feel worse if I were at home alone day in, day out, knowing my husband's dead body is less than a hundred feet away from me.

I've put the little energy I have left into being hypervigilant around Nina. I have been walking on eggshells and anticipating the moment when everything about that night comes flooding back to her. But to date, there's been no indication she has the first clue about what she did. Even when I capitalised on her blank memory and told her that her dad had moved out, there wasn't a flicker of recognition in her eyes about what actually happened.

However, she's struggling to make sense of Alistair's sudden departure. She cannot understand why, when they were so close, there has been no contact between them. So I am the only person she can direct her anger at. She has been flying off the handle at the slightest provocation, she slams doors, listens to her music at an unbearable level and does nothing to help around the house. These aren't just ordinary teenage tantrums; they're indicative of something running much deeper. She has made it clear in no uncertain terms that I am to blame for driving her dad away. And I have no choice but to take it on the chin. Because I'd rather face the brunt of her tears and mood swings than have her remember any of that awful, awful night.

Meanwhile I have been trying to continue with life and my job as best I can. I keep making excuses to leave the reception desk, then I lock myself in the bathroom and cry my eyes out. It's where I am now, sitting on the closed lid of a toilet, my arms wrapped around my body, as if giving me the hug I so badly need that nobody else can offer.

When I am alone, I keep replaying my final confrontation with Alistair moments before his death. Nina's reaction was absolute proof that something traumatic had happened to her in there. I think of our last conversation and the fear in his expression; his was the face of a man who had been caught red-handed doing the worst possible thing he could do to a child.

Over and over, I keep asking myself if that was the first time or if it had been going on for years. Had there been red flags staring me in the face all along and I was too trusting or too ignorant to have noticed them? I rack my brains, but I swear I never saw Alistair behave inappropriately around Nina. He didn't look like a child abuser; he was just an attentive, loving husband and a father.

When Nina was born, he was besotted with her and that never changed as she grew up. She'd sit on his lap and watch football matches on TV with him, they'd sing along to ABBA records, bake together and he'd take her to the cinema to watch Disney films. Sometimes when I felt excluded from their club, I'd remind myself that Nina was lucky to have had the love of two parents while I barely had the attention of one. How could she have continued to adore him after what he did to her? Had she started splitting herself into two as a way of dealing with the two versions of her dad? And when she heard me confronting him that night outside her room – had that forged those two Ninas into the furious shadow I watched execute her father?

I didn't think it was possible to fall out of love with someone so quickly, but now all I feel is hatred towards the man I once adored. I refuse to think about the good times or the love and the intimacy we shared. I'm not going to search for him in the identity of my daughter. As far as I am concerned, he never happened. I won't miss him or grieve for him or imagine how our life might have been. I am rewriting our history. It has always been and always will be just Nina and me. I am not sorry that he's dead, only that it wasn't me who killed him.

CHAPTER 64

MAGGIE

TWENTY-FIVE YEARS EARLIER

I find what I am looking for in Dr King's office. He has an extensive library of medical journals and books. Some are old and bound in leather covers; others are modern textbooks lined up beside folders of papers and back issues of *The Lancet*.

I volunteered to work late tonight and as soon as the last GP left the building, I locked the doors behind her and drew the blinds shut. Then I made my way inside Dr King's room and began my search. I need to know what I am dealing with.

I haven't said a word to Nina about what happened the night she killed her father three months ago. And she finally appears to have bought into my lie that he's simply abandoned us. However, protecting her from the truth has come at the expense of our relationship. And I suspect the part of her brain that's burying what Alistair did to her isn't able to hide it completely. It's starting to reveal itself in the way she's punishing me by engaging in sexual activity. One of the school mums told me she saw Nina and Saffron with a group of older-looking boys drinking cans of alcohol at the Racecourse last week. I'm convinced I saw love bites around her neck. But I was too afraid to confront her about them and risk upsetting the apple cart.

I get to work immediately, sifting through then replacing each book and journal on the shelves in exactly the same position as I found them. Hours later and when I'm two-thirds of the way through, I stumble across a possible answer. The book dates back to the early 1980s and lists every recognised mental health condition. It describes symptoms and potential causes, alongside case studies and suggested methods of treatment. My eyes scan up and down each page as I pore over each one. Finally, I locate something resembling Nina's behaviour.

'"Psychogenic fugue",' I read aloud. '"This psychological state occurs when someone loses awareness of their identity. Often, they participate in unexpected movement or travel. However, when consciousness returns, they often find themselves somewhere with no memory of how they reached it. It is similar to amnesia, but is frequently found in people who have experienced dissociative identity disorder. That is a condition created by the brain as a defence against trauma to help disconnect from extreme psychological distress. Events often include natural disasters, conflict, extreme violence, domestic abuse or a history of child abuse."' Even reading the words 'child abuse' makes me shudder. But I continue. '"Victims are physically and mentally escaping an environment they find threatening or unbearable. Psychogenic fugue can last for hours, weeks or even months. And when it has run its course, it is unlikely they will remember what happened."'

I pause to digest this new information. Nina ticks every box.

'"The condition is so rare that there is currently no standard treatment for it",' the passage summarises. '"The most effective therapy is to remove a person from the threat of a stressful situation to discourage any future threats.'"

I take a deep breath as I realise I'm left with two options. I can take Nina to see a professional, and potentially subject her to more psychological trauma as they encourage her to unlock her repressed memories. Or we continue as we are, with me trying to keep her away from stressful situations. I decide to protect my little girl myself. I can't risk unlocking the box she has consigned her dad's abuse to. I cannot bear to see those hollow vacant eyes again or have her find out what she did to the man she adored. It's going to be an uphill struggle, especially with the pressures teenagers face. And what's life going to throw at her when she moves into adulthood? How am I going to protect her for the rest of her life? It's impossible. But I must give it my best shot. I have to prevent her from remembering the past to stop her from ruining her future.

CHAPTER 65

NINA

I have spent most of the evening holed up in the downstairs toilet. I can't recall a time when I've had such a chronically nervous stomach. I throw cold water over my face to try and calm myself down. I've only just doused the room with a can of air freshener when I hear a knocking at the door. Dylan is about to return to the house for the first time since the day he was born.

'Come in, come in,' I encourage as I hold the door open. I wonder if Maggie saw him parking his car outside and walking up the drive. I hope so, because it'll be killing her not knowing who he is.

He slips off his jacket and hangs it up on a peg.

'Are you not wearing the one I bought you?' I ask.

'Not tonight, no.'

'That's a shame. I'd like to have seen you in it.'

'Another time.'

'Is there something wrong with it? I might be able to exchange it.'

'No, it's fine, Nina,' he says firmly, and I lead him into the kitchen.

'Okay, well, welcome, it's lovely to have you here at last. I hope you like beef Wellington.'

'Yes,' he replies, but there's something a little offish about the way he says it. Perhaps I'm being super-sensitive because I'm so anxious. I'm determined to ensure tonight goes perfectly because I have something to ask him. I'll have to choose my moment, though.

'So this is the house where I was born?' he says, peering out from the kitchen window and into the garden.

I nod.

'And out there, that's where you were told I was buried?'

'Yes,' I say quietly. 'Would you like to see it?'

His head turns quickly and he looks at me as if I'm mad. I know it's an insensitive suggestion. Who would want to see their own grave?

'No, thank you,' he replies. 'Why did you never move away from here? I don't think I could have stayed once I found out the truth.'

'It's just one of those things,' I reply. 'Sometimes you get stuck in a rut and it's hard to get yourself out of it. And for so many years, I thought you were here and I didn't want to leave you. You were all I had.'

I don't think he knows how to respond so he doesn't acknowledge it. 'I would like to see the room where I was born though.'

'Okay.'

Time and time again, I've put Dylan off visiting the house because of Maggie. The soundproofing makes it impossible for any noise upstairs to penetrate down here, and vice versa. But still I was reluctant to take the risk. However, because he has been so insistent of late, I finally gave in and agreed.

I lead him upstairs to the bedroom I've had since I was a child. Not for the first time when we're together, I'm a little embarrassed by how little my life has progressed. I stand at the doorway as he enters and looks around. I explain to him again how swiftly he was taken away from me, but he doesn't seem as interested as he has been when I've recalled the story before. Perhaps I'm becoming repetitive.

'Do you have photos of my grandparents?' he asks. 'I didn't see any downstairs.'

'They're all down in the basement, Dylan. I can have a look for them the next time you come.'

'It's Bobby,' he replies abruptly.

I've been making that mistake more frequently recently. He offers a smile as an afterthought but it's disingenuous.

'Bobby,' I repeat. The nickname his family has given him still snags in my throat. In my head he will always be Dylan.

As we make our way downstairs, he passes the partition wall and door that leads to Maggie's floor. I see he's curious as to what's up there so I beat him to the punch. 'It keeps the heating bills down if I keep that section of the house closed. It's a big house for one person.'

I don't know whether it's being here that's making him awkward, but something is amiss even when we tuck into dinner in the kitchen. I'm generating all our conversations and if I'm being honest, it has been like this the last few times we have come together. I've tried to shrug it off and convince myself I'm wrong, but Dylan no longer appears to share my level of enthusiasm for our get-togethers. They've slipped from fortnightly to monthly, and several times, he has cancelled at the last minute. I feel him slipping through my fingers and I don't know how to stop it from happening. Perhaps I should be flattered – he no longer thinks of me as a novelty but a regular part of his life and this is how he behaves with everyone he loves. Still, it doesn't settle comfortably with me.

'Is everything okay with you?' I ask, and he nods. 'It's just that you seem a little distant.'

'I went to see Jon Hunter's grave yesterday. I found the location on a fan site.'

I hesitate. It's the last thing I expected him to say. 'Why?'

'I don't know. Perhaps to get some closure, I'm not sure.'

'And did it work?'

'Not really. He doesn't even have a headstone. It was just a raised bed of soil. I left a bunch of flowers on it. It was the only one.'

'I think you have to wait until the ground levels out before you can fit a headstone.'

'Where are my grandparents buried?'

'Not far from here. What about Jon? Where did they bury him?'

'You don't know?'

'No.' My face reddens.

'The village where his parents still live. Great Houghton. I thought about going to see them.'

'Why didn't you?'

'I don't know. Perhaps raking up the past isn't always a good thing.'

I recall making the trip there myself after Jon refused to grant me a visiting order to see him in prison. Even when I explained who I was and that I'd lost his baby two years earlier, they wouldn't believe me and refused to talk their son into seeing me. They told me I wasn't the first girl to turn up on their doorstep with a 'sick fantasy relationship' and that I wouldn't be the last. Then they demanded I leave, and I never returned. I am unsure of what else to say to Dylan, so we eat in an uncomfortable silence for a while.

'How are your parents?' I ask eventually.

'They're good,' he replies.

'Have you given any more thought to telling them about me?'

He shakes his head. 'Like I've said before, it's not the right time.'

'It's been two years now.'

'I know.'

'You have every right to want to spend time with me. What's the worst that could happen if you told them?'

'They'd be upset.'

'Don't they want you to be happy?'

'Of course.'

I steel myself for what I'm going to suggest. I've rehearsed it many times but I need to make it sound so casual, like it has only just come to me in the moment. 'You know that if you told them and if you needed some space afterwards, you could always come and stay here.'

Dylan stops chewing; he's hesitant. 'Thanks,' he replies.

'I mean, it's not like I don't have the space. It would be lovely to have you.'

He nods, but I fear it's more out of politeness than genuine gratitude. I need to sell him the benefits.

'You can could come and go as you pleased, if you had any friends who wanted to stay over, that'd be fine too. You could redecorate a room to your taste . . . whatever makes you comfortable. It'd be your house just as much as it is mine.' I stop when I sense I'm becoming too animated, too pushy. But the idea of having my son live with me excites me. 'Is the food all right?' I ask instead.

'It's great,' he says.

'Only you've not eaten much of the beef. Have I overcooked it? I have some steak in the fridge if you want me to fry that instead . . .'

'No, it's fine. I try not to eat too much red meat.'

'Really? Why? The iron is good for you.'

'My grandfather had bowel cancer a couple of years ago so we try and avoid it at home.'

'Well, if it's hereditary it's not going to affect you, is it? There's no history of bowel cancer in your real family.' I fail to mention the lump in Maggie's breast that is quietly causing a division in the house.

'They *are* my real family,' he responds.

He doesn't understand what I'm trying to say so I try to clarify. 'I understand why you might think that, but technically they're just the family who took you in. You and I are related by blood.'

He puts his knife and fork down on his plate with a clank. 'They did more than just "take me in", Nina. They gave me a home; they gave me a life.'

'Yours wasn't a life to be given away. And if they can't cope with how close you and I have become, then perhaps they don't have your best interests at heart.'

'Like I've explained to you many times before, I don't want to hurt them.'

'I know that, but maybe putting their feelings first isn't always the right thing to do. What about how you feel? Or how this affects me?'

'You?'

'Well, yes. It's not nice being someone's little secret. It's as if you're ashamed of me.'

'I'm not . . .'

'So you'll tell them soon?'

'I didn't say that.'

'You can come here to live—'

'To live? A few minutes ago you said it was "to stay".'

This is going from bad to worse, and now he's making me muddle my words. 'Live, stay, it doesn't matter. You would enjoy being here, you'd bring new life into this dusty old place.'

'Nina,' he says firmly. 'You can't use me to get out of your rut. It's not fair.'

'I . . . I'm not,' I stutter. 'I just like spending time with you.'

'And that's what we have been doing. But sometimes you can be . . . overbearing.'

'When?'

'You make me feel guilty if I don't stick to your plans. You call if I haven't replied to your texts within fifteen minutes. You get upset if I don't message you before I go to bed. You've turned up at the office to see me unannounced. You keep buying me expensive presents I don't need. It all makes me feel a little . . . awkward.'

He's referring to the designer jacket we saw on a shopping trip to Milton Keynes. He'd been offhand with me that day so when he expressed an interest in it, I looked it up online the next day and ordered it. It cost me a week's wages but if it made him happy, it was worth it. However, when I saw him next and presented it to him, he refused to accept it and asked me to stop buying him things. So I sent it by post to his office instead.

'I do it because that's what parents do. I love you.'

'And then there's tonight and you constantly reminding me that my parents aren't my blood relatives. I know they're not and it doesn't bother me. But it's like you're trying to place a wedge between us so that you can have me for yourself.'

'You're my son. I like being with you.'

'I know, but parents learn to give their kids space too.'

'What for? Why do you need space from me?'

Dylan sighs and shakes his head. 'I think it's time I left,' he replies, and dabs at his mouth with a napkin before rising to his feet.

'Don't go,' I say quickly, and follow him into the hallway where he reaches for his coat. 'I'm sorry, it won't happen again.'

'I have to go early anyway because I'm going out later.'

'Who with?'

'A friend.'

'What friend? Why didn't you mention it earlier?'

'I'll speak to you soon.'

And without giving me a peck on the cheek or so much as a goodbye, he closes the door quietly behind him.

CHAPTER 66
MAGGIE

Three weeks have passed since I last saw the man in the white car arrive at the house, then leave soon after. And in the back of my mind, I fear he's not going to return. However, I haven't let my doubts stop me from making preparations in case he enters the house again. My plan involves the bathtub screw, but instead of using it as a weapon, I'm using it as a tool.

Since the idea came to me, I've spent every morning waiting patiently by the window for Nina to leave the house for the library. And once she's out of sight, I make my way down the staircase to the soundproofed partition wall and get to work.

I chose a section furthest away from where Nina might potentially catch sight of it, at the bottom, close to where the skirting board once was. It's neither illuminated by the light coming through the reinforced glass of the Velux roof window nor the bulb at the top of the stairs. The other side of the partition wall is the closest spot to the dining room.

My screw has been galvanised to prevent it from rusting when in contact with water, making it strong. The tip is as sharp as a needle and will take some time to wear down. So I have been using it as leverage to prize away a small section of the wall. The cardboard egg box in that section came off easily, but underneath was a layer of board that had been glued to another board, and that had been attached to the existing plasterboard. From that first day, I knew it was going to be a challenge and I had to be patient. But Lord knows, I have the time and the motivation. I want to survive this lump and I can't do that if I remain trapped up here.

I've been placing a towel under my workstation, collecting debris and rinsing it down the sink rather than trying to flush it away and have some remain at the bottom of the toilet pan. Then before Nina returns home each day, I stick the egg box to the wall with toothpaste and cover my tracks.

I never work when she is here, even at weekends, and only take breaks for lunch. It means that by the end of each day, my legs and arms ache from spending it on all fours, crouching and chipping away at the wall with such a tiny object. I hope it'll be worth it.

My lump has been aching more than ever lately, and I don't know if it's because I have pulled a muscle while working or if something more sinister is happening. I don't want to admit it to myself but I think it's likely to be the latter. Because in the bath this morning, I found a second lump, this time under my left armpit. I am trying to remain calm about it because panicking won't do me any good. But its discovery has given me an added determination to continue with my plan.

My daughter has made her position perfectly clear. She would rather watch me die a drawn-out excruciating death shackled to this house than help me. She is crueller, more spiteful and vengeful than I have given her credit for. And it brings to my surface a resentment of her that I didn't think it possible to possess. If I want to get out of here, I must do it myself.

Now, I stand back and look at what I've accomplished. I've cut away less than a square inch. It's hardly up to the excavation standards of *The Great Escape*, but I'm not senile enough to think I'm going to burrow my way out of here. No, my goal is to clear enough of the soundproofing that when her friend next comes to the house, he can hear me shouting for help through the gap I've etched away. My life is in the hands of a stranger who doesn't yet know I exist.

CHAPTER 67
NINA

My skin is already cold to the touch and the falling drizzle isn't helping. It sticks to my cheeks and mats my hair. But I don't look for shelter. Instead I remain where I am. I just need a few more minutes. Then I'll be ready.

The house ahead is located at the end of a horseshoe-shaped gravel driveway. I count half a dozen cars parked bumper to bumper in front of the three-storey property. I'm assuming it was once a manor house and at some point in its history, it was broken up into three separate homes. They're still an enviable size.

I pull the hood of my coat up over my head. I want to feel warm again, and the inside of that home looks so inviting from out here in the darkness. From inside those thick stone walls I can hear the faint sound of music playing. I look at my phone. It's only just gone 8 p.m. and the party sounds as if it's in full swing already.

It's a sixtieth birthday celebration and there are banners in colourful lettering hanging from the double entrance doors. Occasionally someone passes the window wearing a paper hat or carrying a drink. Headlights illuminate the garden and I move to one side as a vehicle parks on the grass verge. Three people leave the car; two adults and a boy. I have a *Sliding Doors* moment and wonder, if things had been different, could they have been me, Jon and Dylan? To have had that life.

Once they're a few feet ahead, I take a deep breath and follow them. My handbag hangs from my shoulder and I clutch a sparkly silver bag in the other. The scale of this party leaves me embarrassed by the bottle of supermarket Prosecco I'm bringing to it.

I can't wait to go inside and see Dylan. 'Dylan,' I say aloud. I still enjoy how it sounds when it trips from my tongue. It warms me in the cold air. I've decided I'm not calling him Bobby any more, despite his requests. It's not the name I gave him; it's not the one on his birth certificate. I don't care if he or the rest of the world refers to him by his nickname because the rest of the world didn't give birth to him. And neither did the woman inside that house who calls herself his mother. I reserve the right to call him what I want because I am Dylan's mum.

I'm convinced it's her fault that I haven't seen him in the last three weeks. Since our misunderstanding over dinner at my house, our catch-ups have ground to a sudden halt. His texts have also been less frequent. On the coach up here, I went through my phone and counted them. For every six I send, I receive one reply, and that's often brief and without sentiment. I toyed with confronting him about it so that he's aware of how much it's upset me, but I decided against it. It physically hurts not to be around him more often. I don't sleep well, I've stopped swimming and I've gone back to my unhealthy eating habits. Our separation is making me increasingly resentful of Maggie, too. That's why I'm here tonight, to get things out in the open and put it all right. To get my son back for a second time.

I try and picture Dylan's face when he sees I'm here at his family home. I really think he'll appreciate the effort I've gone to.

I haven't been invited as such, and I'm not daft, I know that I'll be the last person he'll be expecting to see at his mum's party. In fact it's an occasion I only discovered by chance a few weeks before our falling out. He was standing in a long queue waiting to pay the cashier at a petrol station while I waited inside his car. I went through his phone, flicking through his emails like most parents do, when I discovered one he had sent to a male friend inviting him to the party. I took a picture of the message with my own phone.

It was only when I returned home and reread the email that I noticed it contrasted with how he texts and emails me. It was littered with emojis and signed off with two kisses. It was almost flirtatious. I googled the recipient's name and found a handsome blond lad, Noah Bailey, on Instagram. There was a heaviness in my chest when I saw the number of photographs of him and Dylan together. They were clearly in a relationship and had even holidayed in Edinburgh, a trip that my son hadn't seen fit to mention to me.

My first response was disappointment that he was putting yet another person ahead of his mum. His *real* mum. Not only was I competing for attention with Dylan's fake family, but also this boy. He was a complication and he was coming between us. Then after our falling out at my house, I knew that I was slipping further and further down the pecking order. After a few days of dwelling on it, the frustration became too much. I had to say something. I messaged this Noah and suggested he might want to cool it with Dylan as he had other priorities in his life. I heard nothing in return until my son called the following afternoon.

'How could you?' he snapped. 'You had no right to send that message.'

'Well, if I hadn't, when would you have got in touch?'

'I have my own life, Nina. I keep trying to tell you that but you don't listen. You have to give me some space.'

'I'm not saying that you don't have your own life, I'm just reminding you that I've already missed out on so much, I don't want to miss anything else. You owe me that.'

'I'm sorry, but I don't owe you anything.'

'What do you mean?'

'I mean that what your mum did to us was terrible. But in the long run, it was you that she hurt, not me. It didn't do me any harm. And I'm sorry if that sounds blunt or even cruel because I really don't mean it to. But you have to understand – while I'd like you to be a part of my life, you cannot be all of it. If you can't respect my space and my relationships then you can't be in it.'

The sharpness of his words robbed me of my breath. 'Let's talk about this in person,' I begged.

'No, Nina, not at the moment. I think in the long run, a little distance now will do us some good.'

After he hung up, I clutched the phone to my chest and spent the rest of the night in tears, waiting for him to acknowledge his mistake and call back. But he didn't. It's been a week since he last replied to a text, so here I am to talk this through in person.

The doors ahead open and the people in front of me are greeted by a woman with wide-open arms. She offers kisses to both cheeks of each guest before they are ushered inside. As the door closes, I take a deep breath and then slip inside behind them.

'Room for a little one?' I ask, and without giving her the opportunity to respond, I kiss her cheeks first. 'I'm sorry I'm late. You look amazing.'

'Oh thank you,' she says politely, but she has as much of an idea of who I am as I do of her. 'Can I take your coat?'

'Lovely,' I reply, and slip it off while she takes it to a nearby cloakroom. 'Where shall I leave this?' I ask, pointing to the bottle in the bag.

'If you want to give it to the birthday girl herself, I saw her a few minutes ago in the orangery with the girls from the WI.'

The orangery, I repeat to myself. *It's just a fancy name for a conservatory.* I give her a controlled smile and make my way along a corridor and in the direction of the music. I should be crippled with anxiety but I'm not, and that fills me with extra confidence that I'm doing the right thing by being here.

I take my time so that I can absorb my surroundings. It's apparent Dylan downplayed the description of his home. It's beautiful. Everything is painted white and grey and each floor is parquet. The hallway is vast with its crystal light-fittings, side tables, glass ornaments, white potted orchids and family photographs in bejewelled framing. I pause to pick one up – I recognise a young Dylan as he is the only dark-haired child; the rest are blond. I remember what his adoptive mother looks like from the photos he showed me. In another, she is lying on a white sofa, holding him up in the air. His face is illuminated by the widest of smiles and I find myself replicating it. There are more of him and his pretend brothers and sisters taken throughout the years: holidaying in one of the Disney parks, playing with buckets and spades on golden sandy beaches, and at the top of a skyscraper overlooking New York's Central Park. Between them, Dylan's parents and Maggie took away my opportunity to give these things to him.

Eventually I reach the orangery at the rear of the house. It's the same size as the ground floor of my home, only with added flashing disco lights. Guests are dancing and singing along to songs I recognise from the 1980s. Dylan's adoptive parents have a lot of friends. But if I had their money, I'd have a lot of friends too.

I look around but I can't see my son. I find myself making my way back towards a grand wooden staircase that reminds me of the repeats I watch of *Downton Abbey*. I climb them and count eight doors leading off the landing. The walls are scattered with more family photographs of the children as babies. I stop to examine more of my son. He's the cuckoo in the nest. All I need is for him to see what I see and that he could have a better, more loving home with me and not them. In one photograph he is alone and pedalling on a little blue bike and I imagine myself pushing him on it along a path. I remove the picture from the wall and slide the photo from it, placing it inside my handbag.

Only after opening several doors do I finally arrive at Dylan's room. I recognise his coat lying on the bed next to an iPad. I switch it on, use his date of birth as his passcode and examine his search history. Among the football scores, porn sites and his own newspaper's website are many searches for Jon Hunter. I wonder what he thinks when he reads those stories and examines those photographs. Does he see what I see, all those missed years and opportunities with his real family?

I open the doors to his wardrobe, smelling his shirts and rubbing his jumpers against my cheeks and neck. I find a scarf in the Burberry pattern and slip that inside my handbag too. Finally, I spray one of his colognes on to my wrists, wait a few seconds, and breathe it in.

I'm halfway back down the stairs when Dylan appears below me, arm in arm with his adoptive mother. They are laughing together and he doesn't see me at first. The venom I carry for her rises up the back of my throat and I swallow to force it back down.

I wait for my son to spot me, and when he does, he stops in his tracks, the colour draining from his face.

CHAPTER 68
NINA

Dylan's forehead wrinkles as I descend his staircase. He shakes his head as if he doubts what he is seeing. He would rather believe his eyes are playing tricks on him than accept his birth mother is actually in his house.

'Nina,' he whispers.

His adoptive mum looks at him, as if she knows something has spooked him. 'Bobby?' she asks, but he doesn't reply. He is too busy staring at me.

'Surprise!' I say, and make my way down the rest of the stairs and hug him. His arms don't reciprocate.

'What . . . why are you . . .' His voice trails off.

'I thought it'd be a good opportunity to meet your mum,' I reply, the word 'mum' spat out like a mouthful of nails. 'Hello.' I offer her my broadest smile. I hold my hand out to take hers and scrape a finger on the huge rock attached to her ring. 'I'm Nina, it's lovely to meet you. And happy birthday.' I pass her the bag with the Prosecco inside it.

'I'm Jane, and thank you, it's very kind,' she says without looking inside. I can tell she's curious as to who I am, but my son is too gobsmacked to offer an explanation.

'Are you having a good night?'

'Yes, it's been wonderful. Are you and Bobby colleagues?'

I give an exaggerated laugh before he can reply. 'No, I doubt I'd be able to write a newspaper story if my life depended on it.'

'So how do you know one another?'

'Do you want to tell her, Dylan?' I say.

'Dylan?' she repeats and looks to him again. 'Why is she calling you . . .'

And then the penny drops, but with the force of a thousand-ton weight. 'Nina,' she gasps. Her head swiftly turns to me, to Dylan and then to me again. She sees the resemblance. And now she is as pale as my son.

'I'm sorry, I should have introduced myself properly. I'm Dylan's mum.'

Jane takes a step back and releases her grip on his arm. She looks to him for confirmation.

'Is this true?' she asks. But she knows the answer by the look on his face.

The front doorbell chimes and interrupts us. He takes my arm – too forcefully for my liking – and leads me towards a pair of doors and a darkened room. He turns the lights on to reveal a home office. There's a desk on one side and a chesterfield armchair on the other. Jane follows us in and shuts the doors behind us. She doesn't offer me a seat.

'We've not met before,' I continue. 'I was drugged and unconscious when you took my son from me.' She doesn't retaliate because she doesn't have a leg to stand on.

'I don't understand,' Dylan says. 'What are you doing here? I didn't invite you.'

'You two know each other?' a shocked Jane asks, and Dylan nods. 'How did this happen?' She turns to me. 'Did you come looking for him?' It's more of an accusation than a question.

'Actually, no, my son found me, didn't you?'

I cannot deny the satisfaction it brings me to wound her with my words. Now she turns to him and I see the tears forming in his eyes. But he doesn't offer a reply. I don't think he wants to hurt her so I speak for him. 'We've spent a lot of time together over the last two years, haven't we, Dylan?'

'Two years?' Jane repeats, and shakes her head.

'We meet regularly; sometimes I'll come up here and other times, he'll come down to see me. I only live in Northampton so I'm practically on your doorstep. But you probably remember that.'

We are joined by Oscar who charges towards me, resting his front paws on my thighs. He licks my hands as I make a fuss of him. 'It's good to see you again!' I tell him, and catch Jane looking at Oscar as if he too has betrayed her.

'What are you doing here?' Dylan repeats.

'I wanted to meet the woman who's been looking after you.'

'I haven't just been "looking after him",' Jane says. 'He is my son.'

'Not biologically though, is he?'

'I loved him and raised him when you couldn't.'

'The choice was taken away from me, Jane. It was my mother who gave him up, not me. It's a long story that I'm sure Dylan will fill you in on later. But imagine my surprise when he suddenly turned up on my doorstep wanting a relationship with me. *His mother.*'

Each new revelation arrives like a slap to her face. I know that none of this is her fault but I don't care. Even if she didn't want to admit it, surely she must have always known she has only ever had Dylan on loan?

She turns her back on both of us, leaning on the desk and propping herself up with her hands. Dylan tries to comfort her with an arm around her shoulder and I feel a tinge of envy that he hasn't done the same to me since I arrived.

'I didn't want you to find out like this,' he tells her. 'I just wanted to learn more about where I was from.'

'I'm not upset about that, I'm upset that you didn't talk to your dad or me first. Do your brothers and sister know about her?'

'Her?' I repeat.

Jane glares at me. 'About Nina.'

'About his mother.'

'I *am* his mother.'

'Please stop it,' Dylan interrupts. 'Nina, I think you should go.'

'Why?' I ask.

'Because you're upsetting Mum.'

'Dylan—'

Jane turns quickly and yells: 'His name is Bobby, for God's sake. Call him by his name!'

The anger rises inside me and suddenly she is the only thing I see in the room. Tearing him from my arms when I didn't have the strength or knowledge to fight for him wasn't enough for her; now she wants to keep me from him for a second time. She already has everything – a husband, biological children and a house to die for. Why does she want my son too? Between them, she and Maggie have conspired to destroy me. I hate her. Slowly, Jane becomes surrounded by shades of red and black and I'm overcome by the need to punish her; I want to hurt her *so badly*. I want to make her understand what she has done; I want her to know that this beautiful young man belongs to me and not her. I want to keep him from her forever. My fists clench, and without meaning to, my arm stretches towards a glass paperweight on a shelf.

'Nina,' Dylan says, more assertively this time. His voice is enough to shine light upon my darkness. 'Just go home, please. For my sake.'

I hesitate for a moment until I am more myself again. 'But that's why I'm here – for your sake.'

'I don't want to talk to you right now, you're causing too much damage. You have to leave.'

'But she needs to know the truth. We all need the truth. Look what happens when lies get in the way. Look what it did to us.'

I watch as Jane shakes her head and as Dylan pulls her into his shoulder, she cries. She loves him unconditionally and I hate her for it. She was supposed to be furious with him for going behind her back and finding me. She was supposed to ask him to leave, and then he would come and live under my roof. Then we could be a proper family. I don't know how I would have explained Maggie, but there would have been a way; there always is. He would have understood how I've punished Maggie because he and I are the same. Instead, he is choosing Jane over me. And it's killing me.

I watch as he leads her out of the office, up the stairs and out of sight. I know in that moment I will never see him again. The music continues and people pass me by in the corridor but they don't see me. They don't know who I really am. I am nothing to them, and without my son, I am nothing to myself.

CHAPTER 69
NINA

'No, no, no,' I mutter aloud when I check my phone's screen. A white flashing symbol of a plug and a wire indicates the battery needs recharging. I'd left it plugged in overnight next to my bed and turned the ringer up to loud; not that I slept much anyway. But I must have forgotten to turn the socket switch on.

I panic as I move briskly around the library, asking each colleague I come into contact with if they have a phone charger on the premises that I can borrow. With each 'no' it feels as if a snake is wrapping itself around my chest and neck and is slowly squeezing the life from me.

Finally, Jenna upstairs in the small-business support section hands me a charger from her desk drawer. I don't even think I offer her a thank you. Instead, I rush into an empty meeting pod and plug the phone into the USB port of a plug socket.

I've left a trolley containing today's delivery of new books hidden at the very back of the library. I'll get to them later; now, this is my priority. I hover over my phone, waiting ten unbearable minutes before it has received just enough charge to bring it back to life. Then I type in my passcode and wait. Eventually, a text message appears and my heart starts beating wildly. The disappointment is immediate and I want to hurl the phone at the wall – it's from the surgery about a missed dental appointment, not my son.

It has been exactly eight days since I last saw Dylan at his family home. I have tried calling him, texting him and emailing him and he has ignored every message. I even took a train to Leicester to confront him face to face, only to be told by the newspaper's receptionist that he'd taken some time off for 'personal reasons'. I considered paying another visit to his house but talked myself out of it. I couldn't bear to see the woman who calls herself his mother again.

The silence between us is all her doing, I am sure of it. I can picture her, turning on the waterworks, expensive eyeliner streaking down her Botox-filled face like an expressionless, sinister clown. I can hear her telling him how disappointed in him she is for coming to find me without asking for her blessing. Newsflash, you stupid cow, he doesn't need your permission! Who the hell does she think she is to question why he wanted to find me? What is unnatural is forcing him to stay with her!

The rage inside me builds steadily as I imagine how Jane is using emotional blackmail to keep us apart. And the worst thing about it is that Dylan will be falling for it because he won't want to upset her. He, like me, is an innocent party in all of this. We are pawns in other people's games. We don't want to hurt anyone but, in trying to keep everyone else happy, we sacrifice the most.

I miss Dylan now every bit as much as I did the moment Maggie whisked him away from me on the day of his birth. In fact, now it's even worse because I've got to know him. I know how it feels to be someone's parent and to have it whipped away from me twice.

I feel sick at the thought of never hearing from him again. I scroll through my phone and reread our older messages. He has been in my life for such a short period of time, yet he's filled a gap in me the size of the Grand Canyon. I text him one last time. I'm not proud of how desperate I sound. I say anything I can think of to get him back. If he has any love or compassion for me whatsoever, he will reply.

'What's wrong, hun?' Jenna asks. I jump, not having heard her approach.

'I'm fine,' I say, and wipe my moist eyes with my fingertips. It's clear that I'm anything but fine, and she looks at me sympathetically.

'Do you want to tell me about it over a cuppa?'

'No, no, I'm okay, but thank you. It's just stuff to do with my mum.' My colleagues know about Mum's 'dementia' and are sympathetic. I don't like being an object of pity but sometimes, like now, I use it to my advantage.

Jenna nods. 'Well, you know where I am if you need me,' she adds, then leaves me alone.

I take another look at my emails, my junk folder, then Messenger, but none contain messages from Dylan that I've missed.

I return to the ground level of the library and without warning, Maggie's face flashes before me. I shut my eyes, clench my fists and make her disappear. This all began with her lies and separating me from my child. This is her fault. She is the reason Dylan and I are estranged. She is the architect of my misery. Since discovering her lump, she's fooled me into no longer thinking we are on opposing sides. I've been an idiot. She is doing to me what Dylan's mum is doing to him. We are being manipulated. And we have fallen for it because he and I are good people with huge hearts.

Maggie needs to be reminded of her place. Despite the cruelty, the selfishness and the pain she has caused, I still found a way to care. But not any more. She is the person I share the house with, nothing more, nothing less. She means no more to me than the curtains that hide what goes on in there, the floorboards I walk over or the doors we use to separate us.

And things at home are about to take a very nasty turn for my mother.

CHAPTER 70

MAGGIE

What Nina does the moment after she opens the door to my section of the house tells me about the mood she is in.

If she shouts 'Hiya', then she is in a good mood. If she yells 'Is anyone up there?' she thinks she's being funny, and chances are she will be in a brash mood. If it's a simple 'Maggie', she'll be feeling churlish and dinner won't last for long. But if once the door is unlocked and pushed open she leaves without a word, well, those are the dinners that fill me with dread. They're unpredictable – and I sense tonight is to be just that.

My first thought when I hear the door – but not her – is that she's found the hole I have been chipping away at with the screw. I shut my eyes tightly. *She knows what I've been doing.* Last night, the toothpaste I've been using as an adhesive to stick the egg box back on to the wall hadn't been strong enough and it slipped off. I reattached it but now I'm scared it's fallen again and that Nina has opened the door to come upstairs and spotted what it's covering, hence her silence.

I've removed another half an inch of plaster and wood, and I know my objective is close because when I've lain on the floor with my ear pressed to it, I'm just able to hear the boiler inside the airing cupboard gurgling to life. If I can make that out, chances are Nina's friend might be able to hear me when I shout for help. Going by the depth of the gap, I must have reached the final layer of plasterboard. I stopped there because if I go too deep, I risk creating a hole that Nina could spot from the other side. Then all of this will have been for nothing. Instead, I moved on to another section.

Nina's silence is killing me, so as quietly as I can, considering I have a chain attached to my ankle, I move towards the doorway and peek down the stairs. The door is wide open but she's not in sight. I make my descent and as I reach the landing of the first floor, I'm relieved to see the egg box is still in place over the hole.

I've been left to make my own way to the dining room, and once inside, I take my usual seat. The plastic cutlery has returned and the tabletop is also lacking the usual array of vitamins, seeds and supplements. She's used my grandmother's lace tablecloth. I see that it's shrunk and is no longer an ivory colour, more like a washed-out grey. She is punishing me. But if it's not for hacking away at the soundproofing, what does she think I've done?

I don't have time to question it because she appears. The tray she holds contains a large porcelain cooking pot with steam rising from under a lid. I assume it's another stew. There's also a bread knife and an uncut loaf. I offer her a smile and a hello but the corners of her mouth barely rise when she returns the greeting. She's in a foul mood, I can tell.

Nina uses a ladle to fill both our bowls and then hacks into the loaf. She takes a slice for herself but when I reach to help myself, her eyes narrow, which tells me that bread is not on my menu. We begin to eat in silence. The beef and potatoes are overcooked but I don't complain. I wait a few moments before bringing up the latest development with my lump. It's a desperate last-ditch attempt to make her see reason.

'What do you mean, it's *tender*?' she asks, emphasising the word and looking at me as if I'm exaggerating.

'I mean it's sore. Over the last couple of weeks, it's begun to ache, like a dull throbbing sensation. And I think I might have found a second one under my left arm.'

'You either *think* you've found one or you *have* found one.'

'Well then, yes, I have found what feels like another lump.'

When she doesn't ask to verify its existence, it's more evidence of what I've suspected for weeks. Nina no longer cares. But instead of feeling deflated, it strengthens my resolve and my escalating resentment towards her.

'I thought you'd like to know; that's why I mentioned it.'

For the first time tonight, Nina looks me directly in the eye. 'And what do you expect me to do about it?'

Such hostility takes me aback. 'You know what you can do,' I say politely. 'You can help me. We've tried your approach. I've changed my diet as you've asked me to, I've taken your herbal remedies and I've read the books you've left. But whatever this . . . *these* . . . things are inside me, I need professional help for them.'

Nina shrugs. 'You didn't want my methods to work in the first place.'

She is spoiling for a fight. It would be in my best interests to back down, but when it comes to this lump, where has that got me? No closer to seeing a doctor. *So no*, I decide. *I'm going to fight my corner*. 'Of course I wanted them to work,' I say. 'But we've tried it your way and now it's time to try mine.'

'Oh come on, Maggie. Be honest. This has been your plan all along. I bet secretly you loved it when you found the first one because you saw it as your golden ticket out of here.'

'You think I want a lump in my breast? Don't be so ridiculous! I'm asking you to show me some compassion. I know I've made some awful mistakes and that you might not think of me as your mum any more, but whether you like it or not, that's what I am. And I am also a human being who needs your help.'

'There's nothing I can do.' She sniffs. 'I warned you two years ago that you've made your bed and that come what may, you'll have to lie in it. And nothing has changed. I'm sorry.'

She's not sorry at all. And I know with certainty that at that moment, this is definitely it. Nina is never going to change her mind. 'What have I done wrong? Because I don't understand. I thought we've been getting on better over the last few weeks?'

She points her finger towards me. 'I can see through you, Maggie, I can see *straight through you*. You're like all those other women who are constantly manipulating their children, playing the guilt card, trying to get them to make choices they don't want to make to suit their own selfish needs. Well, I'm not going to let you win this time. I won't let any of you win. None of you are going to take him away from me again.'

I have no idea to whom she's referring. 'Who?' I ask.

'You know,' she growls. 'You know what people like you do.'

Something has happened since I last saw her two days ago, but I don't know what I am being held accountable for. I should probably leave it alone, but instead, I poke the wasps' nest with a stick. 'I don't Nina, I really don't.'

'My whole life has been shaped into how you wanted me to live. All you ever wanted is a clone who wouldn't leave you. You didn't want me to grow up and have the things other women my age have. You've robbed me of everything.'

I push my plate to one side. 'Where is all this coming from?'

'You've never really loved me. You're too selfish.'

'You don't have the first clue what I have given up for you out of love.'

'Ha!' she scoffs. 'You don't know what it means to love anyone!'

I know I shouldn't, but I can't hold back any longer. 'And you do?' I snap. 'Your heart is so poisonous and your rationale so warped that you put your need for revenge ahead of everything else, including those who care about you!'

'How can you say you love me when you gave my baby away?'

I'm now so incensed I no longer think about what I say before it leaves my mouth. 'I'm glad I did!' I shout. 'You weren't capable of being a mother back then and what you're doing to me is proof that you aren't capable of being a decent human being now. I did the best thing for that little boy because in the end you would have killed him like you're killing me. You're too selfish to be a parent.'

It happens so fast that my eyes barely register it. Nina grabs her glass and hurls it across the room, smashing it against the wall. Pieces scatter across the carpet. 'Selfish?' she screams. 'You have the nerve to call me selfish! After what you've done? How fucking dare you!'

She rises to her feet and my body draws in on itself, preparing to cower. Except this time, I stop myself. The realisation is sudden – I will not spend the rest of my life, however brief the rest of it might be, recoiling in her shadow. A strength that I didn't know I possessed rises to the surface. I no longer fear the monster I made.

'I fucking dare,' I growl, and now I'm on my feet too.

'You have taken everything away from me,' she shouts, spit flying from her mouth like tiny bullets. 'You should be on your hands and knees praying to God for forgiveness for what you've done to your child!'

'I've been forced to make decisions that have torn me apart, but they were only because *you* left me with no choice.'

314

Suddenly, Nina shoves me hard against the wall. I lose my balance and drop to the floor. Then I watch as she reaches for the bread knife on the table and stands over me, her knuckles whitening with the force of her grip.

I see it in her. The Nina with no control over her actions has returned. Her eyes have glazed over and right then and there, I know that she is unreachable. The darkness has descended and she isn't my daughter any more. Whatever happens next won't be down to the will of the girl I gave birth to, but as a result of the actions of her father, the man who robbed her of her childhood and set the wheels in motion for all that's followed.

Nina raises the knife above her head but I don't try and protect myself. If I am to die in this moment, then so be it. She will need to look her mother in the eye as she extinguishes the light from behind it.

Without warning, we hear it together.

A voice takes us both by surprise. We turn our heads sharply towards the doorway from where it came.

A man is standing there, a horrified expression across his face. 'Nina?' he asks. 'What are you doing?'

CHAPTER 71

MAGGIE

Nina and I are frozen in the moment, unable to move. I remain on the floor and she looms above me with the knife in her hand. The voice is enough to snap her from her psychosis, something I've never been able to do.

We gawp at the unexplained visitor who has come crashing into our twisted world. My daughter aside, he is the first person I have come face to face with since she locked me up. I stare at the slim young man with his dark hair and pale complexion and wonder if my desperate brain is playing tricks on me. I give serious consideration as to whether she's already stabbed me and I'm in the last throes of death and imagining him. Then something clicks. His frame is familiar; he's Nina's friend, and the man I've seen from a distance through my bedroom window. He is the reason I've been carving out a hole in the wall to alert him to my existence. But now that he's standing in front of me, I am inert.

The silence is interrupted by the sound of metal on wood as Nina places the knife back on the table. Then she takes a step away from me as if this might alter her friend's perception of the chaos he's witnessing. I remain where I am. He looks confused and scared.

'What are you doing here?' she asks, the wind taken from her sails.

'You messaged me threatening to kill yourself if I didn't respond.' She cocks her head to stare at him as if she can't recall doing that. 'Lucky your front door was unlocked. What's going on?' he continues.

His piercing grey eyes look at her, then me, and back at her again. I attempt to rise to my feet but my whole body is shaking like a leaf, making it difficult to stand unaided. I shuffle forward on my bottom like an infant, then use my hands to grip a chair and pull myself up. He moves towards me and places his hand under my arm until I'm on my feet. My legs are still threatening to falter so I steady myself against the tabletop. The noise of the chain draws his attention. He can't seem to comprehend why it's attached to my ankle.

'Dylan,' Nina begins, her voice quavering. 'You came.'

I freeze. *What did she just say?* 'Dylan?' I repeat, and look to her and then at her friend. And for a split second, I don't see him, I see Jon Hunter. I gasp and throw my hands over my mouth as I recognise him as the baby I last saw being carried from the basement in the hope that I might save him from this madness.

'You're . . . you're my grandson!' I whisper.

My words appear to be frightening him further and he turns to Nina. 'I have grandparents? You told me they were all dead!'

Somehow, I'm able to put my thoughts in order. 'She's been keeping me a prisoner for two years,' I spit. 'Please, you have to help me.'

'Nina?' Dylan replies. 'Is this true?'

'She's poorly,' Nina retaliates. 'She has dementia and she doesn't know what she's saying. I'm her carer. I look after her.'

317

'I have no such thing,' I hit back. 'I've been locked upstairs against my will. Look.'

Dylan's eyes follow mine to the cuff and the chain that leads along the corridor and back up the stairs to my floor. 'Why do you have her chained up?' he asks.

'For when I'm at work . . . It's for her own safety. It's not as bad as it looks. She's a danger to herself when she's alone – she goes wandering off. And I can't afford to put her in a care home.'

'But you're at home now, so why is she still padlocked?'

'Dylan, don't listen to her, she's lying,' I plead and grab at his arm. 'Please get me out of here or call the police, call anyone, just get me away from her and let the authorities decide who's telling the truth.'

'No, don't,' Nina says. 'She's manipulating you in the same way Jane does, you know I wouldn't lie to you.' She takes his other arm in her hands. 'You mean everything to me. I wouldn't risk that by not being honest with you.'

'Then why were you holding a knife above her when I arrived?'

'I . . . I . . . I was just trying to scare her into doing what she's told.'

Dylan shakes his head.

'You have to believe me,' she begs. 'She might look harmless but you don't know what she's capable of. She killed my dad – your grandfather – then she tried to keep you and me apart . . . She's a monster.'

When Dylan's jaw drops and his eyes blaze with fear, I know that he believes me.

'I gave you away to Jane because she was a good woman and because I was trying to protect you from Nina,' I interrupt. 'You must believe me when I say that my daughter isn't well. Look at what she's doing to me. If you hadn't arrived when you did, I'd be dead.'

Nina's face creases, confusion contorting it, and it's as if what I'm saying is news to her. Her psychotic rage has taken away any memory of what she was about to do to me with that knife.

'Where's the key for her padlock?' Dylan asks, expressionless.

She shoots him a look that displays her disappointment. 'You're not listening to me!' she counters. 'She's fooling you – you don't know what she's like. You can't take her side.'

'But I can't just pretend I haven't seen that you have my grandmother chained up in your house! Whatever's going on in here isn't normal. You both need help.'

Nina opens her mouth but struggles to find the right words because she knows that what he is saying is correct. Nothing about us or this house or our family is normal. It stopped being that way the day Alistair began abusing his daughter.

'Now give me the key,' he continues.

Nina shakes her head and tightens her jaw.

'Nina,' he says more firmly, but she won't back down. 'Mum,' he asserts. His use of the word appears to surprise her. I wonder if it's the first time he's referred to her as this because she begins to weep. I look to Dylan to gauge his reaction but this is unchartered territory for him and he doesn't know to respond. However, I can't allow him to be sidetracked by sympathy for her. I must put myself first.

'The key is in her pocket,' I say.

'Please don't do this,' sobs Nina, slowly shaking her head as he approaches her. 'I've only done what's best. You have to believe me.'

Dylan stands face to face with her. Her nose is running and her cheeks are wet but she doesn't try and stop him when he slips his hand inside her pocket and pulls out the key ring. 'This is the right thing to do,' he says.

'You're going to leave me, aren't you?' she cries, but he ignores her. Instead, he gives me a smile as if to reassure me that it's all going to be all right. And I believe him. He is the one good thing to come out of today's mess. He crouches and slips the key inside the lock.

And then it happens. My grandson who I never thought I'd see again sets me free.

I look to him with such gratitude that I want to cry. Before I can thank him, he says, 'Come on', and without looking back to his mother, he slips his arm around my waist and we make our way towards the landing.

The noise appears quickly; the familiar sound of a rattling chain. Dylan and I turn together, but barely have time to register the metal cuff swinging in the air before it comes into contact with his forehead. It knocks him flat on to his back.

'No!' I scream and my grandson looks up at me, stunned but unable to comprehend what has just happened. I watch helplessly as Nina lifts the chain and tries to hit him again, but this time she's not as accurate and leaves part of the doorframe in splinters. There's something familiar about the deadened rage in her eyes but I don't have time to dwell on it. Dylan's not quick enough to move for her third shot, and this one catches him again but on the side of his head. There's a sickening crunch of metal against bone. This time, she leaves a dent embedded in his skull.

'Stop it! For God's sake stop it!' I plead. 'He's your son!' But she cannot hear me. Nina's face is once again blank and devoid of all humanity. I look to Dylan again and only when he blinks do I know that he is still alive.

I drop to my knees to try and comfort him but the poor boy is in shock. I grab the oven gloves from the table to stem the blood seeping from the dent in his head, which is beginning to trickle down his face. Flashbacks to the similar injury Nina gave Alistair return thick and fast. 'It'll be okay, I promise,' I tell Dylan, but I don't know how it will be. 'Where's your phone? I'll call for help.'

I fish around inside his pockets but he pushes me away and slowly turns himself over. He uses his arms to drag himself towards the staircase. Perhaps he is as scared of me as he is of Nina. 'Oh Dylan,' I beg, 'please let me help you. Please give me your phone.'

Now the only sound comes in the form of his desperate wheezes and his clothes brushing against the carpet. I turn to my daughter. 'Nina!' I shout, but I can't get any more words out before she hits me too with the cuff. She wields it clumsily and it strikes my shoulder first, but I dodge it before it can cause too much damage. But it's second time lucky when it hits the side of my head, full on. My ears ring like church bells and the room becomes murky and threatens to darken further. I fight to remain conscious. I'm aware of Nina crouching over me but I can't focus on what she's doing. *Stay awake*, I tell myself. *Stay awake and help Dylan*. He is now on his front, legs stretched behind him, using his elbows and hands to crawl slowly away from both of us.

As my sight returns, my head is already pounding but somehow, I clamber to my feet. But when I try to approach Dylan, I am too unsteady and fall into the wall. He is in a much worse state than I am and yet somehow he has found the strength to begin pulling himself down the staircase, step by step. Once he has managed the first four, he loses his balance. He slides down the rest, hitting his head against the newel post before coming to land at an awkward angle at the base. I catch a glimpse of his face and his eyes are wide open but he is no longer blinking.

'Dylan!' I move towards him but only get so far before I tumble face down to the floor. A searing pain shoots up my leg from where I must have torn something inside. After hitting me with the cuff for the third time, Nina reattaches it to my ankle.

'Look at what you've done,' I bellow, and turn to glare at her. She is motionless, watching us in satisfaction like a gamesmaster who knows her opponents have no chance of winning but is allowing them to go through the motions.

And now it's my turn to lose control. I grab Nina's leg and start punching it and biting it and clawing at it like a wild animal, until she wrestles free and kicks me full in the face. There's a sharp cracking sound and it feels as if the front of my head will explode. She's broken my nose, I'm sure of it. I taste blood in my mouth and it trickles down my throat, choking me.

'You have killed your son!' I continue, then my head starts spinning again, my hearing becomes distorted and my vision blurs. I want to pull myself to my feet and launch at her again but I can barely make her out as she clamps my head with her hands and drags me to the top of the first-floor staircase. I think she's about to push me down it, but instead she continues to drag me along the landing until we reach the second-floor staircase in my section of the house. Then she slams the partition door shut and locks it.

'Nina,' I scream. 'Nina! Let me out of here!'

I'm still flat on my back and can't see what I'm doing, but I feel around the wall and scratch at the egg boxes, bending my fingernails backwards as I try to tear them off. I pound at them with my fists, knowing that I can be heard from the hole I've made, but no longer caring.

My need for freedom has come at a horrendous expense. Nina has killed Dylan, as I always feared she would. And in begging for his help, I am responsible too. This is just as much my fault as it is hers.

Nina can no longer control herself. When she murdered her father, he deserved it. But Dylan didn't; he was innocent. And so was Sally Ann Mitchell.

CHAPTER 72

MAGGIE

TWENTY-THREE YEARS EARLIER

Elsie is puzzled at the sight of the swaddled newborn on the sofa in the basement. She looks at him and then at me. 'Who's this?' she asks. 'And why are you down here?'

I just about manage to release the words 'My grandson' before the tears fall. And then I blurt out the whole sorry mess. My guilt erupts like a volcano. And too much of it has built up inside me to spare her anything. From Nina's first pregnancy to her abusive father, and why I'd told Nina that her baby was born dead: it all comes out in the wash. I'm circling the edge of a nervous break-down and I need help.

By the time I have finished, Elsie has picked Dylan up and is cradling him. I look at them both, paralysed by fear of what I've just done and what is to come. I'm ready for Elsie to read me the riot act and tell me what I know already: I'm out of my depth and I should contact the police. But sometimes, people have a way of surprising you.

'If it were my Barbara, I think I might've done the same thing,' she says. 'When your baby is born, you make a promise that you're going to put them first and do what is necessary to give them the best life possible. Rightly or wrongly, that's what you've done for Nina. And now you've got to do the same for your grandson.'

'I have to get him away from here.'

'I know, and we will.'

'We?'

'Yes, I'll help you.'

'How?'

'I might have a way. I know a family who could help.'

◆ ◆ ◆

Three days after Dylan's birth and I'm in Alistair's car.

Nina assumes he took it with him when she thought he'd left us, but I move it from street to street each week about half a mile from the house. It's far enough away for her not to spot it.

After stalling it for a second time at traffic lights, I keep my foot on the brake and rev the accelerator. I become aware of the scent of Alistair's Feu Orange air freshener hanging from the rear-view mirror. It has long since dried up, yet the smell lingers in the fabric of the seats. I don't want to inhale anything that reminds me of him, so rip it from its chain and toss it behind me.

A seemingly endless set of roadworks stretches along the dual carriageway, reducing it to one lane, and I'm at the end of my tether. I need to get home quickly. I am stuck behind a bus whose driver keeps allowing vehicles to exit a junction ahead. I hold back from leaving my car, banging on his window and hurling abuse at him.

The bus is not the only reason I'm wound up like a coiled spring. I've been forced to make a decision that will forever change the direction of three lives.

I am going to give my daughter's baby away.

I have witnessed first-hand Nina bludgeon her father to death when she was placed under extreme duress. I know I can't trust her with the stresses that motherhood and a newborn baby will bring. Sleepless nights, teething, illnesses, constantly questioning whether you are doing the right thing, comparing yourself to other better mothers who have got it all together . . . I have been through it all. Nina is too young and too weak to cope.

I know I could help her, but I can't be there for every single day of that child's life. How can I rest easy leaving them alone even for a moment? I'd be constantly at my wits' end, waiting for something to provoke her next psychotic episode. I would never forgive myself if I could have prevented her from hurting my grandson.

If that's not enough to justify my and Elsie's plan, then taking him away from his father, a child molester who impregnated a fourteen-year-old girl knowing that she was underage, also makes a compelling case. If Nina could see through him like I do then maybe she too would question Hunter's influence on a child. The thought of how he might warp its mind, or worse, terrifies me. My faith in men as fathers has been irretrievably shattered since Alistair. I will never make the same mistake again.

It is my responsibility to safeguard Dylan and as far as I can see, it will be in his best interests to be far away from the toxic life into which he was conceived. Besides, there is no going back after telling Nina her child was stillborn because of a chromosome deficiency her body doesn't actually have.

'Shit!' I yell and brake hard; I haven't been concentrating on the road and almost collide with the back of another vehicle. The dozen nappies I purchased earlier at Tesco's fly from the back seat into the footwells. Then it dawns on me – they might be the last ones I ever buy for him.

Dylan has been with Elsie and I in the basement for three days now. Having the cellar and the attic converted into habitable spaces are the only things I can thank Alistair for. Each time me or Elsie leaves, we push a mattress in front of the closed door to keep the baby's cries in here, although Nina is still too drugged to hear much. We started feeding the baby milk produced by his mum via a breast pump. I've lied to her – again, explaining this was perfectly normal even after losing a child. It's only later that I worry the sedatives I'm giving her might be passed to him through her milk, so I switch to formula.

Elsie and I have cared for and bonded with Dylan. And as I held him in my arms last night while he drifted into a warm, milky sleep, I knew that deep down, I didn't want to give him away, I really didn't. In spite of myself, I have fallen hook, line and sinker for the little mite.

When finally I reach our house, I glance at my watch – Nina will need another dose of sleeping tablets very soon. When I return to work I'll take some more scripts from Dr King's office and find an alternative medication to manage her.

I'm sure I locked the front door behind me when I left, but it's already open when I turn the key. Puzzled, I close it quickly and climb the stairs.

'Nina, I'm back,' I say as I approach her bedroom. 'Are you awake? Can I get you some tea or a bowl of soup?' But her room is empty. I hesitate and cock my head to one side, but I can't hear her anywhere else. Something isn't right. 'Nina, sweetheart, where are you?' I shout.

There is still no response. I rush around the house, looking into each of the rooms, finally locating her in the second-floor bathroom. She sits on the edge of the bath with her back to me. She is wearing a green parka coat; her hair is untied and resting on the fur of the hood. I can't tell if she is returning or going somewhere. Her demeanour unsettles me.

'Nina, did you not hear me?' I ask gently. 'I've been calling you.'

She doesn't answer.

'What's wrong, are you in pain?'

Again, she fails to reply.

'Honey,' I say, and now I'm barely masking my agitation. 'Please talk to me.'

Slowly, I make my approach and take in her appearance. It's pale and expressionless, precisely how she looked in the aftermath of Alistair's death. My best hope is that this latest psychosis is a delayed reaction to the trauma of losing her baby. It's only then that I notice fresh mud on the sides of her Dr. Martens boots. They have also marked the white bath mat. She has ventured outside.

'Where have you been?' I ask.

Under her thick coat, her chest rises and falls and I assume this is all I am going to get for now. 'Shall I help you back to bed? You need to rest,' I say. I want to get her back quickly in case Dylan's cries can be heard up here. I place my arm around her shoulders and my hand under her arm and raise her to her feet.

There's a reticence between us that feels like it might last forever. But in the end, she doesn't need to speak. It's the sight and sound of the bloody knife falling from inside her sleeve and to the floor that does all the talking.

CHAPTER 73

MAGGIE

TWENTY-THREE YEARS EARLIER

The speed at which I burst through the basement door startles Elsie. Thinking the worst, I push the mattress out of the way in my haste to get through the door, and find her bottle-feeding Dylan. He is tucked safely in the crook of her arm. Music plays quietly from the radio I left her.

'Whatever's the matter?' she asks.

I want to tell her about the knife and that I thought Nina had hurt the two of them, but I don't. I do not want to scare her and there's only so much madness I can lay at Elsie's feet. Whatever Nina has done now, I must shoulder it alone.

'I'm sorry,' I reply. 'The house was quiet and I panicked.'

'We're okay, don't you worry,' Elsie says. 'He had a little bit of a cry earlier but it's only because he was hungry. How's Nina?'

'I need to spend some time with her. Are you okay on your own with Dylan for a little bit longer?'

She nods and I close the door and catch Elsie kissing my grandson's forehead. She is going to miss him as much as I am. I return to the bathroom where I left Nina. I step over the knife and crouch in front of her, placing her hands in mine. There's dried blood on her fingers and sleeves.

She speaks without warning and it makes me jump. 'Jon,' she says, her voice deadpan.

'What about him?' I ask.

'I've seen him,' she says, and I hold my eyes shut for a moment. 'Where?'

'At his place.'

'Did something happen? Is he okay?'

I wait for reassurance but the bloody knife tells me everything she is not. I clean her up, dress her in fresh clothing, feed her two more sleeping tablets and put her to bed. Then I search her coat pocket and find an address on a scrap of paper. There's a spot of blood on it. I can only assume this is where she has been. I clean the handle and blade, then carefully slip it into my own pocket.

◆ ◆ ◆

Within the hour I am standing in Hunter's flat, staring at his unconscious body sprawled across the sofa.

His legs are spread wide, his head is drooped forward and there is drug paraphernalia scattered across a coffee table. In the flickering of the television's light, I spot a needle still wedged into a vein in his forearm. No matter how much I hate him, I'm relieved to hear him breathing. It means Nina hasn't hurt him.

Suddenly, I'm startled by a noise behind me. My head turns quickly to face it. A door in the hall is slightly ajar and from here, it looks like the bathroom. I'm no fighter but I have Nina's vegetable knife poised and I'm prepared to lash out and protect myself if necessary. However, the noise doesn't appear to be coming any closer. The sound is like that of a deflating tyre, only more infrequent. I make my way towards it, pushing the door open with my foot.

The hinges creak before it stops. Something is blocking it from opening completely. I enter and that's when I see her on the floor. Sally Ann Mitchell, the sweet young girl I've chatted to at the surgery, is staring back at me, her big blue eyes as wide open and panicked as they can be. For a moment, neither of us moves, each waiting for the other to react first.

I have little choice but to make my move. With Nina's knife in my pocket I go swiftly towards her and kneel down for a closer look. She is lying on her left side; her arm is stretched out in front of her as if she is trying to grab for something out of reach.

Her right cheek has a two-inch-long gash across it. Her bare arms and hands are dripping with blood from open slash and stab wounds. Some are surface lacerations, others are so deep I spot muscle tissue. But as I look down at her, it's her pregnant stomach that has borne the brunt of the attack. My daughter has done this. *My Nina.* I lean over the bath and vomit. There's only coffee and toast inside me but I repeat the action twice more before wiping my mouth, taking a step backwards and assessing the situation.

I see hope in Sally Ann's eyes now. She recognises me through her haze; she doesn't know how or why I am here but she is grateful. She thinks I am going to help her. Her bottom lip moves as if she is trying to talk. I put my fingers on her wrist but I can barely find a pulse. She is bleeding out and within minutes she will be dead if I don't help her.

'Say aye be,' she whispers, and a small trickle of blood falls from the corner of her mouth and drips to the floor.

'I don't know what you mean,' I reply gently.

'Say aye be,' she repeats. 'Save aye be.' Gradually I understand her. She's saying, 'Save my baby.'

It breaks my heart to see the poor girl like this. I move quickly back into the lounge and locate a telephone. I'm about to lift the receiver and call for help when it strikes me that I can't. It goes against all my instincts. But I have done a lot of things I'm not proud of lately. More than anything in the world I want to help her and her child. *Almost* more than anything. Because I want to protect Nina more. And getting Sally Ann help will have a catastrophic effect on my daughter.

If Sally Ann survives this, how do I explain my presence in her home? If she knows my daughter and can offer a description that leads to Nina's identification, then that is it for her. She will be locked away indefinitely in a young offenders' institute, a prison or a psychiatric facility. I cannot do that to her, so I leave the phone where it is. I remind myself that Nina isn't to blame for this; her dad is, Hunter is, I am. And we are also responsible for what's going to happen to Sally Ann and her baby. *I cannot help you*, I think as I weep. *God knows I want to, but I can't.*

I turn my head to check the lounge – Hunter is still unconscious and I take advantage of it. I dip the blade of the knife in blood from the bathroom floor. Sally Ann's breathing is becoming shallower and for a second, I allow myself to look at her and she is watching my every move, puzzled, but still expecting me to come to her rescue. I want to explain to her why I can't, but I cannot bring myself to say the words.

Back in the lounge, I use my gloved hands to carefully wrap Hunter's fingers and palms around the handle and flick blood on to his skin to suggest that he is responsible for the frenzied attack. There's a pile of his clothes on the floor, so I stretch them out and smear blood on them too. Finally, I take the knife and push it through the sound hole of one of three guitars leaning against the wall in the corner of the room. Then I stand back and survey the crime scene I have manipulated for the good of my family.

I don't know what else I can do or if this will fool the trained eye of the police, but I must try. I want to stay here with Sally Ann; I owe it to her not to let her die alone. But I can't even offer that ounce of compassion. I have to put Nina's and my grandson's needs above hers. I need to get back to them.

I whisper 'Sorry' to her and then rinse my vomit from the bath and without looking at her, I leave Sally Ann to slip away alone. May God forgive me, because I know I never will.

I'm about to leave the flat when I look at Hunter again and I hesitate. This man is no better than Alistair, someone who is willing to destroy the life of a young girl for his own sexual gratification. How many more lives will he ruin before someone steps in and says enough is enough? As my fury towards him builds up inside me like a pressure cooker, it's only then that I understand I need to be the one to put an end to this. I must step up and protect the next girl.

So I approach Hunter, place my thumb on the plunger of the syringe embedded in his forearm and push whatever poison is left in the barrel into his arm. I hover over him but I don't know what I'm expecting to see; perhaps his heart trying to beat its way out of his chest or him fitting and frothing at the mouth. But neither happens and I don't have the time to wait. I push open the front door and I leave both Hunter and Sally Ann to die together.

I feel no guilt for what I have done to him; he has got exactly what he deserves. Instead, I save my guilt for the people who need it and whom I have failed, like Nina and Sally Ann.

CHAPTER 74

MAGGIE

TWENTY-THREE YEARS EARLIER

'We need to get Dylan away from here as soon as possible,' I beg Elsie. I hear the anxiety in my own voice.

'Are you sure you don't want to think about it for longer?' she asks. 'This is a huge decision to make.'

'I'm absolutely positive,' I reply. 'We can't keep him down here. It's for his own safety.'

'Why, has something happened?' She pales as she looks at me for an answer but when I don't offer an explanation, she knows that it's best not to probe any further. 'I'll make the phone call,' she adds.

Elsie leaves me alone in the basement tearfully cradling Dylan and closes the door behind her. I hear her muffled voice as she talks on the phone in the hallway, but not what she is saying. I can't tell her what I found at Hunter's flat. I cannot bring myself to admit what Nina has done now or the extremes I've gone to to cover it up. I can't tell her that I'm worse than my daughter because my attempt to kill Hunter was done consciously. It will be all over the news soon enough. I can only hope that Elsie doesn't put two and two together.

Minutes earlier and as soon as I returned to the house, I asked more about the person she mentioned who might be interested in taking Dylan.

'They're a family I clean for,' she said. 'Jane has three kids of her own but after an ectopic pregnancy she was told not to try for any more. She and her husband have been looking into adoption but the council said they were too old to adopt. They're a good family; he'll want for nothing.'

She went on to explain how they were financially stable, lived on a large estate in the south of the town and that their children attended a private school. It is the security I want for my grandson. 'He'll be safe with them,' she continued. 'I hope it's all right but I took the liberty of calling her when you were out and told her about your . . . situation. All I said was that the baby's mum was underage. She wants to come and meet you both.'

'She can't meet Nina,' I said quickly. 'I won't allow that.'

'I know, I know,' Elsie reassured me. 'I've explained that Nina is going through some "emotional complications" but Jane would still like to talk to you.'

I look at Dylan again. His eyes are open but he can't yet focus on me. I'm glad. I don't want him to see who his grandmother really is. I consider how tonight might be the last time I hold him. Then I think about the frenzied attack on Sally Ann and how I might have murdered Hunter. My grandson should not be around people like us; he deserves so much better. This is the best decision I can make after a series of catastrophically bad ones.

When Jane appears at my front door early that evening, she looks as nervous and as unsure as I do. Elsie ushers her inside and downstairs and I stand holding Dylan, giving the once over to a woman I am entrusting with the life of my flesh and blood. She offers me a sympathetic smile, the kind only another parent can, and as if to say she knows what I am going through. But she can't possibly know. Nobody can, not even Elsie.

I sit on the sofa in the basement, she and Elsie sit on two old garden chairs and we talk. Jane wants to learn as much about Nina and me as I do about her family, which reassures me that she is doing this for the right reasons. She asks if she can meet Nina, but I tell her it's out of the question. 'As far as my daughter is concerned, she wants nothing to do with the baby. Otherwise I'd have helped her to raise him,' I lie. I can't look at Elsie when I say this.

'What about Dylan's father?' asks Jane. 'Shouldn't he have a say?'

'Nina is no longer with him and he has not been in contact with her since the night she fell pregnant. He doesn't know about the baby and Nina is adamant that he never will. She wants what's best for the boy and for herself. And she is convinced that a new life is the solution that suits them all.'

'What about you? How will you cope with this? I'm a mother too, and I can't imagine how I'd feel in your situation. I see from the way you are with him that you love him dearly.'

I'm touched by her consideration. 'It won't be easy, but it's for the best.'

'And what about contact? Will you be expecting us to stay in touch or do you want to visit him? Would you like me to send you photographs?'

I think about it. 'No, I don't think so. It would hurt too much. Dylan needs a fresh start with no reminders of his past. In a few weeks when the dust settles, you should begin the adoption process formally, but I don't want my daughter's name brought into it. Name me as Dylan's biological mother and I'll sign any paperwork you want me to, and speak to any social workers so it'll go smoothly.'

Jane appears reluctant at the thought of having to lie; I must convince her this is the best way. 'If you really want to be a mother again and the council won't let you because they say you're too old, then this will be your only opportunity. How much do you want another baby?'

She wrings her hands and finally nods. 'Do you mind if Elsie and I have a conversation?' she asks, and the two disappear upstairs into the kitchen while I make the most of my remaining time with my grandson.

When they return, I reluctantly hand Dylan to Jane and she's instantly smitten. 'If it was up to me, I'd take him right away,' Jane says. 'But I need to talk to my husband and my children first before we make a decision as a family. Can you give me a few hours?'

'Yes,' I say.

Jane is as good as her word. Just after 11 p.m. and when I've finished feeding Dylan, she and her husband appear and we talk until the early hours. By the time they have finished, they give each other a look as if to say they agree that they are making the right decision. And I know I am too. My grandson and I are to be parted.

'When would you like us to take him?' Jane asks.

'Tonight. Now,' I say. 'Elsie, would you mind gathering his things?'

I ask for a few minutes alone with Dylan, and then it's just him and me in the basement that has become his home. I hug him and kiss him and tell him how much I love him, then dab at my tears as they fall on to his mop of dark hair. Finally, I call Elsie to take him away from me as I cannot bear to watch him leave in another woman's arms. I am grateful he will never see this room again.

Moments later, I hear the front door close, a car engine start and pull away up the street as Dylan's new family leave with their son.

Elsie puts an arm around my shoulders but I tell her that it's all right, I'll be okay. I thank her for everything and apologise for bringing such chaos into her life. And then I return to Nina, still asleep in her bed, completely unaware of what I have taken from her. I pull her duvet back and climb in, curling up behind her, holding on to her and vowing never to let go of her again. For the rest of my life, her safety and mental well-being will be my only priorities.

CHAPTER 75
MAGGIE

I remain in darkness as the hours pass. My ear is pressed to the tiny section of the partition wall I've chipped away at. I don't want to move from here until I know what has happened to my grandson's body.

My neck has stiffened, my head throbs and there's a constant tearing pain in my left leg where I have damaged a ligament. But this all pales into insignificance compared to the pain that Dylan went through in his final moments. My poor, sweet Dylan.

I have screamed until I am hoarse, begged Nina to find him help, and made my fingertips bleed as I scratched away at the walls like a caged rat. But I've heard nothing all night that indicates she is out of her psychosis or has heard my pleas. This is what they call karma, I think, for what I allowed to happen to Sally Ann Mitchell. Perhaps if I had helped her, the gods would have helped Dylan.

I have been crying constantly for what has happened to my grandson. My worst fears all those years ago have been realised. The sacrifice I made to keep them apart has been for nothing because Dylan is now dead. The beautiful baby I cried over as I gave him away is lying at the foot of our staircase because of his mother, my daughter. And for the first time in her life, I despise her for it. I wish she were dead.

I don't know what time it is when I eventually take myself back up the stairs, defeated. I crawl up them one by one and I eventually reach the bathroom. There, I rise up until my injured leg threatens to fell me. I scoop cold water into my hands and pat it on my face, leaving it wet as I limp into the bedroom and pray that the lumps in my breast and under my arm are malignant. I want this to be cancer and I want it to kill me. I don't want to spend a moment longer locked away in this hell. I want to die as soon as possible and let my stained soul fly free.

The end goal of my other escape attempts was to leave my situation, not my daughter. Despite all that she's done to me, I wouldn't have cut her out of my life or have left her alone. Not until today. Now, that's exactly what I want. She carries death around with the casualness of a handbag. It has taken me most of her adult life to understand that all she touches becomes fetid.

Through the gloom I stare towards the window. I've lost hope that I might see the flashing red-and-blue lights of an ambulance, which would indicate that Nina has awoken and realised what she has done. This time, she does not have me to cover up her actions or protect her from herself. She must face up to and live with what she has done. She may have the freedom to leave this house when-ever she likes, but she is trapped with herself as much as I am trapped in this room.

I close my eyes and my brain rewinds and replays the crunch of the metal cuff against Dylan's skull. It's a sound that will haunt me to my grave, which I hope to reach soon. However, I know that despite my many other terrible decisions, I did the right thing in giving him away. The way he saw right from wrong and chose helping me over believing his mother assures me that he was raised with compassion. And that's more than he could ever have received with Nina in charge of his welfare.

There is something else that weighs heavily on my mind. I remember where I'd seen the look in Nina's eyes as she attacked her son. I caught it only once before; in the fraction of a second it appeared as she hit her father over the head with the golf club. Now I can see it's different to what happens when her psychosis takes over. The psychosis completely absorbs her and acts for her. But with her dad and Dylan, she was present in the moment rather than being swallowed by it. I shudder to think what this means.

I shut my eyelids tight until they hurt. If I have my way, they will never open again.

PART THREE

TEN MONTHS LATER

CHAPTER 76
MAGGIE

The dining-room window is open and I hear the sound of bird-song coming from outside. Not so long ago, it would have been the highlight of my day. Now, highlights don't exist. Every echo is white noise to me.

Nina unpeels plastic lids from the Tupperware, allowing the steam and aromas to rise and spread across the room. It makes me nauseous. I recognise the label on the plastic bag as the takeaway that Alistair and I regularly used on Saturday nights. After his death I refused to order from there again, needing no reminders of the life we shared. Given my time again, I'd have disposed of his body elsewhere so that Nina and I could have moved away from this cursed house and started again. I was wrong not to. I was wrong about so many things.

'Help yourself to dinner,' she says. I bypass the rice and beef in a black-bean sauce and take two thick triangles of prawn toast instead. I'm not hungry and I don't really want them; however, my stomach is gurgling like a drain. Perhaps the toast might settle it a little.

Despite my four layers of clothing, I'm freezing. Nina has taken to leaving the heating on during the daytime since the weather turned. But because the weight has fallen off me, I have no fat reserves to protect me from any chill. Much of the time, I keep cocooned inside my duvet.

My days are mostly spent curled up in my bed, staring blankly at images on the television screen, the sound muted, as I'm completely uninterested by what is going on in the world. I've stopped measuring time by the comings and goings of the neighbours because it doesn't matter if it's 8 a.m. or 2 p.m., it's all the same. It's time I don't need or want. I judged autumn by the leaves floating past the window and Halloween by the youngsters dressed in their ghoulish costumes roaming the streets. And when fireworks illuminated the horizon in bright colours I knew it was Bonfire Night. Soon I'll be watching carollers singing songs I can't hear as I spend my third Christmas locked up in here. But I know that I won't see a fourth.

The balance of power between Nina and I has shifted and while she might control my present, my freedom, what I eat, when I'm allowed downstairs or when I might bathe, she cannot control my destiny. And my destiny is to die soon. My lumps have expanded and spread to the lymph nodes in my groin and armpits. I'm in constant pain and my lungs hurt when I take deep breaths. I'm often sick, exhausted and increasingly confused. There are abscesses on my ankles from the cuff that are infected and I'm always coughing. The only satisfaction to be had from this wretched life is knowing that when I'm dead, Nina will have no one left to hurt.

I often dream about Dylan and how I could have done more to save him from Nina's brutality. It's always the same scenario. He will appear at my bedroom door and I will try and scream 'Run!' at him. But a pair of hands I feel but cannot see constrict my throat. He can't understand my warnings and by the time he reads my lips, it's too late. Nina is behind him, wrapping a chain around his neck and dragging him down the stairs and out of sight. It's her eyes that haunt me, full of darkness and purpose. She knows exactly what she is doing. When I awaken, I feel his loss as powerfully as I would have had I kept him close to me his whole life.

Nina rises and turns on the stereo behind me. The opening bars of ABBA's 'Ring Ring' begin and after she sits, I feel the vibrations of her foot tapping against the leg of the table. 'It's been a while since we've listened to this, hasn't it?'

I don't respond, and I don't think she has noticed that I haven't said a word since she came upstairs to change my chain. She continues talking regardless, recounting her day, describing the new books that arrived at the library, what she'll bring home over the next few weeks. I don't care. I have long since stopped reading.

She reaches into her pocket and pulls out two tablets I recognise as painkillers. 'You've barely touched your toast,' she says. 'And you're not supposed to take these on an empty stomach.'

I don't need her to tell me how they work. Last week she tried withholding them from me until I ate, but I didn't give in. Perhaps I was cutting my nose off to spite my face because for the rest of the night, I was poleaxed by the pain. Tonight, my insides already feel as if they are being twisted and I know I'm in for an even more difficult time. I reluctantly do as she says and start to eat.

'That's better,' Nina continues, and pushes the tablets towards me. I want to hurl every swear word I can at her but I hold back. Instead, I swallow my anger with my medication.

Nina has yet to make any mention of Dylan following his death months and months ago. Two days later and when she finally brought me a tray of food, I yanked open the door and demanded to know what she had done with his body. 'Whose body?' she replied blankly.

'Dylan!' I yelled. 'Your son!'

'Maggie, what are you talking about? I don't have any children, you saw to that. Remember?'

I cocked my head and glared at her, searching her expression for an indication that she was being dishonest. But her look was not that of a woman who was pretending. It was of someone who genuinely didn't know what the hell I was talking about. It was as if her brain had erased Dylan from her memory completely. That last psychosis must have been different to the others. When it passed, I can only assume it took away other memories with it. I considered whether trying to bring about their return was a battle worth persisting with. However, if I could unlock the room in her brain in which she had hidden her son, what might I be unleashing when she learned she had killed him? Would she discover she had done the same to her father and Sally Ann Mitchell? Would I really want to be trapped in a house with a person who learns all that about themselves?

'I'm tired and confused,' I replied instead. 'Sorry.'

I passed on sharing dinner with her that night so she brought it upstairs for me. I picked at it, my thoughts dominated by all that I would never know about my grandson. I hoped he had led a good life, a happy life, a life full of love and light. But I will never truly know.

Since then, there have been times when I've considered if Nina's been right all along; that I do have vascular dementia and that I'm trapped inside a prison of my own mind, which is why I've never been able to escape. Maybe this isn't my house; perhaps I'm in a care home, we are unrelated and she is charged with looking after me. Perhaps Dylan's death was a figment of my imagination too, because Dylan never existed. Maybe I'm acting out my relationship with my own mother, with me playing her part. Or perhaps Nina keeps me chained up because she has no other choice, as I am a danger to myself and to others. I've stabbed her, hit her, kicked her;

346

I've done all I can do to leave, yet I am still here. Maybe it's all a result of my own psychosis? Am I the sick twisted one and not her? Am I the unreliable narrator in our story?

My only certainty is that a disease is living inside my body and feeding from me. Every waking moment I am conscious of my cancer, slowly growing, asserting its dominance and spreading into all my nooks and crannies. It can't be long now before it reaches further into my brain and renders me completely useless. I can't wait for that moment to arrive. Because then I will have truly escaped this house and my daughter. Only then can we separate. Only then can we be ourselves. Only then will I be happy.

Only then will I be free of her.

'I almost forgot, I have something for you,' she says, interrupting my thoughts. She picks up a cupcake on a plate from the floor. There's a candle in it shaped in a number three. She pulls a box of matches from her pocket, strikes one and lights it.

'Happy anniversary,' she says, and gives me a smile. I don't know what she's expecting in return but I give her nothing. 'Can you believe how quickly the last three years have gone? Sorry but I didn't have time to get a proper cake made. I'll be better organised next year. Blow it out and make a wish.'

I do as I'm told; I let out a puff of air then I make my wish. And I have a feeling it might come true a lot sooner than I expected.

CHAPTER 77

NINA

Tiny green shoots with snow-white tips are sprouting from the mound of earth above his grave in the garden. I bought a bag of seed mix a few weeks ago then sprinkled and raked the contents into the soil. Despite the cold weather, I've been watering that section regularly and it's paying off. They're going to bring colour and beauty to such a dark spot by spring.

I've been thinking about him a lot lately and have spent time out here to feel closer to him. Maggie thinks that I have blanked Dylan from my memory, but she couldn't be more wrong. He is in everything I do and always will be. I talk to him often, even when I don't get a response. When Maggie's time comes – and I don't think it will be long – I will bury her here too.

I feel a chill in the air so I button up my cardigan and make my way back into the house. I spy Elsie upstairs at her window, making no effort to hide behind the curtains or disguise that she is watching me. She wants me to see her, she wants me to know she is there, watching, waiting, desperate for me to slip up. But I won't. Ever. She knows nothing of what's gone on behind these closed doors,

I'm sure of that. I give her a wave and my broadest smile but she doesn't reciprocate.

I place a large frozen pizza and garlic bread on a tray and slip it into the oven. I swam my fifty lengths this morning so I burned my calories in advance and am rewarding myself. I have about fifteen minutes to spare so I make my way downstairs into the basement, my eyes drawn to the dusty old sofa Maggie never got rid of. It's one of the only reminders left of all the rubbish she's hoarded and stored down here. Most of it ended up in the skip I hired, leaving me plenty of space to make this a more practical environment.

By my feet is a plastic crate containing half a dozen albums full of family photos, but Dad isn't in any of them. Maggie has got rid of almost all of them. When I start leafing through them, I stumble across a family holiday we took in Devon when I was a little girl to see Aunty Jennifer. 'Oh my God, I was so fat!' I chuckle, and point to the rolls on my arms and legs as an infant version of me sits naked on a potty.

More pages follow and fragments of long-forgotten memories appear in dribs and drabs, some making me laugh out loud, others making me feel melancholic. In one recollection, I can't be more than three or four years old and I'm dressed in a pink swimming costume with a sponge in my hand and I'm helping an out-of-shot Dad to clean the car. In another, I'm lying stretched out on the back seats of it, no doubt listening to ABBA or Madonna playing from the speakers, and staring at the back of Dad's head as he drives. I loved him so much.

I've been having dreams about him lately and I keep waking myself up out of them, as they don't feature the man I remember. The landing is dark and I'm standing outside a crack in the door of his office, listening to him telling someone on the phone that they're his 'only girl'. (That's how I know I'm dreaming; he'd never say that to anyone but me.) 'It won't be long before we're together,' he says to whoever it is, and then he spots me and hangs up. He follows me to my bedroom and he's talking on and on, telling me I'm his only girl, I'll always be his only girl (but what about that *other* only girl, then? I want to ask him). He goes on talking, I've never heard him talk so much. He says that while he loves me to the moon, he doesn't love Mum any more and he's leaving us. He's met someone new and wants to be with her. As he disappears, I'm furious that he wants to ruin my perfect world and leave me and I want to make him hurt like he is hurting me. I reach for something . . . but then I wake up and remind myself that he was the kindest, sweetest, most dependable man in the world. And although he's been out of my life for almost twice as long as he was in it, the gap he left was unfillable. Until Dylan appeared.

'You'd have liked him,' I say. 'He'd have been a brilliant granddad.'

Aside from the rise and fall of his chest, Dylan remains silent and motionless. He sits on the floor, his back to the wall, a few feet away from me, but not close enough to be a danger. 'I can show you some more pictures of him if you like?'

He doesn't reply.

'Okay, maybe another time then.'

An onlooker might describe the silence between us as frosty. To me, it's typical because it's like this much of the time. Sometimes, when I come downstairs and I spot him lurking in the shadows of the basement, for a split second, I think it's Jon. I've even caught myself calling him that on occasion. To my eyes, the physical resemblance between father and son is so uncanny, I find it hard to know where one ends and the other begins.

'Okay,' I say, getting to my feet. 'The pizza should be just about ready. Shall we go upstairs and eat?'

Again, he says nothing, but he responds by slowly pulling himself to his feet. I take the handcuffs I bought from eBay and slide them across the floor to him. I don't have to tell him what to do because our routine is well rehearsed. Despite his incarceration, he is bigger and stronger than I am and I'm sure that if presented with an opportunity, he would try to overpower and hurt me to get out of here. But I've learned from the mistakes I made with Maggie. And in time, he will become physically weaker and more compliant.

Dylan places his hands behind his back and affixes the cuffs to his own wrists. 'Show me, please darling,' I ask, and he turns and pulls his hands apart to demonstrate they are bound. 'Thank you,' I say. 'Now come towards me.'

He turns again and does as I ask. I approach him, as always, with one of Dad's golf clubs in my hand. I've only used it on Dylan once, when he tried to thrust his head back to break my nose. He caught the bridge but it wasn't hard enough to cause lasting damage. So I whacked him in the kidneys with the club and he fell quickly to the floor. I remember being struck by a moment of déjà vu, but I can't think why. I've never played golf so I have no reason to have held a club before. Hurting my son caused me more pain than he could've possibly felt, though. But I suppose that's what parenting is all about, isn't it? Doing what's best for them, no matter how much it hurts you.

I swap the shorter chain for the longer one and follow him up both sets of stairs until we reach the dining room. When the light catches his face, I note his eye socket is still slightly sunken from where he broke it in the fall down the stairs the day he found me and Maggie together. It's likely it will always remain this way, but not to his detriment. It gives him character.

There's very little I can recall about what happened that night. I remember a furious argument with Maggie and the next thing I know, Dylan is lying at the bottom of the stairs and Maggie is locked in her section of the house. I immediately thought the worst and that my son had been taken from me for a second time. It was only when I reached him that I saw him blink and he begged me to get him help. Despite my confusion, something told me that if I did as he asked, I'd never see him or Maggie again. By making one telephone call, I'd lose the only two people I have in my life. So I didn't do it. And it was the best decision I ever made. Instead, I dragged him down into his new home, the basement.

It hasn't been easy. As I did with Mum – and she with me – I sedated Dylan for the first couple of weeks with the remaining Moxydogrel, then extra sedatives I bought online. I stitched up his head wounds guided by a YouTube video and when he tried to escape the first time, I chained him to a disused gas pipe coming from the basement wall. It isn't an ideal scenario but until Dylan comes around to my way of thinking – which I know he'll do eventually – I have little choice. I am only behaving as any good mother would do, keeping their child safe from harm.

Upstairs, Dylan takes a seat in the dining room and I lock the door behind me. On my return I bring the pizza and garlic bread, and I've treated us to a brand of beer and cheesecake he's been pictured with on Instagram. Before opening the door, I check the app on my phone which is linked to a small camera hidden on top of a bookcase to double-check I'm not going to be ambushed when I enter. It appears safe.

Dylan sniffs at his pizza with the caution of an animal. I don't blame him; I've been forced to use powdered sleeping tablets in his food a handful of times when he's become particularly restless or combative. But not today.

'Shall I put some music on?' I ask, but I don't wait for his reply before I turn the stereo on. 'This was my dad's favourite album. He used to love ABBA.'

'You say that every time,' he mutters.

'I'm sorry.'

Dylan looks up to the ceiling. 'How is my grandmother?'

'Maggie's good,' I lie. She isn't, and she is getting worse. She is decomposing before my eyes and doesn't react to the help I offer. We have long since stopped talking about her lumps and bumps because I refuse to discuss them any more. My online research says it's likely the stress she brings upon herself is manifesting itself in her worsening health. Some people just don't want to help themselves.

I have considered telling her that Dylan isn't dead and is living two floors below her because it might give her the will to live. I've even considered allowing the two of them to be in the same room so that we can all eat dinner together as a family. But now isn't the right time, not while Dylan is carrying so much misplaced anger. I don't want them plotting against me. Perhaps when he reminds himself I'm his mum and not the enemy, he might be in a better frame of mind for me to allow them to meet properly.

I saw Jane, the woman who adopted him and tried to keep him away from me, making another appeal on the local news last night. She's desperate for anyone who knows about 'Bobby's' disappearance to contact the police. Bobby is gone for good, Jane, because 'Bobby' never existed. He has always been Dylan, no matter how much you've fooled yourself into believing he's not.

She was holding a candlelit vigil outside their local church and renewing the family's appeal to find him. Clearly she refuses to believe the text messages I sent her from his phone saying that he needs some time to himself. *Why won't she just give up?* I thought. *Take the hint, woman, he doesn't want to see you!* I ended up smashing the phone and flushing the SIM card down the toilet so the police can never trace him back to here.

They did turn up at the house once, about six days after he vanished. Fortunately, I had him under heavy sedation in the basement so all parties were unaware of one another. They told me police cameras had picked up his car registration plate in Northampton, but I denied he was ever at the house, informing them we were estranged. I even invited them inside to take a look around, but they didn't come any further than the lounge. If they'd looked inside the garage, they would have found his car. If I knew how to drive further than from the road outside to my garage, I'd have disposed of it by now.

Before I begin eating, I cut into Dylan's pizza and feed him pieces with my fork. And I hold a beer bottle to his mouth when he needs to drink. He looks at me as if he hates me but he knows that he needs me to do this for him. Besides, I was robbed of the chance of helping him to thrive as a baby. Now it's finally my time and I must take my opportunities while I can, because it won't always be like this. As soon as he accepts this is where he belongs, the cuffs won't be necessary. We will be just a regular mother and son, eating dinner together like every other ordinary family.

ABBA's 'The Day Before You Came' plays and of all the times I've heard it, it's only tonight that the lyrics resonate. The singer is describing her mundane existence before a man she loved came into her life and changed everything. Before Dylan sent me his first Facebook message, I was her. And now I'm not. I have everyone I need. My mother is upstairs where she can do no more harm; my beautiful, wonderful boy is safe downstairs; and my father is asleep outside under a soon-to-be-beautiful blanket of colourful flowers.

How many people are fortunate enough to have three generations of one family all living together under one roof? Not many, I'm sure. So I don't take any of this for granted. I am a very, very lucky woman.

EPILOGUE

NINA

Two novels I've been waiting for arrived in the delivery van this morning. *Life of Pi* and *Flowers in the Attic* are both for Maggie, so I volunteer to refill the shelves and I hide them in my usual spot in the War and British History section.

I start thinking about tonight's dinner. It's Dylan's turn to eat with me and because he's been looking a little pallid of late, I'm going to pick him up a steak fillet from Waitrose on the way home. It should add a little iron to his blood as I don't want him becoming anaemic. Choosing tomorrow evening's dinner with Maggie won't be so difficult. She doesn't eat much more than a sparrow, pecking at her food or pushing it around her plate with a plastic fork. Nevertheless, feeding three people on one wage means my purse is taking quite the hit these days. But that's a small price to pay for what I get in return from them.

The sudden appearance of Benny startles me and for a moment, I think I've been caught squirrelling away my books.

He looks concerned. 'Nina, there's a phone call for you,' he says.

'Who is it?' I ask as I follow him to the library reception desk.

'I don't know, but she said it was urgent and that she didn't have your mobile number any more.'

'Any more,' I repeat, my curiosity piqued. I head behind the counter and pick up the receiver. 'Hello, Nina Simmonds speaking. How can I help?'

'Oh Nina, thank God. It's Barbara, Elsie's daughter.'

'Hi Barbara,' I reply with genuine surprise. I can't remember the last time we spoke, and it's certainly never been by phone. 'Is everything all right with your mum?' I quietly hope that it's not and that she's called to tell me Elsie has suffered a particularly painful death.

'You need to get home right away.'

'Why, what's wrong?'

'I'm so sorry to be the one to tell you, but there's been a fire.'

'A fire,' I repeat, the words failing to register even when I say them aloud. Perhaps I misheard her. 'What do you mean?'

'Nina,' she says more firmly. '*Your house is on fire.*'

MAGGIE

I stand by the window and take in the view over my street one last time.

All I've loved about this ordinary little cul-de-sac in this ordinary little town I now hate. It's not the street's fault, it's not the house's fault. It's all my fault. And hers. If I had a second chance, I'd do everything differently. I'd have found Nina the help she so badly needed and I wouldn't have let my grandson slip through my fingers. Of all our stories, his is the most tragic. He lived the life I wanted for him when I let him go. Yet he still found his way home. He went full circle and left the world from the same place as he entered it.

I slowly make my way down the stairs and to the first-floor landing. For reasons unknown to me, Nina never bothered to fill in the hole I had dug out of the plasterboard, perhaps thinking there was little point, as no one was likely to enter this house again.

I tear many pieces of cardboard from the soundproofing egg boxes and push them through the hole and into the other side of the wall. Then I remove a box of matches from my pocket. Nina had been too concerned with trying to get one up on me with the incarceration anniversary cake to notice as I swiped the matches from the table.

I strike one, light a piece of cardboard and then drop it through. I put my ear to the wall and listen to the fire crackle as it spreads to the other pieces. The carpets in this house are so old they're not fireproofed. They stretch all the way downstairs to the ground floor and to the doors of the lounge, kitchen and basement. It won't take long before the wooden doors go up in flames either. I take Nina's memory box, rip its paper contents into pieces and scatter a trail of them up my stairs. I strike another match and watch in delight as her past slowly takes light. Now she won't even have those first thirteen years of innocence to cling on to.

Then I retreat to my room, careful to leave the door open. I lift myself on to the bed, lie back and close my eyes. I take a little comfort from knowing it will be the smoke that kills me, not the flames. I'm sure my lungs will burn for a few moments as I cough and splutter, but this really is the best way.

There is nothing I can do for myself and there is nothing more I can do for Nina. She thought that she was lacking a son and that when she found him, it was the missing piece of her puzzle. But she was so, so wrong. What she was actually missing was a self, only she couldn't admit or confront it, even when she sent Dylan to his death.

She wasn't the only one who was wrong about herself and what she needed, because so was I. Only now can I see that my knowledge gave me the freedom I craved. Not in a physical sense; but up here in my head, here where it counts, I have always been a free woman. All along, it's Nina who has been incarcerated. Without offering her insight or nudging memories, it is *me* who has kept *her* locked up in her own prison. I have created and nurtured this monster and now I am extricating myself from its grip.

For the first time, I am putting myself before Nina. I am taking control of my future by ending it, here and now. I am doing this for me and I am doing it for the memory of my grandson. I take in the deepest of breaths and smile because I know, at last, there are so very few of them left.

NINA

My taxi is halted at the entrance to our cul-de-sac by a uniformed police officer. I throw a twenty-pound note over the driver's shoulder, open the door and run towards the blackened house a hundred metres away. I'm stopped by two more police constables and a line of yellow tape tied between two lamp posts on opposite sides of the street.

'I live there,' I yell, pointing to the building ahead. 'My son and my mum were inside. Where are they now?'

'Let me see what I can find out,' says one of the PCs calmly. 'But until we're given the all-clear by the fire officers, I'm afraid you can't go any further.'

As he leaves, the other officer says something to me, but I'm not listening. I'm focused on two ambulances with their rear doors wide open, parked behind the fire rigs. Four paramedics chat among themselves while they await further instructions. I don't see Dylan or Mum inside either vehicle. Perhaps they are being treated inside the house?

I look back at it and gawp, wide-eyed at the enormity of what's happening. My family home, the place where I loved my father, lost and found my son and punished my mother, is grey, black and charred. Fire officers in yellow coats and hard hats enter and exit what's left of it. The blaze has been extinguished but has left an unrecognisable charcoal shell in its wake. The air around me smells like burned wood and acrid plastic. There is glass from broken windows and roof tiles scattered across the lawn and pavement. Water trickles past my feet, carrying away small shards of debris that once formed part of my home towards the drains and out of sight.

'Please let them be okay, please let them be okay, please,' I say aloud and pray that for once in my life, God is feeling charitable. 'They're all I have.'

It's only then that I notice the neighbours lined up in the street, watching me talking to myself. They are staring at me with a mixture of pity and relief that it's not their property in ruins. Barbara looks at me with sympathy but Elsie shoots me a glare of disdain, like this is my doing and that finally I have my comeuppance.

The little girl, the one Maggie was convinced was being abused, is also here, staring at me, hollow-eyed. There's a patchwork of yellow-and-blue bruising leading up the child's right arm and under her T-shirt. Her mother is resting her hand on the child's shoulder but as I look more closely, her knuckles are bent and white, as if she's digging her fingertips into the girl. In that moment I know I should have believed Maggie.

I want to say something to the girl, but a uniformed fire officer is approaching me. 'Are you the homeowner?' he asks.

'Yes, well no, it's my mum's house, but I live here with her. Where is she? Where's my son?' I am so frightened of what he's going to tell me that I want to be sick.

He escorts me under the taped-off area towards the ambulances and out of earshot of spectators. 'Can I ask your name?'

'Nina, Nina Simmonds,' I stutter. 'Why isn't anyone telling me what's happened? Where is my family?'

'Ms Simmonds,' he says softly, 'I'm sorry to tell you but my team has discovered two bodies inside the property.'

My legs buckle beneath me and I drop to the floor like a bag of spanners. I hear him shout something and a paramedic rushes towards us. The two men lift me to my feet and help me towards the ambulance. I sit on the tailgate; I'm crying and hyperventilating and I struggle to get my breath. They encourage me to inhale deeply but when I do, smoke and perhaps the burned bodies of my family catch in the back of my throat. Twice, I'm sick into a bag. All I can think about is how frightened Dylan must have been when he understood he was powerless to stop what was happening around him.

'Would they . . . would they have suffered . . .' I begin, but I can't finish.

'It's likely smoke inhalation would have got to them, not the fire itself,' he says. It offers the tiniest shred of comfort. 'But we won't know until the autopsy.' I shudder at the thought of them cutting into my perfect little boy.

'How did it start?'

'There will be a full investigation in due course but at the moment, we are working on the theory that it might be the result of arson.'

'That doesn't make any sense. It's impossible.'

The officer hesitates, mulling over his words. 'It appears to have been started deliberately from somewhere *inside* the property.'

'What? Where?'

'A preliminary map of origin suggests it was the partition wall between the first floor and the staircase leading up to the attic.'

'Mum's bedroom is up there, but she doesn't have access to anything flammable.'

'Is she a smoker? Does she use a cigarette lighter, or matches?'

'No, she's not . . .'

And then it hits me with the weight of a wrecking ball. Our dinner last night. I was too busy goading her by lighting a candle on her three-year anniversary cake to remember to put the matches back inside my pocket. Mum must have grabbed them while I was distracted. She has set fire to the house to kill herself and get away from me. Only she has taken with her the grandson she didn't know was in the basement. Even in death she has found a way to devastate me once more.

My body folds in on itself and I don't think I will ever be able to stand upright again. Dylan was my heart and his grandmother has torn it out and stamped all over it again. It's too much for anyone to process.

'Ms Simmonds,' a voice asks. I look up. A young man in a white shirt and tie flashes me a warrant card. All I see of him are his eyes. They are two different colours. They scare me. 'DI Lee Dalgleish,' he continues. 'May I have a word?'

I nod, but I am in no fit state to say anything more.

'My colleagues tell me that you lived here with' – he consults a notebook – 'your mother and your son?' I nod again. 'However, your neighbours have told us that they haven't seen your mother since she moved away from the property some years ago? And that as far as they are aware, you live here alone.'

He waits for an answer I don't give.

'Two bodies were found, one in the basement and one up in the attic,' he continues. 'Was there a reason why the deceased might be in those places?'

'Why are you asking me these silly questions?' I sob. I never want to talk again.

'Because their bodies were found with chains attached to their ankles.' I feel what little strength I have left slipping away from me. I don't have the energy to respond. 'Did you know about this, Ms Simmonds?' he persists. 'Do you know why they were incarcerated?'

'They live with me,' I whisper. 'I look after them. They're my family.'

I begin to feel the smoky air between us chill, and a shiver runs from the base of my spine up into my neck. 'I'm cold,' I say, and my eyes look up until they meet his. One is hazel, the other is pure grey, the same shade as Dylan's and Jon's eyes, and just as piercing. They can see through me, they can read me. *I can feel it.* Then suddenly, the colours begin to alter; his irises are darkening and my head tilts to one side as I look more carefully because I don't understand why. Somebody else drapes a blanket over my shoulders but I don't acknowledge it.

The last thing I hear is the clinking of metal, the same noise Dylan's handcuffs made. I'm fixated by why this policeman's whole

362

body is now under a shadow yet the sky and everything that surrounds him is red. I think he's still talking but I can't hear or focus on him properly; instead, the dimming light and colours ahead fixate me.

Someone takes my wrists in their hands but my skin is numbing. I'm slipping away from myself, and I can't stop it. I know I'm moving forward yet it's as if I'm being pulled backward into a tunnel. Everything in front of me is becoming smaller and smaller, darker and darker, until there's nothing left but me, alone.

And all I see is black. Just black.

ACKNOWLEDGMENTS

The plot of this book was developed in a somewhat unusual location for me. The idea of having two people living together who hated one another had been circling my head for a while, but it really began to take shape when my husband and I were on a road trip to California. We found ourselves camping in Yosemite National Park and began to discuss the idea in detail on long walks up waterfalls, mountainous trails and bike rides. The final part of the plot was developed while staying at my mum Pamela's house after she'd undergone an operation to remove cancer. So the first people I would like to thank are my partner in crime and in life, John Russell, for being my sounding board, and my mum for the strength she showed during her successful fight against the disease. Also, the staff at Northampton General Hospital for saving her life.

No book goes from laptop screen to press without a lot of hard work behind the scenes. Thanks to my editor Jack Butler for your faith in this book along with your initial notes, and to David Downing and eagle-eyed Sadie Mayne for helping to shape the final product. Of course, thank you to my publishers Thomas & Mercer and for your unsung heroes, including Hatty Stiles and Nicole Wagner.

Since embarking on my career, I've developed an incredible readership, much of it down to word of mouth and online book clubs. I would like to thank Tracy Fenton from THE Book Club; Lost in a Good Book; The Fiction Cafe Book Club and The Rick O'Shea Book Club. You are all so supportive.

Gratitude as always to some of my author friends for keeping me going when the hours were long and I needed a distraction, usually on Twitter. I love my chats with Louise Beech, Darren O'Sullivan, Claire Allan and Cara Hunter; such a talented bunch of writers who inspire me.

I'm grateful to Dan Simpson Leek and James Winterbottom for their adoption advice, to Anne Goldie for her midwifery suggestions, to Sue Lumsden for walking me around a doctors' surgery and Kath Middleton for preventing me once again from looking like a fool.

My thanks goes to my early readers, Carole Watson, Mark Fearn, Rosemary Wallace, Mandie Brown, and my self-titled 'groupies' Alex Iveson, Deborah Dobrin, Fran Stentiford, Helen Boyce, Janette Hail, Janice Kelvin Leibowitz, Joanna Craig, Laura Pontin, Louise Gillespie, Michelle Gocman, Ruth Davey and Elaine Binder.

And finally, my eternal gratitude goes to Beccy Bousfield. You have given John and I everything and asked for nothing. Thank you, from the bottom of our hearts.

ABOUT THE AUTHOR

Photo © 2018 Robert Gershinson

John Marrs is an author and former journalist based in London and Northamptonshire. After spending his career interviewing celebrities from the worlds of television, film and music for numerous national newspapers and magazines, he is now a full-time author. *What Lies Between Us* is his seventh book. Follow him at www.johnmarrsauthor.co.uk, on Twitter @johnmarrs1, on Instagram @johnmarrs.author and on Facebook at www.facebook.com/johnmarrsauthor.